MOTEL SEPIA

. . . . for peace among all people

"When a stranger sojourns with you in your land, you shall not do him wrong. You shall treat the stranger who sojourns with you as the native among you, and you shall love him as yourself, for you were strangers in the land of Egypt: I am the Lord your God."

Leviticus 19:33-34

A novel by
DALE KUETER

authorHOUSE®

AuthorHouse™
1663 Liberty Drive
Bloomington, IN 47403
www.authorhouse.com
Phone: 1 (800) 839-8640

Published by AuthorHouse 07/30/2016

ISBN: 978-1-5246-2036-3 (sc)
ISBN: 978-1-5246-2034-9 (hc)
ISBN: 978-1-5246-2035-6 (e)

Library of Congress Control Number: 2016911963

Print information available on the last page.

This book is printed on acid-free paper.

Acknowledgements To:

My wife, Helen, for many suggestions, loving patience and moral support.

Mr. Richard Reed of Cedar Rapids, whose memories of Motel Sepia and general support for the book meant a great deal to me. His parents were Evelyn and Cecil Reed. Historical background of their family, taken from Cecil Reed's book, *Fly in the Buttermilk*, (co-authored by Priscilla Donovan, published by University of Iowa Press), serves as foundation for a fictional storyline and dialogue.

Mr. Lyell D. Henry, professor emeritus at Mount Mercy University in Cedar Rapids, whose recollections of Motel Sepia inspired the idea for the book. Mr. Henry also provided resources.

Ms. Emily Johnson and Ms. Vanessa Shelton, whose keen eyes, sharp editing and persistent suggestions smoothed the book's rough edges.

Mr. Ed Gorman, a prolific and successful mystery writer who took the time to read the *Motel Sepia* manuscript and encouraged this project along.

Dr. Percy Harris, Linda Sanders and Dr. James Randall who helped me immeasurably in rebuilding 1955 Cedar Rapids history and culture.

Mr. Charles Jelinek, retired Cedar Rapids police officer, who clued me on police communication and habits, particularly during the mid-50s era; and Police Detective Ron Johnson who explained the art of reading fingerprints.

Mr. David Halbrook and Mr. Julian Toney of Belzoni, Miss. They provided some historical background on the Mississippi Delta region and guided me on the proper pronunciation of the town (Bell-zona) and the Yazoo (Yay-zoo) River. And Barbara at Delta Burial in Belzoni who explained the nature of black funerals.

Personnel at the Cedar Rapids and Marion libraries, African-American Museum of Iowa and the Carl & Mary Koehler History Center.

"Motel Sepia" main characters

Roy and Lillian Sanders – owners and operators of Motel Sepia
Aldo Arezzo – Chicago mob accountant who retired in Naperville, Ill.
Jeremy McNabb – captain at the Naperville Police Department
Curtis Moore – young, unemployed black man from Cedar Rapids.
Deron Campbell – Chicago black in summer school at Coe College, Cedar Rapids
Mike Kreiji – owner of the Czech Inn restaurant in Cedar Rapids
Dorothy Dotson – waitress at the Czech Inn
Charlie Jelling and Kenny Wilson – Cedar Rapids police officers
Louis Byrne – detective lieutenant at Cedar Rapids Police Department
Virgil Howell – black fingerprint expert at C.R. Police Department
Jerry Morgan – reporter at *The Gazette* in Cedar Rapids
Eddie Ralston – bigwig in Chicago underworld
Joe Ellis – mob enforcer and hit man
George Dawson – owner of George's Gourmet Restaurant, Cedar Rapids
George and Viola McDowell – black travelers from Chicago and Motel Sepia guests
Monica and Harold Erickson – white Wisconsin guests at motel
Vernon and Ida Taylor – black motel guests from Mississippi
Ann and Bob Dolan – white motel guests from western Iowa
Matt and Caroline Kilburn – white motel guests from northeast Iowa
Jennifer Jennings – college dropout and Chicago mob moll

Introduction

Cedar Rapids, Iowa, in 1955, was no more a hotbed of civil rights than Chicago was a model for low crime.

When it comes to interracial engagement, Cedar Rapids has evolved pretty much like any other city where historically 90 percent or more of residents are white. While the city and Iowa have a history opposed to slavery and segregation, both also have a record of hateful incidents and unequal opportunity. Among the most infamous in Cedar Rapids was a bitter neighborhood fight regarding sale of a lot to a black physician in the 1960s.

Like nearly everywhere, blacks and whites in Iowa have come closer in the last half century. Still, a recent national poll showed that barely one third of whites have a black friend and vice versa.

There is an old theory that who we are and where we fit into life's scheme depends in large part on where we've been. Modern sociologists might suggest otherwise, that this concept that we transport much of our character, habits and culture from childhood and adolescence into adulthood, is waning. In other words, the influences we had growing up may be less and less significant in who we turn out to be. Education and pervasive communication have, I believe, revised some of our old beliefs and eliminated others. Some of that is good, some otherwise.

I'll leave it to you to decide what is good, but surely the decline in racism and general acceptance of diversity must be included, though some degree of prejudice and even malice linger in many of us. While we may be more open-minded, I believe modern communication and culture has also pushed us, ironically, to be more inward looking. I sense that for many *my* world seems to take preference to *our* world.

Can we change? Can absolutes shift from black or white to gray? Can avarice find charity; hate move to acceptance? And can morality, in all its colors, be embraced in the midst of all culture? In the end, our attitudes toward people outside the comfort of our families can abundantly reveal our true natures.

Motel Sepia is a window on public interaction in 1955, a time when life was much more constricted. While the world was opening up, the vast majority of people were socially and economically confined to their neighborhoods. Taking an extended vacation, going somewhere other than a relative's house, was unusual for most and challenging for some.

This was especially true for black families. While restlessness for equality was well into germination, the Civil Rights Act of 1964 seemed a long way off. Jim Crow was alive and well, openly and in the hearts of many Americans.

The Motel Sepia was a real business operated by a real black couple – Cecil and Evelyn Reed – just outside the eastern limits of Cedar Rapids. It was opened to give black travelers a place to stay. Others were welcome, too.

According to Lyell Henry, professor emeritus at Mount Mercy University in Cedar Rapids, Motel Sepia was one of only a half dozen places along the Lincoln Highway (U.S. Route 30) between Chicago and San Francisco that was publicized as accepting black customers.

Black people in the mid-1950s were generally referred to as Negro and in some instances, as colored. The terms of the period are used in this book.

While the book draws on aspects of the Reeds' life (including Cecil Reed's ancestry, as outlined in his autobiography, *"Fly in the Buttermilk"*), the names, dialogue and storyline have been created to produce a fictional account of life in the 1950s. The crimes related in *Motel Sepia* have no basis in fact or connection to the real Motel Sepia or any other business.

However, there is nothing fictional about Cecil Reed's boundless drive to advance – even if a small step at a time – the standing of blacks while simultaneously promoting the relationship between blacks and whites.

– Dale Kueter

Chapter 1

June 1952, Cedar Rapids, Iowa

"Andre, you get on in here right now! Playtime is over. Was over 15 minutes ago. Time to get cleaned up and go to bed. No arguin' either, hear?"

Lillian Sanders, hands on hips, chuckled to herself. Who could blame kids, recently freed from the structural rigors of school, from wanting to romp outside until darkness consumed nearly every corner of summer's 9 o'clock sky?

For 11-year-old Andre, there was more to the lingering than shucking off the constraints of a long school year. He kicked at the dust and pondered how to explain a rip in one knee of near-new pants and elderberry stains on the other.

The robins in the woods toward Indian Creek dispensed their distinctive night song, a shrill chorus that some would describe as an annoying, disjointed cacophony. In the distance was the more soothing, rhapsodic melody of the whippoorwill, an almost beckoning call to years gone by.

For a few minutes, as a gentle northwest breeze caressed the already sleeping oak leaves, Lillian pondered the age-old question: where had time gone?

Here she was, 41 years old, married to a man who had a thousand ideas to change the world, and bit by bit, she had to acknowledge, he was inching ahead. She wasn't thrilled by some of his prospective enterprises, and told him so. Like most couples they plowed forward in life, rejoicing in the good times and riding out the bumps. She giggled silently and wiped a strand of hair from her still sparkling eyes.

Over the years, like autumn accepts winter, she had cautiously taken to his incurable itch to try something new. Some people hate change. But for Roy Sanders change was a challenge, not always something within reach today, but not always something too distant for tomorrow.

Patient change.

Testing new ideas, to him, seemed as natural as breathing. Sometimes his notions were a breath of fresh air. On other occasions, they were a whiff at wishful thinking. Failing, in his mind, was not trying at all. She naturally savored what to her was his best idea – boldly approaching a new girl in town. That was nearly 20 years ago. Her mind drifted back. She focused on his gangly charm. It still tickled her fancy.

The Rev. Richard Rollins, Lillian's father, had just become the pastor at the African Methodist Episcopal (AME) Church in Cedar Rapids. The family moved down from Minneapolis some 10 days before. While adults in the congregation were sizing up their new minister, Elroy Sanders was giving the eye to the pastor's oldest daughter.

Young Roy (few called him Elroy) did not suffer a lack of confidence. When he first saw her, he was convinced. Her attractive looks, especially her petite figure, distracted his church meditation. Delilah herself could have strutted up the aisle, but Roy's eyes were focused on Lillian. Her black hair, with ends rolled casually on her forehead and falling with a curled tease over her ears, gleamed. The brown of her eyes was deeper than the color of her skin. She walked with elegance in her blue dress peppered with small, white polka dots.

In the fashion of young men overwhelmed with natural attractions, he pledged to himself right there that she would become his wife. While the Rev. Mr. Rollins was soliciting amens from the congregation, Roy said amen to Lillian. On the Rollins family's second Sunday in town, he forthrightly asked if he could walk Lillian home after services. He was sure it would impress her, and just as importantly, influence her parents that church was his choice for a "first date."

Going to parties and dances could come later.

Roy's father, Thomas Edward Sanders, had purchased an old Buick, a sharp-looking, deep blue that concealed some minor scratches and rust. Its square shape was distinguished by a short-billed front visor and bug-eyed headlights. While his Dad purchased plates for the car every year, oddly, neither of Roy's parents drove.

Nearly 19, Roy was allowed to drive the family to church and other places. But not on dates.

It was not uncommon that people walked to events. Lillian and Roy would often hike to nearby youth parties and dances. Sometimes, for fancy, dress-up functions, they would accompany another couple and hire a white taxi driver named Frank for a trip to the light fantastic. For $1.25 Frank would take you downtown in his 1930 Kissel. Nothing like arriving in style. By double-dating, your cost was cut in half.

"What did you say about kissin'?" his mother asked him once after bending a wary ear to talk about the Kissel taxi. She gave it the motherly translation.

"No, no, Mom. Not kissin'," Roy informed her. "It's a brand of a car, Kissel." Lillian had to laugh when she recalled the exchange between Roy and his mother.

Her memory trip was detoured by a honking horn from the nearby highway that screeched through the evening air only to be absorbed by the country quiet. Life is like that. Change suddenly interrupts routine and then becomes part of the ordinary. Chemistry is a fascinating science, she mused.

"How did they let such a pretty girl escape from Minnesota?" Roy whispered in her ear one night not long after they met. They were dancing. She still remembered how his eyes dazzled, almost in a spellbinding way.

Talk about being swept off your feet! Lordy! And was he a dancer! He could cut a rug and have it installed before the final verse. In his late high school years, Roy and two siblings organized themselves into a dancing and singing act called The Faststep Trio.

His sister, Maddie, played the piano and, depending upon the audience, would sometimes toss in sporadic lyrics in Czech or German. Roy and older brother Walter did the high-stepping. The group occasionally hooked up with a white, hillbilly band leader for shows. Maddie would dress in a gingham Aunt Jemima gown, while

Roy and Walter donned waiter outfits. That's when they played to white crowds. They had flashier costumes when entertaining black audiences.

"Just call me Snake Hips," he had brashly told Lillian shortly after they met. Some of his gigs during high school were as far as 100 miles from Cedar Rapids. Classes at Washington High School, home chores and a two-hour road trip made for long days.

"When you are young you have energy to spare," he told her. He continued to dance professionally after they were married.

His father always preached the value and need for work. As a young teen Roy polished shoes at the 12-chair stand at the John Adams Hotel in Cedar Rapids. On University of Iowa football weekends, when the hotel was filled, he'd make as much as $16. Men and women dressed up for games like they were headed to a fancy ball. Some men wore suits and hats, and women donned fancy dresses.

Roy and his friends also raised money through boxing matches. His mother opposed it. She detested boxing, especially the format Roy entered. The last man standing could make as much as $100, an enormous sum.

Roy even worked at a beauty shop owned by a white woman. He cleaned, mixed shampoo solutions and did general maintenance. And he marveled at the mysterious ways of both men and women when it comes to tinkering with hair. Why, his curiosity begged, did some women spend hard-earned money for permanents to curl their hair while some black men underwent conking, a process to remove hair curl?

Unlike most teenagers, Roy listened and learned about the nuances of race. Father Pat Carmody, one of his shoeshine customers and chaplain at Mercy Hospital, suggested that "listening is a sacrament." Roy liked that notion, once Father Carmody explained the meaning of sacrament. He became alert to the manipulation of language, how whites conversed with each other and how they talked with black people. He took note how Negroes changed their words and voice, depending if they were talking to whites or other colored.

He studied how people responded to ethnic jokes. Was reaction to a racial joke different than when a Bohemie joke was told? Cedar Rapids Czechs, most of them descendants of immigrants from the Bohemia region of Czechoslovakia, made up a sizeable portion of the city's population. Jokes often portrayed them as being more pedestrian, even slow of mind.

He entered these experiences into a subconscious account that collectively guided his own behavior. Roy, in his internal bookkeeping, called it a formula for sensitivity and patience. It helped shape his reactions and responses. He believed it was in his best interests to use that approach in a culture dominated by whites. It was a highly unusual process for a teenager of any race.

It was during the dark days of the Great Depression when Roy and Lillian first met. Romance was a happy contrast to a world in economic and political turmoil. One fifth of the people in big cities were unemployed. Even educated professionals stood in breadlines. Adolf Hitler took over in Germany and formed the Third Reich. In America, a once timid man crippled by polio assumed the presidency and created the New Deal.

While most people talked about jobs and poverty, and were abuzz over Hitler's atrocities and Wiley Post's solo flight around the world, two young people in love were content to focus on each other. Roy knew that pastors stayed only a few years at a particular church, but he wasn't ready to propose marriage. He wanted to be older and more financially secure.

Growing up Lillian's life was as textbook as Roy's was busily uncommon. Besides schoolwork and time spent in home-ec club, she had regular babysitting jobs and those assigned by her father with church youth groups.

"I have a question for you, Mr. Smooth, Dancin' Man," she said one night about a year after they'd met. She recalled exactly where they were at the time, a half block down the street from McKinley High School. And she also remembered she was nervous.

"How should I say this?" she began pensively. Her hesitancy underscored the uncertainty of her direction.

"What's the question?" Roy prompted.

"Well, it's difficult. I'm embarrassed. I –"

"Just go ahead and say it, Lillian. What's on your mind?"

"OK. OK." She took a deep breath. "Why is your skin so much lighter than mine?" she blurted. There. She said it. She thought she knew, but she wanted him to tell her.

"Ah-hah!" Roy smiled. "Think you're gonna get married to a whitish fellow? That it?"

"Well," she halted. "Yes. To be honest, that's it. Sort of it."

"Lillian, Lillian. While you have lips that are soft and trustingly receptive," he said, executing his finest charm, "I also sense," and he switched to a more formal voice, "you have the eyes and perception of a suspicious detective. You are absolutely correct woman."

He paused for effect.

"I'm part white."

She was startled by his abrupt honesty, even though she wasn't surprised by what he had said. It's like eyeing chunked sweet potatoes on your plate, but your taste buds discover cooked carrots. It takes some digesting.

"Related to General Robert E. Lee," he boldly continued in undulating cadence. "Attention!! Right face! Left face! Pucker your lips, baby!"

"Be serious, Roy," she said. "My question was serious."

"I'm tellin' you the truth, I swear on the constitution of the Confederacy. I'm part Indian, too."

Her eyebrows raised and her curiosity spiked. She thought she knew quite a bit about this man she hoped to marry. But apparently not everything.

"Lillian, I should have told you before," Roy began slowly. "My family tree has some unusual branches. I'll try to make sense of it for you."

He inhaled a full two-lung dose of air, blew it back out, and then repositioned his respiratory system so as to support and bring believability to an incredulous outline of genealogy.

"My mother's father, my grandfather, was Henry Lee." Roy looked at her smack below the eyebrows, peering into her pupils for signs of circumspection. "Grandpa Lee was a half-brother of General Robert E. Lee. You see –"

"Come on. You're teasing me."

"No. That's true, Lil. Now pay attention."

"How could I not pay attention? Robert E. Lee, indeed!"

"Lillian," he paused to regain traction. "Here's the explanation. Henry 'Light Horse Harry' Lee, who fought in the American Revolution and was a friend of George Washington, was my great

Grandpa. Later, he was a congressman from Virginia. He had a wondering eye when it came to women. His slave woman gave birth to my Grandpa Henry Lee, making him a half-brother to Robert E. Lee. Now, on my Dad's side –"

"Hold on General Snake Hips," she said. "Stop the music! Story tellin' is a first cousin to a fib, and I'm a wonderin' if you crossed the line. My father gives sermons about stretchin' the truth."

"Lil, it's true. Grandpa Henry Lee died the year before I was born. My sisters told me his background. First off, he was nearly white. I am told he looked like the Lees. He was sent to Illinois as a young man, a free man. My sister told how he received a monthly check from Virginia. He owned property, and led a fairly comfortable life. That was highly unusual for a black man after the Civil War."

"What you're tellin' me is second-hand, then. You couldn't swear on a Bible that it's true."

"I suppose you could say it's passed on, but why shouldn't I believe my sisters?"

"I'm sorry, Roy. You're right. No reason not to believe them. You were goin' to tell me about your father's side."

"Well, my Grandpa Sanders married the daughter of a Sac and Fox Indian. Did you ever hear of the Black Hawk War?"

"No. What's that to do with your grandparents?"

"Oh, nothing. Just that Chief Black Hawk and his Sac and Fox members were forced out of Illinois. This was some time before my grandparents married. When the Indians tried to reclaim their Illinois lands in 1832, the army stepped in. Abe Lincoln was part of the force that sent the Sac and Fox back to Iowa."

"Roy, if you be tellin' the truth, that's one wild family story. Mine is dull compared to that."

She cupped her hand on her mouth, another question taking form.

"Who's this Light Horse fellow? Why did they call him a horse name?"

"Lil, it was a nickname. Light Horse Harry. He was in the cavalry corps during the American Revolution. He drove horses. Commanded two mounted companies. Can't explain the Light part. Maybe his horse was smaller than the rest. I don't know. Later, as a member of Congress, he was selected to give the eulogy at President Washington's funeral.

"So you see," he paused. "I'm no ordinary fella." He let that soak in for a few seconds.

"'Ya know Robert E. Lee was a West Point graduate and had long service with the U.S. Army. But being from Virginia, he decided to join the Confederate Army forces."

"I knew that," Lillian said. "Didn't he resign his U.S. Army commission at the family home in Arlington, Virginia?"

"He did. The home is now part of Arlington National Cemetery. Funny thing is that the U.S. government confiscated the property after Lee refused to pay $92.07 in back taxes. The first Union soldiers killed were intentionally buried near the house. After the war, Lee sued and won the property back. But since it was a cemetery, he sold it back to the U.S. government for $150,000. Crazy, huh?"

Roy stood, did a quick, fancy dance turnabout, clapped his hands and double-pointed toward Lillian.

"Now, let's talk about your family."

After nearly three years of dating, it happened. Lillian's father was transferred to Burlington, Iowa. After another year of long-distance courting, Roy and Lillian were married. He took a job at the Burlington YMCA monitoring steam cabinets and giving massages, and opened a shoeshine stand for extra money.

Roy was already thinking of moving back to Cedar Rapids when Lillian became pregnant. Soon after the birth of their first child, a daughter, the couple purchased a two-bedroom house in Cedar Rapids. It cost $1,500 with a $125 down payment. With his dancing gigs, shoeshine operation and cleaning business, Roy had accumulated some savings. Still, the mortgage made things tight.

Members of the Elks Club, where Roy had frequently entertained, provided baby furniture and diapers for the new parents. Some even helped paint the baby's bedroom, all of which surprised the young couple.

Iowa wasn't the South. Schools were not segregated. Yet Negroes were pretty much confined, by choice or social bias, to the Oak Hill neighborhood southeast of the city's downtown. Coming to their house, Lillian reflected, and helping paint was wonderful and unexpected, a gesture of welcoming and acceptance.

A barking dog down the road intruded on her musings and jolted her back to the present.

Why did those early days of marriage seem so long ago? How is it that the future seems to fly into the past? The present is so preciously brief.

Lillian stared at the swaying willow trees, seeing everything, seeing nothing. Gurgling Indian Creek had witnessed generations. It tumbled along as if immune to time. A distant star, set in eternity, twinkled to life in the eastern sky. She was happy.

"No more warnings, Andre," she yelled. "Time for bed. Now."

Chapter 2

June 1955, Naperville, Ill.

Aldo Arezzo's Sunday morning agenda was as predictable as a Chicago Cubs collapse in mid-season.

The direction and pace of his early-morning, three-mile stroll seldom varied. He relished the routine because it contrasted with the chaos that had filled his existence for years. Now his life had transformed into the ordinary. The more he could wrap himself in the ordinary the better he felt.

Exiting his concrete driveway, he launched his six-foot frame in a warm-up walk down the streets of Naperville, Ill., inhaling the day's cool, virgin air before the summer sun climbed high and hot. He didn't believe in running, which he visualized would turn nimble cartilage into brittle gristle and hasten the deterioration of his 60-year-old knees. He didn't need any more wear on his body.

He savored the complete scene. Dew danced on the newly clipped lawns. Shadows, while shrinking like melting snow in a January thaw, still possessed some depth, lingering remnants of a moonless early June night. The solitude of 5:30 a.m. soothed his senses and caressed him like a full-body rub-down. The peace penetrated the pores of his body as he walked, almost meditatively at first, with eyes half shut.

Aldo glanced upward at the big elms, which in some places spread their limbs like a canopy over the avenue. Were they stretching, limbering up, he wondered, before a busy day of bouncing in the wind? Or were they awakening to some form of flora rivalry, competing for attention in a leafy and wealthy suburb where appearance was everything? After three blocks, he stepped up his pace.

He was glad he had shunned a lightweight long-sleeve pullover in favor of a faded blue T-shirt, an Arlington Park race track freebie that had been in his old-clothes bin for years. A bank sign said it was already 68 degrees, notice that the late spring hot spell was still unbroken.

Arlington Park. It was another place where he had performed "bookkeeping" of sorts for his employer. The shirt's lettering had frazzled so that the logo now read "Arling Park." The "ton" had tumbled off into history.

The only sounds were pleasant repeats of every early Sunday morning in the summer. Wrens spit out their unique warble, a joyful welcome to a new day. Cardinals talked it up in one or more of their familiar languages. Aldo was less entertained by robins and their ubiquitous attempt at out-chirping the entire feathered chorus. And those damn sparrows. Their chirp was plain and boring, and, he thought, as pervasive as their poop on park benches.

Traffic on the town's streets was sparse. What few cars there were carried people to early church services, the golf course or coffee shops. A 1955 two-toned Chevy Bel Air, sparkling new, honked as it pulled up to a Chicago Tribune newsstand.

Aldo admired the sleek sedan. If he were to buy one, trading his 1953 black Ford Fairlane, it would be that same turquoise and white combination. It had to be the best looking Chevy ever, he thought, his head slowly turning as his eyes fixed on the car like it was a 22-year-old blond bombshell.

A sound in the distance launched his imagination in another direction.

Standing tall in morning's musical range came the muffled long and short whistles of an approaching train. Was it a Chicago, Burlington and Quincy unit lumbering through the heart of town, or a Chicago and North Western passenger train, its warning whistle struggling to bypass the buildings and trees north of Roosevelt Road?

A railroad buff, his mind backtracked nine years to April 26, 1946. It was more than a train wreck. It was a train disaster of historic carnage. One CB&Q passenger train traveling 60 mph smashed into the rear of another just west of Fourth and Loomis. The latter had stopped to check a suspected safety problem. The toll: 43 dead and 125 injured.

Maybe the waning whistle to the north was that of the North Western's newly named *Kate Shelley 400,* headed west across the plains and through the mountains bound for the west coast. Where were people going? And who would they see? Perhaps he should take the family on a train trip. Did anyone on the train know why it was christened the *Kate Shelley?* He knew the story.

One of the North Western's passenger train routes runs due west to Clinton, Iowa, and then on to Omaha. In 1881, a flash nighttime flood weakened a high railroad trestle in central Iowa. A track maintenance crew checked the bridge around 11 p.m. In the process, the structure collapsed. Their locomotive-driven rig plunged 150 feet to the raging creek below.

Fifteen-year-old Kate Shelley, a native of County Offaly, Ireland, lived nearby and heard the crash. Her father worked for the railroad and she knew an eastbound passenger train was due about midnight. She raced to the scene, saw what had happened, and then ran another half mile in the rain and dark to a small depot where train officials were notified. The passenger train, carrying 200 people, was stopped.

Approximately 74 years later, just a few months ago, the North Western named a train after her.

At last, Arezzo pondered, some sense of recognition had been bestowed upon the teenage girl. He breathed deeply to restore oxygen depleted by his brisk step. It's like the person who works 35 years for a company and shows up every day, even when sickness should have kept him home, only to gain a puny pension and proverbial watch at the end. He was that person.

For more than three decades he had been labeled the "number cruncher," the mocking moniker given to accountants who fight financial forays in boring, mechanical remoteness. His opinion was never sought. All that people care about is that they get paid. All the big shots care about is that they get their whopping salaries and stay clear of the Internal Revenue Service. His bosses had other goals, too. Make sure everything in the books appeared legal.

To do that he had created a coalition of incestuous dummy corporations, an enterprise of entanglements that would dazzle Rube Goldberg. This corporate concoction had not only provided masterful pretense for his bosses, but furnished the fiscal machinery to cleverly cover any extracurricular money transactions that might pay uncharted dividends for him.

That was all in the past. Two years ago he arranged with his physician to feign a heart attack. His doctor suggested he retire early and he did. He and his wife, Marge, left Chicago and moved west 25 miles to the capital of suburbia. Their two grown children had good jobs and their own families. Three grandchildren, a comfortable ranch house and nearby golf courses rounded out his notion of idyllic life.

He was proud of himself. Some people went to the YMCA for swims and others of greater wealth belonged to health clubs where they hired sleek, young people to rub off their fatty tissue accumulated at fancy luncheons and country club soirees. Many more wandered the golf courses in the western suburbs exercising their legs and lexicon. He liked golf, but not on a crazed weekend.

Aldo's idea of peace and relaxation, with exercise being a bonus, was a walk in the park. That's what he'd tell his wife, part of the Sunday morning ritual, on the way out of their bedroom as she sprawled out to a different position and consumed almost the entire width of the bed. "I'm taking a walk in the park," he'd say. "Be back in a couple hours or so."

It was not unusual for him to find a park bench where he could rest and think, especially how life could have been different had he taken his CPA credentials on a different track. But bad decisions and untimely debt had routed him in a direction that had gripped him in a vise-like headlock that may as well have been administered by a Marigold Gardens pro-wrestler.

He had to laugh at such imagery. Marigold Gardens was a north side Chicago dancehall that morphed into a famous venue for professional boxing and wrestling. For years he had gone to wrestling matches only because the boss asked – make that directed – him to go, wanted him to handle the "financial" part of the "evening's entertainment." As a dance spot, the Marigold never waltzed into the same ballroom league as the Aragon and Trianon, but it had some big name bands.

Instead, its fame came from the likes of Antonio "Argentine" Rocca, Lou Thesz, and Gorgeous George, theatrical hulks who rivaled any performers at the Chicago Theater. The alleged eye gouges, body slams, Cobra clutches, full Nelsons, bear hugs and infamous "sleeper" holds were beamed across the Midwest by Chicago television. It rivaled Saturday night at the movies.

Today, like many Sunday mornings, Aldo's walk detoured into a breakfast place where he satisfied his brain's call for black coffee and a fresh bagel smothered with cream cheese and strawberry jelly. It would also give him a chance to scan The Trib's baseball standings. By the time he returned home, Marge would be in church. He claimed he found his religion in nature.

Damn! The Cubs lost again. After beating the Pirates – big deal – 6 to 2 at Forbes Field on Thursday, they lost the second game in a row to the Dodgers in Brooklyn. Still, their record was 32 and 23. Could this be the year? Warren Hacker pitched a good game Saturday, but not good enough to beat Dodger ace Billy Loes. Jim King hit a three-run homer for the Cubs, but that was it. Ernie Banks was 0 for 4, and Miksis 0 for 5.

He continued to scan the newspaper. My God! More than 80 spectators killed in a crash at the Le Mans car race. Aldo liked cars, but he thought car races were a waste of gasoline. Murder. Never a shortage of that in Chicago. How many go unsolved? Quite a few, he suspected. Not suspected. He was lying to himself. He knew many killings were never explained. Cops and prosecutors didn't spend much time on ne'er-do-well victims or dead men believed to have ties to the criminal world.

Naperville's groomed avenues were like a park interrupted by cars. Arezzo's walking path eventually led to the sprawling Centennial Beach area where his mind directed his feet on a zigzag route along ponds and flowers that looped back on a homebound path.

He was weary of the hoopla surrounding the inauguration of Chicago Mayor Richard Daley, tired of the constant talk about bomb shelters and frankly worried about plans to turn Naperville into an even bigger bedroom boom town. He had to admit there was good news. Their grandchildren would be getting the new Salk vaccine to prevent polio.

He crossed over to Porter Avenue and then ambled north on Webster and past Naper Settlement. He had completed some two miles when he turned west onto the groomed grounds of Grace Episcopal Church. While early-service people prayed inside, he adored the splendor of God's creation outside. On the quiet backside of the church lot, he slowed and stopped at a park bench.

Looking upward, he simultaneously paid homage to a knurly oak. He didn't notice the man approach.

Before he could sit down, an arm girdled his neck and a solid hand clutching a course rag collapsed roughly around his mouth and nose. He instinctively struggled against the person's overpowering grasp and headlock. In seconds, his breathing was cut off. The cloth over his face contained some sort of toxic substance – perhaps chloroform – that caused his body to quickly limp into submission.

Arezzo was no weakling, yet his body could not combat the combined strength of his attacker and the noxious substance that permeated the cloth and drifted into his respiratory system.

He dropped to the ground and glanced upward, in a fog. The drug magnified the unusual stoutness of the assaulter, and launched tremors in Arezzo's body. Still, his weakened senses assembled a misty notion of his assailant.

"Well, well, Mr. Aldo Arezzo, the comfortable Mr. Aldo Arezzo," his attacker said. There was a pause in the man's gravelly bass voice. His eyes reflected profound evil. Veins in his neck bulged as blood rushed to fuel his obsession with mission, his covenant with death.

"I am a messenger from Eddie Ralston," he said with a calm but deliberate swagger.

Arezzo didn't require an introduction to either Ralston or his paid goon. He knew their history, and he knew that their combined moral assets were less than those of a depraved jackal.

He also was certain that his life had come to an end, that his casual comment to be home in a couple of hours was now an empty promise. A hazy image of his wife's face, her beautiful eyes, the sheen of her hair, forced their way into an otherwise aura of pending horror.

"You surely remember him, Eddie the Rhino Ralston?" said the voice that conveyed words as though filtered through fine sandpaper. "Eddie says to tell you that your bookkeeping system stinks. He has this persistent opinion that you cheated the company out of thousands of dollars, but the good news is that he is generous and you needn't pay it back."

The big man, his entire countenance carved by a profound vileness, dropped the sedated rag and thrust his left hand forward.

He grabbed Arezzo by the hair. In a singular motion, he yanked back his victim's hazy head and slammed the body against the metal arm rests of the park bench. Arezzo lost consciousness and sank back to the ground.

The attacker violently jammed his left hand beneath Arezzo's jaw, and like a vise pinned him to the bench seat. With his right hand, he thrust a wide-bladed knife deep into Arezzo's torso. Blood spewed outward instantly, some splashing on the attacker's right hand. Another slash hit new abdominal arteries, and in seconds the pristine church lawn turned into a recoiling scene of death.

The juxtaposition of murder and church, sick and satanical at best, boosted the killer's spirit.

More thrusts, really unnecessary to accomplish the task but a requirement of punitive power, penetrated the body and the Sunday morning's serenity.

Aldo Arezzo's dreams died quickly.

Chapter 3

June 1952, Cedar Rapids

"For the last time, Andrew James Sanders, get into this house."

When mothers, arms folded, shift from your nickname to your full baptismal name, you had better pay attention.

"By the time you get all that scruff scrubbed off," Lillian said, "it'll be 10 o'clock. And put your ball and glove away where it's supposed to be. Tomorra' you'll want that stuff again, and if it ain't where it supposed to be, you'll be a yellin' 'Where's my glove, Mom? And you'll expect I'm your maid!"

Who said boys were easier to raise than girls? Fiddlesticks! Boys eat twice as much and dirty twice as many clothes. Only you have to tell them to change. They require repeating things two or three times before they hear you. They take twice as long at everything – to finish their chores, come in from play, get to bed at night and get out of bed in the morning.

To Lillian's way of thinking, Karen, now 15, was a model child. Andrew, nearly 12, and his 8-year-old brother, Joseph, worked overtime to either collect grass stains on their clothes or rip out the knees of their overalls.

Busy, she pondered, was a feeble description that lacked the full dimension of her day.

Lillian wasn't complaining, just expressing the thoughts of every mom. She was satisfied with her life, satisfied with this Mr. Snake Hips and all his ideas. Her petite figure had yielded to the physical pressures of three pregnancies. But she was comfortable in knowing that he loved her, that she was still attractive to him, living what her father had called "the marriage mystery of two becoming one."

She glanced to the rear of the house. A bank of benign clouds stealthily ascended from the western sky, covering the path of the recent fading sun. They quickly lowered the curtain on an ideal June day, and hastened the onset of night. Indeed, where had time gone?

She was happy. Life was good. Roy always seemed to find enough work to keep the family pantry stocked and an adequate supply of knee patches.

Over the years, in addition to his cleaning jobs and floor maintenance, he had worked as a short order cook at a restaurant next to the State Theater. He also washed dishes. When the chef departed, Roy took over that job plus the cooking. After that he had moved on to Old Hickory, a barbeque and night spot on First Avenue east. There he cooked and some nights entertained with his siblings.

Lillian had worked, too. She altered clothing and decorated the windows at a downtown dress shop. When Roy landed a job at the Moosehead Tavern, she washed glasses and did the cleaning there.

Roy was goal-oriented. He liked to work. He liked to fix things. It was noticed. In less than a year, Roger Colson, a member of the Elks Club, asked Roy to take over management of the Moosehead. Colson claimed his tavern had the longest bar in Iowa. No one seemed to dispute that. But Colson was noted for something else. Unlike most Iowa bars, he allowed black patrons. They had to sit in a certain area, but Roy saw it as one small step forward for Negroes.

With no big commotion, Roy Sanders, as smooth as a dancing man, was finding his place in white society. At the same time, with the help of white friends, he was slowly advancing the cause – he believed – of all Negro people. He translated a few black customers at an Iowa bar into a much broader meaning, gave it more far-reaching implications on life's stage than would the average person.

Nevertheless, one day while looking over the tavern's books, he pondered the pace of integration. It was measured and methodical, like getting some people to pay on their bar bill, or as his Dad would say, "slower than molasses in January." Many things, it seemed to him, should be apparent without a whole lot of fussin': integrated schools, equal treatment in jobs, at public facilities, in housing. Equal application of the law.

But it was also evident that changing people's minds and hearts was neither easy nor quick. Every human life, he argued to himself, should be treated equally. When a child is conceived – black, white of whatever – he or she shouldn't have to first prove his or her value and equality in society. Why, his mind searched for understanding, did so many whites routinely cast an entire people as some low- value, back-shelf commodity?

How long, he wondered, would it take for Jim Crow laws to change? Would it require another Abraham Lincoln to dissolve segregation, as the Emancipation Proclamation had outlawed slavery? How would the future of Negroes in Cedar Rapids, Iowa, and America, unfold? What would it take to get people of all races to move closer, in all aspects of life?

He and Colson had become friends, more than just employer and employee. Colson and his wife had been among those who had helped paint at the Sanders house. Why couldn't more blacks and whites have casual friendships? That didn't mean whites and Negroes had to marry, the front line of fear. It didn't even suggest they had to live next door to each other, though that would be nice.

It was not a one-way street, Roy knew.

"Why do you spend so much time with white folk?" a Negro neighbor had asked him a year after they had moved to Cedar Rapids. "You gonna turn lighter than you already are."

Roy tried to observe his mother's law about respect. He measured his response.

"My business is with everyone," he told the neighbor. "It doesn't make me more white or less black. It has always seemed to me that it's not the color of a person's skin that ultimately defines a person, but what's on the inside. But I'll take care to watch out. I'd hate to turn pure white."

Lillian had laughed when he told her about the encounter. "I'll be watching the bathtub water," she said.

She spotted the unhurried Andre stumble in the kitchen door, oblivious to a newly mopped floor. Had she placed a big "42" on the floor, she thought, it may have stopped him in his muddy tracks. That was Jackie Robinson's number, a magic number for Andre Sanders and thousands of other Negro youngsters.

"Ever consider I may have just cleaned this floor?" Lillian asked her son. He responded with a puzzled look, as if she were speaking in Italian, and proceeded to tromp across the sparkling linoleum. She leaned on the mop and laughed. That's one thing that will probably never change, she said to herself. Boys are blind to cleanliness.

Andre was lanky and growing strong, so much like Roy, except he preferred sports to dancing. And there wasn't any debate that Roy was a far better dancer. He had a sense for it. He understood dance entertainment, coordinating movements with others, putting on a show. He knew how to dance and how to manage dance. The combination had served him well.

As manager of the Moosehead, he quickly learned the money side of the tavern business and how entertainment could attract new customers. The Moosehead became a show bar, one of the area's hot spots. He booked bands through a Chicago agent, which led to the King Cole Trio coming to the Moosehead. Even back then it was clear that Nat King Cole was headed for fame.

Born in Montgomery, Ala., Cole grew up in Chicago. As a teenager he was already hanging around jazz clubs. The music program at DuSable High School in Chicago fed his arts appetite. The jazz pianist began playing professionally before he was 20.

Roy, six years older than Cole, had followed the young musician's rise in popularity. When Cole came to Cedar Rapids, he had just recorded his first big vocal hit, "Straighten Up and Fly Right."

Roy not only managed the bar club, he and Lillian cleaned it. He installed a sound system and handled repairs. He arranged housing for entertainers and even produced radio commercials for the Moosehead. A short time later he formed his own band. He played bass, taking gigs at other bars, including black clubs, on nights he had off from the tavern.

Working for Colson was an education. Roy learned how to manage a business, employees, entertainers and perhaps most significantly, how to manage himself and his time. His entrepreneurial engine kicked in. He began to service jukeboxes. That led to playing records at parties, which spawned a dance hall business where he played records and Lillian served sandwiches.

After Andre was born, and their income situation looking good, Roy and Lil decided they needed more space. In 1944, they purchased a two-story house in the same block. Within a year, Roy started a floor maintenance business, using his three-stall garage for operations. Polishing the floors took on a whole new meaning for this dancing man.

Sander's Floor Maintenance shop thrived. Over the years it became Sander's Floor Care Store. He obtained floor maintenance contracts at city hospitals and many businesses, employing more than a dozen workers. The store sold floor cleaning products for the home. Roy and Lillian Sanders became well-established figures in the Cedar Rapids business community, even members of the Chamber of Commerce. This was unusual in a city with a black population of about 2 percent, like water being receptive to oil.

However, the realities of racism reared in 1949, when the couple sought to purchase an acreage east of the city. Again, they desired more room for their growing family and businesses. Fear took over among adjoining white property owners. They attributed their anxiety to the belief that values of their homes would decline if a Negro family moved next door. The Sanders believed the people just weren't ready for black neighbors.

Roy, always the one-step-at-a-time ambassador, wondered what could be done to allay concerns and meet the challenge. Patience, he repeated to himself. His entrepreneurship was only exceeded by his thirst for racial harmony.

The tract the Sanders hoped to buy was owned by Mike McGarry, a white barber. Years before, Roy had shined shoes at Mike's shop. Perhaps Mike would speak to neighbors, explain that the Sanders had a respectable business history in Cedar Rapids.

"You are going to have a tough time with that old German, Joe Kuster," McGarry had warned him. "He sits out there in his yard almost every day, smoking his pipe and eyeballing his investment. He's a good farmer. He'll tell you so. First to have crops in, and first to take them out. First to have hogs marketed. His son does most of the work now, and that gives old Joe even more time to daydream about his way of doing things.

"You know, Roy," McGarry reflected on one occasion, "I don't think Joe has gotten over the ribbing from neighbors after the Germans lost the war. And as usual, some took it too far and called him Heinie and gave him the Nazi salute. Even though two of his boys were in the Army. But I suspect I'll turn into a leprechaun before he changes his mind about a Negro family moving in down the road."

McGarry, it turned out, was mightily surprised. And so was Roy. While Joe Kuster didn't lead a welcoming parade for the Sanders family, neither did he oppose them as neighbors once he learned Roy was a respected businessman. McGarry's middleman harmonizing worked. Neighbors became less guarded, if not fully accepting.

The Sanders were able to purchase 15 acres from McGarry. For Roy it was confirmation of patience giving birth to success. The property included two houses on the southwest corner of Bertram Road and Highway 30 and an undeveloped area on the southeast corner.

"This is what I have in mind," Roy told McGarry shortly after the transaction. "I want to show these new neighbors that our family is looking for the same things they are, a place where kids can play and have fun. I want to build a play park, with swings and slides, perhaps a merry-go-round. Maybe a midget car race track. Everybody will be welcome."

McGarry's smile told Roy all he needed to know.

The following year, after the Sanders had moved in, the play park became a neighborhood project. It was curious how fears had dissolved. The Elks club donated a ping-pong table. Roy's one-time schoolmate, George Nissen, the founder and president of Nissen Trampoline Co., set up a trampoline at the playground. To celebrate what Roy called another small step forward, Lillian proposed a picnic.

"Can you believe how many people came?" she said, as the couple cleaned up after the gathering.

Lillian had gradually embraced Roy's ideas and optimism that Negroes and whites could get along as regular neighbors.

"Maybe," she chuckled, "this was the first black-white potluck in the history of Cedar Rapids?"

Yes, time flies.

"Mom, why do we have to come in so early?" Andre filed a formal appeal. He may as well have taken his case to the U.S. Supreme Court.

"Did you put away your baseball stuff?" she repeated, dismissing his petition by ignoring it. "And don't forget to wash your hands and face, and behind your ears. Maybe you should jump in the tub and get a complete scrub-down. Go ahead, now. Where did you get all those stains on your pants?"

Only yesterday those pants were swinging on the clothes line, free of grime and the remnants of hard play. His short trousers danced in the sun next to Roy's long coveralls. She glanced at the wires strung tautly between two iron poles. The clothes line and its dangling apparel told stories of their own, who had been where and who had done what.

Andre's telltale slacks always seemed to leave little to the imagination. He did everything in high gear. He enjoyed the open spaces, and she was glad.

1952. She never dreamed she would have a house in the country with a big yard where kids could run their legs off. The children were healthy. Roy's businesses were going well. There really hadn't been any major racial incidents at their country home after the initial cool reception out on Fifteen Acres. That's what Lillian called the place, Fifteen Acres. Never did she think she and Roy would own a beautiful two-story house and 15 acres.

There was that nasty bump in the road over a parking ticket. One of Roy's truck drivers at the flooring business had accumulated five parking tickets. The vehicle was registered in Roy's name. Police stopped Roy and Lillian one night as they were headed for a church meeting and confronted him about the unpaid tickets. Roy said he was unaware of the parking tickets, but that he would take care of the matter.

One of the officers knew Roy and said he would check with the traffic department to see what they wanted to do. What the couple heard next astonished them.

"Send the nigger in," said a male voice over police radio."

The Sanders weren't naïve. They knew bigots weren't foreign to Iowa. Still, they were surprised. Shocked, really.

Roy paid the fine, but the lingering hate word was far more painful. Should he say something, tell somebody in the police department? If he said nothing, was that any small step forward?

The wound healed but the scar remained, and life went on. Lillian filed it in her "things happen" column. Roy carried a profound hurt, a deep disappointment in what had become his community, the community where he and Lillian were raising their family and had a business. They were active at the church. They had many friends. You can't just let setbacks control your life.

Sometimes life seemed like this Greek character they studied in high school. You work hard pushing the stone to near the top of the hill, only some days it rolls right back down, threatening to squash you in the process. Roy hadn't told Lillian, but what bothered him as much as anything is that he didn't report the matter to the police chief.

Lillian loved Fifteen Acres. Roy did, too, but for reasons beyond its natural beauty and quiet. He saw it as a place of respite and independence, where the kids could run and yell without fear of disturbing the neighborhood. He loved it for what it was and what it could become.

Frequently Lillian would walk down to Indian Creek, which bordered the east side of their property, and listen to its music and absorb its canvass of color. She could meditate there. Occasionally, she would sit on the bank, remove her shoes, sink her feet into the clean, cold water and close her eyes. The gurgling creek massaged her feet and soothed her mind. The wind whispered through the willows. The trees swayed to this symphony, casting blips of sun here and there, shifting the spotlight from dancing leaves to sparkling water.

It was a place where Sac and Fox Indians once pitched their homes, planted their corn. They were the objects of discrimination, too. They had been shuffled around, sent away, never being accepted as humans and neighbors. Now the tribe lived on a large settlement west of Cedar Rapids on property they had to purchase. They were still poor, but they had their own homes and a place to celebrate their own culture.

Lillian felt settled. At least until last fall. That was the first time Roy had mentioned the idea of opening a motel.

Two weeks after the family had returned from a trip out west, one night at supper, his brain wave advanced a new business idea in the middle of chomping on mashed potatoes. She was amused by this man's drive and crafty approach.

"Lil," he said cautiously, "what would you say to buildin' a motel on the property across the road, along Indian Creek?"

He shifted his attention from the roast beef to Lillian's eyes. Usually he was pretty good at reading her face.

She didn't look surprised, or like a veto was forming on her lips. But neither did she appear receptive, ready for a full buy-in. She didn't look anything, except that her one slightly raised eyebrow may have suggested growing trauma from being broadsided by another of Roy's big ideas. Or, her look may have concealed a laundry list of doubts. How, he thought, was she able to raise just one eyebrow, anyway?

"It would be a place where black people could stay while they're on vacation," he resumed his proposal. "Maybe a row of cottages, some for couples, some for families."

His blueprint was growing. His eyes were expanding.

"We're right on the Lincoln Highway," he said, "a coast-to-coast road. What better location? We could involve the whole family in the operation. People of all color could stay here."

Roy resumed his assault on the roast beef. He waited as Lillian chewed on his latest business idea, giving no hint of how she felt.

"We'd call it Motel Sepia," he said.

Chapter 4

June 1955

"**I**'ve not seen such a vicious stabbing in 20 years on the department."

Naperville, Ill., Police Capt. Jeremy McNabb stepped back from the gruesome murder scene, looked away and shook his head, partly in revulsion at what he'd seen and partly in dismay that one human being could inflict cruelty to another in such dimensions. The dead man's torso was ripped open.

"My God!" McNabb shuddered.

It was as much supplication to the Almighty about an incomprehensive, ghastly act as it was a phrase of exclamation. McNabb was not one to use casual profanity.

A slight breeze touched the oak leaves overhead as if to bestow consolation. How could such a divine Spring morning incorporate such a gruesome expression of human brutality?

Again he looked at the corpse. A few more plunges of the murder weapon, a knife whose lethal capabilities were well known to its owner in McNabb's quick assessment, and internal organs would have spewed onto the church lawn.

"I would ask if you called an ambulance," McNabb addressed Patrolman Dave Lundgren, "but this man can't be put back together. Any idea who he is?"

"I did call the ambulance," Lundgren replied, "but you are right. There is nothing outside the grace of God that can help him." They stared at each other. "And, no I don't recognize the victim."

"Who discovered the body?"

"Someone called the station. A man who identified himself as Frank King."

"Hmmm. Frank King. Do we think this Frank King is an innocent passer-by, or perhaps the killer?" McNabb asked. He had already formed his best guess.

"Dispatch asked Mr. King where he was calling from, but he hung up before giving an answer," Lundgren said. "All he said was that he found a 'sickly' man in the park on the north side of Grace Church."

"That," said McNabb, "tells me he was the killer, the fact he hung up. Call in as many officers as you need. Check every drug store and news stand in the area, any store that is open this time of day, and see if they noticed anything unusual, someone using a pay phone. Ask about vehicles that seemed out of place. Oh, one other thing. Contact the dispatcher again and ask if he heard any sounds, background sounds, that might help identify where the call was made."

"Will do, captain."

"And please, one other thing."

"Yes?"

"Have a couple of officers come over here immediately," McNabb directed. "Church services are going to be over in a few minutes and we're going to have a major scene on our hands unless we divert attention from the crime area. Throw up some barricades at both ends of the block to eliminate drive-by gawkers. I think officers can keep walkers away from the area."

He pressed his teeth together in rhythmic fashion, and the outer hinges of his jaw throbbed like a pensive frog. He rubbed his clean-shaven face in search of understanding, as if some insight could be summoned.

"This is unbelievable," McNabb said. "We haven't had a murder in this town in ten years. This looks like Cicero."

Lundgren had been on a routine Sunday morning patrol, usually a boring assignment that required a minimum of five cups of coffee to stay awake. He was near the church, a route taken mostly by habit and the proximity of a nearby doughnut shop, when dispatch alerted him to "a man down, possible heart attack, on the lawn area near Grace Episcopal."

There was no one around the church grounds when he arrived, except for what looked like a sleeping bum sitting on the ground and leaning on a park bench.

The guy, Lundgren had made a quick assumption, wandered over from the railroad tracks and was planning to panhandle church goers. What a great plan: Nice morning. People in a good mood. People with money in a good mood. And the frosting on the cake was that they had probably just been instructed on the needs of the poor. Maybe the guy had a degree in Bible Studies and a minor in psychology.

He had parked the squad car and walked over to the area where the man was lying. Closer observation quickly changed Lundgren's offhand assessment. No bum. No heart attack and no leisurely Sunday for him and the Naperville police department. It was a grisly scene.

After gathering his senses, he called back to the station. He suggested that Capt. McNabb and the chief of police be alerted immediately.

"One other thing Lundgren," McNabb called once again. "Have Dispatch get a hold of Mike O'Conner. He's the fingerprint expert, or at least knows more about it than anyone else in the department, and as one of the elder statesmen in the station he may recognize the M.O. or remember a crime of similar dimensions. A murder of this style suggests several things to me."

"What would that be, sir?"

"Well, this is not a first-time murder. No novice here," McNabb said. "The killer knew how to kill. He knew the location of vital organs. I believe he knew the victim, was aware that he would be in the proximity of this park area near the church on a quiet Sunday morning. He could have caught up with the victim in a secluded, wooded area. But the killer wanted to make a statement. He's the guy, we'll find out, who called the station."

"You may be right," said Lundgren. "What you are suggesting is that this was planned, perhaps a hired killing. Maybe the wife finds out he was messing around with another woman and wants to put a stop to it, a permanent stop. Perfect timing. She goes to church on a quiet Sunday morning and prays that the deed will be efficiently and professionally administered. That means no suspicion directed at her."

"That's possible," replied McNabb, again looking at the victim and the gaping wounds in his chest and abdomen, "but I doubt it. Usually such a scenario involves, literally, a hired gun, not a knife that could rip the heart out of an elephant. Look at where the clotting blood hasn't obliterated the wound. That stab point right there suggests a wide blade, a serrated blade, used with tremendous force. Our killer is a man, a strong man. I'm guessing there was more to his mission than knocking off a cheating husband.

"But enough speculation. We need to get moving."

Within 10 minutes police were erecting barricades and shutting off traffic in the block next to the murder site. That done, one officer stood near the sidewalk and the other on the lawn closer to the church door. The north side of the church, because of hedges and slopes, offered virtually no access to the crime area. McNabb wanted nobody from the general public traipsing over the scene.

He was by himself now, except for that lifeless form and repeating thoughts about man's ability to kill one of his own.

Outside of war, what sort of person is willing to intentionally end human life, to ignore that human life is unique and special? You could look all over the world and never find a person just like the victim, a man who has been so violated that his very soul appears to be exposed. To kill like that, McNabb thought, requires one to look upon a subject as having no value. What does it say about the killer? He must be the embodiment of moral indifference. Can anyone with an ounce of moral fiber justify such an act?

Maybe war is an invalid excuse. McNabb's younger brother was wounded in North Africa. The two often discussed war and killing. Sure, Hitler had to be stopped. Millions died and millions more suffered because of the thirst for power, the desire for supremacy. Stopping that had to be done. Still, too many leaders and others quick to back war as a solution never spent time in a trench, never witnessed a body without a head, never cradled a dying man.

It was unusual for a cop, but McNabb strongly opposed capital punishment. He was among a growing minority who doubted if executing a convicted killer was any deterrent to murder. Otherwise, it was purely an act of revengeful punishment that said as much about the accusers as the accused. He had to acknowledge that it was this kind of murder – the brutality of it – that generated support for the death penalty.

The morning sun started to crank up the day's thermostat. Cottony clouds that appeared to have been chewed on by some atmospheric rodent posed no barrier to the bright rays. Nearby Quarry Lake would have a busy afternoon as summer shifted into high gear.

McNabb walked the short distance to his car. He retrieved his black raincoat, and returned to the crime scene. He gently placed the coat over the dead man's body.

It was almost 8 a.m.

People would soon be leaving Grace Episcopal Church. McNabb saw an officer walk between the church entrance sidewalk and the crime scene. His partner stood near the far street barricade. He believed the two would be able to steer church goers in other directions. The church parking lot was opposite the murder scene.

"Where do you want me to post?" the officer yelled at McNabb.

"I would say just off the church entrance walkway. People will see you and wonder what's going on," said McNabb. "I think most will go to their cars. If someone does approach you, tell them we are checking on a reported injured person. Oh, if the priest comes out front, would you ask him to come down here? Thanks."

Several minutes later, people began to leave the church even though McNabb could still hear the closing hymn. Soon, the rest of the congregation exited the building. As he predicted and hoped, no one approached the police officer. No one walked toward the crime scene. Several glanced in McNabb's direction, but their curiosity ended there. Some spent several minutes visiting with the presiding clergyman.

McNabb watched as the officer approached the minister, talked briefly, and then accompanied him to the murder scene. They walked slowly, silently. McNabb looked around, and then walked 50 feet toward the two advancing men.

"Hello, I'm Father Don Wright," the priest said, extending his hand to McNabb. "I'm the assistant pastor here at Grace. Is there some sort of trouble here this morning?"

"Father, I'm Capt. McNabb. I think we've met before."

"Are you a member of Grace Church?"

"No," McNabb said. "I am a parishioner at St. Joseph's Catholic Church. I believe you were at a school safety meeting where I talked. Last year?"

"Could be, Captain," Wright said. "I meet a lot of people and I have to work at matching names and faces."

"Well, that's what I'm hoping you can do," McNabb said. "I hate to shock you like this, but a man was found dead this morning in the park area near the church. It appears he was murdered."

"Blessed be God. Captain, I've never had experience with a homicide. Do you think it is one of our members?"

"We don't know, Father. I hate to impose on you, but perhaps you could look at his face and see if you recognize him. The sooner we can identify him the sooner we can advance our investigation. There is no billfold or ID on him. Just some keys, a couple of $1 bills and change in his pocket."

Father Wright glanced away and then upward to a nearby red maple tree. His face began to take on the color of its crimson leaves.

McNabb knew immediately that the priest was a stranger to the ugliness of murder. Dealing with natural death was one thing. A bad accident, or worse yet, a vicious homicide death like this, was entirely different for the trained and untrained.

"Don't feel you have to look at the victim now," McNabb said. "You could come down to the hospital morgue later."

"No, no. There is no good time for this sort of thing."

The three walked the short distance to the park bench and body. McNabb took the priest's forearm. Once there, the officer looked at the clergyman. Nothing was said, but the priest understood and nodded. McNabb slowly pulled the black covering off the dead man's face, and Wright studied the lifeless form. After 15 seconds, he drew away.

The clergyman's mind was a collision of thoughts. Five minutes earlier he was greeting parishioners. Thirty minutes ago he was preaching on the gospel – on the importance of every human life. "*Do not fear those who kill the body but cannot kill the soul*," the reading said, "*rather fear him who can destroy both soul and body in hell . . . So do not be afraid; you are of more value than many sparrows.*"

Do not be afraid? His insides were shaking. This was new territory for him. It would be for most people. How does God allow such cruelty? Was this a faith crisis? No, God created man and all his foibles. Even the option to hate. But how can good live next door to evil? Dear God give me strength.

"I don't think he is one our members," said Wright, backing still further from the ugly scene. "At least, I don't believe he is one our regulars. But I can't say positively that I've never seen him before. This is a town of more than 10,000. I just can't say."

"That's fine, Father," McNabb assured. "If you have any recall about his identity, give us a ring at the station. Again, I'm sorry to drop this on you so quickly. Sometimes, after reflection, some aspect of a person's face will match up with a name or another person's name. Thanks for your help. The officer will see you back to the church."

Chapter 5

August, 1952

Roy Sanders loved sourdough bread, especially when it was toasted.

He placed two slices in the old Westinghouse toast maker, and then poured his first cup of coffee of the day. Thanks Folgers. He glanced out the kitchen window and squinted as the rising sun tried to poke its way through the mass of elms and willows along Indian Creek. It was his favorite time of day.

They had lived out on Fifteen Acres, as Lillian called it, for three years. To Roy's way of thinking, the early morning was the time nature merged all of its beauty and ability to mesmerize. It was quiet. It was peaceful. The entire landscape seemed to be in unmolested harmony. The sun was barely up, but he saw it as the highlight hour. A man could think at this time of day without interruption from anyone or anything.

In the distance he spotted the muscular root of an old oak tree adjacent to the stream. He chuckled. It bulged out above ground, arching like a leg testing the water with its toes. It was determined to get its share of life-giving moisture.

Little Joe had tripped on the intransigent mass of splinters one morning, and Lillian's suggested the old root be severed at the trunk. Delay came to the rescue. Roy wouldn't tell her, but he admired the tree and its root for enterprise. Joe could walk around it.

Now the door of a new day was open. It really was early-morning magic that launched, in Roy's mind, another prospect for opportunity to bloom. It pulled at him, a siren that speaks to the inner self. He took coffee in hand and heeded a summons to the stream like August follows July. There, in the middle of a contemplative harbor and fresh time, was the fitting space to nurture a new idea.

Long ago, he had concluded that this solitude was no accident. Rather, it was the invisible hand of God sustaining perpetual order among powerful but communal forces. It was the dawn of another chance. God must be pleased, too, with His work, Roy thought. Maybe with one exception. Roy's mind drifted to philosophical deliberation. Did God ever regret giving man reason and free will? Did the Creator ever scratch His head in dismay?

No, he decided. Not to the question about head scratching, but to the matter of free will. God, Roy answered his own question, wants us to make up our own minds. We have to decide to believe or not. We must select truth or something else. Cheat or be fair. Work or be dependent. Be charitable or cling inward. We have to determine for ourselves what's important. We can belittle other people or boost and inspire them, segregate or embrace.

Roy ran his left hand over the stubble of his unshaven face. He picked up a pebble and casually tossed it into a part of the stream where water had pooled. He watched the widening ripple. Every action we take, he pondered, produces some form of reaction. Newton's Law applied to human interaction as well as inanimate objects.

Parts of the ripple bumped into the surrounding bank and were repelled, while other parts filtered through reeds, engulfing them gently. Another section of the growing undulation was quickly swallowed by the force of moving water, the main flow of the stream.

Roy envisioned himself as the ripple that bumps things gently.

He watched.

Did the pebbles he tossed during some 40 years of life leave any mark on his family, his community? He never intended to make a big splash. On the contrary, small successes satisfied him, little steps that may produce bigger ripples. The important thing was to do something to advance the relationships between people, between races.

Perhaps, he surmised, we are all products of ripples, the various waves of experience handed down by family and those we encounter every day. One cannot live in a vacuum. We cannot exist just by and for ourselves. Ripples intertwine. They cannot be bound and isolated.

He liked the stream's metaphoric behavior. He liked where he was at in life.

Life is good, he thought, even on bad days. Then the day, taking a cue from the stream, became his allegory. A day, a single frame of time, is really more than that. It begins with the first light, struggling to break through. In its ordinary span, a day takes on many shapes and casts a sundry of shadows as it progresses to its designed end.

"Caw! Caw! Caw!"

The crow dislodged him from his musings, and a chipmunk scurried along the bank to remind him of the busy day ahead. By the time he returned to the house, his toast was cold. He reinserted it for a round two warm-up.

Roy, though his father-in-law was a minister, didn't regard himself as a highly religious man. He never missed church on Sunday and frequently attended Wednesday night services. He never preached about religion or race. He adhered to the notion that example was more successful, more effective. One step at a time. More than once his mild-mannered approach on race issues was misread as indifference.

August, after a scorching July, was an unexpected weather improvement. Still, Iowa's corn crop, because of the unusual heat and dryness, was predicted to be below normal yields come fall. Oats and hay also had suffered from lack of rain. Fifteen Acres, outside the city limits by several miles, was bounded to the north, south and east by a seemingly perpetual carpet of rolling farm fields. The only interruptions were the meandering Cedar River, a major Iowa watershed, and its gurgling tributaries like Indian Creek.

Across the gravel road from their house, to the east, lay a broad grassy area with native bushes and flowers. Sweet Williams had mostly run their course. Coneflowers and Black-eyed Susans were showing off late summer coifs. To Roy's dismay this section, sandwiched between Indian Creek and the county road, also featured bull thistles. They stood proud and obstinate, sporting purple flowers and a strong will to survive. He tried slicing them off at their base with a shovel, but their roots stubbornly pushed up again the following year.

Roy didn't want to switch on the WMT early-morning radio news for fear of waking up the family. It was tempting, though, to tune in and learn if CBS had any positive information out of Korea.

Two years ago President Truman had ordered U.S. troops to aid South Korea following invasion by Communist forces from the North. Now the war had ground to a deadly stalemate along the 38th Parallel. China's entry into the war on the side of North Korea had boosted the bloodshed and all but squashed sporadic hints of a ceasefire.

Truman's approval rating plummeted to 22 percent, lowest ever for an American president. He had decided against seeking a second full term after being trounced in the New Hampshire primary by Tennessee Sen. Estes Kefauver. Then only late last month Democrats picked Illinois Gov. Adlai Stevenson over Kefauver to face war hero Gen. Dwight Eisenhower.

"Dad," a sleepy whisper interrupted Roy's meditation. "How come you always get up so early?"

The voice descended from the stairwell. Simultaneously, the quiet was suspended by the clank of the toaster, reporting its job was done. Roy looked at his son with the rumpled look and exposed bellybutton.

"This is the best sleeping time of all," little Joseph proclaimed, rubbing his eyes as evidence.

"Come here, Joe," Roy motioned to his 8-year-old. He hugged him and gave thanks. "If this is the best sleeping time, why aren't you sleeping?"

"I don't know, Dad. I woke up and tried to get myself back to sleep, but it didn't work."

"What's on your mind? What's keepin' these eyes open so early in the day?" Roy asked. He ran his fingers lightly over Joe's eyelids.

Joe rubbed his eyes, clearly a sign that sleep pulled on one side. But things rolled around in his head and tugged the other way.

"Why do kids in school make fun of me? Why do they say we are black kids and look dirty? Why do they say we are stupid? And some call me "nigger." The kids in our neighborhood don't do that. We just have a good time out here. I don't want to go to school anymore."

Wow! This will wake you up faster than hard-to-stir coffee, Roy thought. Why do some children have to be mean? Why does Joe have to be the target? Andrew never came home with such issues. If he had them, he didn't talk about it.

"Joe, how would you like a piece of sourdough toast smothered in butter and grape jelly?" Roy asked, with his son's questions still tumbling in his mind. "And I think there's some orange juice left."

Joe smiled a little as his father rose to get a glass and the orange juice. The jelly and butter were already on the kitchen table, along with an unpeeled banana.

"Dad. You like jelly on your toast, too, don't you?'

"Joe, you got detective blood just like your mama. Sure, I like jelly. I like to have toast with my jelly."

They laughed, but the questions were still in the air. Roy didn't want to dodge them, but how do you explain to a 8-year old that some people are racist and that some children can be mean. Joe was old enough to understand that the word nigger had horrible implications. He knew it was a word that was flung with intent to hurt.

What he didn't know is that the white schoolmates who uttered such insults, always boys it seemed, probably didn't know what they were saying. It was a word they had heard somewhere, probably at home, and one they understood to have biting results. Instead of a fist fight and a punch in the nose, it was a word-sling and a punch in the self-worth.

"Sometimes people say things because they want to hurt you," Roy began, unsure of where he was going or if any of it would be comforting for little Joe. "They feel they have to hurt someone because maybe they don't feel so good about themselves. Maybe they have to show off to their friends by tryin' to hurt other boys. Did you say something to them that caused any problem?"

"No, Dad, I didn't say anything," Joe replied. "I don't even play with these guys. I don't even know their last names."

"Joe, I didn't think you would start anything. And I'm glad you didn't retaliate. I'm proud of you, and I love you."

"But Dad, it makes me feel like I'm a no-good snake, worse than other kids," Joe said, casting his eyes downward. "I was glad that Mike Murphy took my side. He said these guys were odd balls who probably weren't smart enough to come out of the rain. That would be pretty dumb, alright."

"Joe, I like this Murphy guy."

"Well, Dad, it wasn't exactly a new experience for him. He said they once called him a stupid Mick and cat licker. What does that mean?"

"It means," Roy opted for the easiest explanation, "that Mike was right. These guys are odd balls who are suspicious of anyone who is different. If you said you like jelly on your toast, they would claim peanut butter is better. If you said climbing trees is the best fun, they would say tossing rocks is better. You say up, they say down. You can't win with a contrary person, Joe."

"What does contrary mean, Dad?"

"That's somebody who likes to disagree," Roy explained. "Now, if you are not going to eat that jelly toast, I will."

There would come a time, Roy knew, when he would have to give Joe a better and more profound explanation of racism and the way life was for Negroes. For now, he turned his attention, and Joe's, to a deer that was strolling up from the creek bed and heading for Lillian's sweet corn. Like radar, the deer's nose guided him to the garden morsels.

"Your Mom is not going to be happy when we tell her that Rudolph's buddy was down poaching her corn," Roy said. "We probably should chase the rascal off before he calls his friends. Deer cause a lot of damage to gardens and trees, Joe, and it gets worse every year. Either shoo him, or I can get my rifle and we'll have some deer sausage for winter."

"Oh, don't shoot him, Dad," Joe pleaded, even though he had a good idea his father was teasing. "Mom wouldn't like that either."

"Let's put it this way, Joe. Do you like sweet corn?"

"Yeah. I like sweet corn better than toast and jelly."

"Well," Roy prodded his son. "What does that say to you?"

"It says we have to scare the crap out of that deer and get him out of our garden," Joe responded quickly. "Let's go on the road and grab a handful of gravel and toss it."

"That's a good idea, son. I pick tossing rocks over climbing a tree and watching him munching our corn."

Joe gave his father a puzzled look and then raced out the door ahead of him, mind set on loading his fist with gravel and taking aim.

The fall passed and the cold of winter descended upon Fifteen Acres. Roy had no time frame, no schedule for delivering a family speech that had been ruminating in the back of his mind for months. The entire presentation, and that's how he envisioned it, would culminate with a proposal that he had mentioned briefly to Lillian a year ago.

His early morning talk with Joe last August had rekindled a spark that ushered this long-brewing idea from the back shelf of his brain to the front. The more he thought about it, the more excited he became. Still, Lillian's lack of enthusiasm, to cast her reaction back then in the best light, kept his plans sequestered.

Motel Sepia.

He dwelled upon those two words and his imagination fired up. His entrepreneurial juices began to flow. He had been successful in building a flooring business. He was respected in the business community, the first black member of the Cedar Rapids Chamber of Commerce. He was sure he could get a loan and the necessary building permits.

A week before Christmas the gestation of the motel idea and his courage peaked in tandem. It was a chilly Saturday morning. No school. No work, if you didn't count Lillian's to-do list. Roy was awake and usually up by this time. His mind rotated between thoughts of his family speech and Lillian, who was snuggled in bed next him. She is so wonderful, he told himself for the millionth time, always – well, almost always – supportive of his ideas and projects.

He shifted to a strategic position and kissed her softly on the lips, exploring the possibilities of a familiar routine that really wasn't routine, but more like their own, private unwritten script. He gently moved the straggled hair from her eyes. She responded with a sound that he had memorized.

"What?" she said with a whisper. "No sourdough toast and grape jelly this morning, Mr. Snake Hips?"

Roy laughed. Her famous quick wit, exiting from a sleepy, semi-conscious form, threw his sex drive into neutral. He wasn't sure if he should go forward or back up. The power of his blossoming idea took over.

"Do you remember when I mentioned Motel Sepia to you some months ago?" he blurted out. The question wrestled its way through doubt. Sure, the idea had been taking root for some time. He even dreamt about it one night. But now, like a leg cramp, it muscled its way smack dab into the middle of potential romantic avenues. The question, he quickly learned, detoured spontaneity.

"I remember," said Lillian, in a tone that removed potential passion from the radar screen.

She shifted away and pushed herself to a sitting position in bed.

"You may recall I was not all that excited about the idea," she said. "It seems to me to be an awful big gamble. We're doing fine with our floor businesses. We are established and respected. Why do you want to toss a new challenge into the mix?"

"Lillian, the business is practically runnin' itself," Roy said. "We have the land across the road, and it's not doin' much except providin' a wonderful display area for thistles. We can put up four or five bungalows, independent units for travelers. Instead of stayin' at a cramped motel in town, they could be out in the country next to a bubblin' brook and wide open spaces."

"How do you know anyone would stop?"

"Why not? One of the busiest highways in the country passes right by our door," Roy shifted into his sales gear. "Highway 30 probably carries more traffic than any other East-West road. We could advertise in the *Negro Motorist Green Book* as well as the new *GO Guide*. They have listings for hotels and motels that accept everyone."

"I see you've been doing some homework," Lillian noted. "Are you going to take in white travelers, too?"

"Sure. That's the whole idea, Lillian. We would be open to anyone. We get the black travelers and white travelers to mixin', people from any land and any culture, and next thing ya' know we have a regular United Nations here. Besides, there are not enough black travelers to make a go of it. Oh, I can see it now, Lillian. It –"

"Hold on there, Roy!"

Lillian folded her arms, never a good sign.

"Back your bus up to reality. There's a reason not many places take both blacks and whites. Many whites are not too fond of mixin' with Negroes, and there are Negroes who just soon not be stayin' at a lodge next to whites. Lots of people rather be with their own kind, especially when they are travelin', and don't want any extra problems."

"What extra problems?" Roy inquired. "Not askin' them to sleep in the same bed or stay in the same buildin'. Everybody would have their own place. Maybe outside in the yard we could make little patio areas by the cabins. There they could talk, get to know one another, find out we ain't gonna poison one another."

"And," she continued, "when a white family pulls up and sees the place is owned by a Negro, they just simply gonna rejoice, I suppose, sing Hallelujah."

"Who says we have to open the corporate charter and list all the board of directors and investors?"

Roy was slightly put off by Lillian's negative attitude. He knew there would be issues. Some would pull in, discover the situation, and leave. Others might stay, but wouldn't visit with someone of another race if Russia dropped an atomic bomb in the middle of Iowa.

"Lillian, just think back a couple of years ago when we traveled west." By now, they were both out of bed and getting dressed. "We had a difficult time in some towns finding a place to stay. Some nights we had to sleep in the car. You packed sack lunches every day because we didn't know if restaurants would allow Negroes."

Roy pulled on his coveralls and Lillian slipped into a plaid cotton dress that had seen its share of cleaning, painting, gardening and whatever other chores needed doing.

"I know. I know what the routine was," Lillian said. "Keep your voice down. The children are still sleepin'."

They went downstairs and in unrehearsed rhythm casually walked to the front window. They gazed at the new day, at Lillian's dormant garden and the frozen but obstinate bull thistles across the road. A pickup truck turned off the highway onto Bertram Road and rattled past their house on the corrugated gravel. It kicked up dust like it was passing through a talcum factory.

"Old Elmer is headin' down to the river to try his luck at ice fishing," Roy said, breaking talk about the motel. "Maybe I'll go join him. He probably has plenty of chicken livers and stink bait to wake up hibernating catfish."

The conversation was in neutral, stuck in uncertain ground and looking for a map. It was as if the music had stopped and all the dancers were frozen in mid-step. Roy finally unplugged the silence.

"Now Elmer is white, and I know he wouldn't mind staying at Motel Sepia."

"Maybe Elmer could be your concierge, providin' he was cleaned up from the catfish bait." She let him mull that for a minute. "Why do you call him Old Elmer? He's only a couple years older than you are, Roy."

"Well, I'm getting' to feel old, Lillian. Put on 10 years just this morning."

She didn't see the humor.

"I read someplace that between Chicago and San Francisco there are only five hotels and motels that advertise they will take Negro travelers," Roy continued his lobby. "That includes motor courts. Remember, we stayed at Hotel Chieftain in Council Bluffs, but in eastern Colorado, we slept in the car. In Utah, we slept in the car. In one California town, we stayed with a Negro family.

"That's not unusual," Roy continued. "Probably more Negro families stay in Negro homes when they travel than anywhere else. In some cases, homes have been turned into a commercial business and they advertise. It's a way for these families to make extra income."

"I know all that, Roy. My aunt in St. Paul sent me a clippin' from the *The Minneapolis Tribune*. It was a story by Carl Rowan, and he writes how many of these hotels in bigger cities, who take only Negro travelers, are owned by whites and run by Negroes. They are nothing but a flea factory, but where else can our families go? 'Protected by the tariff of racial seclusion,' was how Rowan put it."

"Yea, well, Rowan himself often had to stay at private homes or Negro colleges, especially when traveling in the South," Roy said.

The couple moved their discussion to the breakfast table. They savored bacon and eggs, a combination usually reserved for their weekend mornings. Motel Sepia was put on the back burner while breakfast sizzled.

"Could you please pass another slice of sourdough bread?" Roy asked. "Negro families," he resumed the main subject, "because of Jim Crow laws, are restricted in many ways when they travel – the few that have the means to travel.

"Lil, we had to travel nine and 10-hour days sometimes to find sleeping accommodations. Usually it was from urban area to urban area. We couldn't stop to explore what was around the bend because we had to be at our overnight quarters by a certain time. Maybe someday we'll be welcome at every small town motel in America, but that ain't the case in 1952."

"Roy, I'll bend this far," said Lillian, making it clear she was done talking about Motel Sepia this day. "Find out if you can build something on your bull thistle patch, what it would cost to put up the cottages. Maybe the highway people can tell you about travelin' traffic. What's advertisin' gonna cost? What would you expect to charge to cover expenses? Two dollars a night? Three dollars? Telephones in cottages? Ice boxes? Who would manage it and who would clean it?"

"Lillian, you are a good bookkeeper," he said, pushing away from the table. "You could keep the records."

Chapter 6

June 1955, Cedar Rapids

"**A**re you nuts, man? That's the worst idea since Eve picked apples. Don't do it! Don't you do it! Don't even think of doing it!"

"Why not? I'm goin' nowheres on a fast train right now, anyways."

"I'll tell you why not. First off, they'll grab your ass before you get a block away. Second, it just happens to be a crime for which, in your case, you will get the maximum penalty. Being Negro, that'd be life in prison. Third, should you escape permanent incarceration at Alcatraz it would be a mistake that follows you like a bad case of athlete's foot. Fourth, your mama will kill you before the cops get to you. And there are 100 more reasons why it's an idiot idea."

"Deron, I'm guessin' we be far apart on this kind of thinkin', an livin' in general. We diffrant. Hell, you even talks funny. We both Negro, but we diffrant. Yo Daddy got a decent job. Mine took off when Mama was pregnant wif me. After Washington High School, I worked half dozen diffrant jobs. Goin' nowheres."

Curtis Moore crumpled his napkin and tossed it on the table. He adjusted his green cap with a Quaker State logo and looked out the rain-splotched restaurant window. He was in a mood gear shifting from complaining to grouchy. They had talked about job prospects and life in general before.

"'Sides, maybe they buy into my story," Moore suggested. "Maybe, I make the news. Become famous."

"Neither the police nor any judge is going to give your story five seconds of consideration on a day when they've got nothing else to do," Deron Campbell replied. "You would go to jail. Period. Case closed."

Moore was currently unemployed, a fact that bothered him since the jobless rate in Cedar Rapids, Iowa, was one of the lowest in the nation. He had heard it more than once: If you really want a job, you can find one. Often, the reminder came from his mother. He found jobs. The problem, and he wasn't sure what all went into that, was that he couldn't keep one.

Part of it was his fault. He admitted it to himself, if not to anyone else. He overslept one morning and was late for a watchman's job at Smulekoff's downtown furniture store, not exactly a prescribed action for job retention. He worked nearly a year at Allen Motor Co. washing cars before an argument landed him back on the streets. It was his fault. He mouthed off to a supervisor. Then he landed a job at the new Kentucky Fried Chicken restaurant. He loved taking home leftovers, but hated sliding around the greasy floor. And he didn't like being bossed by a woman. So, he quit. His mother was furious.

A friend steered him to City Hall to apply for a job with the Parks Department. He didn't get it. Applied too late, they said. Maybe. His mom worked in housekeeping at Mercy Hospital and kept an eye out for jobs there. No luck. The Rev. John Jackson at Bethel AME Church knew the manager at Rapid Placement Service, a job finding agency. No success there.

Moore had thought seriously about enlisting in the Army. Following the Korean War peace agreement in 1953, the military draft remained in effect, but few were being called. Volunteers maintained military manpower needs. Now, in 1955, Congress had adopted the Reserve Forces Act. It required six years of combined active and reserve service, for regular service personnel as well as the National Guard and Reserve. He didn't fancy that kind of commitment.

Moore liked Deron Campbell. He liked Campbell's modest but cool clothes, especially his bright pullover shirts and blue jeans. He admired Campbell's neatly groomed hair and envied his confident calmness. Campbell was the one away from home, away from familiar surroundings, yet he appeared as relaxed and secure as if he were at a family reunion.

However, Campbell's comfort level magnified Moore's discontent at where he was in life. Another thing that bugged Moore was

Campbell's inclination to calmly twirl a spoon or knife as if to demonstrate self-confidence. At first it befuddled Moore. About the third time it became annoying, and he said so.

"My Dad" Campbell attempted to explain his quirky tendency, "preached we shouldn't have a one-gear mind, that we can work on one thing and think about another. He said the brain is fully capable of talking, gesturing and even dancing if the occasion called for it."

Moore listened, but wasn't buying right off.

"Mom," Campbell continued, "would point out that you shouldn't talk with your mouth full of food. By contrast, Dad said he could ponder why a car is having starting fits while at the same time fix its brakes."

Moore raised his eyebrows in sustained puzzlement.

"Think of it this way," Campbell suggested. "Dad said one time. 'Did you ever notice these guest jugglers on the Ed Sullivan Show? They juggle balls and at the same time tell jokes. Their body and brain are involved at the same time. I like to think we can juggle our work to fit the time.'

"I guess Dad meant a person can be involved with more than one thing at a time."

"Oh, I s'pose I understand," a skeptical Moore responded. "Some smart aleck guys tell me I cain't walk and chew gum at da same time. Dat's screwy. I don't even like gum." He laughed. "Your Dad's theory could be OK unless you're talkin' 'bout girls. They don't like bein' juggled with anythin', 'specially if another girl be involved."

"I can't disagree with that," Campbell nodded.

The two met at least weekly at the Kozy Inn restaurant. Moore enjoyed hearing Campbell's stories about Chicago, where Campbell's father owned and operated a successful gas station and auto service business on the city's south side.

Aside from being Negro, Moore and Campbell had little in common. Moore, 22, was small city. Campbell, 20, was big city. Moore had struggled with high school studies, and despite his mother's urging couldn't imagine his future. Campbell was a 3.5 GPA student in college, and with strong support from his family had set his sights high – perhaps business, but more likely in the arts.

Moore was slender but strong, about 5 feet, 11 inches tall and 180 pounds. He had an impish streak, and his mother declared him lacking in common sense. Still, he had been liked by classmates, especially those boys who admired inventiveness that was a tad off center.

Campbell's 160 pounds was distributed on a sleek frame, a runner's physique, with good looks to match. He wasn't averse to pulling pranks on friends or even horsing around with those he knew, but his taste for practical jokes was minimal. More prominent in his character was uncommonly mature judgment equipped with a sensitive switch for turning off potential trouble.

There were acquaintances who looked at Moore as mischief waiting to happen. Indeed, at age 15 he was the unlucky chap in a trio accused of attempting to break into a car outside Armar Ballroom in Marion, Iowa. The other two hightailed it, leaving Moore looking at a security officer's flashlight. His fingerprints were the only ones found on the grey Chevy.

Due to his age and cooperation, and because it was a first offense, Moore was given a suspended sentence. Neither police nor prosecutors believed his story that the three were simply looking inside the car, not trying to break into it.

Campbell, on the other hand, spotted potential trouble a mile away and tried to dissolve it before it thickened. His Dad bragged about his son's uncommon common sense and savvy at problem solving, but his Mother sometimes worried if he'd ever stray from the practical and predictable.

Maybe not yet firm friends, Moore and Campbell enjoyed each other's company. They met in mid-May, just after Campbell arrived in town. Campbell had accompanied his aunt to a potluck supper at Mt. Zion Baptist Church. Moore was there with his mother, one of the organizers of the gathering. They were among the few young men present, incentive enough for their getting acquainted.

If opposite personalities attract, this was a preordained friendship. Food was the natural conveyance. In a short time, their comfort level grew. They not only talked about Campbell's classes, but shared likes, dislikes, weaknesses, disappointments and hopes, subjects beyond trivial talk to profound notions often kept hidden from family and close friends.

Where Moore tended to see the glass as half-empty, Campbell saw it not only half-full but brimming with potential. And, he saw Moore as someone not half-empty, but as a struggling young man with latent talents suppressed by self-doubt. Offsetting that, in Campbell's mind, was Moore's penchant for spawning wildcat ideas that portended pain, distress or worse.

In addition to liking each other's company, both savored those huge pork tenderloin sandwiches that made the Kozy Inn famous. It was impossible for the standard bun to corral the Kozy's perfectly seasoned breaded tenderloin.

"Good thing we're not sitting on some picnic bench in the park," said Campbell, glancing out at the weather's gloomy weekend exhibition. The early drizzle had thickened in intensity.

For Moore, Chicago seemed like some fantasy land a million miles away, a huge city with unending excitement and entertainment. But he had no family there. His grandparents, that is, his mother's parents, moved to Cedar Rapids from Tennessee. He had some uncles and aunts there. They sometimes visited Iowa, but Davenport and Des Moines were as far as he had ever ventured. Both trips had to do with high school sports.

He was fascinated by Campbell's enthusiasm for baseball. He wished he could get that excited about anything.

Moore sipped on a 7 Up. Campbell swirled the ice in his fountain Coke and launched a speech about the greatness of Ernie Banks and baseball in general. He portrayed himself as being among the biggest fans of the Chicago Cubs shortstop, the team's first Negro player.

Being a Cubs fan didn't make Campbell any friends at school back in Chicago or in his south side neighborhood, where the vast majority were partial to the White Sox. Campbell relished that contrast and the accompanying commotion it created.

His love for baseball went as deep as an Ernie Banks home run. It extended to the heart of the game, the way it was played, the nuances of the national pastime, the stats and strategies. Though he never played the game, it drove him crazy, for example, when an outfielder missed the cutoff man, allowing a runner to reach second base. Or, when someone failed to back up a play. And, when a batter failed to move a runner along with less than two out.

His baseball monologue was producing a glazed look in Moore's eyes.

"Don't misunderstand, Curtis," Campbell pitched more small talk. "Minnie Minoso is a great player for the White Sox. He hit .320 last year with 116 runs batted in. But Banks is hitting .295 and on his way to a 40-homer and 100 plus RBI season, and is a better fielder. By the way, did you know Minoso's full name is Saturnino Orestes Armas 'Minnie' Minoso?"

"I didn't know that," said Moore, whose boredom with baseball talk was beyond extra innings. "But isn't .320," he attempted a show of interest, "quite a bit better batting average than .295?"

"Maybe, but Banks is doing better this year," Campbell said, backing off like a hitter who just swung and missed at a change-up third strike.

Moore was more interested in Campbell's classes at Coe College, particularly discussions in sociology. That was another thing about Moore that surprised Campbell. Moore was smarter than he let on. It was one of those sociology sessions, and Campbell's review of it, that set off Moore's imagination and planted a seed that swelled uncontrollably in his mind. It became almost an obsession.

The notion grew to where he envisioned himself as the focus of an experiment. He wasn't going to let Campbell talk him out of it.

Campbell had no Saturday classes, and Moore had no desire to job hunt. They had almost finished lunch. Campbell frequently treated.

"You want anything else?" Campbell inquired. "I'm thinking about another Coke, and may watch some baseball."

The Kozy's management didn't mind if customers hung around to watch Saturday's baseball TV game of the week, still a novelty after two years of telecasts. The Kozy, a short distance from Coe, was one of the few restaurants in town that featured both air conditioning and TV.

"Naw. This is enough," Moore replied. "Thanks, though." His mind drifted back to his future. He just couldn't assemble a plan.

"Deron, you got an education," Moore said. "You a smart person. You knows things. You gonna go someplace. Me, I'm just a Negro who might as well be a slave. I'm a slave to my situation. I'm a slave to my lack of education. I'm a slave –"

"Damn it, Curtis, stop that plantation pouting," Campbell injected. "Frankly, I'm getting tired of hearing how good I have it and how bad your life is. The truth is there are damn few Negroes who were born just after their mama had dinner at the country club, unless, of course, she worked there and ate out of sight of its members.

"I realize your Dad ran off, and that made it particularly difficult for your mama and you. But that's done with. It's over. No amount of review is going to change that. Ernie Banks says you have to find happiness within yourself. I believe that. Curtis, you have to deal with reality. Reality says you're not likely to get any big favors in a white man's world. You have to convince yourself that you have talents, or you can obtain them through education, and they can be converted into a job.

"Reality also says," and Campbell looked Moore square in the eyes, "that your idea – this wild scheme, and I hope you drop it now – is the dumbest since the South fired on Fort Sumter."

When he had finished his mini-sermon, Campbell rued his preacher attitude. He wasn't walking in Moore's shoes. The essentials of life were never in doubt for him. He never scrubbed grease pans where fried chicken fat stuck like dollar bills in a banker's pocket. He worked as a mechanic at his Dad's shop, changing oil and other minor duties, but it wasn't drudgery.

Campbell was one of the fortunate young Chicago Negroes. He was in college, a junior-to-be at Chicago Teachers College, a school some 60 blocks south of The Loop. In the spring of 1955, at the invitation of his aunt in Cedar Rapids, he applied and had been accepted for summer school at Coe College. The campus was only eight blocks from where she lived. The arrangement was OK with his parents, Coe being affiliated with the Presbyterian Church and having stricter than normal guidelines for college students. And, he could live with a relative.

It wasn't just a parental leash being employed, either. Campbell had established his own moral guideposts, and they contrasted considerably from those of many of his high school classmates. He wasn't opposed to fun. He liked girls but knew there were rules. His Dad had listed those more than once.

"Mind your manners." That was his Dad's parting advice before he left on an infrequent date. Deron knew all the territory that covered.

"You gotta smoke?" Moore inquired. "All this jawin' 'bout life and jugglin' make me hungry for a puff. I can discuss better with a smoke."

"Did you ever see me smoke, Curtis? No," Campbell said with disgusting emphasis. "If you haven't seen me smoke you can deduct that I don't smoke. If you'd quit smoking, you could save yourself a lot of money. Besides, cigarettes make your clothes stink. Hell, they make your whole body smell worse than fried roadkill."

"Fried roadkill, eh?" Moore chuckled. "That pretty good. Maybe, I'm thinkin', you sneak a weed behind the chemistry building at school one time. Just as a experiment you know, not that you'd enjoy it. No, no."

"Actually, I did try a Lucky Strike one time," Campbell replied, "when I was a freshman in high school, and almost puked. My Dad smelled it when I came home. He said he didn't know I was such a cool cat as to replace fresh air with pollution and offered to buy me a full pack. I guess that cured me on the spot."

Campbell didn't like cigarettes or alcohol, and much preferred Coca Cola to beer. Many young men smoked. For that matter, a great number of adults smoked. To his way of thinking, booze and cigarettes were mostly tools for young guys to assume the role of adults, to act outside their normal skins. Fire up some Kentucky Club tobacco in an opaque Meerschaum pipe, and you were equipped to be BMOC.

What he did like, besides baseball, was dancing – social dancing, jitterbugging with a flare. He did his talking with his feet, and they said plenty. Maybe, just maybe, he had a career in drama or dance. However, dancing, he found out, didn't fit with the strict history of the Presbyterian Church.

Coe had been affiliated with the Presbyterian Church since the late 19th century when a wealthy packinghouse owner, T.M. Sinclair, paid off the debts of the Coe Collegiate Institute. That's when the Presbyterian Synod assumed responsibility.

"Curtis, I'm sorry for coming on so strong," Campbell said as Moore disposed the last of his tenderloin. Mustard on his chin was the only remaining evidence of the sandwich. The rain cast Campbell into a reflective mood.

"I don't want to sound so high-minded, making like W.E.B. DuBois at a NAACP meeting," Campbell said. "But you must understand that this idea of yours is trouble, bold-faced, all caps, underlined trouble."

He wished now he'd never said anything about that sociology class discussion on the sensitive relationship between black men and white women in the South. In some places, black men could not gaze at white women for fear of retribution. What would happen in Iowa, the class pondered as part of the conversation, if a black man kissed a white woman?

It was a question that fascinated Curtis Moore. He latched onto it, not just as an academic issue for reflection, but one to be put to a test. Twice he had mentioned to Campbell that it would be "cool" to watch the reaction of white people if he, Moore, kissed a white woman.

Campbell felt compelled to warn him again. He didn't want his venturesome friend to solicit a new kind of trouble.

"It's like throwing spit balls at the teacher and claiming it was a physics exercise on seeing how far wet, wadded paper will fly," Campbell continued his attempt at persuasion. "Like smoking a cigar in front of your mama and telling her you are practicing how to create smoke rings. That would be a raw exercise in blowing smoke. It ain't going to work."

"How'd j'you know my mama don't like cigar smell?" Curtis laughed. "And who dis Do Boy fellow anyways? Ya sure do talk funny."

Chapter 7

Cars filed by on First Avenue East, Iowa's busiest street.

Campbell looked out the restaurant window and watched the spray of one car envelop the one behind. It, in turn, conveyed the misty mass to its successor, and on and on the showery parade proceeded. Where, he wondered, were people going on such a miserable, wet day?

Some young men at Coe were sponsoring a car club session. Because of the rain, the meeting had been moved inside to a room at Stewart Memorial Library, so named because it was a gift of the former chairman of Standard Oil Co.

To Campbell, cars were not a hobby. He saw them purely in practical terms, transportation and the source of his family's income. Cars could spin some young men into a tizzy. They could gaze and swoon over the curves of a '54 Mercury like it was Marilyn Monroe in the flesh.

The June rain also put a damper on weekend gardening and lawn tending. No kids' ball games today. No picnics along the river at Ellis Park. The Cedar Rapids Raiders baseball game at Veterans Stadium would be in jeopardy.

Cedar Rapids' history with minor league baseball dated back to 1891 with a team called the Canaries. Campbell had been out to the stadium three times.

"Not much work or anythin' else gonna be done today," Moore said. "Maybe jus' as well have another 7 Up. I'm gonna make a wild guess, but pretty soon we gonna see cats and dog comin' out of the sky. But, as the farmers say, all this rain good for the corn."

Outside the city, in Iowa's multitude of small towns, farmers gathered at local coffee shops to praise the rain. In periods of overly wet weather, they would assemble at the same places to cuss the rain. Corn was well on its way to "knee high by the Fourth of July," and oats would soon produce heads and then turn gold on its way to harvest and threshing.

Campbell had zero interest in farming. He didn't know the difference between a Duroc and Hampshire and couldn't distinguish a Holstein from a Guernsey. What's more, he didn't care. He was a big city kid and proud of it. He enjoyed Coe College, and his favorite class featured Professor Jansen and his sociology ramblings.

Jansen's summer class focused on two themes, interfaith relationship and interracial behavior. Most people would prefer to avoid both subjects like an assault of halitosis. Race relations was the current topic.

Of the 15 students in the class, Campbell was one of two Negroes. That didn't bother him. In fact, the class makeup intrigued him, particularly in light of assignments put forth by Jansen. He asked students to write about their own experiences and attitudes with people of other races. He challenged them to assess what they believed a person of another race thought about them.

Campbell thought the responses would be fascinating. How honest, how forthright, he wondered, would students be? There were no women in the group, a fact not part of the professor's subject matter.

Eight in the class, mostly from Iowa, came from small towns with no Negro residents. Iowans were mostly white Protestant descendants of European immigrants. Their experiences with other races would have been almost exclusively in Cedar Rapids or on visits to larger cities. And in Cedar Rapids, with only two percent of its population Negro, the chances of an interracial experience were slim.

Was there a connection between community demographics and acceptance? Were race relations generally and individually any different in cities with greater numbers of minorities than in cities like Cedar Rapids? And, what about Iowans in and around small farming communities? Would they be more circumspect of someone who looks different? Were Negroes on Chicago's south side wary of whites who come into their neighborhood?

Campbell had spelled out to Moore the various questions raised in Jansen's class. Moore was engrossed by the subject. The class had also reviewed Iowa's current status and history in race relations.

Iowans, while having the propensity to be fiercely independent, also hold the reputation of being neighborly and open minded. Some might claim their collective tolerance, given the lack of immersion in racial contrasts, hadn't really been put to the test. Perhaps there was truth in that. Yet, it was also true that Iowa was unlike southern states where Jim Crow lived in the open.

Separate public facilities for Negroes didn't exist in Iowa in 1955. No one insisted Negroes sit in the back of the bus. Lunch counters were, in theory, open to anyone, even though just eight years before a black woman in Des Moines was told by a fountain attendant at a drug store that the business "was not equipped to serve her." However, the woman sued and won.

Negro students could attend any school, but housing patterns produced what in essence was a segregated education system in some places. Iowa presented no outward obstacles to voting. At the same time, it would be naïve to suggest that discrimination didn't exist – in housing, jobs and in the private confines of individual hearts and minds.

"Iowa's early history was a contrast in openness," Campbell said. He outlined for Moore what the class had reviewed.

When the first Territorial Assembly gathered in Burlington, Iowa, in 1838, it virtually excluded Negroes from the state. To settle in Iowa Negros had to certify that they were free persons and post a $500 bond against becoming a monetary liability to the state. The Assembly also prohibited racial intermarriage and enacted other restrictions that were race specific.

Still, there was another side to Iowa's collective attitude toward Negroes in the state's early history. Before Iowa became a state in 1846, there was the matter of Ralph. Records only referred to him as Ralph.

Ralph had been a slave in Missouri, but his owner allowed him to travel to Iowa, a free state under the Missouri Compromise, providing he pay $550. Ralph worked in the Dubuque lead mines and hoped to earn the $550 and buy his freedom. Years passed, and he failed to pay the money. His owner sent bounty hunters to bring him back to Missouri.

On a writ of habeas corpus, Ralph's case ended up before the territorial Iowa Supreme Court in 1839. It found that Ralph should pay his debt, but held that "no man in this territory can be reduced to slavery." The court rejected the argument that Ralph was a fugitive slave, reasoning that by allowing him to leave Missouri and reside in a free state, his owner could no longer exercise any right over him in the Iowa territory.

By contrast, the U.S. Supreme Court faced a similar question in 1857 when it rendered the infamous Dred Scott decision. However, unlike the Iowa Supreme Court's ruling regarding Ralph, the U.S. Supreme Court upheld the rights of the slave holder and ordered the slave returned.

Though Iowa was a free state, there was a good deal of soul searching and political bobbing and weaving blended with subtle and open hostility to Negroes when delegates in 1844 debated the state's first constitution and the question of citizenship. Citizens at first rejected a proposed constitution that barred Negroes from voting and holding office, but approved a similar draft two years later.

Influence of southerners in Iowa's Third General Assembly in 1851 led to a bill that banned settlement by free Negroes. Those already in the state could stay, but newcomers were to leave within three days.

Curiously, the law was not included in the 1851 Code or its revision in 1860. It was to become effective upon publication in the Mt. Pleasant *True Democrat*, a newspaper with an anti-slavery editor. Mysteriously, it never made it into print. The would-be law ultimately was declared null and void, and Iowa's Negro population tripled by 1860.

Iowans, tired of pro-slavery maneuvers, elected Whig James W. Grimes as governor in 1854. While campaigning, Grimes had promised that he would "war and war continually against the abandonment to slavery of a single foot of soil now consecrated to freedom." This was the signal for a decided change of opinion in Iowa.

"I know lot of that stuff," Moore said. "We studied 'bout that Ralph guy and Dred Scott and early history. Forgot most of it. I'd be more interested in today. What happenin' now? What else this professor ask you?"

"Well," Campbell responded, "Professor Jansen wants to know our personal experience. For example, have I met enough English, Germans, Poles, Italians, Greeks, Irish and other whites in Chicago to discern differences in their relations with Negroes?

"What, in turn, are Negro attitudes toward whites? Do some Negroes hate whites like some whites hate Negroes?"

The two young men exchanged inquisitive looks.

"Have I personally," Campbell continued, "been the target of racist actions or slurs, he wants to know. Have I witnessed others suffer bigotry? Is Jim Crow active on the south side of Chicago in 1955? Do I know anyone denied equal rights? Am I aware of whites who are treated differently by Negroes because they are white?

"How about my neighborhood? Do any whites live there? Am I aware of any interracial marriages?"

"Those all good questions, I guess," Moore broke in. He took a gulp from his 7 Up. "It be December 'fore you get all the answers. What 'bout others in the class?"

"Other students have to ask themselves similar questions," Campbell said.

Only the hard-headed would argue that Iowans in the mid-1800s were, in general, a great deal more tolerant than those in the South when it came to race relations. Before Iowa abolitionists made their opinions known, there was too much specific and ancillary evidence to the contrary. But the notion of slavery, that any human life could be regarded as less than human, was met with broad contempt in Iowa.

Some 13,000 Iowans died for the North during the Civil War, and part of the evidence of that sacrifice covers a large knoll at Vicksburg National Cemetery. The firing upon Fort Sumter had produced an amazing response as Iowans volunteered in numbers beyond the expectations of Governor Samuel J. Kirkwood. Most Iowans were supporters of Abraham Lincoln and opposed slavery. Confederate sympathizers were mainly confined to Iowa's southern borders.

Still, when Alexander Clark, the second black lawyer to graduate from the University of Iowa Law School, offered to organize a company of Negro volunteers in 1862, Kirkwood told him, "It's a white man's war".

Only after President Lincoln issued the Emancipation Proclamation and slavery became a defining issue in the war was Clark successful in forming the first company of black recruits.

But what about conditions in Iowa in 1955?

Campbell continued a rundown of issues being examined by the class. Did white students ever witness discrimination, racial or otherwise? Were they perpetrators of it? Did any ever hear the epithet "nigger," or say it themselves? What about acceptance of Catholics and Jews? Were all ethnic groups in Iowa treated with respect?

"That sure coverin' a lot of territory," Moore reflected. "I wish I coulda been in on the kissin' talk."

"Curtis, forget about that nutty idea, and come up to my room a piece," Campbell said. "We can listen to music, maybe a little Blues by the new man on the block, Bo Diddley."

Campbell had brought his inexpensive, black and gray RCA record player with him to Cedar Rapids. It only played 45s.

He looked at Moore and read a big question mark on his face. Who was Bo Diddley?

"Don't dig Diddley? OK. We'll try somebody else. I know, man. How about the hottest song in the country? I have the single of 'Rock Around the Clock' by Bill Haley and His Comets."

Moore smiled and Campbell knew he had struck a chord. Bill Haley had teens and young people everywhere jumping. It was a strange new beat that sent the young gyrating and howling, and parents bellowing in objection, puzzlement and retreat.

"Or there's another new guy, a Negro, who's getting popular," Campbell said excitedly. "Have you heard of Chuck Berry and his song, 'Maybellene?' I've got that record, too. It's just out!"

"I should prob'ly be gett'n home, Deron," Moore said, pushing his chair away from the table. "The rain seems like it let up, and I should skedaddle 'fore it opens up again. Thanks for the offer, though. Maybe some other time.

"You sure didn't watch much of the ball game on TV," Moore pointed out to Campbell.

"East coast teams, again," Campbell said. "I'm not as interested as when the Cubs play."

"When ya plan to finish the report for Professor Jansen?" Moore asked. "Tell me, what you gonna say? How ya be treated by white folk? They sit down nex' to you in Chicaga? How 'bout here in Cedar Rapids? Ya ever be called 'nigger'? Colored people get same treatment in Chicaga as white folk? Do ya even go to their neighborhood?

"Hell," Moore rambled on, "I know couple white kids in school, but dats 'bout it. How many you know? Really know? Do you have any white fren's? Can little Negro kids join hands with little white kids on Chicaga playgrounds? Never seen it here."

Campbell suddenly realized that Moore was a whole lot smarter than he first judged. He looked across at him as he finished his Coke. Don't measure a person by the way they talk, he thought.

Campbell lived in a virtual sea of black people. He had no white neighbors. Chicago proper had 3.6 million residents, 15 percent of them Negro and nearly all concentrated in specific sections of the city.

The so-called great migration from the South to Chicago started during Reconstruction. Most settled on the city's south side. By 1910, 78 percent of the 40,000 Negroes in Chicago lived in the Black Belt, a narrow stretch of neighborhoods south along State Street. In 1919, riots followed the movement of Negroes into white neighborhoods.

By 1940, the collapse of tenant and sharecrop farming in the South, and a switch to machines picking cotton, sent more Negroes packing for the promised land. The resettlement became the mantra of *"The Chicago Defender,"* the newspaper voice of Chicago blacks. What Negroes found in the big city were segregated neighborhoods and schools, and often job discrimination.

But Campbell's family was not among the recent newcomers. His father's parents had moved up in 1912 from Warren, Ark. His mother's family came two years earlier from rural Pontotoc, Miss.

The Campbells lived on the south edge of the Grand Boulevard neighborhood, not far from Chicago's famous Bronzeville. Bronzeville had been a magnet for southern Negroes in the second decade of the 20th century. It developed into a center for Negro culture in Chicago.

"Hey, Curtis, have you ever seen Jet magazine?"

"No, can't say I has. What it be, some fancy write-ups of high society colored folk?"

They laughed.

"No, man," Campbell said. "It's a small news magazine published in Chicago with items about Negro life. Oh, it has some articles about the kinda hats Negro women wear and hair styling. But it also talks about music, sports, jobs and culture. And, we also have a newspaper, *The Defender,* which a few years back wrote editorials urging President Truman to integrate the military. Truman did, or as much as a law can do."

"Haven't seen it either," Moore said. "But Mama take the local paper. She say only dumb people don't read, don't know what goin' on. She say if you don't read the paper you don't know what rascals to vote out of office. I read it. I like the funnies.

"From now on, I gonna look for Chicaga Cub news, see how's they doin'," Moore added. "See if this Ernie Banks fella any good like you say."

Moore picked up a copy of the Friday evening *Gazette* that Campbell had found on the restaurant counter. He scanned the sports page, but found nothing about the Cubs or Ernie Banks.

"How's come no news 'bout the Cubs?" Moore inquired. "Maybe the sports editor don't like the Cubs."

Quiet moved in as the young men digested the conversation of the last hour. Finally, Moore rose to leave.

"Ya know what, Deron?" Moore folded the paper and placed it on the back of the table.

"One of these days some colored person gonna create some hell 'bout discrimination. He gonna call the card. He gonna file a lawsuit if he can't get a job 'cause of color. He gonna march to the mayor's office in Chicaga and demand better housin'.

"Heck, in the South," Moore continued, "somebody may even try to sit in the front of the bus. Who knows?"

"How do you know it's going to be a he?" Campbell asked.

"I don't. Now don't be fool'n wif me. Maybe it be a she. You know what I'm talk'n 'bout. Somebody or sombodies gonna yell foul. Somebody gonna push back. Ya think on it, Deron. It'll happen. Times chang'n. Ya think on it when ya write that paper for Professor Jansen.

"I'll tell ya what's crazy?" Moore ran on. "I heard on the news other day that in Selma, Ala., and you knows this happen in other suthern' towns, too, a Negro has to guess how many jelly beans there is in a jar 'fore he can vote. Now Deron, that is plain crazy. No white person has to guess how many jelly beans. Hell, I grab a han'ful and run. Put that in your professor paper."

"Okay, Curtis, maybe I'll do that," Campbell said. "In the meantime, you give plenty of thought to what I said earlier. No goofy ideas. Get yourself a job and make your Mama happy. I'll even check at Coe to see if they have any jobs available. These professors know rich people in town and someone who might be hiring. But no stupid stuff, OK? I'll see you later."

In much of the South in 1955, as it had been for years, if a Negro male looked at a white woman for longer than a white man deemed appropriate, the Negro could find himself anywhere between a beating and death.

Curtis Moore knew that. Deron Campbell knew it. Was it really any different in places like New York, Chicago or Iowa?

That's what Moore wanted to know. He as much as challenged Campbell to make it a prime point of deliberation in Professor Jansen's class. It was the notion of a sociological demonstration, putting the question to a test, that Moore couldn't get out of his mind.

What would happen, Moore queried Campbell several times, if a Negro in Cedar Rapids kissed a white girl? Not a prolonged press of the lips or passionate embrace, but a simple peck on the cheek?

Campbell had to admit there was intrigue in the proposition. But the likely trouble, serious trouble, far outweighed any experimental benefits. He knew one thing: he wanted no part of it, in Chicago or Cedar Rapids.

"Let me give you a piece of advice, Curtis," Deron looked him square in the eye. "What you're saying may be an OK topic for classroom discussion, but it sure as hell would be a stupid idea, or experiment as you call it, to try in real life. Don't, I repeat, don't be an idiot."

His voice had become louder than he intended, and it provoked a bigger response than he had expected. Curtis, his face turning red, looked down on the still-seated Campbell. He pointed a finger at him and then began wagging it as he searched for words.

"You and I have had some good discussions, Deron, but I'll tell you this: I don't need any Uncle Tom shit from you."

Others in the restaurant began to stare.

"I gets enough crap without you calling me out as stupid and idiot."

Curtis glared at Deron.

"I'm just trying to keep you out of trouble, Curtis, that's all."

"Well, why don't you mind your business, Mr. Big City Boy, and I'll mind mine. How's that for equality?"

"What seems to be the problem over here," the Kozy Inn manager inquired, drawn by the raised voices.

"No trouble on my part," Curtis replied. "Jus' ask Mr. Cool College guy here. He has all the answers," and he headed out the front door.

Chapter 8

Naperville, Ill.

Naperville Police Chief Ken Zimmerman had envisioned a morning on the links. The telephone call from dispatch changed his Sunday plans and those of the entire Police Department. The chief arrived at the murder scene 12 minutes after being notified and not too long after Capt. McNabb's visit with Father Wright.

"I believe you are right, Jeremy." Zimmerman said grimly. "As much as I hate to say it, this has all the marks of a professional killing. If that's the direction we're headed, it's foreign territory for us. What is the latest information you have, and how do you suggest we proceed?"

"Chief, I've never seen anything quite this violent," McNabb told his superior. "It's difficult to put into words. Not only did the killer wish to make a statement, in my opinion, he wanted it in big headlines on the front page, for all to see. This was a notification sent in bold face. The question is, to whom?"

"We've never had any significant problems out here with organized crime," Zimmerman said with authority. "Maybe some numbers running or barbershop pools, but nothing that smacks of big-time hoodlums. Are you thinking along those lines?"

Zimmerman was old-school cops. His Dad had been on the police department in Elgin. His older brother, Paul, was on the fire department in St. Charles. The family joke was that Ken Zimmerman had worked his way down the Fox River to Naperville law enforcement. He was employed five years on the department at Wheaton and now 25 years on the Naperville police force, the last eight as chief.

He was well respected by fellow officers and by the community. He knew the people, and he knew the territory. Like just about everybody else in Naperville, city employees were well-paid. Cops, too. What was not to like? Crime was below average in this white-collar community, and pay was the best in Chicago's quilt work of ethnic, racial and socio-economic neighborhoods and suburbs.

If Naperville had a highbrow reputation, as many suggested, news of a gruesome, gangland murder just outside a church on an otherwise lovely June morning would more than sully that perception. It would be outlandish, like having a flea-infested hotel in the middle of shiny downtown Naperville.

Chicago newspapers, bored by murders in the near-Loop area, would give top billing to the story. It was gore in the midst of gold, opulence defiled by blood. It was man bites dog. It would not be an item in next week's Naperville Chamber of Commerce bulletin.

"I think we will have more answers, and probably more questions, once we determine his identity," McNabb said, lifting his police cap with one hand and scratching his head with the other. "Chief, please take a look at the deceased and see if you recognize him. I think I've seen him around, but I'm not sure."

McNabb again pulled back his raincoat to reveal the dead man's face. The victim's countenance retained that surprise look, one of shock and foreboding expectation.

Zimmerman motioned that the body cover be removed entirely. He looked closely at the staring eyes of Aldo Arezzo. The chief's gaze shifted to the bloody and battered chest and abdomen. It sent shivers through his own body.

As McNabb had done, he shook his head in disbelief. He focused on the face again, and wondered, without word, if the man had died quickly or suffered for minutes. The massive physical trauma suggested the victim did not suffer long.

"I think he is a golfer," Zimmerman said quietly. "I'm sorry," he paused. "Was a golfer. Like you, I'm not positive. But I believe I've seen him at the course, maybe the one over at Wheaton. We have a camera at the station. Have one of the officers snap a picture, get it developed right away, and circulate it at nearby golf courses. We may hit on something. And we need to get pictures of the full crime scene."

There was silence as both men confronted the private thoughts that crisscrossed their minds. McNabb again pulled the make-shift covering across the body.

"I tend to agree that this was a hit job," the chief continued. "The ferocity of the stabbing, with no attempt to conceal the crime, called in by a Frank King? Not Frank Mendoski or Frank Sullivan, but Frank King? It all points that way." He directed his attention elsewhere. "Look at the blood marks on the park bench. Is that a partial print?"

"It sure looks like it, but it's rather large for a finger," McNabb said. "I've asked Mike O'Connor to come over. He should be here as soon as he collects his fingerprint gear."

"I think I'll put out a quick query to departments all over the Chicago area," Zimmerman said, his detective skills kicking in. "What do you think? Ask around if this crime resembles another. The more I think about it, the more I'm convinced this is a signature crime, an attempt by the killer to be unique, in a sense, to leave his stamp, his credentials."

"That's a horrifying projection, but you may be correct," McNabb said. "We could be dealing with an amoral monster."

Chapter 9

August 1955, Cedar Rapids

Mike Kreiji leaned on the laminate-topped order counter and swabbed his sweaty forehead with his grease-splotched apron.

It was fortunate that the Health Department didn't come around late at night to inspect. He laughed to himself. Was there any place on that once white apron to wipe the last ounces of perspiration from his drained body without smearing himself with a variety of glop and grime?

Even the apron strings looked suet-soaked.

It had been a busy day and a busier night. He was perplexed, really, at the heavy stream of customers for a Thursday night. There were no advertised specials. No big events in town. The Cedar Rapids Raiders minor league baseball team opened a three-game home series with Evansville. The movie, *"The Night of the Hunter"* starring Robert Mitchum, was the feature at the Paramount. Baseball and movie fans? Perhaps. Even the late-evening traffic on Mount Vernon Road was above normal.

The Czech Inn was not a fancy place. The building had more makeovers than Bette Davis. Like the actress, it held a special attraction, particularly among those who appreciated both good food and a reasonable price.

Maybe we're doing something right, Kreiji mused. He was exhausted and ready to close shop.

"Dorothy," he said evenly through the order window to the kitchen. "Don't forget to turn off the fryers and ovens."

Not that Dorothy Dotson would. She had worked at Kreiji's restaurant for 15 years and knew the end-of-the-day routine like Steve Allen knows a punch line.

She, too, was tired, beat. Her body felt as limp as a soup sandwich. Her arms had labored to lift the rack for the last batch of fries. But Dorothy wasn't a complainer. She was the kind of person who saw work to be done and did it. She was poor at delegating, an adherent of the theory that she could do it quicker and better than taking the time to ask someone else. She was the biblical Martha, except she smoked Viceroy filters and savored manhattans. And she could cuss.

Running a restaurant is hard work. Customers may not realize it, don't even think or care about it, but the business of feeding people – and keeping them satisfied so they will return – is one of the toughest jobs on God's Earth.

Dorothy and Mike, during a lull one rainy day, compared the business to that of a politician. You are only as good as your last vote, or last meal, and voters, or customers, run the gamut in their approval rating. Make a slip on a crucial legislative issue and the opponents will have you for lunch. Make a slip at the lunch counter, and customers will vote for a different restaurant faster than a lobbyist can pull out his billfold.

"I think I'd rather be in the food business," Mike told Dorothy. "There is less that goes to waste."

The two were on automatic shutdown, their bodies numb with fatigue. Dorothy's mind focused on a hot bath and soft bed. As usual, both had come in to help with the noon lunch rush. There was a regular morning shift that opened the place at 6 a.m. The evening staff, largely made up of pinch-hitter students from Mount Mercy and Coe colleges, customarily dwindled to where only Dorothy and Mike remained.

Kreiji inherited the Czech Inn Lounge from his parents. He was well-acquainted with the ups and downs of business and the particular challenges of operating a good eating place. He had watched his father worry and weather the bad times, and rejoice and expand in the good times.

Now was a good time. People were in a buoyant mood in Cedar Rapids, as well they should be. Anyone who really wanted a job could get one. Collins Radio Co., like much of the city's industrial sector, was booming. In fact, Collins, launched in 1933 not far from the Czech Inn, had grown significantly in 22 years to become the city's largest employer. Arthur Collins, at age 21, founded the company in the basement of his home. World War II sales to the military thrust his high-powered radio transmitters into permanent prominence.

The city's huge food industry labored to satisfy the appetite of a growing nation and a fledgling export market. Quaker Oats operated the world's largest cereal mill in Cedar Rapids, an operation that provided many jobs and a signature smell. It cast a toasty fragrance over the city compared with the less-than-rosy emissions from the packing house. Blended, they produced a non-ambrosial ambiance that some called nostril numbing, but the mayor believed to be the "smell of money."

Beyond the benefits of a robust economy, Kreiji had a solid base of Czech customers – in a city with 20 percent Czech heritage – and a spot on the busy Lincoln Highway, the nation's first cross-country road. Add that all together and the bottom line showed a mighty fine profit for the Czech Inn, enough for Kreiji to put his own sweat equity in neutral, and let others run the place.

But that was not in his constitution. He carried all the Czech genes that comprise hard work and individualism.

Times were good if you ignored the ruminations of the Cold War. Active hostilities between the Communist sphere and the West were in a two-year lull with the end of the Korean War, but that didn't mean verbal sparring between the two sides wouldn't erupt into something worse somewhere else.

Congress, early in 1955, authorized President Eisenhower to use force to protect Formosa. Shortly thereafter, the president sent the first American advisors to South Vietnam. While war was in recess, the world seemed to be once again choosing up sides, with growing hemispherical bombast and nuclear talk.

That was the picture. Unprecedented prosperity lived with renewed anxiety. Bomb shelters co-existed with a home-building spree. It was a time of fancy new Chevys and Fords and the incessant sounds of Elvis Presley, Bill Haley & His Comets and the latest sensation, Pat Boone. Rock 'n' roll was trying its best to drown out apprehension and fear.

Kreiji's customers were talking more about the new Disneyland in California than they were of bomb shelters and nuclear war. Since the end of World War II, Walt Disney had been pondering a place where children and parents could frolic, and finally this magical spot had been born. A 160-acre orange grove in Anaheim had been transformed into new rivers, fairy tale castles, groovy rides, flying elephants and giant teacups.

The restaurant was clearing out fast. The few customers from the second shift at the packing house, Wilson Foods, finished their bedtime snacks and headed home. One regular, who worked in the department where they grind up all the leftover parts from butchered hogs into a mixture destined for wieners, had his usual grilled cheese and root beer.

"No hot dog for me tonight," was his standard salutation. He was the last to leave.

"What'dia think, Dot?" Kreiji yelled back to the kitchen. "A trip to the new Disneyland? Do you think Olga would go for it?" he asked, raising his eyebrows to reflect his own doubt.

Olga Kreiji, his wife of 31 years, was as busy with Czech culture as Mike was operating the restaurant. She had about as much interest in the Czech Inn as Mike had in collecting hand-painted Czech Easter eggs. She liked the restaurant's financial security, and he liked her contacts with many potential Czech customers. He honored and recognized the legitimate respect she had earned with her many years of teaching summer classes in the Czech language.

"She might surprise you, Mike," Dorothy replied. "She won't take an airplane. Said she's afraid. You'd have to drive, and that's one helluva long Sunday afternoon swing on the prairie." Dorothy had a way with words.

"Oh boy, here comes trouble," she switched subjects, hands extended upward in disgust. "I hope his order is short and his stay the same. He can be a royal pain in the ass."

Fritz Langerhaus was not the favorite customer of the Czech Inn. He was long on loud, his opinion and other people's faults. He was a bachelor, a circumstance Dorothy said was not surprising, and now that he had retired from Wilson Foods he had more time to circulate the public places of southeast Cedar Rapids and spread his gospel.

"Dobry den," he greeted Kreiji before the front door had closed behind him. Fritz was proud to advance the lone Czech phrase he knew. He snapped his ever-present suspenders, a sign he was in an extraordinarily good mood.

"Jak se mate?" Kreiji responded. "Mluvite Anglicky?"

"Why don't you speak English?" Langerhaus growled, changing his mood as quick as a turn in Iowa weather. He regretted that he had initiated the Czech talk. He adjusted his Pioneer Seed Corn cap and eyed a table.

Mike chuckled to himself. He had asked Langerhaus, "How are you?" and then followed with, "Do you speak English?"

He liked to pull the old German's chain, but not too far as to launch Fritz into a tirade about "foreigners." The fact that Fritz's grandfather had immigrated from near Bremen, Germany, was of no account. Fritz was all-American, as he often reminded anyone who cared to listen, and the proof was that his younger brother fought with the U.S. Army in North Africa against the Germans.

"Hey, Dorothy," Fritz yelled, circumventing the omnipresent green ordering pad that usually catalogued a customer's desires. "How about manufacturing a Reuben sandwich for me?"

He plunked his 250 pounds, led by a sizeable gut, on a chair at a table Mike had just cleaned.

"Go heavy on the kraut, with the pickle on the side. Don't want to contaminate the kraut," Fritz chortled at his attempt to be funny. He tossed off the episode of Czech talk like bad karma, and restored his jovial self.

"And add a plateful of French fries. Oh, how 'bout toasting the rye?"

Two things were in Fritz's favor, sort of. Dorothy was cleaning out the French fry rack, and she had a smidgen of corned beef left. She was going to throw it out, but now she calculated that she could slather on enough Thousand Island dressing and a couple of slabs of Swiss cheese to cover for the deficiency of meat. She didn't mind charging Fritz full price for a half-order.

"I can cover it," she addressed Kreiji before he had a chance to inform Langerhaus on Czech Inn ordering protocol and the lateness of the evening.

"Thanks, Dorothy," Kreiji responded.

Dorothy didn't think of herself as better than Langerhaus or anyone else. She just didn't suffer fools well. Maybe that's why she was divorced. She now lived with her aging mother.

Cedar Rapids was a blue-collar town, and she was comfortable as part of the hoi polloi. Her social home was the church circle, its regular bake sale and the Monday night bridge game. She didn't work at the restaurant on Mondays. It was closed on Sundays.

She had been a good student in high school and was an avid reader, even now. She loved books. It wasn't something she advanced in conversation, trying to impress friends by releasing her hidden knowledge. She simply was not the forward type. Neither was she shy. Once someone else opened a subject, she felt comfortable at giving her opinion. Even then, it was in modest proportions.

However, people would make a big mistake to judge her as ordinary. She may look vanilla on the surface, but inside Dorothy – close friends called her Dot – was a woman of many contrasts. She had her hair cut and permed at the beauty parlor, followed results of car races at Hawkeye Downs, though seldom could attend, and occasionally went to the Sunday afternoon performance of the Cedar Rapids Symphony.

Dorothy inherited her diminutive stature from her mother. At 5-foot-2, she was one of the shortest people in her class at Wilson High. But if shoved, she would shove back. Or, as her father summarized her, "She's a feisty one." Joe Dotson had worked at the packing house until his death five years ago.

Dorothy assembled the Reuben quickly, barely warming the bread and interrupting the toaster's normal cycle. She glanced at Langerhaus and reviewed his huge nose. His long, wooly sideburns matched his eyebrows. She wondered if he brushed his teeth or had even been to a dentist in five years. There was an upside to Fritz now that he was retired. His shirt usually wasn't stained with sweat and the accompanying waves of body odor.

For a second Dorothy admonished herself. Who was she to judge him? She had been happily married, for 28 years. What happened? Was the divorce her fault? When their daughter left home, it seemed the bond of marriage left, too. Why? Failure to talk, do things together? Maybe neither one really worked at it. But that's the past. Now her life revolved around her mother and beautiful new granddaughter, Jillian.

She glanced at Langerhaus and suddenly felt sorry for him. She had a better life. Fritz lived alone. She doubted if he had many friends. She felt ashamed for her quick conclusions, her broad paintbrush that colored him something less than human. Maybe he gave generously to his church or to the Salvation Army. Maybe he volunteered at the Jane Boyd Community House. She doubted that, however. Nevertheless, she slathered another layer of mayo and second slab of cheese to his Reuben. They also concealed the dearth of corned beef.

"I'm going to put the 'Closed' sign on the door so we can wrap this up," Kreiji said for the benefit of both Dorothy and their last customer. He looked at Langerhaus. "Eat fast, because we're already five minutes past when I turn into a pumpkin."

"I wouldn't be in too big a rush there, my friend," said Langerhaus, glancing through the restaurant's front window as Kreiji walked back to fetch Langerhaus' Reuben. "It looks like you have another customer headed this way. More money for the Bohemie's bank account!"

Bohemie, by tradition in local culture, was a dual-edged term. It carried a complimentary signature that recognized the innate hard-working, home-owning, bills-paid nature of Czech people. It also had a derogative side, one that suggested a lower rank in the social stratum, bourgeois at best, a down-the-snoot appraisal. In this town, Bohemie jokes were the Irish and Polish jokes of another place.

Langerhaus, no country club member himself, intended neither admiration nor disrespect.

Kreiji stopped to follow the cue and looked back. He didn't like what he spotted as he reversed course. Just that quick, a man with a hood over his face bolted in the door. It soon became evident his primary business was not to satisfy a growling stomach.

The man's left hand fidgeted in the pocket of his black jacket, and it appeared to Kreiji he was concealing a gun. He held a plain blue cloth sack with his right hand and walked straight toward Kreiji, ignoring Langerhaus.

"Jus' move real slow to your cash reg'ster, like nothin' is out of kilter, and put about $10 in this here bag," the man ordered. "This a simple matter, simple request. You, ma'am, come 'round out of the kitchen and step out here in the front where I can see you. And bring that sandwich wit ya. And you, Mr. Pioneer Seed Corn hat," he gestured toward Langerhaus, "you be staying on yer ass where you are."

The man launched into an almost subliminal hum as if he were casually walking through the flower beds at Bever Park Zoo. His demeanor, outside his direct intent of robbery, was more like a person on a Sunday stroll than a Thursday night heist.

"Do what he says," Kreiji said to Dorothy as he walked over to the cash register. He looked at the man, a slim fellow about 6 feet tall, and then picked up the bag from the counter and put in a $5 bill, some ones and change. He didn't count it.

"Everythin' goin' well with the business?" the robber asked. Kreiji thought he was being a smart aleck and thought best not to respond. "You gotta nice place, hear lots of good things about the Czech Inn."

The man talked through a fairly large cutout in the hood's fabric, an opening that revealed a pencil-like mustache. There were tiny slits to accommodate his vision, too small for Kreiji to see the color of his eyes.

"And lady, hand over that sandwich. I's hungry like a hobo." His voice would put him in a choir's tenor section, but at the moment he was singing trouble.

He took a big bite out of Fritz Langerhaus' Reuben. Salad dressing oozed out of the corners of his mouth. Some stuck on his mask-like hood, creating a clown-like picture. With his left hand still in the pocket of his unzipped jacket, he motioned in Kreiji's direction.

"Move along there Czech rest'rant man." He took another bite of the Reuben. "Hey, this pretty damn good ma'am," he munched with a nod toward Dorothy. "I shud pay you for this. It's pretty damn good."

The intruder's criminal conduct, aside from the concealed hand, seemed almost disarming to Kreiji. While precise in purpose, his actions displayed no overt hostility, no threatening bellicose, and, at least to this point, no physical harm. He seemed as relaxed as a turtle basking in the sun, except his hooded head bobbed with alternated attention between the Reuben and the cash register.

It all added up as peculiar to Keiji. He didn't misread the man's intent, but it was also clear this fellow hadn't graduated from the Sing Sing School of Sin and Skullduggery. There was nothing hard about his manner. Asking for "about $10" seemed especially strange.

Kreiji had removed cash from the register several times during the day and placed it in the safe in the basement. He estimated there was nearly $100 taken in since his last deposit to the safe. Thursday was his appointed time for the weekly trip to the bank, one day before checks were distributed to the help.

He handed the money bag to the robber.

"And I thank ya very much," the holdup man said to Kreiji. "I knowed this is a good place to eat. Mighty fine sandwich. I'll just take the rest wit me."

He wrapped the remainder of the Reuben in the wax paper it came in, and placed it in the money bag. Langerhaus hadn't moved a muscle, fixed by the audacity of someone who would steal his Reuben.

"And you ma'am," the robber said. "I thank ya." He walked toward Dorothy, still keeping his left hand out of sight and the cash bag tucked under his right arm. "Come here," he wiggled his finger at her.

"You've got the money, now leave," Kreiji pleaded. "There is no use harming Dorothy or anyone else."

"I's sure not gonna hurt her," the robber said.

He walked up to her, leaned on the glass counter and kissed Dorothy Dotson on her right cheek.

"That sure a good sandwich," he told her.

Then he left.

Dorothy's face was adorned with astonishment and Thousand Island dressing.

Chapter 10

1953, Cedar Rapids

Roy Sanders was as joyous as a meadowlark immersed in a cloud of grasshoppers.

He felt like handing out cigars to passersby on the Lincoln Highway. While there were some delivery pains, he and Lillian had given birth to Motel Sepia, a place where all travelers could spend the night. The first two units were in place, and by the week's end the Bob Severn Sign Co. planned to complete erection of the 12-foot high neon nameplate.

The word "MOTEL," in a vertical letter arrangement, would occupy the top two-thirds of the sign. "Sepia" would be spelled out below in smaller letters, horizontally in a signature style font.

Eventually canvass awnings would grace the front windows of the cabins. Patio tables and chairs and charcoal grills would add charm to outside front entry areas. The one-bedroom cottages contained a small sitting section. The toilet area included a shower. Cabins were not air-conditioned.

"Whooohee," Roy hollered against the crisp early-morning breeze. He stood along the highway, near the bridge over Indian Creek, arms flailing as if he were performing some sort of voodoo baptism. His exclamation echoed off the willows and elms that lined the creek and bounced westward to the main house. He didn't say another word, but merely stared in a sense of satisfaction.

Lillian saw him, smiled, and decided to join the reverie. She wasn't all that enamored about starting up on a new business that meant more work for the entire family, meaning mostly her and Roy. She was excited because Roy was excited.

The azure March sky appeared to have been colored by a throng of kindergarteners, all armed with blue crayons. Only lingering puffy clouds from an overnight shower mottled the painting. Roy's spirit ran high. He breathed in the freshness of a new day, nature still sparkling from the rain's polish. The rain-soaked daffodils along the house, brave first-bloomers of Spring, drooped as if doubting their decision to stick their heads out in such chilly environs.

But Spring meant renewal, and Roy's mood was renewed beyond any influence caused by the vagaries of weather. The Iowa Department of Agriculture had issued a hotel license in February, and changes in zoning had finally been approved.

A car zipped by, and someone waved. Roy waved back as the vehicle sped eastward on the concrete ribbon.

The Lincoln Highway, officially listed as U.S. 30, was the first cross-country road for automobiles. Roy was surprised to learn that one of the first segments of the Lincoln Highway in Iowa, part of the so-called Seedling Mile projects, was constructed about six miles east of his property in 1918.

Highway officials also told him that the very first part of the Lincoln Highway was built in 1913 in New Jersey. The last segment was completed in 1938. They gave him summer and winter traffic counts.

What they didn't tell him was that there were already plans for rerouting Highway 30 around the south side of the city. Had he been aware of that information, Motel Sepia may never have been born.

"We did it!" Roy shouted as Lillian approached. "Lil, we are going to be in the motel business. I told you we could do it. As they say down at the teen center, ain't that hunky dory?"

"Well, we ain't done it yet," she said, throwing a dash of reality on his excitement. "They are putting up the buildings, but the business part remains to be seen. Getting customers on a regular basis and keeping the place maintained, that's the hard part. Talk to me a year from now, and I'll give you a report on the business end."

Roy had to chuckle. Where he saw sky and pie, Lillian envisioned life's bumps and humps.

"I will agree that the investment is less than I expected," Lillian softened her assessment. "It was the right decision to buy the already constructed cabins from that closed motel on Sixth Street Southwest and move them out here rather than building new ones. And, we'll save money by not putting telephones and TVs in every unit. If there is an emergency, customers can use our house telephone."

One of those bumps in Lillian's crystal ball had already turned out to be authentic. Roy had expected no difficulty in rezoning the Motel Sepia property from agriculture to commercial, but the application for rezoning lingered for months in county offices. When a friend, a white friend, investigated the matter, the issue suddenly was resolved.

Roy expected to open Motel Sepia – at least some of the cabins – sometime in March or April. Family members and perhaps some hired help would do the cleaning and maintenance. Lillian would be the official manager and bookkeeper. Roy had already placed a brief ad in the *Negro Motorist Green Book*.

The caption in the ad said: "SHADIEST SPOT IN IOWA." It was in small letters above the large words, "MOTEL SEPIA."

"On coast-to-coast Highway 30," the ad continued, "3 miles east of Cedar Rapids, Iowa." The telephone number was listed, and in the lower right-hand corner the name, MRS. LILLIAN SANDERS, Prop.

"This is excitin' Lil," Roy said, a grin from ear to ear. "I think people will be pleasantly surprised when they find Motel Sepia. It's out in the country, away from busy town streets. There are lots of shade trees and a bubbly brook nearby. If they want, they can go for a leisurely walk down to the river. We have swings and a trampoline for kids. Why, it's like staying in a park."

"Oh, I don't doubt some will be surprised," said Lillian. "Especially white folk when they find out the motel owner is Negro. Whether that will be pleasant or not, I'll defer to your optimistic side."

They walked back to the house. Whatever the fortunes of Motel Sepia, the adventure was about to begin. Roy's floor cleaning business had been a success. His newer floor installation business was a success. Why not Motel Sepia? It was true. He had become an established businessman in Cedar Rapids. That advantage wouldn't apply to white travelers though.

"Don't you feel good that we are providing a place for Negro travelers to stay?" he asked Lillian.

"Of course, Roy," she said mildly. "But if we depended on Negro customers for our floor businesses to succeed, we'd be starvin'. That's just being honest, Roy."

He didn't answer.

"I want to plant some vivid flowers in front of the cabins, brighten what is pretty much a forest green right now," Lillian said, changing the subject. "Those weedy coneflowers don't appeal to me. What color should I buy?"

"How about black and white to match our customers' complexions?" Roy shot back without much thinking.

There was not a lot of woman's touch to bestow on a floor installation and cleaning business, but she was already envisioning how to brighten up both the interior and exterior look of Motel Sepia. She pictured green living rooms with orchid trim. She petitioned Roy for recessed fixtures in the ceiling.

"Yes, I think I'll get the deep red zinnias," she said imagining outside plantings, "and perhaps some marigolds and pink petunias."

As the new entrepreneurs in the motel business soon found out, there are not a lot of vacationers in April and May. Business picked up in the summer months, but not enough to make Lillian and her financial statement comfortable. The zinnias grew, but Motel Sepia's income did not.

A feature article in the local newspaper about the Sanders' endeavor to provide housing for black travelers was nice, but it didn't reach the people from Chicago, Omaha and beyond. Her attempt to gain national publicity for Motel Sepia in *Ebony* magazine was met with silence. Nor did they receive acknowledgement from the American Automobile Association.

Lillian sent out postcards and other promotional material, but in the end it was the nearness to Highway 30, word of mouth and repeat business that kept the doors open. Slowly, business grew to allow purchase of two more buildings in 1954. By 1955, there were 10 rental units. In the summer, an average of six were occupied, with about one-third being Negro travelers.

More black families were hitting the road for vacation, and for them the Motel Sepia was like an oasis in the plains of Middle America.

Chapter 11

August 1955

$\mathbf{K}$reiji calmly dialed the Cedar Rapids Police Department, before the robber was out of sight.

It was the first time the restaurant had been robbed, at least in his memory, a highly unusual fact for a business open at night and situated on one of the city's main east-west streets and a national highway. The Lincoln Highway brought truckers and visitors from across the country into the heart of the city.

Dorothy was still standing by the counter, more in shock because the robber had kissed her than from the crime itself. She grabbed a paper napkin from one of the tables and began wiping the salad dressing from her cheek. Kreiji, talking to the police switchboard operator/dispatcher, turned away from her to hide a burgeoning smile that threatened to erupt into outright laughter if he wasn't careful. She grabbed a second napkin to finish the facial mop-up.

Langerhaus, uncharacteristically quiet, remained at his table, Reuben-less. He knew better than to comment on either Dorothy's Thousand Island cosmetics or his lack of something to eat. Kreiji, minutes after requesting that Langerhaus not linger at closing time, had now asked him to remain. Police would want to question all three and anyone else in the area. However, the dry cleaning store next door and the wholesale electrical shop on the corner had closed six hours earlier.

There was a possibility, albeit slim, that other workers getting off the night shift at Wilson Foods or medical personnel at nearby Mercy Hospital had seen something, perhaps even the robber as he walked westward from the restaurant. Mercy's parking lot was three blocks west of the Czech Inn. It would have to be a nurse, nurse aide or some other hospital staffer who didn't leave immediately after 11 p.m., someone whose windup work detained them an extra hour.

"All I know is that when he exited the front door, he turned west," Kreiji told the police attendant in answer to questions. "I didn't see how far he traveled, if he changed direction, or if he was picked up by an accomplice or had his own car parked nearby. I know that's not much help. I do know that less than a minute ago he took off with $10 or so, a $5 bill, some ones and change."

"Was he armed?" the dispatcher inquired.

"I don't know that either," replied Kreiji. "He didn't show a gun, but he may have had one in his left jacket pocket."

"Can you describe his appearance?"

"He was wearing a black jacket and grungy blue pants. He had a gray hood pulled over his face, a sort of nylon mesh." Kreiji paused to search his memory for other details. "Oh, he wore a plain purple shirt. I think it was purple. It may have been bluish. I should point out that no one was harmed."

"OK," said the dispatch officer. "We'll send someone right away."

With that, the police contact hung up and switched his attention to radio communications. The officer had double duties, running the switchboard as well as handling dispatch and other radio transmission chores. He and the desk sergeant were the only officers on the first floor of the two-story, beige-brick police station on the city's near west side. There was no one in records and traffic, no one in the upstairs juvenile department and, at the moment, no one in the detective bureau.

Cedar Rapids was too small to have neighborhood precinct stations. However, its rapid population growth had outsprinted its police force numbers. The official 1950 census had counted some 72,000 residents, but estimates now ranged upward to nearly 80,000. The Police Department had 64 uniformed officers, six detectives, two men working juvenile cases and the command staff.

Weekday nights in August were generally quiet. School hadn't begun. Some of the bored high school guys gathered at one of the First Avenue car lots to exchange boasts of purported conquests and clank their beer bottles. As long as representatives of rival schools didn't show and produce a rumble, cops seldom bothered them. Occasionally, to satisfy parents and school officials, they would stop and confiscate remnants of six packs.

Tavern fights were the most common bump on smooth summer nights, and the occasional robbery.

"Car Six, Car Six, come in please."

Car Six was the Loop patrol. Cedar Rapids called its central downtown area the Loop. It mimicked the downtown name of its much bigger neighbor, Chicago, 230 miles to the east.

The Cedar Rapids Police Department had five two-man cars on any given shift, one covering the Loop, two patrolling the balance of the east side and two responsible for the city's west side. Four more officers had walking beats in the inner Loop, assignments that concentrated on a 10-block area. Others worked traffic, station assignments or weekend overlap.

"This is Car Six, go ahead," responded Patrolman Charlie Jelling.

"What's your 10-20? Over."

"We're at Third Avenue and Sixth Street. Over."

"Car Six, please proceed to the Czech Inn on Mount Vernon Road. We've had a report of a robbery there. Suspect possibly walking toward the west, wearing gray-hood, black jacket and blue slacks or jeans. Use caution. Subject may be armed. Over."

"Ten-four headquarters. Out."

Jelling and his partner, Kenny Wilson, were about seven blocks from the restaurant. They did not turn on the siren or emergency lights as they picked up speed. The distance was short and there was little traffic. They shot south on Tenth Street for five blocks, then cut left and east on Mount Vernon Road, keeping an eye for anyone matching the suspect. Anyone, really. At this time of night anyone became an automatic suspect just by wandering around the neighborhood. They saw no one.

Automatically, Wilson reached into the upper left pocket of his blue shirt and pulled out a pack of Lucky Strikes. With one hand, he coaxed a cigarette out, tapped an end on his watch crystal, and stuck it in his mouth. He pushed in the car lighter, and in moments it popped out. He lit up and inhaled deeply.

Wilson yanked the 1954 Ford Crestline police cruiser across the west-bound lane of Mount Vernon Road and up into the parking lot of the Czech Inn. The dashboard's circular clock showed five minutes after midnight. They were supposed to be heading home instead of working a robbery call. Up to now, this particular four to midnight shift had been a breeze. Hitting the sack would be postponed for at least two hours.

Meanwhile, officers in another eastside patrol car had been directed to scan the Mercy Hospital area and, as time went on, expand the search to nearby houses and apartments.

"I thought you were going to quit smoking," Jelling said, looking at Wilson. "Could you roll down your window all the way to clear the smoke?"

"I tried," Wilson said, cranking the window handle. "It ain't easy."

"Well, I could have it worse," Jelling commented as the cruiser pulled into the restaurant lot. "At least I'm not walking the beat down by Central Fire Station."

Slowly, the squad car encircled the Czech Inn, giving special attention to the alley at the rear. There was no sign of anything up and down the alley, walking robber or get-away car.

"What the hell are you talking about?" Wilson looked over at his partner, giving that brow-raising, are-you-going-loopy look.

"I've told you about the time I was checking doors down at the old warehouse," Jelling said, "the one near the fire station on First Street. I know I have. Wow! Your memory! For a guy in his late 20s, your recall is sick. You've got bygone bethinker! What? The old cranium in neuro-neutral?"

"For crissakes, Jelling. Tell the story or shut up."

"That warehouse, the one down by Central Fire. I was checking doors, found one open, peeked inside and –"

"And what?!!"

"I saw rats bigger than tomcats," Jelling laughed. "I told you that story a dozen times. Your memory's melted. I'm not sure I'd want you testifying on my behalf."

The pair had been patrol partners for about a year. Jelling, 26, had been on the force only two years, getting badge No. 57 in March of 1953. He was the talkative one, yammering about this or that. And he was good with the verbal jab. Wilson could dish it out, too.

Wilson parked by the front door, switched off the ignition and exited the cruiser. He inspected the front of the restaurant, and then proceeded west down the street to see if the robber had dropped anything or if there was any evidence as to where he may have cut across yards. Jelling went inside, examining the doorway as he entered.

"Good evening. I'm Officer Jelling. My partner, Officer Wilson, is taking a look outside."

"Thanks for coming, Officer," Kreiji stuck his hand out and the two men shook hands. "This is my head cook, Dorothy Dotson." He nodded toward the counter.

"And this is Fritz Langerhaus, who came in about 11:45. Everyone else had cleared out by that time, and we were shutting down the place."

Jelling acknowledged both, but did not greet them formally. He gave a glance around the restaurant's interior, walked back to the counter area and poked his head into the order window. He returned to the cash register and strolled the length of the area behind the counter, then walked out to the main seating area.

"Guten auben, Herr Fritz," Jelling said. "Wie geht's?"

Langerhaus' reputation was not confined to the near east side. Jelling was aware of his prejudices and his adamant rejection of anything foreign. In a town with many people of Irish, Czech and German descent, and a healthy sprinkling of Greek, Italians and Lebanese, there was always opportunity for disagreements. Blend in the dominant Methodists, Lutherans and Presbyterians with the Catholics and Greek Orthodox, and Saturday night at certain taverns could be interesting.

The city also had small Jewish and Muslim congregations. The Mother Mosque of America, the oldest standing mosque in the United States, was located in northwest Cedar Rapids. The small black population, about two percent of the city, was concentrated in the near southeast quadrant.

"Guten auben to you," Langerhaus replied. "I'm doing fine."

He was not anxious to continue any German talk, coming perilously close to the end of his Deutsch vocabulary.

"Mr. Kreiji, why don't you just start at the beginning and describe as best you can what happened," Jelling said. "We'll get more formal statements tomorrow, but right now just briefly run through the situation. Fritz, we'll talk to you later."

Wilson tossed his cigarette into a flower bed at the front entrance and walked in, making his own quick review of the restaurant's environment.

"Well," said Kreiji, "like I told your dispatcher, we were getting ready to close, and Fritz sees this person approaching the front door. He –"

"You didn't tell the dispatcher that I saw someone coming," Langerhaus interrupted. "You didn't mention my name at all."

"OK, OK!" Kreiji snorted in disgust.

"Mr. Kreiji, just tell the story your way," Jelling advised. "Fritz, we'll get your full statement in due time."

"He walked directly in, wasted no time in asking me to put money in his blue bag," Kreiji continued. "He asked for $10. I thought that was strange, requesting a specific amount. I grabbed a $5 bill, some ones, halves and quarters. I think there was more than $100 in the cash register. I'm not sure how much."

"The $10 request is odd," Jelling agreed. "Usually, they want everything. Describe the person the best you can. "You said 'he.' You are sure it was a man?"

"Oh it was a man alright," Kreiji replied. "And I think he was Negro. He had on a black jacket, unzipped, a gray hood over his head with slits for his eyes and a large section cut out for his mouth. His left hand was in his pocket, and he motioned it around as if he had a gun. I didn't see a gun, mind you, but he wanted you to believe that."

"What about the rest of his clothing?" asked Wilson. "Was he wearing a cap? Did he have gloves?"

"No cap," said Kreiji. "Like I said, he had this gray hood over his head. His pants were blue, but it looked like he'd been wrestling in the dirt. Oh, and he was wearing a purple shirt."

"No, Mike," Dorothy spoke up. "It wasn't purple. It was more magenta. And his blue pants were more like dress slacks. They were cuffed and had a neat crease. Yes, they were a little dirty, but I didn't see any holes in them. I would say he once wore those slacks to church."

"Yes, ma'am," said Jelling. "Wore them to church."

"He knew who I was," said Kreiji. "He called me Mr. Czech restaurant man."

"That suggests he's local," Wilson said. "How about a description? Fat, slim? Tall, short? Young, old? Wearing any jewelry? A watch?"

"I'd say he was around 6 feet tall, slim and mid to late 20s, maybe 175 pounds," Kreiji replied. "He had no jewelry that I saw, and I can't say if he wore a watch or not."

"He had a wrist watch," said Dorothy, "and the band was gold. I saw the edge of it when he partially pulled his left hand out of the jacket pocket. And he was not in his 20s. I'd say he was older. Younger guys don't wear pressed slacks with cuffs. And he was wearing polished black loafers."

"Yes ma'am, older, pressed slacks and polished black loafers," Jelling repeated as he made notes on a small pad. "Did you see a gun, ma'am?"

"No, I didn't. If I had, I would have told you," Dorothy said. "He was holding up the place, but it didn't seem threatening. You know what I'm saying? He almost seemed like a gentleman. He wasn't loud like some men, some customers. He didn't push anyone. Didn't threaten anyone."

"Don't forget, he liked your Reuben sandwich," said Kreiji, a little aggravated by her saintly description of the robber. "This guy orders up some money and a Reuben, Fritz's Reuben, at the same time. After taking a couple of bites out of the sandwich and placing the money bag under his arm, he walks over toward Dorothy, leans on the counter, stoops down and gives her a big kiss. You left that part out, Dorothy."

"Oh, and he really liked Dorothy's Reuben," Langerhaus chimed in. "Best sandwich he ever had. That's what he told her. And it was my sandwich!"

Neither he nor Kreiji mentioned the Thousand Island dressing left sparkling on Dorothy's cheek.

"He gave you a kiss, ma'am?" Jelling looked at Dorothy for confirmation, a suppressed smile primed for release. He looked downward, fighting images that stoked indecorous snickers. Think of something else, he coached himself.

"You didn't say if he was wearing gloves," Jelling said, addressing no one in particular.

"Well, his left hand was always in his jacket pocket, but I don't think he had any glove on his right hand," Kreiji responded.

"Did you say he leaned on the counter, that glass counter?" Jelling inquired.

"Yes, as he approached Dorothy," Kreiji said. "I thought the man was perhaps going to strike her, although there was no indication he would become violent. But who knows? He walked about right here and placed his right hand on the counter."

Kreiji pointed to the counter section where Dorothy had been standing.

"He leaned over and gave her a kiss on the cheek."

"You already told him that," Dorothy sent a non-appreciative glare toward Kreiji. "One other thing, officer," Dorothy continued. "Your partner asked if the man was wearing gloves. He wasn't, at least on his right hand. And I doubt if a man would wear a glove on one hand and not the other. Do you suppose?"

"I'm sure you're right, ma'am," said Jelling.

"And his hand was black. This man was Negro," Dorothy said leaving no doubt.

"OK," said Jelling. "I think we're done for now. Like I said, we'll have you come into the station tomorrow, or I should say later today, to give a full statement to detectives. One other thing, could you keep the restaurant closed until our fingerprint man, Virgil Howell, has a chance to dust your counter – the place where the robber leaned on the glass."

"We can do that," Kreiji said, "but I hope this all gets done early in the day, or I will lose a lot of business on top of the money stolen."

"We'll have Howell over here first thing in the morning," said Jelling. "And the three of you can come down to the station, oh, I'd say around 9 or 10, if that works for you. We'll type up the information you gave us and provide a copy for the detective assigned to the case. Still, he'll want you to give a full report, repeating what you told us. Incidentally, another car has been checking the area between the restaurant and the hospital, and blocks north and south.

"Mr. Langerhaus," Jelling nodded in the German's direction. "Do you have anything to add? Do you disagree with any of the description?"

"No, sir," said Langerhaus. "I agree with Dorothy. The robber was Negro, and he may have not been threatening, but he was still a robber. And kissing Dorothy, a white woman, smearing her face with dressing? That's even worse."

"Thanks for mentioning the kiss part again," Dorothy sneered at Langerhaus. "You are such a gentleman. You know Fritz, as long as you want to discuss kissing, you should know that I'd rather get a peck on the cheek from a prickly pear cactus with bad breath than from you."

With that the police officers left.

"OK," Kreiji addressed Dorothy and Langerhaus. We may as well leave, too. I'll see the two of you at the police station about 9, or shortly thereafter. I'll have someone from the morning shift post a closed sign on the front door and wait for the police fingerprint guy."

Dorothy made a quick check of the kitchen, ensuring everything was turned off, put some containers back on the proper shelves, and walked out the front entrance after Langerhaus. Kreiji locked the doors and left.

Chapter 12

Virgil Howell didn't own a car.

He once had a 1942 Chevy, one of those black models manufactured before all production turned to war goods. He had purchased it used at Rapids Chevrolet, but after 10 years it needed major repairs, and Howell didn't want to spend the money on it or a replacement vehicle. Unmarried, he managed to arrange for rides of any distance. He walked most places – to church, the grocery store, to friends' houses and to downtown stores.

Howell lived alone in a story and half frame house on Fifth Street SE near Eighth Avenue, just seven blocks from his favorite restaurant, the Butterfly Café on Third. He seldom ate at Kreiji's, even though it was slightly closer. He preferred the Butterfly because of its exquisite butterscotch pie. He bought his groceries at Charlie's Food Market on Eighth, a little more than a block from his house.

Virgil was a native of Savannah, Mo. His family later moved to St. Joseph, Mo., where he was graduated from high school. After service in World War I, he moved to Cedar Rapids. He had been the janitor at First Lutheran Church for many years before joining the Cedar Rapids Police Department in 1945. At age 57, Howell was no rookie looking to mix it up with some young Saturday night trouble maker.

Rather, he took a job in records and ultimately began teaching himself the art of fingerprinting. He spent his own money on a correspondence course. That was eight years ago. Howell was the first Negro on the Department, a fact not overlooked when he was hired by Chief Will Kendra. Cedar Rapids' population was two percent

Negro, and Kendra believed it smart public relations to have a Negro police officer.

Howell was no stranger to Kendra, a member at First Lutheran. Moreover, Howell was gaining a reputation as a speaker and historian on American Negroes who had left their mark on the country. He was assembling a book he had tentatively titled, "Famous Black Americans." He was also delving into his own ancestry in anticipation of writing that story one day.

His parents were born into slavery in Missouri shortly before President Lincoln issued his Emancipation Proclamation in 1863. Howell discovered through family records and interviews with his grandmother that he was a direct descendent of a teenage girl – a princess of the Jaloff tribe in Gambia – who was sold into slavery. Indeed, he was among the fourth generation descended from black royalty in Africa.

Kendra was aware of Howell's background, having heard him speak of his ancestral research in a lecture at Mount Mercy College. After that, he urged Howell to develop the full story of his roots with the goal of authoring a book. It stimulated Howell's already surging writing juices and search into family history.

"Car Six, Car Six, what is your 10-20?" the daytime dispatcher radioed.

"This is Car Six. We're heading east on Third past Armstrong's Department Store. Over."

"Car Six. Please make the usual run down to Eighth Avenue and pick up Officer Howell. Over."

"Will do," the Car Six patrolman replied. "Out."

Howell was in good enough physical shape to hike the 14 blocks to the police station, but most of the time he was given a ride by a friend or a squad car came by. On this particular day, the detective bureau wanted Howell in early so he could proceed to the Czech Inn to dust for fingerprints.

When he was transferred out of records, Howell became the first Negro in the United States to serve as head of a police department bureau of identification. His self-education in fingerprinting had paid off, and he was proud of it. The ID Bureau was a single room barely larger than a janitor's closet. Yet to Powell, it was like a suite in the FBI Building in Washington, D.C.

He had set up shop, complete with a microscope, photographic equipment and even a dark room. Files matching names and prints had been established. His fingerprint kit included the latest in ink pads, powders, feather brushes and lifting tape. Lifting tape is similar to Scotch tape, only clear and more durable.

The peculiar ridges that form fingerprints were first identified by a Czech psychologist in 1823. However, the concept of fingerprinting was not used until 1858 in India. A fingerprint bureau was established in Calcutta in 1897. Fingerprinting began at the Cedar Rapids Police Department in the late 1930s, but not in a significant way.

A New York City police official introduced the fingerprinting of criminals to the United States. The Scheffer case of 1902 was the first in the U.S. where the identification, arrest and conviction of a murderer was based upon fingerprint evidence. The accused killer had been arrested previously, and his fingerprints filed some months before. Those prints were compared to ones found on a fractured glass showcase at the murder scene.

After arriving at the P.D., Howell went upstairs and grabbed his kit and camera. The ID Bureau was part of the detective division. He obtained a copy of the report made by officers at the scene shortly after midnight and in minutes was back in the patrol car for the ride to the Czech Inn.

He rapped on the front door of the restaurant about 6:30 a.m. A uniformed officer introduced Howell to the lone employee. Howell thanked him for keeping the business closed until police could finish their inspection.

He read the robbery report during the eight-minute trip from the station, and had a cursory picture of the crime, particularly the various movements of the suspect during the time of the robbery. He honed in on the counter, shifting his focus to the glass section toward the end. Howell was delighted.

Immediately, he spotted distinct palm and fingerprint images, even though the area was illuminated by only the natural light from nearby windows and his flashlight. Of course, the big question was if the fingerprints belonged to a restaurant employee, some other customer or the robber. He would have to secure prints from Mike Kreiji, Dorothy Dotson and others who had worked there the day before. It was part of the process of elimination.

A magnifying glass revealed several sets of fingerprints on the glass counter. Some were faint and smudged. One stood out. It featured the classic tented arch on the small and fourth fingers and a prominent scar on the upper side of the palm, about a half inch below the finger crease. To the left of the prints was a smear that looked like food of some kind.

Before dusting, Howell photographed the fingerprints as a precautionary step. Lifting a latent print was not always successful. He then took his feather brush and carefully applied white dust over the fingerprint area. The prints popped out like zits on a teenager following a chocolate binge. Howell pressed the lifting tape on the powder, pulled off the image and placed it on a white card.

The process went well. Satisfied that he had preserved an excellent image, he scanned the glass top for other evidence but saw none that interested him. Based on information from Mr. Kreiji and Mrs. Dotson regarding where the robber had leaned, he was content with his work.

"Mr. Robber," he said to himself, "I've got a nice picture of you." At 7:45 he called for a ride back to the station, and thanked the restaurant worker on the way out.

At almost exactly 9 a.m. Thursday morning, Dorothy Dotson walked into the police station and approached the window of the desk sergeant. It was her first time at the Police Department, and she was a little nervous. Not much shook her. She had sometimes felt like she was in jail while sweltering in the heat of the restaurant kitchen. Dealing with customers can simultaneously build confidence and create thick skin. She had weathered plenty smart alecks.

"You're acting like you've just poisoned a good customer," said the man right behind her. It was Fritz Langerhaus, one of those smart alecks.

"Relax, Dorothy," Langerhaus assumed the role of counselor. "They won't hold you here long if you're telling the truth," he laughed, blowing Chesterfield smoke in her direction.

"You know, Fritz, perhaps no one has ever told you, although I sincerely doubt it," Dorothy looked him square in the eye, "but you can be a real pain in the ass. And the fact you blow cigarette smoke at people makes you a complete asshole. Just think, if you'd quit smoking, you'd save yourself 25 cents a pack and be a half-assed jerk."

Before Langerhaus had a chance to express his shock, the desk sergeant broke in.

"Folks, I hate to bust into a friendly conversation, but is there a reason you are gracing these premises?"

"I'm here to answer questions about our robbery last night," said Dorothy.

"And where was this robbery?"

"At the Czech Inn on Mount Vernon Road," she replied. "This man came in shortly before closing, and –"

"Hold it, ma'am. Just have a seat over there and we'll get you squared away," the officer said. "And you, Mr. Funnybones, to what do we owe the honor of your presence?"

"Same thing," said Langerhaus, "the robbery at Kreiji's."

"Where?"

"Oh, pardon me. The Czech Inn."

"I see. Why don't you sit on that bench at the other end of the waiting room, and we'll see if we can avoid World War III until one of the detectives comes down to see you. Thank you very much," he said, motioning them to sit.

Five minutes later Kreiji entered the police station and approached the desk sergeant's window.

"Yes sir, how may I help you?" the officer inquired.

"I'm Mike Kreiji, owner of the Czech Inn Restaurant. We had –"

"You had a robbery," the sergeant said. "I already know about it, and your two friends here," he said with a sigh and raised eyebrows. "You should really be more careful with the company you keep. Please sit down. I'll let you pick the place and hope for the best."

Kreiji seemed a little puzzled, but walked toward Dorothy and sat next to her.

"What was that all about?" he asked her.

"You don't want to know," Dorothy said curtly.

Several minutes later, Detective O'Neil walked down the exposed stairway and introduced himself to the restaurant trio. They shook hands and proceeded to the upstairs detective bureau where the trio repeated their robbery stories.

Again, Dorothy spent what Kreiji thought was an inordinate amount of time telling how nice the robber was, how "non-threatening," as she framed it, he was. He felt the need to counter such a soft outline of what happened.

"Detective O'Neil, I don't mean to sound argumentative, but this fellow wasn't a missionary. He held up our place and poked a gun in my face," said Kreiji.

"You don't know that," said Dorothy. "I mean that he had a gun."

"Damn it, I do know it," Kreiji said emphatically. "I was scared. He could have harmed anyone of us, especially you, when he went over, and, and kissed you."

Dorothy blushed. The last thing she wanted was for the interview to focus on kissing and a face full of salad dressing.

"What I meant, Mike," she continued, "is that we don't know for sure if he was armed. It appeared he had a gun or something in his jacket pocket. All we know positively is that his left hand was in the pocket, and he waved the hand and pocket around in a single motion. He may have had a gun. Maybe he didn't. Did either of you see a profile of a gun in the pocket?"

"It was a real nice kiss," said Langerhaus. "She deserved it because she makes a scrumptious Reuben sandwich."

If Dorothy Dotson had been anywhere but in the middle of a police station, the homicide on her mind likely would have unfolded. She could have spit bullets, but forced her mouth in the shut position.

"I didn't see a profile of a weapon," Kreiji acknowledged, "but I wasn't concentrating entirely on his pocket. I also watched his hooded face and listened to his directions to put money in that blue sack of his. Robbery is robbery. I'm not buying this business that he was Mr. Nice Guy."

"Mr. Kreiji is right," said O'Neil. "Robbery is a serious crime, no matter what the amount. I believe we have everything for now. I'm going to give you my direct telephone number, and if there is anything else that should go into the report, any details you think we should be aware of, please call right away.

"Read the statements on the report that you gave last night to Officers Jelling and Wilson, and if all the descriptions and other information are correct," O'Neil asked, "please sign at the bottom. I would like all of you to sign." He pushed the report across the table.

"Our fingerprint man was at your restaurant earlier this morning. I'm sure he has completed his work by now, and that will all be part of the record. Thanks for coming down."

Ordinarily, Bill Morgan, who covered police, fire and municipal court for *The Cedar Rapids Gazette*, is on the beat by 9 a.m. This Thursday morning, before making his rounds, he wanted to finish a Sunday feature about a judge who kept court records in the trunk of his car. That delayed his arrival at the police station by an hour.

The Gazette is an afternoon daily that covers a large section of Eastern Iowa, from the Minnesota border south to two counties north of Missouri. It focuses on Cedar Rapids and Iowa City, home of the University of Iowa, and competes on the east with the *Davenport Democrat*, to the north with the *Waterloo Courier* and to the west with the statewide *Des Moines Register*.

The Register's attempts to boost its circulation in Cedar Rapids were hampered by staff limitations. Hence, it was unable to give daily attention to local government and institutions. That included the Cedar Rapids Police Department. Nevertheless, the newspaper picked its fights with calculated cunning, getting a hard story scoop here and a compelling feature there.

Nothing irritated *The Gazette*'s city editor Ty Franklin more than spotting a story, especially a police story, in *The Register* before it appeared in *The Gazette*. Veteran reporters claimed he gained the Ty moniker because of the ever-present bow ties that adorned his neck. One back-row newsroom wag attributed the name to the boss's ability to tie a reporter's guts into knots.

Franklin was old-school. He advised reporters of their shortcomings in a manner so that the entire newsroom was informed. He handed out accolades with the paucity of a Pulitzer Prize judge. Few reporters, Morgan included, had escaped his wrath. Still, he was respected for his news judgement and tenacity.

One morning, Franklin locked on a *Register* story about a flim-flam operation that was targeting Cedar Rapids' elderly. Smoke rolled from his nostrils as he approached Morgan's desk. Noisy newsroom chatter sputtered to a halt. Typewriters suddenly froze. The only sounds, oblivious to human drama, came from the constant chatter of the Associated Press, United Press and weather teletype machines.

Newsroom eyes zeroed in on the scene.

"Goddamn it, Bill," the boss issued his salutation. "We can't have stories second behind *The Register*. Look at this," and he pointed to the scam story. "We should have had this first. You know –"

"But Ty –"

"There are no goddamn 'buts' about this. This is all pretty simple. They had the goddamn story, and we didn't. You go there every day. You develop sources. You –"

"But Ty –"

"Bill," Franklin summoned his windup words, "we should have had the story. That's all there is to it."

"Ty," Morgan finally found a verbal break to make his case, "you should know that I didn't work yesterday. It was my day off."

Franklin walked away giving no acknowledgement to Morgan's testimony.

That was some weeks ago. Now Morgan, one of *The Gazette's* best writers, scanned the police log with an eye for the unusual.

The log is a summary of every complaint, traffic accident, crime and neighborhood spat. If a reporter wanted more information on a particular matter, he would seek the full report on the case. If neighbors duked it out in a dispute over fallen fruit on the property line, Morgan wanted the full statement.

One Saturday night, Morgan had zeroed in on a log entry about an 87-year-old woman who was arrested for shoplifting two pair of Hanes hosiery at a grocery store. Her home address indicated a better part of town. Why, he thought, is an apparent well-off grandma pilfering nylons?

The newspaper's policy was not to run shoplifting arrests, unless, of course, the mayor, president of the country club or some other well-known person was involved.

Morgan saw this case was different. Why, he wondered, did she do it? He pursued the matter and talked to the woman the following Monday.

The elderly woman was horrified by his questions. She hadn't told her husband of her arrest. She hadn't told her visiting daughter and granddaughter. She didn't know why. She just did it. There was no explanation. She couldn't sleep. All she saw, day and night, she told

Morgan, was the vision of two police officers walking toward her. She didn't know what to do.

She was relieved when Morgan told her he had no plans to identify her in any story. But he did want to write the story from the angle of how a simple misdemeanor could cause such anguish. And, if she would like, he said he would accompany her to court where the judge most likely would give her a deferred sentence. She accepted his offer.

His story chronicled her deep pain, the constant vision of two approaching police officers, and her torment during a weekend visit with her granddaughter and daughter that should have been a time of rejoicing. It was a story about human frailty, an inexplicable action and the crushing of a person's spirit all because of a lousy pair of stockings.

As for Morgan, some alleged newsroom pals gave him the business, razzed him about being soft in reporting about old ladies "who were crooks."

One stuck the needle in deep.

"She probably had a rap sheet a mile long," he said.

"Whoa, what's this?" Morgan pointed to the log.

"Are you asking about the robbery over at the Czech Inn?" the desk sergeant responded.

"Yeah. What's this about the robber kissing the waitress?"

"Talk to the detectives," the sergeant said. "They have the full skinny."

Morgan went upstairs.

"Hey, O'Neil," he said, walking into the detective bureau. "Could I see that report on the robbery at the Czech Inn, please? What's this business about the robber kissing the waitress?"

"Well, that's what they said," O'Neil replied. "I don't make up these reports. They said a guy comes in shortly before midnight, walks directly to the owner behind the counter, demands money, and before leaving grabs a sandwich from the cook and kisses her on the cheek. I'm surprised he didn't curtsy and take a bow. It's a new one on me."

He handed the report to Morgan.

"It says here he asked for $10," Morgan noted. "Isn't that on the strange side, too? Don't robbers usually try to break the bank, get all they can get?"

"I guess he thinks his kisses are worth only $10," O'Neil offered. "Either that, or he was half drunk."

"Anybody say that?" Morgan asked.

"No. In fact, it appears this fellow took pains to be courteous," O'Neil explained. "He complimented Mr. Kreiji – he's the owner of The Czech Inn – on running a good restaurant and lavished praise on the Reuben sandwich prepared by Mrs. Dotson. Nothing about slurring of words or drunkenness."

Morgan took additional notes about the robber's description. He knew he had a good story. Ordinarily, a $10 robbery story would land deep inside the paper. This one, Morgan correctly sensed, would make page one.

"Kissing Bandit Robs Czech Inn," the headline read.

Chapter 13

Naperville, Ill.

Police officers aren't any different than the rest of us when it comes to Mondays. Unless, of course, you work the weekend and have Monday off. In that case, Monday has all the solemnity and high regard of Sunday.

But this was no ordinary Monday for the Naperville Police Department. There was a murder, a horrendous killing, that needed to be investigated, and that meant there was no such thing as an off-duty cop in this small suburban department. Everyone was assigned to check some angle, some person, some of the few known facts, in a team attack on one of the worst crimes ever to touch this growing town.

Deputies from DuPage and Will counties were helping. Detectives in other suburbs, and in Chicago itself, were checking records to see if the MO in this murder matched any killings in the past.

It even had the attention of the *Chicago Tribune,* which normally ignores murders. It carried a brief story on page one of its suburban section.

"Captain, we may have a lead as to the dead man's identity," a runner from dispatch informed Jeremy McNabb. "It came in last night."

"Why are we just learning about this now?" McNabb questioned the young staffer. "What time did the report come in? Why wasn't I called? Who took the call?"

"I don't know, sir."

"I'm sorry," McNabb said, knowing the messenger shouldn't be skewered. Besides, most of the answers were on the slip handed to him.

The call was taken at 9:36 p.m. by Joyce Powers, a part-time summer intern. The caller was a Marge Arezzo of Naperville. Her address and phone number were on the report. She said she last saw her husband before going to church Sunday morning.

"Would you please get me the phone number of Miss Powers?" McNabb asked the runner. "Thanks for bringing the report to me."

In two minutes, he was on the phone with Powers. Her explanation was that she had received a report of a car accident a few minutes after the Arezzo call. She said she had placed the first message aside while attending to the second matter. An hour passed, she said, before she remembered the Arezzo call. She decided, because of the lateness, it could wait until morning.

McNabb instructed her, as civilly as possible, on the importance of letting the officer in charge know immediately something as important as that of a missing person. Time could be everything if there was a kidnapping or someone had run off the road.

Powers recognized her mistake and apologized. As for the caller, Mrs. Arezzo, "she didn't sound all that excited," the intern said when questioned by McNabb.

"I didn't ask her any questions, just took down what she said. She said she arrived home from church about 10:30 and her husband – his first name is Aldo or Eldo I think – was not there. She said she checked with family and friends in the afternoon and made other calls, thinking all along he would show up. He didn't. Should I have asked her more questions?"

"No," McNabb said. "You did fine, except for forgetting about the call and then not passing the report along to the night desk sergeant."

He didn't tell her that Mrs. Arezzo's husband may be at the hospital morgue.

As soon as he hung up with Miss Powers, he called the Arezzo house. The phone was picked up on the third ring. Mrs. Arezzo's description of her husband matched that of the dead man. She said he had gone out for his Sunday walk and outlined his usual route.

"He sometimes stops for coffee and a bagel, and if he sees anyone he knows, he can talk and lose track of time."

"I'd like to stop by and visit with you for more information," McNabb told her. He didn't want to tell her on the phone that he was pretty sure she was a widow. "Is now a good time?"

"By all means, officer," she replied. "What did you say your name is?"

"Capt. McNabb. Jerry McNabb. I've been on the Naperville police department for some 20 years."

She confirmed the address on the report.

"I'll be over within a half hour," McNabb said.

"Do you have any information on my husband?" she asked. Now there was serious worry in her voice. "I can't imagine where he'd be. Has anyone else called about him?"

"No. No one else called," McNabb said. "I'll tell you what we know when I come over."

With that, he said goodbye. He checked with other officers working the case for new information. There was nothing. The case, other than the cryptic signals left by the killer, was full of empty blanks.

Arezzo, or the man now believed to have been Arezzo, had been seen at a coffee shop on Main Street. He had come to the place before. A waitress said he was alone. She remembered nothing unusual about his actions. McNabb was about to leave when Mike O'Connor entered his office.

"Mike, good morning. Find out anything?" McNabb asked. "I was just about to head over to the Arezzo home. I think we may have identified the victim."

"Good," O'Connor replied. "I won't keep you. Just wanted to mention that I lifted some prints from the park bench. It appears to be a partial of two fingers, perhaps the fourth and fifth digit, or what most people call the ring and little fingers. And I think they are fingers on the right hand. They are not pronounced, but I think I have enough to determine the pattern."

"Fine, O'Connor. Keep working on it. I don't need all the technical details right now. Where did you find the prints?"

"On the metal bench, on the left side of the victim," O'Connor said. "I'm assuming the killer was facing his mark. Hence, his right hand would be on the left side of the body. He may not have seen the seepage of fluid from the body on the bench, but that helped highlight what images we were able to obtain. I'll work on it. I know an expert in Elmhurst. See if he can help."

"Are you sure the prints aren't those of the victim?" McNabb asked.

"Yes. I already took the dead man's prints. These don't match, fingers or palms."

"OK," McNabb said, heading out the door. "See you this afternoon."

Ten minutes later McNabb was at the Arezzo house, a modest ranch on a tree-lined cul-de-sac. There was a flag pole in the front yard, but no flag flying this day. Mrs. Arezzo opened the front door before he exited the squad car. This was police work that he hated, telling parents their child had been killed in a car crash, or, in this case, telling a woman her spouse was dead. He carried the heavy news, looking straight ahead.

"Mrs. Arezzo, I'm Capt. McNabb." He removed his cap.

She returned greetings and the two went inside. McNabb looked at a picture of the couple in the hallway. It was final proof of his suspicions. She directed him to a blue sofa in the living room. He sat down, opposite a two-cushioned couch that matched the sofa. A mahogany table separated the pair.

"Could I get you a cup of coffee, officer?"

She was wearing a yellow, sleeveless blouse and tan slacks. Her hair was tied in the back, pony-tail style. He could tell she had been crying.

"No, thank you," McNabb said. There was a long pause. "Mrs. Arezzo, your husband was retired?"

"Yes. He retired two years ago. Heart condition." She slid a magazine to one side and lowered herself to the settee.

"Who did he work for?"

"He was chief accountant for Circle Midwest Industries in Chicago," she answered. "He was a CPA and headed a small staff that maintained books and handled billing and payroll."

"What is the company's line of business?" McNabb asked.

"I'm not sure of what all they're involved in, but I know it has a truck operation and delivery service in the Chicago area, and I believe the company does some sort of metal casting. I was only at Aldo's office once. He preferred to meet for lunch or coffee away from the office area."

"Do you know if he was to meet someone Sunday morning? Perhaps decided to go golfing?" McNabb suggested.

"Not that I was aware of," Mrs. Arezzo replied. "Just his usual Sunday morning walk, or 'stroll in the park' as he liked to call it. He didn't like to golf on Sundays. Too busy, he said."

"Did he have regular golfing partners?"

"Yes, there were several retired men that he usually played with." She mentioned their names and McNabb made notations on a small pad.

"Any other regular friends? Card clubs? Bowling?"

"Aldo didn't have a big circle of acquaintances," she answered. "He liked family gatherings, the quiet of home. When we play bridge, it involves people I know from church."

"Mrs. Arezzo," and again McNabb searched for words. "I know this will be difficult, but there is no easy way to tell you." He shifted forward on the sofa and looked into her eyes.

"We think your husband is dead. We believe the body of a man we have taken to the hospital morgue may be that of your husband. Would you come with me to confirm that, to see if you can identify this person?"

Marge Arezzo cupped her hands over her mouth and began to sob softly.

Chapter 14

It had been nearly a week since the August 17th robbery at The Czech Inn in Cedar Rapids, and police were no closer to solving the crime than they were on the first day of the investigation.

While it certainly was not in the urgent category of a murder, the possibility that a gun had been involved elevated the restaurant holdup as more serious than a break-in or burglary in the minds of cops.

Cedar Rapids was not a high-crime focal point in the Midwest. It was the state's largest industrial center, a primary factor in the city's low unemployment and lower than average crime rate. Its downtown served as the major commercial hub for Eastern Iowa. Its education system was regarded as excellent, and the overall income level considerably above the state average.

It had well-known entertainment venues such as the opulent Paramount Theater, stately movie theaters and for 34 years proudly supported a 70-plus member Symphony Orchestra.

For sure it wasn't Utopia. For starters, the city was founded by a horse thief with the benign-sounding name of Osgood Shepherd.

As a railroad center, with major lines running through the heart of the city from all directions, there was ample access for the transient, ne'er-do-well or anyone to import devious intentions. As in any community, there was a constituency that believed the best living came out of the pockets of other people, whether a business schemer or wallet snatcher.

Unlike its Midwest metropolitan kinfolk – Chicago, Minneapolis, St. Louis and Kansas City – Cedar Rapids did not light up the night with fancy clubs and regular big-time show people. There were some who claimed that the overwhelming focus on work, the near devotion to business, and a broad, conservative-leaning culture, kept a lid on show palaces and big-name glitz.

Regular night life in The Loop centered on the movie theaters, bars and the weekend dances at Danceland. Stores normally closed at 5. There were some fine downtown restaurants, including Baranchanus, Ross's Steak House and of course the Butterfly, but none with regular evening attractions. The sidewalks were pretty well rolled up by 11 p.m. Most late-hour eating or drinking was left to outlying taverns and road stops.

Charlie Jelling and the rest of the night shift police staff pretty much knew them all and which ones were the most likely to summon their help. A tavern in the river flats section was a noted trouble spot.

"When you enter there," he had often cautioned whoever was his partner, "go in low. Stuff may be flying – shuffleboard pucks, cue sticks, anything portable – and so will fists. There are a lot of fights there."

When Jelling first joined the department, Chief Kendra gave his rookie a piece of advice. Jelling was short and wondered if he was big enough to tackle some drunken giant.

"If you find yourself face-to-face with some big bruiser," Kendra offered, "hit him low and knock him down. Then you'll be the same size," he laughed. It was advice that raised Jelling's eyebrows, if not his confidence.

More frequently, the cops were running down a kid that should have been home. Or they cared for a drunk, maybe locked him up for the night so that he wouldn't be hurt by someone, or himself. Jelling had a regular customer, a college graduate who was an alcoholic. The man always dressed up in a suit and tie to pursue his binges. Often Jelling took him to jail or the man's home. They became friends.

"Car Six, Car Six. Come in, Car Six," the radio squawked.

"Go ahead, dispatch. This is Car Six."

"Proceed to Lincoln Truck Stop on Sixteenth Avenue West," dispatch directed. "Report of a robbery. Man possibly armed. Use caution. MO similar to Kreiji's caper the other night. West side car is on another call. Over."

"10-4 dispatch. We're headed over the river. Out."

Twelve minutes later, Jelling and Wilson pulled into the huge truck operation, a combination of fuel pumps, trucker supplies and restaurant. Wilson eased the cruiser around the perimeter of the complex, again looking for anything suspicious, before parking near the main door.

As planned, Jelling went inside, and Wilson made a walking exterior check. Both had plenty of prospective witnesses to interview. Dispatch had asked Lincoln Truck Stop night Manager Bob Pincotti to keep everyone in place until officers arrived. There were about seven customers inside the building and three truckers outside.

"Any of you fellas see a man run out of the restaurant?" Wilson inquired of the cluster of drivers standing at the refueling station. The damp, night air conveyed remnants of diesel fumes. Flickers of light from passing vehicles on the nearby street bounced off the parked trucks and the assembled group.

Two of the drivers shook their heads in a negative response, but a third said he saw "a figure in dark clothing" walking west away from the front entrance as he parked his rig about 11:30.

"Can you describe him further? Wilson asked. "Was he carrying anything?"

"He might have had something under his arm," the driver said, shrugging his shoulders in punctuated doubt. "I couldn't see that well. The lighting out here is not the best. I'd guess he was about 6 feet tall, on the slim side."

The trucker took a draw on his cigarette and let the smoke filter out of his nostrils and into the polluted night air.

"Was he wearing a T-shirt, sweat shirt, shorts, blue jeans?"

"He had on slacks of some sort, I think dark slacks, but I can't say for sure. And I'd say a long-sleeved shirt," the trucker continued. "It could be he was wearing a hooded jacket. Like I said, he was walking away from me. I only saw his back side. Anyway, his arms were covered."

"Anything else?" Wilson asked. "Did you see a weapon of any kind?"

"Nope," the trucker answered. "He just walked west, and I didn't pay any attention to where he went after that. I didn't see him get into a car. I guess I just looked at something else after a few seconds."

Wilson took their names and telephone numbers and gave them the phone number for the detective bureau.

"If you remember anything else, anything at all, please give us a call." He then joined Jelling inside.

Jelling had already gathered the same information, names and telephone numbers, from those inside the restaurant. The questioning revealed a tall, slim suspect who wore a dark jacket over dark blue slacks and had a grayish hood concealing his head and most of his face. Two people, including waitress Meg Sharp, made mention of the hood's large frontal cutout.

"There were small slits in the hood for his eyes, but you could see his mouth," said Sharp. "He gave a big smile once."

"Heck, you know what caused that big smile," said Pincotti. An impish grin spread between his ears, a smirk that couldn't be pried off with a crowbar. He looked at Sharp. "That was after he gave you a big smooch on the cheek."

That drew a laugh from the others.

None of the witnesses could say for sure if the man had a gun. All agreed his left hand was in his jacket pocket and that made it difficult to determine if a weapon was involved or not. No one described the ordeal as violent or even that they felt threatened. Curiously, none could say if he came in the front south entrance and passed through a general merchandise area, or if he entered from the west directly into the restaurant section.

"Wait a minute," said Jelling. "Let's back up a little. Are you saying the robber took time to plant a smacker on Miss Sharp's cheek after taking your money?"

"Yep," said Pincotti. "I was alone at the cash register. He came up, tossed a felt-like bank bag on the counter, and asked for money. I didn't argue with him. I put what I had in the bag, handed it to him, and then he walked over to Meg and gave her a peck on the cheek. I'd smile, too, after kissing Meg. Who wouldn't?"

Again the gallery guffawed.

"You," she shot the manager a look that could maim, "would have to give me a lot more money than he took to get a kiss."

That drew an even louder round of laughter.

"Mr. Pincotti, did you see a gun or some other weapon?" Wilson asked.

"Well, in my opinion he was armed."

"What do you mean, 'In your opinion'?" Wilson followed up quickly.

"The man had something in the left pocket of his jacket," Pincotti said, "and he pointed it at me as he tossed the bag with his right hand. I assumed he had a gun."

"It could have been just his hand, with his left index finger made to look like a gun," Wilson suggested.

"I don't think so," said the manager. "That's not the way I saw it."

"Was he wearing gloves? Could you see his right hand?" asked Jelling.

"He had no glove on his right hand." And his hand was black. The robber, I'd say, was a black man."

Sharp and several others agreed.

"Did he lean on the counter?" Jelling inquired.

"Well, he was standing right there," Pincotti pointed to the area next to the counter and cash register. "He may have."

"We will check the top for fingerprints," said Jelling. "I know you are a 24-hour operation, but we'd like to cordon off this counter area until the fingerprint man gets here in the morning. Would that work?"

"We can work around that," said Pincotti. "Anything else?"

"The detectives will ask you to go through this again," said Jelling. "I'm sorry, that's just the way it works. Oh. How much money was taken? Do you have any idea?"

"My estimate," Pincotti replied, "is something around $30 or $40. We clean the cash register of large bills and checks every hour. We did that at 11 and there was not a great deal of gas or food sales after that. I don't think we had any truckers fill up since that time. Most of them are pulled over and asleep by now. U.S. 30 gets pretty sparse by 11 p.m. Sometimes I wonder why we're open all night."

With that, Jelling and Wilson left. Back in the squad car, they looked at each other. Jelling scratched his head.

"Are you thinking the same thing I'm thinking?" Jelling said with a perplexed look. Both started laughing.

"You mean about the kiss on the cheek?" Wilson blurted as he turned the key in the ignition.

"Yeah," said Jelling. "This job never ceases to amaze me."

Chapter 15

This time the story of the kissing bandit cleared the confines of The Gazette's circulation area.

The local paper called it into the Associated Press, and from there it sped nationwide. The "Kissing Bandit," whether or not he sought notoriety, was a headlines hit.

The account even made the roundup briefs inside the staid *New York Times*. "Prairie Lips," its 14-point lead-in said.

On the other hand, *Chicago's American* splashed the romance and robbery story below the fold on the front page. "Stealing a Kiss," it blared.

Cedar Rapids police were bombarded by calls from dozens of papers. A newspaper in Melbourne, Australia, wanted details "aboot this here outback caper." Even a fashion weekly and monthly magazine probed for particulars about the Kissing Bandit's tendencies in haberdashery and cuisine.

One slick monthly offered Dorothy Dotson, the kisser's first "victim," $100 if she would pose close with a Reuben sandwich and display a cheek daubed generously with Thousand Island dressing. She declined.

"I'll be Mayor Daley's old grandmother," Eddie Ralston laughed as he read the *Chicago's American* story of the Kissing Bandit. He flecked ashes from his fat Havana into a green glass tray big enough to be classified as a lethal weapon. He inhaled again and dispensed "O" rings, smoke signals that an idea had blossomed in the conniving section of his cranium.

"Judy," he yelled at his secretary, who was also sometimes confidant and sometimes other things. "Get me that puke Ellis on the phone. What the hell's his first name? Is it Joe? Yeah, Joe Ellis. Get that maniac Ellis on the horn and renew my subscription to the *American*.

"Great greetings to Colonel McCormick!" he chortled with scorn. His abundant jowls bounced in rapturous delight. "You'd never see *The Tribune* tarnished with this kind of story. Too damn entertaining." His laughter created sizeable tremors in his corpulent mid-section, sufficient turbulence to dislodge cigar ash. He mirthfully brushed it off his black slacks.

Ralston was so tickled by the news story out of Cedar Rapids, Iowa, that he read it three times, the last out loud to Judy. She listened as if it were a steamy yarn from *True Story* magazine.

"Oh, that's sweet, Mr. Ralston," she chirped.

"I wonder, Judy, how would you look with a little Thousand Island dressing delicately painted on your cheek, or," and he gave her a leering glance, "or some other spot?"

She didn't respond.

"I think, Judy, that Mr. Kissing Bandit just became a member of our payroll. Not officially, you understand, but how do they say, vicariously? Tell Ellis to get his ass over here as soon as he can. Today!" Ralston ordered. "And tell him he doesn't need to dress up!"

It took several hours before the secretary was able to locate Ellis and pass along Ralston's directive. It required only 25 minutes for Ellis to reach Ralston's place. Ellis jumped out of the taxi and walked briskly toward Ralston's small office. He knocked, with some nervousness, on The Man's front door. To his surprise, Ralston answered.

"Why it's Joseph," Ralston said in a tone that was born out of smugness. "Come in, my boy. It's good to see you again," he provided a veneer disposition as though he had just cleaned up on the last race at Washington Park. "What can I get for you? A drink? A cigar?"

"No thanks, Mr. Ralston, I –"

"One of your problems, my boy," Ralston interrupted him, "is that you never accept hospitality. It's one of the most important things in the world. Do you know that courtesy and hospitality open more doors than force? Would you believe that gifts and giving produce a greater return than guns? You ought to think more about that, my boy. You'll have a more satisfying career, with less wear and tear on the body. Do you get my meaning?"

"Yes sir, I do," Ellis said, his stomach grinding with sour rejection of Ralston's thesis, though his face presented acceptance. "OK. I'll have a beer."

"Good, good," Ralston responded. "It's more fun doing business in a joyful atmosphere. Judy," he shouted to the next room. "Judy, will you please bring us a couple of Atlas Praegers. Or, maybe I should say, 'Atlas Praeger Got It! Atlas Praeger Get It.' That's their slogan, my boy."

Ralston laughed at his lame attempt to sing the brewery's famous jingo.

"And bring us some beer nuts, too," he bellowed.

The two men sat in a small room off the front entryway, what Ralston called his office. The Man sat in an old wooden swivel chair that had a two-inch flowery pad to soften its business side. His desk was battered and messy and dark enough to appear as if it had survived the Great Chicago Fire. The walls were a combination of dark wainscoting and flowered wallpaper. It was a sure bet that nothing about the décor would show up in *The Tribune's* home section.

Windows with wooden blinds flanked both sides of the desk, giving Ralston a panoramic look at the street outside. They also provided illumination to an otherwise dimly lit room.

Ralston motioned Ellis to sit on a maroon-colored couch that was long enough to nap on and appeared to have served that purpose many times. He settled deep into its sagging midsection, the point where worn springs reflected The Man's posterior at rest. Ellis was not comfortable. Ralston sat several inches higher in his chair, not a coincidence.

"You don't mind if I smoke a cigar?" Ralston asked, as he took another draw on the ugly black stogie.

He wasn't really looking for approval from Ellis. The question was regarded as perfunctory courtesy by Ralston. He was like the railroad baron who sized up a life raft and an approaching elderly woman as The Titantic was sinking: "Do you mind if I go first?"

Ralston was in charge of the script, as well as playing the key roles.

"Joseph, do you remember the story of the Trojan Horse?"

"I'm not sure Mr. Ralston. Did he run at Washington Park?"

"Not the one I'm thinking of Mr. Ellis," Ralston replied with condescending disgust. He took another puff and blew smoke directly at Ellis.

"Surely, my boy, you had some history in school and heard of the war between Troy and the Greeks. In order to gain entry to the barricaded city of Troy, the Greeks constructed a large hollow horse, filled it with soldiers and parked it at the front gate. The Greeks pretended they were abandoning the battle, and the leaders of Troy looked upon the horse as a trophy.

"Do you know what happened next, Joseph?"

"No, sir."

"The idiot sons of Troy opened the gates and danced around the horse as if it was a god. Do you get the picture now?"

"Yes, sir," said Ellis, looking down at the tattered rug. "I assume the Greek soldiers jumped out of the horse and invited the rest of the Greek army in."

"Ah," Ralston looked Ellis smack in the eyes. "You are a quick study, my boy. I am going to send you to the head of the class." His look carried undisputed authority. "You are going to be a Trojan Horse, my boy. I want you to visit our good friend George Dawson. Remember him?"

"I remember our talk about Mr. Dawson and his unpaid bills," Ellis responded with hesitance, "but I don't understand this business about a horse."

Ralston tossed the *Chicago's American* front page to Ellis and asked him to read the story of the Kissing Bandit. Ellis read the item, and returned a puzzled look at Ralston.

"Now, here's what we're going to do, Joseph," Ralston continued his joyous romp through simulated high theater. "I should say, here is what you are going to do."

Chapter 16

Joe Ellis usually consumed a big dinner before going to work.

There was something about heading off to the job that stimulated his gastronomic juices. He had strict rules about not mixing alcohol and business. As much as he liked a brace of Jack Daniels, escorted by a cold Blatz beer – especially before eating – he never indulged before work. That renunciation did not come from outside influence. It was self-imposed, governed by his need to maintain a keen mind in a dangerous occupation.

Ellis, 33, made good money and spent most of it. He gratified himself by donning the finest suits, styles by either Hart Schaffner and Marx, or the light weight imported Coronado. He preferred Robert Talbott ties and wore only stylish Jarman Miracle Mesh shoes. For a man who spent nine years in a drab Marine Corps uniform, including a hellish year in Korea, he had become a walking model for men's fashion.

The prim attire disguised his depraved soul.

Ellis diligently managed his Marine Corps physique, preserving his slim but powerful form by regular visits to Chicago health clubs. It served his job, but more importantly, it nurtured his pride. He had become an expert in self-adulation.

Uncommonly muscular, Ellis was a svelte 195 pounds. There was no fat on his 6-foot frame. He had his hair trimmed regularly, with specific attention to grooming his bountiful eyebrows. Unattended, they quickly transformed into the likeness of stalwart caterpillars.

He had no immediate family. Ellis was the only child of parents killed in a car crash while he was in the service. He had no ties to extended family and didn't want any.

Initially, he planned to put in his full 20 years in the Marine Corps and retire at the ripe age of 40. However, his independent streak followed him one night into a bar near Camp Pendleton. An ensuing fight involving an officer led to an option he accepted. Sometimes a sergeant has to back off. That was not part of Ellis' nature. At first opportunity, he quit the Marines and returned to his native city's south side.

With no attachments to home after high school, he had entered the Marine Corps to prove his toughness – not to others, but to himself. There was no motivation from Semper Fi and legendary Marine dependability. Ellis wanted to demonstrate to the Corps that he could withstand the fiercest drill instructor and any challenge sent his way. He accomplished that and along the way groomed his reputation as a loner.

He flourished as a one-man operation in Korea, a sniper who carried out assignments by literally calling his own shots. He was thrust into danger, beyond the perils of a forward observer. When an artillery round from his own unit kicked up death next to his position, it reinforced the notion that he alone was his ticket to survival.

Upon discharge, he found employment almost immediately. His aptitude and attitude attracted him to a special line of work, like a magnet seeks metal. Or, perhaps more appropriately, like a wolf is drawn to sheep. At first it was simple kinds of chores, such as emphatic conversations with dirt-bag street drug dealers and convincing visits with slimy loan sharks, business talks where there was no room for misunderstanding.

But then Ellis was promoted to more serious work. When talk doesn't produce results, other steps are necessary. In classic Chicago persuasion, he was adept a breaking fingers, and when ordered, rearranging internal organs.

Except for his boss and a few co-workers, Ellis' life was void of acquaintances. None of those he worked with were really his friends. It was a lifestyle that served his narrow view of values, if you want to sully the term. He was his own best friend, and he would do anything for himself. He had never really loved a woman in a profound sense.

To him, women were merely entertainment, objects of pleasure, things. Commitment was not in his vocabulary. Sexually, he acted more like a barnyard animal, and it caused him no pause.

His job fit his character. As a bonus, the boss would occasionally grant him carte blanche from the organization's prostitute stable. It was almost a blessing for his parents, religious Episcopalians, not to witness what their son had become. He was the opposite of everything they had hoped for and stood for.

They had attended Holy Eucharist every week. They believed, like Catholics, that the host becomes the body of Christ, and the wine becomes the blood of Christ. They responded with serious dedication to the church's social ministry, especially hospital volunteer work.

Joe Ellis had no interest in church social ministry. He was devoted to forcing people to follow the mob's mission.

His primary entertainment centered on the horse races at Washington Park. His father had been an ardent White Sox fan, but for Ellis baseball was just one more instrument for betting. He had no concern, no particular curiosity in Sox second baseman Nellie Fox's batting average, except to the degree that it served Ellis' betting average.

America had had its fill of punk criminals, Bonnie and Clyde-like mush brains who robbed and killed joyously as if it were a Hollywood production. Ellis envisioned himself as a serious, suspender-snapping, suave, respected member of the criminal country club, a capo in waiting. He smoked designated hits, not fancy cigars.

There was another mark in his character, so secret that even he shunned its existence. Deep inside Joe Ellis there was a germ of dread, an atom of anxiety that he shielded with layers of independence and unprincipled pluck.

When Ellis turned three years old, his mother hired a clown to entertain at his birthday party. For some reason, the clown showed up with a loud "boo," and young Ellis didn't stop crying for an hour. That night, and for several years after in the face of dark nights and creepy sounds, his mother sang or hummed *Twinkle, Twinkle Little Star* to soothe his fears.

He never forgot the calming influence of those simple strains. Even as a toughened sniper, his rifle scope focused on a target, he would hum that jingle to counter any anxiety. Often he had visions of directing a bullet in the middle of that clown's head.

The taxi dropped him off shortly before 7 p.m. at the doorstep of Gene & Georgetti's, one of Chicago's best known steakhouses. Located just north of the mammoth Merchandise Mart, it drew customers from around the world. It was a place where the likes of Lucille Ball and Frank Sinatra ate, and Joe Ellis fancied himself worthy of such company. He ordered a T-bone, rare.

He would have savored a Jack or two, but he stuck to his rules. Instead, he ordered ginger ale as he waited for his Caesar salad.

Ellis hated ginger ale. Even more, he despised the notion that there were rules, even if they were his own rules. He loathed having to bend his desires to serve the wishes of someone else. But he knew it was necessary in the crime business just as in any other business.

He shunned a refill offer on the ginger ale and took his meal with deliberation. He was in no hurry, but neither did he want to be late. Rules, you know.

It was 8:30 when he entered St. Hubert's Olde English Grille on West Jackson. Again, he was to meet The Man.

Ellis wasn't nervous. He was long past getting uptight about meeting anyone or anything. For one thing, he had been a good employee, paying heed to the No. 1 rule in business – never make the boss look bad. More importantly, his pride walked before him, clearing the way of any skittish feelings and emitting a steely presence that did not waver even in nefarious quarters.

Ellis walked slowly to the back of the restaurant. He knew where The Man would be sitting. The Olde English Grille was a famous hangout and meeting place for some of Chicago's more illustrious underworld leaders. In some ways, Ellis and The Man, known in newspapers as The Rhino, were an odd couple. Not that they were a couple in any social sense or other meaning except, two people, boss and employee.

For one thing, Eddie Ralston had a squatty build and was a firm flouter of any suggestion that pointed toward healthy living. Why would you abuse oneself by exercising at a health club, or shun the pleasures of fatty foods and a Cuban cigar only to get knocked off by some competitor's hired gun? He believed in enjoying life to its fullest, so long as he could enjoy life.

Moreover, The Rhino, a nickname Ralston obtained because of his tiny ears and ample jowls, believed in violence as a last resort – unlike Ellis. That anomaly in the gangster world made him stand out like Miss Manners at a pie-eating contest.

That did not subtract from his ruthless reputation. He could make opponents suffer by cunning design – placing blame in wrongful places, directing rumors like a traffic cop works a busy intersection, destroying businesses with financial juggling and creative paperwork.

Ralston subscribed to a doctrine he attributed to Al Capone: Anybody can use a gun. Rather, he believed in a process he described as "civilized hurt."

"The Rhino can kill with a gun if it is compelling, but he likes to negotiate with cash when possible," he told Ellis when they first met. "Go the extra mile to make a friend instead of an enemy."

Unlike some mobsters who craved the limelight, he worked to avoid attention in the press.

At that first introduction to Ralston, Ellis had to force his attention away from The Man's hands. Neither the small ears nor jowls distracted him. But, Ellis noticed his hands. It wasn't the fat diamond ring perched on his stubby middle finger that beckoned attention. Rather, each of his hands had a tiny sixth finger, an appendage that stuck out from the base of the little finger. They just dangled there.

Ellis looked away.

Why did they call him Rhino? It would have been more appropriate to tag him as Six Fingers.

Can you imagine how many bullets old no-shoot Rhino would drill into your body if you called him Six Fingers? Mr. Nice, aka Six Fingers, would make you look like Swiss cheese. Here he was meeting him again, and Ellis instructed himself to avoid staring at the hands. Look at his ears. No, better yet, look him in the eyes. He could do that. He wasn't afraid.

Ralston was of Scotch descent, the fourth of five children. His family was poor. He dropped out of elementary school at age 10 and got a job selling newspapers. He soon tried his hand at petty theft and became involved with the world of Chicago street gangs. By age 14, Ralston was in the custody of a Chicago judge who attempted to interest the young hoodlum in a law career. Though that failed, Ralston picked up judicial lessons that proved of great value later on.

During the next few years, Ralston was involved in jewel thefts and burglaries, actions that landed him in jail for short stints and expanded his criminal education. Once accused of felony burglary, an offense that would have carried a much stiffer sentence, Ralston convinced the prosecutor to reduce the charge. According to stories that circulated in the mob world later, when he rose in gangsterdom, he had cut a deal with the D.A.

"You attempt to get me indicted for burglary, and I will weep before the grand jury," Ralston purportedly told the prosecutor. "They probably won't indict me because I am only 16. Even if you get me to court, the do-gooders will state that because of my extreme youth I ought not to be sent to prison. However, if you reduce the charge to petty larceny, I will plead guilty. I'll get a light sentence. You'll get a conviction that looks good on your record. Everybody will be happy. What's more, you will receive a suitable gift before the case goes to court."

In the 1920s, with tutoring from a small-time gangster, Ralston matriculated to the lucrative field of bootleg liquor. He soon had a job with Capone's outfit. After that, it was on to racketeering and the more serious side of Chicago crime.

In 1933, Ralston was indicted for income tax evasion. On the run for 15 months, he finally surrendered in Iowa and pled guilty. He was sentenced by a federal judge to 20 months in Leavenworth. He served 14. Because of his connections, the Chicago Outfit assigned him to more and more difficult and sensitive matters. Perhaps the most complicated came in the1940s when the Chicago Outfit reportedly asked him to secure paroles for four prominent mobsters who were behind bars. Several faced new indictments.

Ultimately, through acquaintances in Missouri, Ralston allegedly offered a deal to quash the new indictments and push the paroles along. The offer was said to involve a high judicial appointment for the prosecutor. When the legal dust settled, Ralston was given credit by the crime syndicate for pulling off the deal.

Ralston's stock boomed on the mob market. Whether he really had any impact on the judicial nomination was argued for years. Later, it was even a subject of FBI probes.

By the early 1950s, when Ellis first met him, Ralston was riding high in the Chicago mob hierarchy. To the outside world, Edward Ralston was listed as vice president of development for Circle Midwest Industries. To Ellis, he was vice president of trouble shooting and quality control.

As Ellis approached him at the rear of the Olde English Grill, Ralston was poised to become the Outfit's chief political fixer, strategist and master schemer. He had won the favor of some of the nation's largest labor unions, established a footing in gambling and recently dined with a Middle East emir. He had big shot friends in labor unions and at the country club, and knew high rollers in both local and national politics.

While many of Chicago's crime bosses owned estate-like compounds, and some had Wisconsin hideaways, Ralston had spent most of his life in a nondescript bungalow along the city's south shore. Yet, he was highly respected throughout the syndicate. His "system" placed great trust in the corruptibility of government officials.

"The difference between guilt and innocence in any court is who gets to the judge first with the most," he once told Ellis. Still, when push came to shove in a business with plenty of pushing and shoving, Ralston's hardness was exposed. Ellis was about to learn that.

"Joe, good to see you again, my boy," Ralston reached out his right hand while remaining seated in a booth. Ellis didn't savor the "my boy" moniker but said nothing and accepted the hand greeting. Some of Ellis' criminal peers called him "Brows," a reference to his bushy eyebrows. That angered him even more.

"Please sit down," Ralston said. "May I order you anything?"

"No thanks," Ellis replied. "I just ate a short time ago."

"Good. Good. How about a cigar, then?"

"No, I'll pass on that, too," said Ellis. "But thanks."

"Suit yourself," said Ralston. "We'll get right to business, then. You know I despise violence, but any time you become weak, you might as well die. I'm not ready to die, and I'm not going to be weak."

"I understand, sir," Ellis nodded his head in agreement. "Weakness is one of the worse sicknesses in the world, especially when it comes to business dealings. If given an inch, people will run over you every time. My motto is to run over them before they run over you."

Ralston placed his mammoth paws on the table. He was sporting a long- sleeve white shirt, open at the neck, and tan seersucker pants. The impeccable creases on the shirt's sleeves looked as if they were applied by a street roller. Fancy gold cuff links in the shape of a heart dazzled at his wrists. His unusually dapper appearance embellished his cryptic history.

"Well, that's where you and I differ," said Ralston. "I believe in giving a man a chance to show his good faith, to demonstrate that he is part of the team. If he fails, well, then, other steps have to be taken. That brings us to the issue at hand. I've given this individual more than one chance, and he's treated me as if I were a fucking bill collector. Let me put it this way. His bills are way overdue, and my interest rate is going to be exceedingly fucking high."

During the next 15 minutes, Ellis received his instructions. He was to go to Iowa and settle the matter for good. Clear the books. Since The Man was being stiffed in a long-time financial arrangement, it was time to reverse the roles. Except, this transaction would be deadly permanent.

The stiffer would become the stiff. And, The Man emphasized, it would serve as a message for all others doing business with him.

Ellis was delighted with the assignment to commit violence. However, there was one part of The Man's directions he despised. The hit would have to be executed so as to divert any attention from Chicago.

Ralston ordered Ellis to develop a plan that would make the killing appear to be part of a robbery, and certainly not connected to the intricate business web known as organized crime. And Ralston wanted veto power over Ellis's plan of execution. Ellis was given one week to propose a plan. All this oversight and micromanagement of a simple murder aggravated Ellis, but he had no choice.

The target was one George Dawson, a long-time character on the back side of honesty whose repertoire of illegitimate businesses included drug dealing, loan scams and betting. He was a second-tier hood in Chicago, but had compiled first-tier debts with Ralston and The Outfit.

It's one thing to not pay your utility bill or grocery tab. The food store will discontinue credit. The gas and electric company will merely shut off your heat and power. Being in arrears to the mob meant they could shut off your lights for good.

Dawson was as shady as an elm-canopied street. His business model was to prolong debts and invest the money instead in new schemes. He had had some success. As long as he paid some of his debt to Ralston, he believed, any drastic developments could be forestalled.

But that dance was about to come to an end. He had waltzed around too many warnings. By moving to Iowa, where he had opened a fancy restaurant in Cedar Rapids' east end, he thought he could further insulate his past.

It was the worst miscalculation of Dawson's soon-to-be-ended life.

Chapter 17

Spring 1955, Oak Park, Ill.

"George, this is one of the wildest notions you've ever had! Jus' cause we can afford it now, with the kids grown, don't mean we should be doin' it. Goin' off on some long journey, makin' like we was some sort of modern day Lewis and Clark. We could get lost! What if the car breaks down? What if we can't find a place to stay? And the cost! I can think of a thousand better uses for our savin's!"

Viola McDowell was not a timid person. Her opinions flowed as freely as Niagara Falls. For weeks she had shared her mind about what she sometimes labeled "your scheme," and now she streamed forward with her latest summation – for what in George's mind seemed like the hundredth time.

"Vacation is a good time to paint the hallway and make serious on your promise to clean up the garage!" Viola continued. "Nex' thing you know half the neighbors in Oak Park will be gettin' up a petition to haul away what you keep storin' in that garage. For goodness sake, watch out for that truck! He's taken more than half the roadway. I keep telling ya, this travelin' thing is dangerous. I jus' keep wonderin'. Should we be doin' it? What will people think?"

She really wasn't asking questions. She was draining her thoughts.

"For cryin' out loud, Vi, this ain't covered wagon days!" George finally broke in. "We ain't takin' the Oregon Trail. What will people think, you're sayin'? You make it sound like we're headin' out as if it was before we was married, contemplatin' some secret sexual tomfoolery with your father lookin' over my shoulder. Like we was two young people who – wait!"

He glanced over to the passenger side of their 1953 Chevy Bel Air, giving her a sneaky, semi-lustful look of anticipation. He had always called her Vi, and not just because it sort of bugged his mother-in-law, who cherished the full "Viola," the baptismal name given her oldest daughter.

"Vi! That's a great idea! Whooee! We'll call it our second honeymoon. The neighbors won't be talkin' 'bout my messy garage. They'll be sayin': Why George, you ole rascal. I'll tell 'em 'bout this big trip, our second honeymoon, romantic cottages along the way, and they'll say, 'George, you ole rascal'."

"George, you said that twice. Now I know for sure your headin' down that long slide into senility," she said, but then she caved in to his silly side and laughed. She punctuated the laugh with a "hmmm hmmm" that carried a tinge of naughtiness of her own.

It was really the first big vacation Viola and George McDowell had ever contemplated. Except it was mostly, almost exclusively, George's contemplating. They had been on short trips with the kids to Wisconsin and visited relatives in Indiana and Tennessee. Once the family went to the Black Hills, but this, a trip to the West Coast, was something extraordinary.

George had been mulling the notion for several years. Only last winter had his fortitude and excitement coalesced with sufficient force and maturity to where the idea could finally be exposed to Viola.

It was at supper one evening during late February. Viola thought he was joking. Then she looked at him again, and still thought he was joking. As he kept rattling on, and she kept listening with a skeptic ear, sizing up his face, tuned in for counterfeit inflections in his voice, probing for any hint of deceptiveness, she discovered that he was serious.

Oh, yea. George was copiously serious. You could almost see the seriousness oozing out of his eyes.

Now it was May, and his idea had fully bloomed. George was anxious to gather his travel designs into one big final bouquet of concrete plans and get on the road. He had completed months of oral overtures, tendered reams of written material and proffered a spreadsheet of financial data for Viola's benefit.

She was the household's vice president of finance, and he knew the money part had to be solid. If the expense side exceeded what she believed the savings account could comfortably handle, Vi would veto the entire thing faster than Jackie Robinson could steal second base.

He figured 4,500 miles round trip and tossed in 500 more for side ventures. Gas, he figured, would average 23 cents a gallon. While the 32-page Chevy manual made no mention of gas mileage, George knew from experience he could get close to 15 miles to the gallon on the highway. The tank held 16 gallons, so he could go more than 200 miles before looking for a gas station. He pegged the total fuel cost for the trip at around $85.

He expected they would be on the road a minimum of 15 nights. That's the part that freaked Viola. Housing was the least attractive element about the trip for George, too, away from the comfort and coziness of his own bed for more than two weeks. But there was one thing that would cushion the foreign feeling of an on-the-road bed – his own pillow. George never went overnight anywhere without it.

Viola laughed at him, but he made her pledge never to divulge his little secret to friends at church or his colleagues at Wendell Phillips High School.

George, 58, was the principal at Wendell Phillips, one of the best-known high schools in Chicago. He had taught American history at several schools before accepting a similar position at Phillips. After 25 years of teaching he took a job in administration, and for the last several years he was the school's top official. He looked upon this planned expedition project as a real-life history project.

He was taking his full three weeks of vacation, plenty of time in case the trip went beyond his calculations.

While George knew he would have a new crick in his back after that many nights away from his own mattress, Viola worried about the chink in the checkbook. George figured $10 a night for accommodations, and $15 a day for food. He totaled those estimates at $375. Both figures, he judged, were on the high side, but he knew prices would be steeper out west.

George, whose job taught him that if things can go wrong, they will, plugged in $100 for emergencies. That included car troubles, getting a flat tire fixed, or worse. He didn't tell Viola, but that also covered a trip to a hospital if something more than first aid was needed. His last category was "trinkets and beads," a classification devoted to souvenirs, clothes and unexpected "needs."

His bottom line guesstimate for the trip was $560. He believed that was beyond what they would spend, but he'd calculated it that way, hoping to avoid any of Viola's 'I told you so's'.

"Now Vi, don't go making this a guilt trip," George chided. "This is what we've been working for once the children were raised. Go some place exciting. Turn off on the less-traveled road. Head for the horizon. California, here we come!"

He was pumped.

George and Viola McDowell were like two peas in a grenade. They were close and loved each other deeply, but sometimes outsiders gathered a different picture. Friends sometimes wondered how they stayed together, seeing that they frequently were one bite away from each other's throats.

But they, especially Viola, savored such close encounters. They detested anything sterile and fake. No airs. No cutesy smile outside and churning gut inside. It wasn't simple and the same time not all that complicated.

George and Viola lived the mystery of marriage. That's how he explained it to a church friend. Two people, George said, become one in marriage, but they are still two people. His formula was to be honest, forgive and kiss. Love, he said, overlays the whole thing. His favorite reading from the New Testament was Paul's instruction to the Corinthians, Chapter 13. George usually accompanied his theories about marriage with a hearty laugh, adding to the mystery.

He had worked diligently in schools for more than 35 years. When they were first married, Viola did the house cleaning for several white families. He figured they earned what he called a *real* vacation, one he defined as putting more than 1,000 miles on their two-year old car and in the process make no stops to visit relatives.

His original plan was to do just what Viola had facetiously referred to – follow the Lewis and Clark trail up the Missouri River to Great Falls, Mont., then west across the Rockies into Utah and Oregon. In some places, you could stay in wigwams or outdoor camping sites. There were western barbeque celebrations. Would they accept Negroes? He didn't know, and Viola wasn't the wigwam type.

Alright then, he decided. It was California.

"Cool off your engine there, Mr. History Professor," Viola piped. "I still have a lot of questions lookin' for answers. Many places don't have motels and hotels that will take Negroes. Thought 'bout that? Places to eat? Same thing. Car troubles? Would we be able to get help everywhere?"

George loved that Chevy Bel-Air, even though its six cylinders and automatic Powerglide transmission were sluggish. Some faculty guys and one at church, too, particularly Ford owners, derisively called it power slide. They bugged George that he could take a short nap in the time the Chevy would do 0 to 60. It was light blue with a long chrome strip that flared into a white band on the back fender. He wished he had gotten a convertible, but Vi would have had a fit.

"Don't you be worrying any 'bout our Chevy," George responded. "We'll have it all checked over before we leave. The boys at Oak Park Mechanics will have it humming like new. Only 12,000 miles on the tires. It don't spit no oil. Battery good. Why, it's like a smooth-running chariot right out of the pages of Roman history."

"George, don't dramatize. What about places to stay? Figured that out? Do we have to pack lunches?"

"Well," George down-geared his enthusiasm, "I think we will be fine, but that's something we'll check out at the travel agency. They have books that tell exactly what places will accept Negros. And in those towns where there are no places for us, books give addresses of Negro families that will take in Negro travelers. I don't see it as much of a problem."

"This won't be like driving a school bus down the streets of Oak Park," Viola continued her weakening lecture as they approached the travel agency on Lake Street. "I know you told me you did some research on the route and where we might stay along the road, but how sure are you of all this?"

"Vi, Vi, Vi, it's all settled. We're a shootin' straight west on the Lincoln Highway, the Abraham Lincoln Highway," he added with flair, "west across Illinois, over the mighty Mississippi, past Iowa's bountiful farms, Nebraska's flatlands and Colorado's mountains. The next thing ya know, we'll be in California.

"This will be a fun adventure, Vi," he continued, "and the time to take it is now. We're healthy, we can get around. We're still quite a few miles from the sweet by and by, at least I hope so. And," he paused, now more seriously, "I know motels where we can stay."

He pulled into a parking place, just down the street from the travel business.

He was hoping her attitude about the trip would get an improvement injection from the travel agency. At a minimum, he was trusting the agency stop wouldn't reveal Vi's hard-nose detective face and produce an overall backfire in plans.

McDowell knew the problems Negro people faced no matter where they traveled. It was 1955, and a whole lot of progress had been made in race relations and legal advances for Negroes. But not every place was like Chicago. Jim Crow laws were unofficial dictums on buses, trains and trolleys in many states, and not solely in the South.

But the automobile, for those black families who could afford one, granted a new freedom. Buzzing along, inside a car, a Negro could avoid the routine of racial restrictions. Except on overnight trips. That could be iffy.

'Miss Melanie,' was how she introduced herself. She was one of several advisors at the largest travel agency in Oak Park. Formally, the suburb was known as the Village of Oak Park.

"Welcome, Mr. and Mrs. McDowell," Miss Melanie greeted the couple. She flashed a broad smile at George, knowing in an instant who was the main driving force behind this venture.

"I know you are going to have a wonderful time," Miss Melanie began, tossing an even greater glow toward George, her approach and bearing cultivated in business school. "And I'm here –"

"I know why you are here Miss Melanie," Viola interrupted. "It's your job to convince people where to go, where to stay and how to spend their hard-earned savin's. What I want to know is exactly where we can stay when we go, if we go."

Miss Melanie was quick to translate that while George was the enthusiastic one, Mrs. McDowell was the eventual decider. Her smile was reduced by 50 percent as she looked at Viola.

"You are right, ma'am, to be concerned about accommodations." George frowned. "But," continued Miss Melanie, "you shouldn't overly worry about where to stay. We have many guides to help you. In fact –"

"Look, Miss Melanie," Viola said, locking on the young woman's dark brown eyes. "This may be our first long trip. I mean, this *may* be our first long trip. We ain't decided. But this sure wouldn't be our first time totin' a suitcase. We've been out of town before. We have a good idea of what's goin' on out there."

"Now, Vi," George thought it was the right time to jump in. "Miss Melanie has been in this business for a few years and is well aware of the problems. Give her a chance to explain, to show –"

"George, hush," Vi countered. "*Ebony* magazine jus' ran an article about travelin' issues. You read it yourself, George. A survey claimed that 3,500 motels, places all over America, said they would put up pet dogs, but only 50 said they would accept Negroes. How does that make you feel? Ready to jump up and click your paws, George?"

George had experienced this side of Viola before. Still, out in public, while focusing on his dream vacation, her volley nicked his pride and caused him to shrink in silence. He couldn't argue with the truth, but sometimes one has to look truth in the eye and proceed. He had students like that. There were some who just refused to study and learn. They weren't going to improve their brain no matter what. Finally, you just acknowledged that and went on.

Viola's black hair glistened, and a vein on her forehead heralded another round of incoming opinion. Like a turret on a tank, she swung her aim back to Miss Melanie.

"That same article conveyed droll 'breakthrough' news from Kansas and Oklahoma," Viola fired. "Give me a drum roll, Miss Melanie. Ready?" Hands on hips, she gave the travel lady another glare. "Last year, a Kansas tourist court allowed a Negro couple to stay on the condition they disappear before daylight. An Oklahoma motel admitted a Negro family after they agreed to pass as Mexicans during their stay.

"You see, Miss Melanie, what's chewin' on my underwear?"

"Viola!" George recovered from his shell-shock. "It's not Miss Melanie's fault that many places still choose to discriminate. On the contrary, she can help identify places that don't discriminate. Why do we have to concentrate on the negative? Things are getting better, and we need to support places that do accept us."

There are some things they don't teach you in travel guide school, and Miss Melanie just discovered one of them. How do you thaw a frozen tongue when your brain has taken a direct hit? She fumbled for a reply.

George came to her rescue.

"We are aware, Miss Melanie, that there are publications that list places where colored folks can stay," he began, hoping his deep voice, employed several decibels below Viola's, would calm the travel lady and return the entire visit to neutral territory. "Perhaps the best known is *The Negro Motorist Green Book*." He looked for an endorsing nod from Miss Melanie, but saw none. She still suffered from shell-shock.

"But *Ebony*, for several years, has published its own *Annual Summer Vacation Guide*," he continued. "You probably get it. New ones come out in June and should soon be available. It lists hotels, motels, resorts and even beaches that allow Negro vacationers. Some new motels that accept Negroes are even being built in Dixie."

Miss Melanie seemed slightly more relaxed, but decided to give the meeting five or ten seconds of silence while the smoke began to clear. She shuffled some papers on her desk, purely as a diversionary tactic, and reassessed the situation. Obviously, it was Viola McDowell she needed to address

"Mrs. McDowell, everything you have said is true. As a Negro travel agent, I wish I could assure you that traveling had no race hassles," Miss Melanie began to explain slowly. "But that's not the way it is. It's much better than 10 years ago, but when you start with close to nothing, you still aren't far away from nothing. But what your husband said is also true. I will give you a number of travel guides that specialize in places where Negroes can stay. Some include YMCAs, churches and private homes."

George appreciated Miss Melanie's revised approach, minus the travel school smile. Viola seemed to have shifted away from cutting cynicism, almost as if she had taken a mild sedative. She was listening, with satisfaction. Everybody was on the same page, maybe.

"I have all the maps you will need, for all the states between here and California, with extra information on national and state parks and other attractions," Miss Melanie rolled on in new-found fortitude. "These guides will tell you where you can stay. They don't list places that deny accommodations to Negroes, and they don't list places where it is uncertain.

"No gas stations will deny you fuel, but some may have separate rest rooms for black people. As for restaurants, I recommend you ask at the motel or tourist camp where you are staying," she advised. "They most likely will know. Or, you can call the local library or AME church. Phone books won't be of help. I think you will find that most gift shops will be glad to take your money."

Miss Melanie folded her hands, placed them on her desk and gently leaned forward with professional aplomb. She directed her gaze at Viola, purposefully avoiding George.

"Now, Mrs. McDowell, I would recommend that you make a rough outline of how far you want to travel each day, things to see and do. That way you can select ahead of time the places that will accept colored people. I call it managed travel, and I can do that for you if you wish. Do you folks have a target place for the first night?"

George chuckled at the travel lady's new found vigor and scheme. She was swamping Viola with harmonious accord, information and service. It was really a site to behold. Here's Viola, vigilantly on guard against sales hokum and high talk, being surrounded and seemingly receptive to the one-two travel school pitch.

Viola was nodding in acceptance, as if she were succumbing to a shoe salesman. Her once formidable attack caved to what the guys at the car repair shop would call a sucker punch.

George perked up the Chevy's Powerglide transmission to 40 mph as they rolled toward home, a stack of travel information in tow. He had some rethinking to do. Miss Melanie had raised a few detours, but fears of a full roadblock by Vi had subsided. Yet, the matter of where to eat every day was a bigger issue on his plate than before. And George liked to eat.

"I love the idea of the breeze coming in my car window," said George, glancing at Viola and hoping to maintain some of the fair winds raised by the travel woman.

He rolled down his window all the way. The air was not only cooling, but carried the refreshing notion of freedom. It swept, uninhibited, across George's face and cut an invigorating path through his tight-clipped hair.

George moved his right hand across the top of his head, rubbing his scalp in an unconscious gesture of combing his mind in search of more avenues to allay Vi's concerns.

"I read an article by a Negro travel writer who I think sums up what I mean, Vi. He said that race is most completely ignored on the public highway, that effective equality seems to come at about 25 miles an hour or above. I like that. I like that a whole lot."

Chapter 18

"**P**ut on a pot of mornin' thunder," George McDowell requested as Vi entered the kitchen. "I'll get the eggs and bacon goin'."

Both liked their coffee black and strong. Their recipe never varied. Five heaping scoops of Maxwell House in the General Electric percolator produced the desired taste. And no cream or sugar.

Friends at church, knowing the answer, liked to ask George, "You want sugar and cream for your coffee?"

"Naw," he would reply with a grin. "Just black, like me."

It was a spectacularly happy day for George. Vi had reviewed his trip budget. More importantly, she had agreed – or more accurately, didn't disagree – with his estimates.

Still higher on the assent scale, she concurred that they could afford the trip and do some repainting later on. She also acceded that the guide books and other materials provided by the travel agency's Miss Melanie offered sufficient confidence in finding overnight accommodations.

Coffee bubbling, Viola sat down at the kitchen table and in everyday fashion perused the Irv Kupcinet column in the "*Sun Times.*" George flipped the eggs, then sauntered over to his wife, kissed her on her blazing black hair and moved his hands downward over the front of her housecoat.

How can this woman, he wondered, so wonderful in every way, sometimes get mired in skepticism? Maybe that was harsh. Perhaps her upbringing generated an extreme caution that sometimes evolved into an automatic "let's not" rather than "let's go for it."

George was a disciple of the latter, more adventurous, more willing to try new things. Viola was comfortable with what her mama called "the fo' sure." She was cozily content in the familiar, a product of Tennessee poverty and uncertainty.

"You better keep an eye on them eggs, George," she redirected his focus. "I don't like 'em runny, but I don't like 'em fried to a frazzle, either."

George skipped back to the stove, happily basking in pre-vacation exuberance. As often is the case, anticipation can be almost as exciting as the actual event. Thoughts of mighty plains and majestic mountains were interrupted by a splash of bacon grease.

"What did the Cubs do yesterday?" George asked.

Viola flipped to the tabloid's back side.

"Good news," she said.

"You mean the Cubs won?"

"No. You forgot. They didn't play," she added with a giggle. "Remember, it rained. The baseball gods shined on the Cubs."

Ernie Banks could have hit four home runs to help the Cubs trounce the Dodgers in a Sunday double-header. It wouldn't have elevated George's euphoria one scrap.

The big decision was in the bank. He and Viola were headed to California.

They had planned to leave in late July, but the school board called an emergency meeting to discuss finances, particularly how to replace the main building's boiler. That led to several more sessions before the matter was settled.

George wasn't happy, but it goes with the territory, he had told Viola. By the time the contracts were signed for the repair work it was mid-August.

The new school term didn't begin until Sept. 13, allowing just enough time to make the trip. And, if they did arrive home a couple of days late, the associate principal could handle opening week.

Finally, on Monday, Aug. 29, departure day arrived. George's metabolism was tingling.

"Did you give the front door key to Beatrice next door?" Viola asked as they were about to exit suburban Chicago.

"Yes, I did," said George. "That's a question that you might have asked 20 minutes ago." Silence. "You did unplug the coffee pot?" he asked.

"Yes, and I suppose, George, that question isn't 20 minutes too late?"

Viola looked at George and smiled. Some people might read her unrestrained tongue as hostile and, in George's case, the tosser of stones in the path of marital bliss. That would be a mistake, close acquaintances would argue. They would say Viola presented unvarnished honesty, unwavering friendship and profound loyalty. She was hard-working and charitable. And, she loved George with all her heart. But she was independent.

"I can't help thinkin', George, how lucky we are. Sure, we've had our tough times. But we had good parents, parents who insisted we stay in school. They had rules and the courage to enforce them. I'm not sayin' that we didn't kick over the traces a time or two, but on the whole we behaved, got jobs, saved some money, raised our family and stayed off the dole. We've been lucky."

George wanted to say something, but he sensed Viola's impromptu discourse wasn't over. He was right.

"We drive out of the city, and I see these kids walkin' along, mostly, I suspect, poor kids. Maybe they look at our car and think, 'Those folk are goin' on vacation, maybe headin' West.' They say, 'I sure wish I was in the back seat, sneakin' a ride through them open spaces, seein' the mountains rise out of the horizon, look with awe into the Grand Canyon and then watch the waves roll in on the Pacific Ocean. Jus' leave my troubles behind'."

The momentary quiet blended with the hum of the Chevy's tires on the grooved pavement.

"I suspect they might think that," she said. "Some of these kids never been west of Harlem Avenue."

He still said nothing, but his return glance said all she needed to know. George had many of these sort of kids in his school. Many just needed a chance to sneak a ride somewhere. Many just needed love and security.

"George, remember the opening line in Zora Neale Hurston's book, her most famous one, *Their Eyes Were Watching God*?" Viola asked. "Didn't you have to read it in high school?"

He nodded.

"Well, I thought of that line as we drove past them kids. '*Ships at a distance have every man's wish on board*,' she wrote. I felt that's what they was thinkin'. We're lucky George."

Viola switched on the car radio and was hunting for music, really any kind of music, except rock and roll. She preferred big band and jazz. The tuner yielded nothing that fit her fancy.

"Why don't you dial over to WNBQ?" George suggested. "It's about time for the news update with Alex Dreier."

Dreier was Chicago's "Man on the Go" and the city's most respected radio reporter. George never sought the news on any other station.

Viola had a different favorite radio personality, Franklyn MacCormack. He hosted a late-night program that featured romantic poetry and classical big bands.

George would be sending up his own snoring sonata while Viola listened to MacCormack's regular readings from Elizabeth Barrett Browning. She loved hearing the broadcaster's signature lines.

"*Why do I love you?*" MacCormack's resonating bass voice would intone. "*Let me tell you the ways.*" Brief, audible breathing followed. "*I love you not only for who you are, but what I am when I am with you.*"

That could push George into fortissimo snoring.

"Where is it we're heading?" Viola wanted to know.

"Across Illinois and part way through Iowa," George replied. "You'll get to see a lot of corn, Vi."

"Actually, I get to see quite a bit of it at home, George."

"That's the spirit. This is gonna be a long trip, Vi, so we'll be in each other's presence and talkin' more than ever. Think up lots of topics. Did you bring along any crossword puzzles? I want to finish '*The Blackboard Jungle*', and I brought a couple of other books, '*The Leatherstocking Tales*' and '*The Urban Social History of the Middle East*.'"

"Well, George, that last one sounds exciting."

Viola landed on WNBQ.

"*– temperatures in the low 90s, with the rest of the week being only slightly cooler. Now,*" the news broadcaster said, "*the latest out of Mississippi and the disappearance there of Chicago Negro teenager, Emmett Till. Till, you may remember from late reports Sunday evening,*" *left his Chicago home just over a week ago. He was visiting his great uncle, Mose Wright, in the tiny town of Money in the Mississippi Delta region. According to Wright and others, two white men had come to Wright's home in the early hours of Sunday and kidnapped young Till at gunpoint."*

"This is gonna cause all hell to break out in –" George said, but was halted by Viola.

"George, hush."

"We have now learned a few more details," the announcer said. *"It has been reported that Emmett Till and a cousin last Thursday had joined some local sharecropper boys in buying candy at Bryant's Grocery in the town of Money. The store is owned by a white couple, Carolyn and Ron Bryant. Carolyn was alone that day, according to authorities. It was said Till bragged about having white friends in school, and one of the locals dared him to talk to Mrs. Bryant.*

"From there the information is disputed. Some say young Emmett whistled at the white woman. Some say he may have grabbed her hand. In any case, Mrs. Bryant ran out the door and the boys fled. Ron Bryant learned of the matter when he returned home Saturday after hauling shrimp to Texas. He eventually found out that young Till was staying with relatives. He went to Wright's home and took Till, who is 14.

"The Leflore County, Miss., sheriff is investigating the disappearance and circumstances surrounding the kidnapping. According to the sheriff, Bryant admitted to taking Emmett Till from his great uncle's yard, but claims he released him outside his store. We'll have more on the kidnapping in tonight's news report.

"In world news, President Eisenhower will meet with allies to discuss –" Viola turned the radio off.

"George, for once I agree with you," Viola said solemnly. "I think this Till kidnapping case is gonna be like a civil rights snowball at the top of a hill. Maybe they find him alive, and that'll be that. I sure hope that boy is alive."

Again there was silence, a roaring unease provoked by the ominous news out of Mississippi. They both sensed the potential tumult if the kidnapping turned out to be a lynching. Many Chicago Negroes had relatives in the South, and all were aware of the delicate state of race relations. Black people were pushing to expand their place in American society. Whites, especially in the South, were pushing back to defend the crumbling 90-year old cultural aftermath of Civil War Reconstruction.

"Just where are we stayin' tonight?" Viola asked, breaking the somber atmosphere. "I know you've mapped this out, you and Miss Melanie."

"We did," George said. "And we mapped out the trip, with options, for many nights after tonight. Vi, would you pass me one of those fig bars you packed. I feel a slight pang in the bottom of the breadbasket."

"Seems to me you're afflicted with that lots of times. Tell me again where we stayin' tonight. I think you left that out."

"Tonight Vi, we'll be stayin' at the Motel Sepia in Cedar Rapids, Iowa.

Chapter 19

"I've got an idea Monica," Harold said with an ogling glance at his wife as they traveled down Highway 52 in southern Minnesota. "When we get to the motel in Cedar Rapids tonight, let's play Trinity Lutheran Hospital parking lot."

At first she didn't connect the dots.

"What's this about a parking lot?' she replied, leaning her ear toward the driver's seat to make sure she understood what he was talking about. He looked to his right again, this time shifting his eyes to her bare legs, before refocusing on the road ahead. She had gorgeous legs, and the tan cuffed shorts exposed a good portion of them.

In typical male geographic fantasy, he explored in all directions before his eyes landed on her sumptuous lips.

"Harold, pay attention to your driving or you'll end up in some farmer's hay field. Parking lot? What are you jabbering about?"

"Where did you go to nurses training?" he plunged ahead, prolonging his proposal as if directing a scene from a play. In a sense, that's exactly what he was doing. He was creating a plot that in his view held great promise for the evening.

"I went to Trinity Lutheran School of Nursing in St. Paul," Monica replied, still puzzled. "But what does that have to do with a parking lot?"

"Think back, my dear wife," Harold said, chuckling at his own artistry and deviousness. "What happened in the nursing school parking lot?"

Harold and Monica Erickson had been married for 20 years. She worked as a pediatric nurse at a hospital in Eau Claire, Wis., and he sold insurance for Wisconsin Mutual. They were too busy raising kids and paying bills to take a real vacation before now.

Oh, they had spent weekends in the Cities. They recently saw "Oklahoma," a musical romance that Monica loved and Harold tolerated, at the Strand in St. Paul. He would have preferred watching a Millers baseball game at Nicolet Park. Monica, on the other hand, didn't roll summersaults when on another weekend they toured the Schlitz Brewery in Milwaukee.

"What's not to like about free glasses of beer in the hospitality lounge at the brewery?" he had argued rhetorically after the alehouse tour. She had a polished comeback.

"You're such a big baseball fan, Harold. I would have thought you would want to see the Milwaukee Braves and Hank Aaron."

Now, in late August 1955, they were headed for a week's vacation in Nashville, Tenn., and a dreamed-of visit to the Grand Ole Opry at the downtown Ryman Auditorium. They had watched country stars on the NBC Television Network and planned to see Little Jimmy Dickens, Cousin Minnie Pearl and Chet Atkins in person.

Harold thought he could howl "Howdee!" with as much shrill as Minnie. Both liked Atkins' unique guitar style.

They could relax, confident that their teenage daughter would keep her 8-year old brother in line. They were staying with grandparents.

"What happened," she smiled, getting the full drift of his little drama, "is you tried to push your luck. But good Lutheran girls have their boundaries. They know Russian guys with Roman hands. You never got very far past the kneecap, did you?"

Both grew up in western Wisconsin, she in Eau Claire and Harold on a dairy farm outside River Falls, 10 miles from the Mississippi River.

For a time, he had his hopes set on a baseball career and even played briefly for the Eau Claire Bears. The Bears belonged to the Northern League, first affiliated with the Chicago Cubs and then with the Boston Braves. When the Braves moved to Milwaukee in 1953, the Bears became the Braves. Harold was cut by the Bears in his second season.

He took his UW-Stevens Point CPA degree, which had been primarily employed in figuring baseball stats, to a local insurance agency. After 10 years, he was the owner.

Wisconsin Mutual, based in Appleton, Wis., concentrated on whole life insurance. In recent years, it began providing home, farm and automobile coverage, and that's where Harold was writing most of his business. He believed that if he could sell casualty and liability protection, it would be much easier to convince customers about life insurance.

Monica rolled down the window of their 1953 Mercury Monterey, which last week had acquired a noticeable dent in the right front fender panel. It was Harold's fault. He struck a light pole in his own agency's parking lot. It tickled Monica, but she earmarked her mirth in case of future needs.

The excessively warm air of late August swept her black hair into a rippling serenade that caressed her smooth neck, and reminded Harold of Elizabeth Taylor in "Father of the Bride." Not Taylor's hair so much, as it was shorter, but the actress's skin, like Monica's, was as soft as a duck's down.

"If I remember correctly," Harold said with Major Hoople confidence, "I once massaged the upper thigh of your right leg in that parking lot, and with some ingenuity and dexterity. I recall you attempted to block my maneuvers by crossing your right leg over your left leg, which, of course, made your right leg vulnerable. That would have been above the knee, Missy."

"Wow!" Monica responded, unimpressed. "You are such a technician. If I remember correctly, you were on the receiving end of a not-so-gentle shove. And your crazy bone smacked the steering wheel and sent you into a howl. I thought I was going to have to take you to the emergency room. And, as I further recall, you never tried it again."

"Wanted to."

"Maybe I did, too. But we both know where that would have led."

"Yeah? And where's that?" he asked with a fake, quivery voice accompanied by Groucho Marx-like up and down eyebrow movements.

"It would have led to a spoiled honeymoon, that's what," she said, looking to redirect their conversation. "There's the Iowa border welcome sign. We could stop briefly at Luther College in Decorah. I almost went there. Who is the governor of Iowa? Leo Huff? Or something like that?"

"Why are you interested in Iowa politics?" said Harold with more than slight annoyance.

She was shutting off his hormonal tap, already hampered by middle age. Part of his chest had slid down to his stomach to create a small front porch, and it didn't take a magnifying glass to see that he was more than a few hair follicles short in the attic.

"We were talking about parking lots and legs," he whined. "To answer your question, no, it's not Leo Huff, it's Leo Hoegh. Hoegh as in, I don't know," he sighed in exasperation.

"Ployg, p-l-o-y-g. And, no, we won't have time to stop in Decorah. Not if we want to get to our motel in Cedar Rapids by 5!"

"What's a p-l-o-y-g?" she said, enjoying her needle-work.

"Monica, you know darn well what it is," Harold groused. "It's a strategy that's been ground to near extinction by a dispassionate spouse. As in ploy plus ground. As in any approach or tactic that I was developing for a romantic evening has run off the road. Now, do you want to go for naming Iowa's assistant governor or whatever they call them?"

"Gee Harold. Whatever happened to the smooth talk about legs? And I am not dispassionate!"

Giovanni Battista Belzoni was a renowned archeologist and explorer. He was born in 1778 in Padua, Italy. As a young man, he pursued several interests in Italy, the Netherlands and finally in England where his quest intersected with a woman who he wooed into matrimony. In classical style, they had abundant love, but no money. The couple traveled with a circus for a while, but fate led them to Egypt.

There, Belzoni developed a fascination for archeology. At Thebes, along the Nile River, he subsequently uncovered the 7-ton bust of Ramesses II. In cooperation with British officials, the massive monument was dragged to a boat on the Nile and shipped to the British Museum in London.

Mr. Belzoni died – and some say was murdered – in 1823 at the age of 45, without an inkling that a town in the state of Mississippi in the United States of America would be named after him.

It could also be said that Vernon Taylor, an avid fisherman who decided to become a student in mortuary science in 1937, didn't know a catfish's lick about Giovanni Belzoni, that is, until there was a feature story on the man in *"The Belzoni Banner"* newspaper.

Taylor moved to Belzoni in 1940, worked there as a mortician for 10 years, and then opened his own business, Taylor Funeral Home. For a region of some 4,500 souls, Taylor provided the services of mortician and funeral home director for about 3,500 of them. That was the approximate Negro population in the Belzoni vicinity. No one knew the exact number because a precise count was never made by census takers.

Like everything else in Belzoni and Humphreys County, Miss., funeral homes were segregated. Whites had theirs; Negroes had theirs.

"Ya'll positive the back door was locked?" Ida Taylor asked her husband as the couple drove north on U.S. 61 outside Clarksdale, Miss. "Got all your fishin' gear? What is it, a half-dozen poles? Prob'ly the first stuff you put in the car. And you're sure you made it clear to Will to stay on our side of town?" she inquired over the hum of their 1952 Ford Crestline.

Will, their 16-year-old son and only child, was staying with her parents during the week they would be in Minnesota. He had precise orders to keep his travels restricted to the Negro district of Belzoni, and more specifically between school and his grandparents' house. That meant the north side of town.

He was to avoid the downtown area and the white section of Belzoni. Most of the town's white population, except those who operated cotton plantations on the edge of the community, lived in an area called Brooklyn on the east side of the Yazoo River.

"Woman," Vernon said softly, "we are more than an hour from home and it's the second time we've gone over that territory. Everythin's fine. Will is fine. Your parents are fine. Everybody's fine. Let's just concentrate on havin' a good vacation."

He could understand her concern. Teenagers don't always follow the prescribed path. Get in with the wrong group and bingo, you find yourself in trouble in short order.

But he was confident about Will. He was a good kid, Vernon said to himself. He was a good student and a good football player. His Junior year at McNair High School would begin in September. but football practice started in a few days. After graduation, it would be off to mortuary science school or Alcorn State and dentistry. Either would be fine with Vernon.

"He will do as your parents say," Vernon said, glancing at his wife.

What nagged both of them, but Vernon wouldn't say it out loud, was the recent violence in Humphreys County and the Mississippi Delta. Late summer of 1955 witnessed a swell of tension between Negroes and whites in Mississippi and all through the South. Both sides were restless in a changing society. Still, there was such a thing as worrying yourself to a tizzy.

What made the anxiety razor sharp were recent killings close to home. The Reverend George Lee, a grocery owner and NAACP field worker in Belzoni, was shot and killed at point blank range on May 7 while driving his car after trying to vote.

A few weeks later another Negro, Lamar Smith, was shot and killed in front of the Lincoln County Courthouse in Brookhaven, Miss., just south of Jackson. Smith, a 63-year-old farmer and World War I veteran, was killed in broad daylight, before witnesses, after voting.

Both men had been active in voter registration drives. No one was arrested in connection with either murder.

Vernon and Ida had intended to leave on the weekend, but Ruby Brown changed things.

Ruby, 86, had been sick for months, and when her son called to say she had passed, Vernon didn't give a thought to letting others handle funeral home arrangements. Ruby was a stalwart in the Belzoni Negro community and a prominent member of Greengrove Baptist Church. That's where the Taylor family also worshiped.

The funeral was Saturday, Aug. 27. The Taylors had everything packed for their trip. It was just a matter of loading up the car, a quick chore that was shifted to Sunday morning. The plan was to stay the first night with her sister and brother-in-law in St. Louis, travel to Cedar Rapids, Iowa, the second night, and then reach Minneapolis the third day.

There they would hook up with his younger brother, Tom, who had already informed him that Minnesota fish were twice as big and twice as hungry as those in Mississippi. While the men were off fishing and telling lies to one another, Ida and Eunice, Tom's wife of two years, would go shopping and take in the area attractions.

The complete itinerary, with projected arrivals, departures and telephone numbers, was deposited with Ida's parents.

Vernon looked over at Ida. He just had to say it, he had to mimic her ultra concern over matters already reviewed several times.

"Ya sure now your sister knows we're comin'?" he shifted his voice to a slightly higher tone, with just a dash of slyness. "It wouldn't be very nice to just show up at their place. And ya know for sure she said to come in time for supper? That would be even more embarrassin'. Knock on the door and the nex' thing my stomach grumbles. 'Oh, hi, sis and Vernon,' she says with a surprised look. 'Is there something I can do for you? Ya'll lost?'"

"Vern," Ida said with undisguised disgust and a pause for emphasis. "When you die, what funeral home do you want me to use for processin' and funeral arrangements? Where would you like to have your poor soul dropped off?"

He had to laugh at her quick and cutting response. Usually, she would put up with his rambling tease, but this time she trumped his baloney.

"Ida. You are an amazin' woman. You are so predictable, and yet you are so unpredictable. I knew there was a reason I married you."

"If you think that's butterin' up, Mr. Would-Be Funny Man, you'd better look for better material," Ida said matter-of-factly. "I do have a question about this Motel Sepia in Iowa. What do you know about it? You're sure they accept Negroes? Now, that would be embarrassin'. Get there and they take one look at us and say, 'Gosh, we're sorry. We just rented the last room.'"

"First off, Motel Sepia doesn't have rooms," said Vernon. "They have cabins, a half dozen or so. Each unit has a bedroom, bath and sitting area."

"Sound expensive to me."

"No, it's no more expensive than the usual motel room, which most of the time is not available to us anyways. The place is owned and operated by a Negro couple," Vernon explained. "That's why I know we can stay there. And, it's not some back woods place. It's right on the Lincoln Highway and near the road we'll be taking to Minneapolis."

"And how do you know all this?" Ida inquired.

"I did some callin'. Funeral director in Chicago tells me that Motel Sepia had a mention in the *"The Negro Motorist Green Book."* Seems the place opened in 1953."

"Doesn't have bugs? You know I hate bugs."

"Ida, when I called, I didn't ask them if their cabins have bugs. I wouldn't be surprised if there are the usual brands of multi-legged creatures that occupy places near the woods. It is in the countryside."

Vernon paused.

"They were also nice enough to switch our reservations to accommodate our change in plans. They didn't say if the weekend spiders will still be there when we arrive tomorrow."

Chapter 20

$\mathbf{B}$en and Ann Rooney Dolan lived on a century farm, six miles outside Red Oak, Iowa.

He was the fifth generation of Dolans to till the 275 acres of moderate-to- good soil, much of it whisked in by westerly gales after the Ice Age. Winds scooped up Missouri River basin loams after the glacier melt and deposited them on what eventually became the Hawkeye State.

To be sure, the soil quality on the Dolan place didn't match that of north central Iowa, such as in Grundy County, touted as having the richest and most productive land in the world. But Montgomery County, for which Red Oak is the seat of government and largest town, has served the economic needs of the Dolan clan for more than 100 years. Even in bad times, the farm kept them alive.

Ben's great-great grandparents, who migrated from near Ballyvourney, Ireland, settled on 150 acres in the 1850s. Over the years the place expanded with the purchase of adjoining property.

For the first time, in the prosperous mid-1950s, there was uncertainty if the farm would remain in the Dolan family. None of Ben and Ann's four daughters seemed interested in farming, though that could change. Their only son was killed in World War II.

The couple had no plans to retire. Ben, 60, and Ann, 58, were healthy. Both loved farming and its curious co-joining of both independence and what Ann called "collaboration with God."

Their two-story frame house, with typical triple gables, was comfortable. They installed running water in 1944 and hooked up to REA electricity the same year. Extensive remodeling converted the old kitchen into a bathroom and a former downstairs bedroom into the kitchen.

Other farm buildings were in good repair. The barn had a new corrugated tin roof. Two new wire corn cribs had been erected. The old outdoor biffy was torn down some years ago and replaced by what Ben called a "memorial" Catalpa tree. It shaded a wooden bench. With the demise of the outdoor toilet, he said he needed some similar quiet place where he could sit down, read the paper and meditate.

They own an array of International Harvester machinery, including two Farmall M tractors. Often Ben worked with his brother Leo in putting in crops and harvesting.

Ann operated a tractor just as skillfully as the men did. What she refused to do is slop the hogs. It wasn't the stink, she insisted. She rather enjoyed the curious nature of pigs, even though they lived up to their name at feeding time. Pigs, she preached, were some of the smartest animals around. What she detested were the flies. While no one counted them, it seemed two billion congregated morning and night around the slop barrels.

She had asked Ben to hang sticky tapes around the hog house, but he postponed action on her request for months. He would laugh at her fly phobia, hanging the tapes but seldom replacing them until the next time she raised the subject. She hated flies like frogs loved them. They had fly swatters strategically placed throughout the house. Her usual good sense of humor dissolved when it came to flies, and the whole family knew it.

Once, Ben tried to toss a little levity at what he regarded as her anti-fly affliction. What's a good way, he had asked her, to keep flies out of the kitchen?

"Other than shooing them away from the door before you enter, I'm open to suggestions," Ann replied.

"Well," he pondered, "you could keep them out of the kitchen if you put a little manure in the living room."

She hit him with a fly swatter.

Even though they had known each other in high school, they had married late. Ben was a slow mover in the romance department, and Ann was a no-nonsense woman who wasn't easily wooed. But when they fell for each other, it was an all-out crash. Their courtship lasted three months. They were married at St. Mary Catholic Church in Red Oak, and 14 months later their oldest daughter was born.

Now they anticipated their 35th wedding anniversary and an extended trip. At their 25th anniversary, Ann's mother had been ill, and it hadn't seemed proper for them to leave on a long vacation under those circumstances. So the celebratory excursion was postponed, and then postponed again.

This time, in August 1955, all seemed to be in order.

"Do couples take a second honeymoon on their 35th anniversary?" Ben teased one afternoon. "Isn't that a little late?"

"This isn't a second honeymoon," she fluttered her eyes. "Every day has been a honeymoon."

They often laughed at their slow beginning at parenting, and once married having five children in 14 years.

"You sure were one fertile woman," Ben said one day. "If my corn crop produced as well every year, we could take a vacation to Paris."

"Me?" she was quick to respond. "Every time you hung your overalls on the bed post I became pregnant."

Even if they could afford to go to Paris, Ben and Ann Dolan were not the types to step out of character or do the exotic. They would never purchase a Cadillac. They were Chevy people, and did not pretend to be otherwise. Impressing others was not part of their agenda. They were highly regarded as good parents, solid citizens and excellent farmers.

The community had rallied around the family when their son, Brad, was killed. At first Ann refused to believe it. The Army said he had been killed in action, and when the family unsuccessfully pressed official sources for more information about what had happened, they learned the awful truth from another soldier. Brad's head was nearly torn off when a front line newcomer eight feet away panicked with a live grenade in his hand.

Ann wanted to see the body after it was returned home, but Ben advised against it. She said if she could only see her son's feet, to touch him, she would know it was him and be satisfied. Ben and the Army convinced her to keep the casket closed.

Thirteen years failed to heal her heart. His picture still hung in the hall entryway of the farmhouse. Every day she paused to touch it.

Trip plans were for Ann and Ben to meet up in Cedar Rapids, Iowa, with Ann's younger sister and husband, Caroline and Matt Kilburn. The four of them would then proceed in the Kilburn's Ford station wagon on an East-Coast trip highlighted by the sites of New York City. Ann wanted to see "Damn Yankees" on Broadway and hoped to get tickets to the Ed Sullivan Show.

Ben had some misgivings about a long trip with his brother-in-law. Their personalities were not exactly in sync. They got along because Ben was tactful and forbearing. Matt was an extrovert. Ben was not. Matt liked to talk without resting his lungs. Ben listened more than he chatted. Matt, to put it benevolently, possessed the uncanny ability of putting his foot in his mouth and then, amazingly, was usually able to extricate his wayward words with minimal damage.

Matt looked at life from a different angle. He thought Ben was hidebound and reluctant to try new things. In addition to using pig manure, Matt believed in applying commercial fertilizer. Ben was cautious, unsure the extra cost paid off. Matt purchased new oats seed nearly every year. Ben took oat seed needs right out of the bin.

People would cringe at some of Matt's remarks, but his good nature and cheery countenance seemed to dissolve most of the bad taste. Occasionally, it took a sour turn. In the presence of outsiders, he would sometimes hint strongly that life dealt Ben a better hand of cards. Such mewl-like talk sometimes drifted to mention that Ben inherited a farm, one larger than Matt's.

Then, in an effort to backtrack, his undisciplined tongue would add to the folly by saying, "But I got the good-looking sister."

"By golly, Ann," Ben said one time, "it seems your brother-in-law shoots for some sort of international record to produce the most embarrassing combination of words in the shortest length of time." But he never voiced strong opposition to traveling with the Kilburns.

Matt, like Ben, attended a rural elementary school. Matt was the smallest kid in school, often the target of bullies. His youthful fragileness at times emerged as insecurity in his adult life. After high school in Elkader, Iowa, he attended Upper Iowa University for two years. That's where he and Caroline met.

His interest in science quickly dissolved into his inherited love of the soil. That coincided with his introduction to a smashingly attractive young lady from western Iowa. By the end of his sophomore year, his mind was overrun by two thoughts, Caroline Rooney and farming.

With the backing of his father, the newly wedded couple obtained a bank loan and set off on the speculative business of farming. They rented for seven years before they spotted a "For Sale" sign on a place less than 10 miles from where he grew up. Caroline loved the idyllic setting near the Turkey River. He loved the challenge and independence. They acquired the farm.

Matt and Caroline had no children. For several years, she had difficulty conceiving. When she did, the baby died shortly after birth. It was traumatic for both of them, especially for Caroline. For months she dwelled on the time leading to her baby's birth. Did she do something wrong, somehow harm this little life growing inside her?

Matt was loving and gentle, but of little help. Then her mind was consumed with images of her baby daughter, thoughts of what her first birthday would have been like, walking, playing, growing up. Caroline cried every day.

Ann believed her sister had a profound fear of pursuing pregnancy again. Those circumstances, she confided to Ben, had to have had an impact on their marriage, too. Ann had proposed the vacation with Caroline and Matt as much for therapeutic reasons as anything else. It would provide an opportunity to visit privately with her younger sister about the lingering pain. Ann could speak from reality, having lost a son.

It would be easy for the casual observer to appropriate all of the wisdom and grace to the older of the two couples, but that would be in error. Caroline, in part to redirect her energy and attention, volunteered at the county food bank and taught religion classes at her church. She led the demonstrations on women's clothing styles at the county fair.

Matt, without a lot of fanfare, had become a conservation leader in the hills of Fayette County in northeast Iowa. He led the effort for contouring and strip farming. Both had volunteered on a program to welcome home veterans from the Korean War and both rang bells for the Salvation Army Red Kettle appeal at Christmas.

The Kilburn farm was near the small town of Elkader. The 172-acre place was much smaller than the Dolan's, and only 93 acres was tillable. The rest was steep hills and timber. Some called the scenic area "Little Switzerland." Matt Kilburn didn't share the charm.

"Ya can't grow good crops on scenery," he'd respond to those glamorizing the hills of northeast Iowa. But, his father's respect for the soil rubbed off on Matt.

"Feel it, smell it," his father had suggested one time when Matt was plowing a field of alfalfa. Like his Dad, Matt came to discover the soil's distinctive and overwhelming power of creation. "Treat it as gold," his father advised. "You will come to know why the American Indian revered it as Mother Earth."

Ben Dolan, mild-tempered by nature and considerate of Matt's family grief, gave wide berth to his brother-in-law's cheeky and sometimes contrary ways. But he was less patient than Ann. He would never mention names, but once while visiting with the parish priest he had raised the issue of people he regarded as impudent. He didn't get the answer he wanted.

"The world isn't just a canvas of black and white," the reverend advised Ben. "There are many hues," he said, "and in between strains of gray that are sometimes difficult to see."

August was a good time for a trip. School had not yet started, and the two youngest Dolan girls could take care of themselves. Ellie, the oldest, was married and living in Omaha. She and her husband had two children. Emily, No. 2, was a writer with the *Omaha World-Herald*. Kara and Jackie still lived on the farm, but had summer jobs in Red Oak.

The oats harvest was completed. Second crop hay was in the barn. Corn was tasseled and needed no attention. The stock cattle could fend on their own in the far pasture, so long as they had plenty of water and a replenished salt lick. Ben's brother Leo would tend to the hogs. It was a given that Kara and Jackie, inheriting their mother's genes, wanted nothing to do with hog chores. That left to them the care of Ann's chickens.

The girls had become used to getting pecked now and then when they gathered eggs. They didn't mind that, and feeding the chickens took little time. What bugged them was shooing them out of trees at dark. Stupid chickens! Ben had fashioned a couple of chicken "catchers," long pieces of No. 9 wire with a curved end designed to slip around their legs. Chickens beyond their reach spent the night outside, come storm or predator.

All was ready. Ann had reviewed all the rules and telephone numbers to the point where her daughters' raised eyebrows became weary. Ben made sure they knew the name of the mechanic in case of car trouble.

"And try to remember to close the garage door," he implored.

"Where are we staying tonight?" Ben asked Ann again, knowing her sister had made reservations.

"In Cedar Rapids, at a place called Motel Sepia," she replied.

Chapter 21

"**M**r. and Mrs. Taylor," Roy Sanders summoned them from the gravel path leading up to Cabin 3 at Motel Sepia. "You have a long-distance telephone call at the main office."

The couple looked up in the afternoon's shimmering sun, using their hands to protect their eyes.

"Just follow me please," Roy said. "Bring your tea along, if you'd like."

The Taylors had unpacked only a half hour before and were sipping iced tea on the cabin's front patio. Tea, lemonade or a soft drink was part of the welcoming ritual arranged by Lillian and Roy. The grassy area near the entrance of every cabin included a small, round table and lawn chairs.

Wafting leaves from several large white oak trees filtered the afternoon sun. They collaborated to produce a kaleidoscope of dancing shade. The quiet repose was accented by marigolds and petunias Lillian had planted along the base of the cabins. The flowers were cordoned off by a one-foot high picket fence. Some of the petunias, lanky from the caress of the afternoon sun, were trying to escape the picket confines.

"I'm sorry we don't have telephones in our cabins," Roy said, looking at Ida Taylor. "Cost you know. I trust you found everything to your liking. If you need anything, just ask me or Lillian."

"Oh, the accommodations are most acceptable," Ida answered as they walked toward the Sanders' house. "And the countryside is so peaceful. I must say, the tall corn makes Iowa appear so bountiful.

I just love the settin', much better than a place in town. Only one request, Mr. Sanders."

"By all means, Mrs. Taylor. What would that be?"

"Well, if you don't mind, the tea could use just a little more sugar? You know us Suth'ners. We like sweet tea," she said, laughing.

"Of course," Roy replied. "I should have remembered. We'll add a spoonful or two or three up at the house."

It was a forced light moment for Ida, an attempt to obscure what was really consuming her thoughts. With her manipulation, she and her husband lagged behind Roy on the walk.

Suddenly, she stopped and whispered.

"Oh, Vernon," she said gravely.

Ida was a perpetual worrier. Even at home, the ring of the telephone at night made her nervous. She always interpreted police sirens as trouble in their neighborhood. If a dozen clouds in the sky coagulated into a dark mass, Ida feared a storm was brewing. It was her nature, the residual of growing up in an anxious culture and time in rural Mississippi.

"Vernon, do you suppose somethin' has happened back home? I just know somethin' has happened. What do you think? What should we do?"

He took her by the hand, firmly but gently, a clear signal to move on.

Vernon Taylor was a slightly built man, about 5-foot-8, and maybe 160 pounds if dressed in his Sunday suit, tie and vest. He was a quiet man, courteous and deferring to others, perhaps to a fault. If anything, he was overly pliant to Ida's periodic paranoia.

"First, we should answer the telephone call," Vernon replied, more sternly than usual. "That way we'll know for sure what the call is about, and we can either worry more or not worry at all," he said in a semi-lecturing tone.

They proceeded in silence. In less than two minutes they were inside the main house, where Roy and Lillian Sanders had cordoned off a corner of the kitchen to use as a small office for operating Motel Sepia.

"This way," Roy motioned. "Right over there. Here, pull up one of the kitchen chairs." In succeeding motions, he shuffled papers to one side of the counter and semi-tidied the small desk nearby.

"Thanks," Vernon said as he picked up the phone.

"Hello." He waited for the voice on the other end of the line. "Yes, this is Vernon Taylor." He cupped his hand over the phone and looked at Ida. "It's your mother," he said softly.

Vernon listened, nodded, and turned to Ida again. He gave no indication of what was being said. After about 30 seconds, Vernon responded.

"Thanks Grandma (He always called her Grandma.) for the update, and thanks again for looking after Will." Pause. Grandma was giving the local report.

"Your timing was excellent," Vernon told her. "We arrived in Cedar Rapids only a short time ago." He suspected she just wanted to check in, to see if the telephone number was correct. Grandma continued her report.

"Yes. Yes, I'll tell her," Vernon said. "Do you want to speak with her? Okay, then. We should be at Tom and Eunice's tomorrow night."

Grandma asked if they had any travel problems.

"None, all is well," Vernon dutifully responded. "We'll call you when we get to Minneapolis. Oh, one thing more, Grandma. Tell Will to stay away from the Dairy Treat. The owners are nice people, but sometimes they get some of these hell raisin' youngsters who drive around the place spittin' gravel and lookin' for trouble."

Grandma said she understood.

"Goodbye, then. And don't feed Will too many of your grits."

Ida was antsy and a little put out that she was not part of the telephone talk.

"What did she say? What's wrong?"

"There is nothin' wrong with Will or your parents," Vernon said warmly. "With this Emmett Till disappearance, she wanted to assure us that all is peaceful in the Belzoni area. It's the talk of the community," he addressed Roy, "but there have been no new problems." He turned his attention back to Ida. "Will is goin' to football practice and returnin' to your parents' home as soon as he's finished. Nothin' to worry about."

Ida seemed somewhat comforted, but it was unnatural for her to slip into a relaxed mood.

The Till case dominated radio and TV news in the Mississippi Delta. It was the lead story Sunday night on KMOX, the CBS station in St. Louis. Vernon was glad to get on the road and away from the salvo of Till reports. Ida wanted to ask if the Sanders had a TV, to see what national news coverage might be, but she decided against it.

"Thanks, Mr. Sanders for lettin' us use your phone," Vernon said. "All seems to be fine at home. Our son is stayin' with Ida's parents, and with racial tensions a little high in Mississippi, she wanted to give us a personal report. Say, Mr. Sanders –"

"Please, call me Roy."

"OK, then, Roy. One other thing. Could you recommend a restaurant in the area, some place, you know, that allows Negroes?" Vernon asked. "Otherwise, we did bring the fixin's for sandwiches."

"I believe most restaurants here serve everyone," Roy said, painting his reply with a brush of doubt. "Some may not open their arms to us, but you can eat there. I'm afraid there is nothin' close except for the Lighthouse and George's Gormet. The Lighthouse, just east of here, is good. The Gormet is 'bout two miles west down the road. But it's on the pricey side and mostly Italian. Bishop's Cafeteria and the Butterfly Café are downtown. Both have good food. Bishop's is buffet style."

He let his guests think about it for a few seconds. As they left the house, he proposed something else.

"Vernon and Ida," he began pensively. "I'm hopin' you can join our other guests later tonight, just for some pie, talkin' and visitin'. I believe we have four other couples at Motel Sepia this evenin'."

Roy paused a second to correct himself.

"Actually, I think we have five couples stayin' here, but one just got married." He laughed. "Not likely to see much of honeymooners."

Ida and Vernon nodded in agreement.

"Lillian makes a fine cherry pie with a wonderful crumb toppin'. Jus' come on up, say about 7. Okay? That way you won't have to order dessert at the restaurant."

Lillian entered from a rear room and overheard the invitation.

"Hello. I'm Mrs. Sanders," she said, extending a hand to both guests. Roy had checked the couple in when they arrived. "Yes, by all means, we'd love to have all of you for a light dessert."

"Pleasure to meet you," Ida said. The Taylors didn't respond immediately to the invitation. Preoccupation appeared to immobilize Ida's ability to answer. She finally looked at her husband for relief.

"Let us think about it," Vernon said. "I do like cherry pie. Almost good as rhubarb pie."

"I hear ya there," Roy smiled, as the Taylors departed. Once they were out of hearing range, he glanced at Lillian with a look that told her a pronouncement of some kind was forthcoming. Her expectation was accurate.

"That's a troubled lady," he said, scratching his head. "You can see it in her eyes, Lillian. She has a distant look, her mind focused on things miles away. She's a woman wrapped in worry."

"And you find that hard to understand?" Lillian said. "If we lived in a place where our family's very lives were in question, you'd worry, too. Maybe we ain't on the country club invitation list here, but we ain't on any hit list either."

On the walk back to their cabin, the Taylors noticed a light green Chevy with Illinois plates, and a blue Mercury with Wisconsin plates in the parking area. Soon after, a black couple exited cabin two. Vernon guessed the matronly-looking woman would have no trouble tipping a scale past the 170 mark. She had coal-black hair. The man was about 6 feet tall, broad-shouldered, probably 220, with plenty of white specks in stubbly hair. They exchanged greetings.

"Do ya'll need any help carrin' your bags?" Vernon offered.

"No thanks," replied George McDowell. "I believe we have everything in except for a few incidentals and Viola's shoes. As soon as I get a team of mules hitched, we'll haul in her collection of high heels, low heels, in-between heels, slippers and whatever other design women wear."

The two men laughed, but Viola pitched George a scowl that would have knocked a lesser man out of his loafers.

"I apologize, Viola," George said. "I think we can get by with a wheel barrow."

"Never mind him," Viola summoned an appropriate zinger. "When he gets off his leash he tends to bark more. My name is Viola McDowell, and this toy terrier of mine is George McDowell. It's a pleasure to meet you."

"Vernon and Ida Taylor from Belzoni, Miss.," Vernon completed the introductions. "Where are you folks from?"

"We're from Chicago," Viola said. "Actually, we live in the Village of Oak Park. We're headin' west to California, the big trip George has been plannin' for I'm not sure how long. And, are you on a trip?"

"On a fishin' trip to Minnesota," said Vernon. "That's where my brother Tom and his wife live, in St. Paul."

"They are goin' fishin'," Ida injected. "You didn't hear him say catchin'. I suspect my sister-in-law and me will be involved in more successful pursuits."

"Sweet truth," Viola chuckled.

"Now, ladies," Vernon countered. "Don't criticize what you don't understand. If people focused on the really important things in life, there'd be a shortage of fishin' poles."

"Ah, Mr. Taylor," George chimed. "I admire your philosophy."

"Say," Ida continued, "do ya'll want to join us for a bite to eat? Maybe we could take a short walk in the area, and after that go downtown. Mr. Sanders says there is a buffet place downtown."

"Count me out for a walk," George answered. "My legs and back jus' filed a joint petition for a rest. Get it, Viola? Joint petition? I was thinking of a quick nap before we eat."

"I'd be happy to take a walk, but not too far," Viola said. "I'm a bit overweight, and my knees are on the wobbly side of apprehensive, if you get my meanin'. I knew George had sleepy knees. What 'bout you, Mr. Taylor?"

"I'll tag along with you ladies," Vernon said, "and when we get back from dinner we can all have cherry pie. You up for cherry pie, George?"

"You buyin'?" George chortled."

"No," Vernon replied. "Didn't Mr. Sanders mention cherry pie to you, around 7 o'clock? Up by the main house?"

"I don't think so," said George. "Viola, did the motel fellow say anything about cherry pie later on?

"As a matter of fact, he did," replied Viola. "You were too wrapped up in the TV sports report when we registered."

"Sounds okay to me," said George. "So long as a couple scoops of vanilla ice cream smothers the cherries. Speaking of vanilla, I see there's white folk renting a cabin here, too. This Motel Sepia not too fussy who they take in," he scoffed.

George gurgled a chuckle or two, unable to contain his impish self. The Taylors said nothing.

"Now, George," Viola began.

"I'm just rambling amongst our own kind here, Viola," he interrupted. "No harm in it. It's called sarcasm. I've heard you use the word 'honky' a time or two, in the privacy of our own house, of course."

"Well, this ain't exactly the privacy of our own house," Viola said pointedly.

"I'm guessin'," Vernon broke in, partly to level off the conversation and also to impart a bit of perspective, "we all say things we wish later we hadn't."

He stared at the ground, not directing his words to anyone.

"I guess God slipped up when he made the tongue faster than the brain."

Chapter 22

"You didn't tell me this motel was owned by colored people."

Matt Kilburn inserted the key into the Motel Sepia cabin door and opened it for his wife. He picked up part of their luggage and they entered.

"You didn't ask me," Caroline responded evenly, "not that I knew. What difference does it make? If the place is clean and there are no bugs, what difference does it make?"

"Well, um," Matt stuttered. "I guess it don't matter. It was just kind of a surprise. When I followed you up to the office, and we walked in, I first thought you were talking to the cleaning lady."

"No, the woman who greeted us was Lillian Sanders," Caroline said. "She and her husband own and run the place."

"Well, after a while I sorta figured that on my own," Matt grunted. "Okay, then. That's settled, I guess. Did Ann say anything?"

"About what?"

"For cryin' out loud, what have we been talking about? Sure as heck not the price of tea in China!"

"Smooth your ruffled feathers, Matt. Ann didn't say anything, except that Lillian struck her as a friendly and graceful person. Are you sure it doesn't clog up your craw that the motel is owned by a Negro couple?"

"Naw, Caroline. You're just trying to read something between the lines that ain't there. Where's the cooler? I need a Grain Belt."

The two went outside and sat at the small table in front of their cabin. As the sun drifted westward, their unit had mercifully acquired shade.

The late afternoon temperature huddled in the mid-90s. The heat blistered man and nature. It was so hot the leaves on nearby trees curled in submission and lost their rustle. Even in the infrequent wisp of a breeze, they hung without emotion. The usually lithe timothy field down the road seemed to be locked in slow motion.

Matt's eyes closed as the cold beer trickled down his esophagus, sending a cool massage to neighboring organs. He decided to have a smoke.

Caroline hated it, but had put her protest of cigarettes on hold. She wondered what cigarette smoke did to lungs. Moreover, they were stinky and costly. Matt "compromised" by rolling his own and limited himself to "no more than a dozen a day."

Soon Ben and Ann, who had arrived earlier at Motel Sepia, toted chairs and joined them. Ben's sun-burned face was bubbling with sweat. When he removed his Kent Feeds cap, it revealed his pale forehead, the familiar no-tan zone that made farmers look like brown and white zebras.

"You'd better grab a beer there, big Ben, to cool off the corpuscles," Matt offered. "Ann's suitcases must have weighed a ton, eh? Ben, did you know this motel was owned by coloreds?"

Ben Dolan, like most farmers, was in good physical shape. He supported broad shoulders on a 5-foot-10-inch frame. His hair was beginning to look like the first snow flurries of winter stuck to a waning lawn. What bugged him more than this evidence of aging was that his hair was thinning. The hairs in his ears seem to multiply as fast as the strands on his head disappeared.

His usual work garb was OshKosh bib overalls, but Ann asked that he not wear his farmer uniform on vacation. Without further discussion, she had gone into Penny's and bought him several pairs of khakis. The cap came along on the trip. He denied to needling friends that he wore one to bed.

"The August sun can really turn on the burners," Ben replied. "I'm glad we have a shady spot here. Caroline, I couldn't have reserved a better place myself," he answered Matt indirectly.

Ben read Matt like a competing bidder at a farm auction.

"Maybe, Caroline, you should make more of the decisions at your house. Could lead to bigger yields in the corn, Matt, and better production from your Holsteins."

"Do you want a beer or not?" Matt asked.

"Thanks, maybe later," Ben said. "Where did you get the iced tea, Caroline?"

"From the motel owner," she replied.

Their attention was diverted by two approaching people, one carrying a tray of glasses and the other a clear pitcher that revealed what Ben was savoring.

"Good afternoon, folks. I'm Roy Sanders, and some of you have met my wife, Lillian. We like to welcome guests with iced tea. Ma'am," he looked at Caroline, "would you like a refill? And how about the rest of you?"

"By all means, Mr. Sanders," Ben said. "I was just eyeballing Caroline's tea. Ann, do want some?"

Ann, Ben and Caroline took tea, but Matt said his taste buds had already become "accommodated to barley pop," so he declined.

"Would any of you like more sugar?" Roy asked. "I made the mistake of not offering more sugar to some guests from the South. They like their sweet tea."

"Not for me, thanks," said Ann.

Ben and Caroline responded likewise.

"Now, where you folks from?" Lillian inquired.

"Caroline and I live on a dairy farm about 90 miles north of here," Matt explained. "Caroline and Ann, that's Ben's wife, are sisters. We're traveling east on the Lincoln Highway to New York City. Gonna see the Empire State Building. At least that's the plan, right, Carrie?"

"That's right, Mrs. Sanders," said Caroline, her large brown eyes conveying the excitement of the trip.

She had fixed her short brunette hair with a little poof in the back and bangs in the front. High cheek bones and dimples punctuated her stunning complexion. Any fellow with average vision could appreciate the rest of her lithesome 5-foot-5-inch makeup. She sported canary-yellow culottes, augmented with a two-inch black belt. It added heat to the late-summer day.

Ann had a more mature appearance, but that didn't subtract from her natural beauty. Her expanding gray hair inserted a look of wisdom. Today, she wore white slacks and a sea-foam green top. It would be bad judgment for outsiders to peg farm women as fashion-handicapped. True, many rural women still converted feed sacks into dresses. Their sewing skills and innate inventiveness truly embraced the notion of making a silk purse from a sow's ear.

"Ben and I live on a farm in southwest Iowa," said Ann. "It's not too far from Council Bluffs."

"Glad to see you're spending some time visitin'," Roy said. "I'd like to get all the guests out here talkin' and enjoyin' the outdoors. Along that line, we would like to invite you about 7 tonight for dessert. Everybody can meet everybody else and be smackin' their lips over Lillian's cherry pie at the same time. Come if you can."

Roy and Lillian bid their goodbyes and turned back toward the office when Matt called out.

"Mrs. Sanders, how did you know cherry pie was my favorite? Are you some sort of soothsayer?"

"'Fraid not, Mr. Matt," Lillian smiled. "Nothin' mysterious about my cherry pie. The recipe is all spelled out by my mama. See you afterward, then."

The two couples sipped their beverages and drank in the pastoral setting as well. There was a soothing power in the rural landscape. It was nearly hypnotic to focus on the dancing fields and swaying willows. Across the road a red-tail hawk clung to the wisp of wind as it glided in search for an afternoon snack.

"This sure is a relaxing place, right out in the middle of farm country," Ben gently gestured at the adjoining terrain. "See along the stream, Matt, how the sycamores elbow their roots in the moistened soil? They appear unperturbed by the unruly willows or the sentry oaks. They all get along just fine."

A blue jay shot through the open spaces of the trees, squawking at something. A pair of cardinals pecked away at a five-foot sunflower at the edge of the road.

"Idyllic place really," said Ben. "Don't you agree, Matt?"

"Ben," Matt joked, "you musta taken several semesters of poetry appreciation at Iowa State."

That flavored the atmosphere and produced some laughs.

"Is everyone in favor of cherry pie at 7?" Ann asked. It was her way of quashing any further exchange of barbs between Ben and Matt. She didn't oppose a little good-natured needling, so long as blood was not drawn.

Chapter 23

Roy Sanders scoped his front yard with undisguised pleasure. Hands on hips, he smiled and took quiet account.

Here he was, in mid-1955, blessed with a beautiful and wonderful wife and three children who behaved as best as children can behave. The flooring and cleaning businesses had done well. He had good employees. He and Lillian were respected within their church and, with the exception of a few racial incidents over the years, the family had been accepted in the community.

Roy had made friends in the business community, and thanks to the efforts of Chamber of Commerce secretary Robert Wellman, he'd been admitted to that prestigious group. Some even suggested that he run for city council, and one prominent Republican proposed he try for the state legislature. That would be something – the first black Republican in the Iowa Legislature.

Maybe, he pondered, operating a motel hadn't been his most profitable venture, but you can't always measure success by money. It was satisfying to see travelers, hot from the late August weather, find some respite in the shady oasis of Motel Sepia.

The screen door on the side of the house slammed and tromping feet followed. The reason for the commotion ran toward him.

"Can I have a piece of Mom's cherry pie?" Joseph asked.

"Later," Roy replied. "Right now, why don't you play on the trampoline or swings. And Joseph, do we need to have lessons again on how to close the screen door?"

There was no answer, just an "Oh, Dad!" look, and he ran off.

Roy glanced skyward. The great cloudless canvas was already changing to a deeper blue in the east, displaying signs of a dying day. The western sky fought off such notions, the sun still beaming its life and heat, acting out its role as the great and permanent spotlight. Tomorrow would be a new scene in the complex and uninterruptable order.

Oak tree leaves waved at him and sprinkled splotches of light and shade. A short distance to the south, trees and weeds near the gravel country road were laden with dust. He was pleased that the county had sprayed a dust-control substance on the roadway along the motel property.

Roy pulled out his big blue handkerchief and wiped his brow. The day's heat must have set another record. When would the hot spell end?

It had been a good move to buy the property out in the country, his deliberation continued, good for the family and good for the business. Maybe he should run for the Legislature. Look over there. White folks and black folks, sittin' near each other, eating cherry pie.

Roy was tickled. Progress. Sure, they were at separate tables. He supposed they just sat down that way. They naturally moved to their comfort zone, whites with whites, Negroes with Negroes.

Had any of them thought about moving, to mix? What was going through their minds? Would any take the initiative to cross over? Had they ever sat down and talked with someone from a different race? Do any of them have friends of a different color? Will mankind ever discover the order in nature, God's order?

"What's goin' through that head of yours?" Lillian said softly.

He hadn't seen her approach from the house.

"You look like you're off in a dream," she said, grinning. "Things spinnin' 'round up there? Wait, let me get a look at your eyes. They awhirlin' like a man put under hypnosis? Sure ya don't have sunstroke?"

"Lillian, you have always been able to figure me out before I figure me out," Roy said. "That's scary."

"I guess that's what happens after 20 years," she said. "Finally two become one, just like it said in the marriage vows."

"If that's the case, why can't I read your mind like you do mine?" Roy replied.

"For several reasons," Lillian zipped back with a chuckle. "First, women are the dominant sex, more complex, and not as easy to read as men. Second, we change our minds more often, dancin' here and dancin' there. And lastly, men just aren't very good mind readers."

"OK, OK. Tell me, what are our guests talkin' about?" Roy challenged. "You so smart, let's see you read their minds. Are they talkin' weather? Sports? Their travels? Civil rights? Family? Hmm? Put it on me, Miss Mystic. Take your time."

"I'm goin' to see if anyone wants more pie," Lillian said.

"No, wait," Roy sought advice. "Do you think I should try to integrate the conversation, suggest a comin' together? What do ya think, Lil?"

"I think you should mind your own business and help me. How's that for integration of Motel Sepia chores? Roy, this is a business. It's not a mission house." She was tired but couldn't show it, hot but had to stay cool. Yet, she had to be honest, say things that she had been thinking for some time.

"Why do you elect yourself as the race relations expert, the great bargainer, the diplomat-mediator? It's good to be friendly with everyone, Roy, but do we have to throw away the color box and pretend there are no differences?" There she said it.

"I know this is a business, and it's a lot of work. And, you do more than your share," Roy said. "But why not use cherry pie and ice cream as sort of a lubricatin' oil, to get these people to slide over to one 'nother and mix? What's wrong with that, Lil? Can't see it would do any harm. I don't see it as meddlin'."

"Well," Lillian looked away in surrender, "you do your 'Come to Jesus' work, go pretend you're in Amen Corner, and pray it doesn't turn into an argument or somethin'."

"There won't be any argument, Lil," Roy said with exasperation. He walked with her to retrieve the ice cream. Lillian grabbed another pie. Together they silently returned to the outdoor tables and their motel guests.

"George, have you and Vernon exhausted all there is to know 'bout Chicago and Mississippi?" Roy asked.

The Taylors and McDowells had returned from the downtown buffet. George was still chewing on a toothpick, flipping it around in his mouth as if he were conducting a concert.

"Oh no," George replied. "But we exhausted all the exclamations on this weather. So we switched to comparin' the merits of grits vs. Quaker oatmeal. Actually, he was doin' the comparin'. I don't like either. Give me bacon, eggs and hash browns for breakfast, seven days a week. Now, we've moved on to the merits of baseball and fishin'. All man talk."

George took time out from his discourse, and directed his tongue instead to a slice of Lillian's pie.

"Let me ask you, Mr. Sanders," George formulated a question between chomps on cherries. "Pretendin' you was a doctor, one of them shrink kind." He tapped his index fingers on the side of his head. "Suppose Vernon and I were sprawled on the lawn here lookin' for advice on relaxation, the best way to forget work, put your mind in neutral. What would you suggest, baseball or fishin'? Vernon and I have a little disagreement here."

"Well, I'd recommend a cold bottle of Schlitz beer and the hammock," Roy quickly replied.

"Naw, naw," George objected with a guffaw and wave of his hand. He almost dropped his pie plate. "Man, we already ruled that out. You must choose between baseball and fishin'."

"Tough question," said Roy. "How much you payin' me for this diagnosis?"

"Hey, we figured it was part of the motel amenities," George joked.

"Sure, OK then. First, I want to make it clear, if you don't like my answer you can't have your money back."

The joshing was detoured when Viola and Ida returned from their cabins. They joined their husbands just in time to hear George propose the hypothetical analysis of baseball and fishing, a pro-con evaluation he claimed would lead to "the truth of the matter." Viola's proclivity for visceral response leaped into action.

"I apologize, Roy and Vernon," she began, a sinister smile taking shape. "George has been out in the sun too long, and when that happens it tends to sauté his judgment. I usually try to humor him through these spells."

"Ah, Viola," George fashioned a comeback. "Pity you never made it as a stand-up comedian."

It was one of those times when observers find themselves suspended in the middle of a couple's chin music, not knowing what to do. After a few awkward moments, controlled smiles evolved into uncontrolled laughter.

"Roy," Vernon was still chuckling, "we should first thank you for recommendin' that downtown buffet. That Bishop's is good food at a bargain. I was surprised that the fried chicken was so hot, crisp and tasty. That is, for a buffet. What'd you think, George?"

"Chicken was OK and so was the barbeque ribs. Yeah, nice place. No beer, though."

George paused to rethink his comments.

"Mind you, the ribs don't come close to the spread at Twin Anchors Tavern on Sedgwick in Chicago, but that's an extraordinary place. My brother says it's one of Frank Sinatra's favorite eatin' places. That's some endorsement."

"George, we've only been there once," Viola stepped in. "And, you said while the food was good, it was too damned expensive. That's a direct quote, George."

"Well, I guess we all have our favorite eatin' places," said Vernon. "My brother in Avon Park, Fla., raves about a restaurant in an old hotel down there. I've never been in the place."

"Say, Mr. Motel Sepia," George returned to the original question. "What about the advice. Baseball or fishin'?"

The toothpick that he had taken on the way out of the downtown restaurant swiveled in the left corner of his mouth like a miniature Louisville Slugger.

"George, I'd have to say fishin'," Roy answered without a lot of enthusiasm. "I've played some baseball and done some fishin'. But for pure relaxin', I'll take fishin'. Unless, of course, you are a big Chicago Cubs fan. Cubs fans are always relaxed because they know the outcome before the season starts. You can snooze in April and wake up in August. Nothin's changed. Cubs are in last place."

"Now, Mr. Sanders," George began slowly. "That was way too long an answer to a simple question. I think I want my money back."

"George," Vernon laughed. "You can't have your money back. That cherry pie is too deep in your insides, brotha."

"I agree with you, Mr. Sanders," Viola again took her turn at bat. "Baseball is boring. George thinks there's more to baseball than spitin' and scratchin'. Why, it's more excitin' to put up Venetian blinds."

"Pay no mind to this Viola person," George began his rebuttal. "First off, she doesn't understand baseball, which is probably the most technical and cerebral of all sports. She doesn't see the attraction of statistics, which may explain her dislike for mathematics. Viola fails to sense the intricacies of baseball, the nuances, when to bunt, when to steal, when to take a pitch."

His lips maneuvered the toothpick in menacing strokes, like Mickey Mantle getting ready for a fastball.

"It's more like when to bitch at the umpire, like you do," Viola injected. "When to yell at the manager. Oh, George, baseball is full of such nuances," she rolled her eyes. "Don't swallow that toothpick, George. I'm not sure extracting it is covered by our insurance."

"Viola does have a point with puttin' up the blinds, that bein' excitin' and all," George picked up the volley. "We almost killed each other early in our marriage as we tried to install blinds at a rented apartment. Blinds, shall I say, that were fifth-hand junk that she bought at some second-hand store. It was our first big fight. At the time, we still had leftover wedding cake.

"Oh, I could see it, Viola," George bolstered his recall with hyperbole. "The divorce counselor askin' how long we'd been married, and we would say, 'Two weeks.' And he would be so flummoxed that he almost forgot where he was goin' next. Finally, he would say, 'Well, just what momentous thing has caused such turmoil in your young marriage?' And we'd say in unison: 'Venetian blinds'."

"Strange things happen, even in the romantic early months of marriage," Vernon agreed. "I was preparin' this body for a wake showin' and services when Ida comes into the funeral home. We were only married a few weeks, and it was her first visit to the mortuary. She immediately objects to the man wearin' a green tie with a brown suit.

"I said 'Honey, that's what the family requested. I don't pick out the clothes for the dead. When someone passes, relatives – in this case the niece was the closest survivin' relative – decide on such things.' Well, Ida 'bout ready to telephone Christian Dior, to see if he approved of that green tie. I bet we spent better part of an hour goin' over this green tie business and all the 'What will people say' parts."

"Make fun if you want, Vernon," Ida said mildly. "But green looks sickenin' with brown."

"What color a tie did you want, Ida?" George risked a question.

"Well, that's the funny part," Vernon said before his wife had a chance to speak.

"It took her 59 minutes and 59 seconds to say that a harvest gold tie would look just fine with a brown suit. Never mind that green had been the man's favorite color, 'green as in money,' the deceased liked to say. He never had much of the latter, so his family figured, let him wear a green tie."

"Sure, sure," George leaned in with a growing grin, absorbing every aspect of this early dispute between the Taylors. "But who won? Did they bury the guy in a green tie or a harvest gold tie?"

Vernon Taylor laughed.

"You have to know that the dearly departed had been quite aged and ill for some time," Vernon said. "It was difficult to make him look 30 years younger, which is what the niece wanted. When I said that was not possible, she decided to keep the casket closed."

"Ah, women!" George said, waving his hands in the air. "I will take another sliver of pie."

Chapter 24

Ben Dolan, the not-so-loquacious farmer from southwest Iowa, took the first step.

It was calculated, not a matter of ambling over to the fence line and shooting the breeze with a next-door neighbor. This was a step over the color line, not particularly bold, yet uncommon. He didn't want to be intrusive or presumptuous. Civility trumped caution.

"Hello, I'm Ben Dolan. Do you mind if Matt and I join you?" Ben had offered his hand to Vernon Taylor after sensing the big discussion about fishing had run its course. When Vernon extended his smaller black hand, Ben added a broad smile.

"Please, Mr. Dolan. Pull your chair over."

"Call me Ben if you don't mind."

Matt Kilburn also repositioned his folding chair.

"Did I hear you say you're from Belzonee, Miss., Mr. Taylor? Where's that?" Matt inquired as he shooed away a gnat. "Kinda remember where Clarksdale is, on Highway 61, I believe. Maybe it's Clarksville. Think we went through there once on our way to Vicksburg."

"Well, you'd be right the first time. It's Clarksdale, and we're quite a bit south of there, toward Jackson," Vernon explained. "We're 'bout 75-80 miles south of Clarksdale, on what they call Route 49 West."

Roy Sanders smiled. His fervor at stirring the diversity pot was yielding results. He looked at the three men, men of different color, talking. What Roy saw in the shade of Motel Sepia gave him internal delight. For a second he thought about joining the conversation, but decided against it.

What was it his Dad liked to say: 'Ya can lead a horse to water, but you can't make him drink'. By golly the horses were drinkin'.

"Belzonee," Matt repeated, scratching his reddish hair. "That doesn't sound like a southern name. In fact, it sounds Italian. What's the Mafia doing in Mississippi? Didn't know they had Wops down there."

Matt laughed. Ben didn't. He looked at his brother-in-law with eyes that could paralyze a Mississippi possum. He didn't think of Matt so much as a bigot but rather a general noodlehead who thoughtlessly succumbed to stereotype.

"You'll have to excuse Matt," Ben looked at Vernon. "He's my brother-in-law, so I'm stuck with him. He's long on attempts at humor and sometimes short on propriety. I'm guessing his ancestors lived so far north they were subject to brain freeze. And on top of that, he's an ex-Marine. Could never accept that the Marines are part of the Navy."

"Well, listen to ole Mr. Bog Trotter," Matt shot back. "Part of the Irish Mafia in southwest Iowa. If you look real close at Ben here, you may spot tater sprouts comin' outta his ears."

Ben laughed and Matt thought he'd scored a hit. Ben was unafraid of taking pokes, and frequently laughed at himself. Matt was more defensive. It was the interplay of confidence and uncertainty.

Vernon wasn't sure which way to direct his reaction, but he figured a smile was safe. He decided to return to the subject of Mississippi.

"Well, Mr. Matt, you are right on that score, too. Belzoni is Italian, named after quite a venerable fellow who gained fame as an archeologist in Egypt."

"Excuse me, Vern. I hope it's OK to call you Vern," Matt said. "I'd just like to point out here to Saint Ben that Scots know plenty about stereotypes and discrimination. We Scots, as everyone knows, are penny pinchers – no, make that tightwads. And the men wear skirts and devour sheep hearts. And all of us, by jiminy, fancy our grog and a woman with tough skin.

"Now, where were we, Vern? Oh yes, Belzonee. So this guy was an Italian who notta havea lot of moola, and had to dig for his money?"

"I give up," Ben said, shaking his head.

"The history books," Vernon continued, passing over the word swapping between Matt and Ben, "say that a man named Alvarez Fisk was one of the first land owners in our area. His place was known first as the Fisk Plantation. Then he changed it to the Belzoni Plantation."

"Why'd he do that?" Matt asked.

"I was just gettin' to that," Vernon smiled. "Mr. Fisk bought and sold land like some folks trade them stocks and bonds. He kept a piece of property on the west side of the Yazoo River and called it Belzoni Landing. Mr. Fisk so admired this fellow known as The Great Belzoni that he named his land holdin's after him. Eventually the town became known by the same name."

"Well, I'll be darn," Matt said, only half pretending he was interested in Mississippi history. "Tell me, Vern, did this Fisk fellow ever find himself up the Yazoo?"

"I think, Matt," Ben injected, "the term is 'up the wazoo,' and it has nothing to do with a river.

"I am not certain 'bout that," said Vernon, "but I believe Yazoo was the name of an Indian tribe that lived along the river at one time. And Matt, it's not YA-zoo. It's Yay-ZOO. The emphasis is on the zoo."

"Well, thanks, Vernon, for clearing that up," Ben said. "Matt surely won't make that mistake again."

"And 'nother pronunciation matter," Vernon explained. "It's not Bel-zon-ee. Rather, Bel-zon-AH. Again, the emphasis is on the last syllable."

"Bell-zon-AH. Got it," said Matt. "And what sort of work do you do in Bell-zon-AH, Mr. Taylor?"

"I own and operate a mortuary, Taylor's Burial," Vernon said, ignoring Matt's belabored phonetics. "Went to mortuary science school down in Jackson 20 years ago, worked in Vicksburg for a while, and opened my own business right after the war."

"I'd imagine you have to study quite a bit of science," Ben said, "and know more than a little bit about the human body."

"True enough, Mr. Ben. Two years of study, heavy on anatomy, physiology and pathology, among other things. Then after that, a year or so as an apprentice. The Jackson school also emphasizes communication, a special way to talk to the grievin' family."

"Well, I can understand that," Ben said. "It's sensitive territory, and there's certain ways to talk to a new widow or someone who lost a child. Not a lot of room for joking."

"Exactly," Vernon nodded. "But, there was some comic relief in school, as you might imagine. We don't do cremation at our mortuary. Some folks don't like the idea of getting a preview of Hades. But we had a course in it. One of our smart aleck students even memorized *"The Cremation of Sam McGee"* and recited the entire poem in class one day.

"I remember one of our instructors recalled an old joke about the fellow who died penniless. Great timin', a friend said."

"The advice I like," said Matt, "supposedly came from Yogi Berra, the baseball player. Yogi said, 'Always go to other people's funerals, or they won't go to yours.'"

The three laughed. Ben broke the lull with a serious question.

"Do you handle funerals for white families?"

"We would, but that doesn't happen in a segregated society," Vernon explained. He wasn't sure if he should elaborate, but then decided to say what he felt and what was reality.

"Our people are more content at Negro funeral homes. And I guess the same could be said for white people. They feel better at a white funeral home. That's the way it is."

He waited to see any reaction from Ben and Matt.

"I'd have to say Negro families feel more comfortable with a black mortician," Vernon tried to explain. "It may sound funny to you, but the truth is they have concerns about practical and cultural matters – like the right skin makeup for the deceased, proper haircut, things like that. And you might notice that we say a Negro person passed rather than died. Or, there was a crossing over."

That gave the two Iowans something to think about.

"I believe that the terms passing and crossing over soften the finality of death," Vernon expanded his explanation, "and give indication of eternal life. It leaves some doors open." He smiled at Ben and Matt.

"And we mourn different than white folk. Sometimes there's lot of emotion, lot of yellin' and hollerin'. Some people even get to rollin' on the floor, and I've seen folks pass out. We don't take death lightly. We rejoice at birth and grieve deeply at someone's passin'."

His remarks hung in the night air for a few seconds.

"Now, ya'll say you are farmers?" Vernon changed the subject.

Ben and Matt explained their farm operations.

"You mentioned the Yazoo Indians in Mississippi, excuse me, Yay-ZOO," Matt corrected himself. "We had the Meskquakie and other tribes in Iowa. Still do. Meskquakie, that is, or some call them Sauk and Fox. They were here first, but they had to buy land for a settlement. How's that for crazy? We chase the Indians from every home they ever made, and in Iowa they have to buy a place for their people. It's another national disgrace."

"Vernon," Ben said hesitantly. "How is life in Mississippi? What's segregation like?"

Wow! That's a brilliant question, Ben thought in retrospect, wishing he could back up and erase his inquiry.

"What I mean is," Ben hastened to add, "do you feel safe? Is every day a challenge at living?"

"Not at all," Vernon answered, fully comprehending that if you don't live with segregation, it's difficult to know segregation. "There are just certain rules. Some are social understandin's, and some are elbowed into the legal framework. Sometimes, I admit, it's hard to know what's what. It's not an ideal arrangement, but change, I believe, is comin'.

"Not all Negroes would agree with me," Vernon added, "but I believe there are a lot of good white folk who want change, too. They jus' can't say it."

Ben, uncomfortable by thinking he had cast Vernon into an uneasy spot, looked for a way out of the subject at hand.

"So, let me get this straight," Matt plowed back in. "You can't drink out of the same public water fountains, as I understand it. You can't sit at the drug store counter and order a malt or ice cream sundae. You can't buy a house in a certain part of your town. You can't even go –"

"Matt!" Ben sought to cut off the barrage.

"No, that's quite all right Mr. Dolan," Vernon looked him directly. "Matt is right. There are a lot of things we can't do, places we can't go. Our children have separate schools, even though the Supreme Court ruled last year that such racial segregation is illegal. There are parks for whites and different ones for Negroes. We sit apart in restaurants and at the movies, the ones that let us in, that is."

Stillness enveloped the men like the August humidity. Fifteen seconds passed before Vernon decided to proceed with his picture of Belzoni.

"Our son, Will, attends McNair High School," Vernon said, "a Negro school, while whites attend Belzoni High. That Brown rulin' by the Supreme Court last year, the one prohibitin' school segregation, ain't found its way to Belzoni.

"Funny thing about the South," Vernon said. "And maybe outside the South, too. Lots of people go to church, but Sunday is the most segregated day of the week."

It was a profound perspective on black-white relations.

"For the most part, we live in the north section of town – some call it Camp Town. During World War II, there was a German POW camp on the north end. That's how it got that name.

"Lotta black folk in our area work pickin' cotton," Vernon explained. "Get $5 a day for farm work. Sharecroppers are disappearin'. Right 'bout now the gins are starting up again. There is one plant, pays good, too, won't hire the Negro. Way it is. We're a small town, fellas, though there's smaller places in the Delta. Remote, that describes us. Remote, and in the summertime, hot and dusty."

"The same can be said about Red Oak, Iowa," Ben said. "It's remote. People in New York and Los Angeles might think that a person could die out here and God wouldn't notice."

Roy stood near the front door of his home, looking across the road toward Motel Sepia and the source of his satisfaction. His joy sought escape. Hallelujah was written on his face.

He had heard some of Vernon's rendering of life in Mississippi, and momentarily contrasted it with his own experiences. But the sight of two white men conversing with a black man overwhelmed him and validated his mission.

"What's that grinning all about?" Lillian shattered his silent self-congratulations. Beads of perspiration dotted her forehead. It had been Roy's idea to serve welcoming tea and cherry pie to motel guests, but Lillian made it happen.

"Maybe Roy," she said in tired tones, "you should go into the kitchen and prepare a couple of pies for tomorrow's crowd."

Chapter 25

The man parked his rental car, a black, four-door sedan, on a Cedar Rapids side street and turned off its lights.

He stepped out, calmly closed the door and proceeded with purpose. His demeanor shifted to that of a hunter, mentally and physically, as if he were setting out on patrol in Korea. He looked in all directions, adrenalin building, and then walked two blocks to the outside rear of the restaurant. His dark clothing blended into the shadows. No one was around.

It was about 8:15 p.m. Daylight was retreating, and while the August heat had sustained its potency, the setting sun was already portending a September calendar.

The first time he arrived at the restaurant, around 6:30, he had studied surrounding streets, plotting exit alternatives. The truth was, he concluded, there weren't many options and that was his first challenge. But this wasn't Chicago. The lack of traffic and scarcity of potential busy bodies offset concerns about egress. Hunger obscured his usual craving for vigilance.

Confident he would be able to overcome what he analyzed as a minor issue, he had boldly and casually entered the place, had dinner and assembled the rest of his scheme. After eating, he returned to the car, switched into his work clothes and headed back for the reason he had come.

The front of the restaurant faced north toward busy Mount Vernon Road. Customers could park either out front or on the west side. The sparsely filled parking lot revealed that business this weeknight was slow.

He selected a south corner of the building, a section not included in recent remodeling, and proceeded to a shade-less window. His small crowbar easily and quietly pried the window free of its casing. The only resistance came from wood weathered by time and petrified paint that had been swashed on years ago. There was no lock. There was no alarm.

The intruder jimmied the window upward, slowly. Satisfied it was far enough open, he carried the pry bar to a nearby hedge and deposited it in thick foliage.

Again, he glanced in all directions. Nothing.

He walked back to the window, thrust his upper body into the opening and carefully wiggled through and into the restaurant's storeroom. On all fours, he waited a few minutes for his eyes to adjust to the near dark interior. Then he rose.

Only a shred of light penetrated the room. It entered on an angle through a window on the west side, originating from a lamp post that was part of the inadequate illumination of the restaurant parking lot.

He flicked on his black Eveready flashlight, equipped with a glow lens that muted its bulb. That and his keen night vision, honed in the military, guided his short steps.

His movement was deliberate. He noted with satisfaction the stacks of soft cardboard boxes and knew intuitively that they would muffle any sounds. But he made no noise, save for his controlled breathing and the soft crinkling of his clothes. Like a mouse approaching cheese in a trap, he masterfully avoided tripping anything that would produce undue disturbance.

The man had a good mental picture of the building. One immediate concern was whether the old linoleum concealed any squeaky sections of flooring. So far, not a squawk.

He reached the door. Slowly, he gave a counterclockwise twist to the storeroom doorknob. The latch withdrew from the strike plate. He eased the door open, anticipating that he would find a hallway. He didn't know who or what else might be there.

Nothing. Two naked lights, pull chains dangling from the ceiling, were on, but there was no sign of anyone.

At the end of the corridor, north toward the street and front of the building, he heard a toilet flush. He remembered being there. It was approximately in the center of the structure. Steadily, he walked past two other side rooms toward another door. A groan in the floor beneath his right foot froze his movement.

He listened. Nothing. He proceeded.

A normal human being would be seized by fright, ingested with panic. The intruder was clothed in self-confidence.

The floor creaked again as it returned to its previous position.

He knew exactly where he was going and how he would get there. He had left nothing to chance. The plan was etched in his mind.

The face of the restaurant owner was imprinted in his memory. He had seen pictures of him. Less than an hour before, he had seen him in-person and heard him talk. He would recognize his voice. It was like Korea. You study the map, assess the situation, make a plan and inject the entire blueprint into the whole of your being.

For a while he had been a successful platoon leader in Korea. He had trained his body and mind as a single force. He had led fearlessly and expected his entire team to be as he was. But not all bodies, all minds, are that malleable and fixated.

Eventually, he left no room for anything less than what he defined as perfection, a fatal flaw of leadership. He became a loner there and he was a loner now, once again in the business of killing.

An hour earlier he had savored one of the restaurant's entrée specials, an inch-and-a-half thick pork chop topped with roasted peppers. It was as good as any steak he had ever had in Chicago. Included in the $1.90 price was a vegetable, and he had chosen mushrooms pizzaiola. He splurged.

For him, breaking a self-imposed rule was a sin, not that sin was part of his vocabulary. Never, never, according to his rule, should one have an alcoholic drink before work.

But he did.

The fine food was wrapped in an ambience of Italian music. *Napule Bella,* he thought, as he finally surrendered and ordered a glass of wine. He caressed his taste buds in the milieu of a dry Tuscan wine. For dessert, he had Italian cheesecake.

What a pleasant surprise, he had thought to himself. The unpretentious sign outside boasted "Gourmet by George" and, beneath that, "The finest Italian cuisine."

He couldn't argue with either claim. And, he had managed to see the owner himself. Except for longer hair, the photograph he'd been given was precise. Now he had seen the man in flesh, natty in his tan pants and blue blazer, proud and seemingly profitable.

Alas, the pleasure of food and drink was over. The time for business was at hand.

The intruder cocked his head to listen, and spotted the sign, "Office," on a cheap wooden door.

That's him. That's his voice. There was another voice, a woman's. The second person is leaving the office? Footsteps.

The intruder carefully slid into a side room. The office door opened and closed. The footsteps stopped. Another door opened and closed, and the click of the shoes faded and disappeared into the restaurant proper.

Mr. Gourmet by George was now alone.

A telephone rang. The intruder carefully stepped back into the hallway, walked up to the office door, toward the voice.

Slowly he turned the knob and opened the door.

George Dawson was talking on the telephone.

"Yes, Michelle. I know how you feel," he said in accommodating tone. "OK, my love."

It was him alright, and this Michelle was displeased about something.

"Mr. Dawson," the intruder interrupted the telephone conversation. "It's nice to see you. I've heard a lot about you." The greeting came in a somewhat muffled Chicago accent.

"What the hell's going on here?" Dawson jerked his head upward. "Who are you? Why are you wearing a mask? What the fuck are you doing, barging into my office?"

The unwanted and mysterious guest calmly but purposefully flashed a knife with an eight-inch blade. He briskly stepped forward, moved the knife toward Dawson's face, and motioned for him to hang up the phone. Dawson obeyed, handing the receiver to the intruder.

"Thank you," the man said, and placed the phone in its cradle. "There is no need to involve a third party. Next, I want you to open the safe behind you. Put all the money in this bag, and we'll proceed to step two."

"Who the fuck are you?" Dawson repeated. "This is –"

"Really, Mr. Dawson. Consider your position. Remain calm and quiet and you may see the morning sun. Surely you remember your skimming days in Chicago. Now is the time to pay what you can. Reach in the safe, and place all the paper money in the sack!" He tossed a blue sack to Dawson, one that looked more like a genuine bank bag.

His voice stayed low but heightened in menace. He handed the fairly large cloth sack to Dawson.

"Quickly!" he ordered Dawson. "I should also indicate the presence of a pistol with silencer in my back beltline. And, of course I have a permit and paid the tax. I abide by the law. Now, do it!"

It was a quiet but stern directive expelled through gritted teeth.

For Dawson, the debit side of his Chicago ledger immediately came into focus. He didn't know the hooded man, dressed in dark clothing, jacket partly zipped. He saw dark eyes through the slits in the mesh hood. He saw dark hands.

None of this mattered to him. What mattered were the knife and the gun. The man's voice tone mattered. So did references to skimming.

He had no doubts of the intruder's intent. He had no doubts about what sort of business transaction this was and where it had its genesis.

The door of the safe had been ajar. In less than 30 seconds, Dawson emptied it of more than a thousand dollars in cash. He passed the bag back to the intruder.

"That's all there is," Dawson said. "Let's get on with your step two. I assume this is where you depart a richer man."

"As you wish," the intruder responded. "Part two." His cold, piercing eyes cut into Dawson's psyche. "But first, place your driver's license in the bag with the money. There needs to be some proof of who made this down payment on past debts."

Dawson complied.

The intruder took the bag and placed it on a chair, and then, with a powerful burst of energy, plunged his left fist into Dawson's diaphragm. The restaurant owner coughed and crumpled forward, his hands automatically reaching for his chest in hopes of bringing relief to a gasping body. He could not breathe. He could not speak.

The assailant's right hand surged forward. The knife penetrated the upper left side of Dawson's chest, instantly severing organs critical to sustaining life. The blade twisted. More lethal damage. It was withdrawn.

The process was repeated, several times, though perhaps unnecessarily. The job was finished.

He eased Mr. Dawson's dying body to the floor, wrapped the knife in a cloth and placed it in the sack with the money. He shut the safe, and left.

As the attacker walked calmly into the back of the restaurant, the head chef noticed the stranger and his dark clothing, the hood and the sack.

Hot grease spattered on the chef's hand as he watched in a daze. Was this a holdup? What should he do? Rush back to the office and have the owner call the police? Should he intercede? Would that endanger staff and customers?

Instinctively, he picked up a bottle of olive oil and poured more in the pan. He looked at it, then back at the intruder.

The chef did nothing, frozen by the man's audacity.

The intruder strode impassively and confidently to the front of the restaurant.

Customer heads popped up from plates. Conversations stopped in mid-sentence. Was this a gag? A real robbery? Just a weird dresser? Like the chef, people were rigid with perplexity.

"'Scuse me, ma'am," the intruder said to the cashier near the front counter.

Before he approached, she had shifted her duties to housekeeping, speedily reshuffling menus haphazardly tossed in the rack by waiters and waitresses.

"Could'ja please move over to that there cash reg'ster and kindly place the cash in this bag?"

The request came in a tone no different than a customer inquiring about the special for the night.

She was startled. She hadn't seen his advance. When the young woman turned around, she nearly fainted in shock. She grasped the counter to regain equilibrium and gather her senses. She took a deep breath and moved to the cash register. With a mechanical motion, she opened it, grabbed most of the bills and placed them in the sack he held before her.

It took no more than 15 seconds.

"I thank you," he said softly.

About a half dozen customers in the front section of the restaurant watched the drama unfold.

The stranger glanced at them, bowed gracefully, and looked back at the alarmed cashier.

He walked up to her. Her entire body shook in fear.

"There's no need to worry, ma'am," he assured her as he moved around the corner of the counter.

He stepped right next to her, kissed her on the left cheek and departed.

Chapter 26

Jean Mallory was stunned. She touched her cheek, where the robber had kissed her. It's as if she were fumbling for a bullet hole she knew wasn't there.

The fear that had numbed her minutes before had faded, but was replaced by a sense of befuddlement. She felt relieved, yet confused to the point of stupor.

It had happened so quickly. Her mind kept replaying the scene. It seemed to her as if she were caught in a brief one-act play that kept repeating without resolve. She tried to move on, but always found herself back at the beginning.

"'Scuse me, ma'am," and then, shortly after, the request for money, followed by emptying of the cash register, his courteous thank you and the kiss.

The kiss.

Rather than a robbery, it felt more like the time in high school when Tommy Keese had yanked away her chemistry book in study hall. Before she could vocally object he had planted an unexpected smacker on her lips. Not her cheek, mind you. Her lips! It was a dare he had readily accepted. He boasted about it as the "best chemistry experiment ever!"

Her mind wandered back three years to that study hall kiss. She hadn't screamed then. You just don't scream in study hall, even if Tommy Keese kisses you.

Was it that bad? Well, yes. I could have killed him, she thought. Maybe the kiss wasn't so bad, but the snickering and bragging afterward ignited fire in her eyes. Sometimes you might want to let friends know that a boy kissed you, but not when he did it before the entire study hall.

"Jean, Jean," a voice attempted to invade her comatose-like state. "Are you hurt? Did he harm you in any way? Jean, can you hear me?"

Doug Brochman, a waiter at the restaurant, had witnessed the final 15 seconds of the dazing drama. He rushed to the front as the intruder-turned-robber went out the entrance. He and Mallory were employees, nothing more, not that he hadn't given her a second look more than once.

She was a sophomore at Mount Mercy Junior College and he was a junior at Coe. Brochman's goal was getting an accounting degree. He hated to spend hard earned cash on any girl. Still, she was cute and his hormones were slowly persuading his pocketbook.

Several customers, including Tim and Cathy Peterson of Kansas City, gathered at the front counter area.

"You had better call the police," Cathy Peterson urged Brochman.

"You – you're right," he stammered. "Of course. Call the police. Would you please keep an eye on Jean?" he pointed to his co-worker. "She appears dazed. Maybe she's hurt."

Brochman ran behind the counter, pulled open a drawer and fumbled through the telephone directory. By the time he found the police department number, the phone began to ring.

He swore under his breath. Damnable timing, he thought. I'll tell them we're closed. I'll get rid of whoever it is fast.

"Gourmet by George," he answered.

He didn't let the caller edge a word in.

"I'm sorry, but we are closed for the evening. We have an emergency. Perhaps you could call back tomorrow."

"This is Michelle Keller," came a woman's testy reply. "Do you know who I am?"

There was a pause.

"Well, dumbo, I'm George Dawson's girlfriend," her alto voice continued, bulging with self-importance. "I need to talk to George. I just want to –"

"Miss Keller," Brochman interrupted. "We have just had a robbery at the restaurant and we need to call the police. Could you call back?"

"Well, I suppose, but I'm a little upset. George hung up on me not too long ago. I'm not used to being treated that way."

"I understand Miss Keller," Brockman tried to incorporate courtesy with urgency, "but I must hang up now, too, because I have to call the police. OK? Goodbye."

That may cost him his job, he thought, but it was the right thing to do.

Brochman looked at Mallory, whose eyes suddenly began to focus on the present. She again touched her cheek, but this time the curtain stayed down. The scene was over, the playlet ended. She was recast in real time.

Mallory blinked her eyes and shook her head as if to shed the fog that had accumulated in her mind. She stared at Brochman.

"Doug, I think you had better call the police," she said, her glazed look no longer apparent.

"Jean! You're feeling better," Brockman said. "Good. I'm in the process of dialing the police now. Why don't you sit in the booth over there?"

By now, chef Tony Ambrose had wound his way to the front counter. He nodded toward Mallory and approached Brochman. Brochman held up his hand so as to stop another interruption.

"I'm waiting for the police to answer," he informed Ambrose, cupping the mouthpiece with his hand. "Perhaps you should go back to the office and inform Mr. Dawson what happened. Jean seems to be doing better. I don't know how much money –

"Police Department?"

Brockman redirected his attention to the voice on the phone.

"Yes, this is Sgt. Miller. How may I help you?"

"Sergeant. This is Doug Brochman. I'm a waiter at Gourmet by George restaurant. It's out on Mount Vernon Road East, past Lape's Florist."

"I know the place," Miller replied.

"Well, we've had a robbery. About four or five minutes ago."

"Mr. Brochman. Was anyone hurt?" Miller inquired.

"No. Miss Mallory is shook up, but that can be expected. I believe she is going to be fine."

"Miss Mallory?"

"Sorry. She is the checkout person, the cashier. The robber ordered her to open the cash register and put money in his bag."

"Was the robber armed?" Miller inquired.

"I don't think so, but I couldn't say for sure." Brochman looked at Mallory.

"Jean. Did the robber have a gun?" She shook her head, no.

"Officer, the waitress who gave the man money from the cash register said the man did not show a gun."

"Good," Miller said. "We'll have a squad car there in 10 minutes or so. Please hold a second."

Miller placed the phone receiver on the desk and clicked the dispatch button. After instructing the roaming Loop car of the robbery, he returned to the telephone line.

"Mr. Brochman, would you please ask any witnesses to remain at the restaurant? Our officers will want to talk to them, or at least get their names so we can conduct interviews later. And, please tell people not to touch the counter or other areas the robber may have touched. He may have left fingerprints that will help in the investigation. Understand?"

"Certainly," said Brochman. "I'll tell everyone."

With that, Miller hung up and recorded the information on the log sheet. Based on the time the call was made, and Brochman's account, the officer put the time of the crime at 8:46.

Officers Wilson and Jelling arrived at the Gourmet by George restaurant around 9. Following protocol, Jelling went inside while Wilson explored the exterior of the building.

Wilson waved his flashlight beam in all directions as he made a cursory inspection of surroundings. Darkness covered most of the scene, but it didn't take him long to discover the open window on the south end.

He shined the light through the window, but saw only stacks of cardboard boxes that held paper napkins and towels. Next, he directed his light on nearby shrubbery, but spotted nothing out of the ordinary. He finished his walk-around and entered the front door.

Jelling was questioning Brochman, the waiter who had made the call to police. Mallory was still sitting in the booth, talking to the couple from Kansas City. Jelling had asked others who witnessed the robbery, or any portion of it, to be seated in the front section.

He turned his attention to Mallory.

"You are Miss Mallory, the cashier?" Jelling asked.

"Yes, sir," she replied.

"Were you harmed in any way? We will want a full description, but first, were you harmed in any way? Did the robber have a weapon?"

"No, sir. I wasn't harmed and I don't believe he had a weapon. I didn't see any kind of weapon." She paused. "I'm doing fine now. I was a little dizzy at first, after he kissed me."

"What?" Jelling responded, his voice rising at the end. He looked at the floor, shaking his head back and forth like a church steeple bell.

"What a familiar ring that has," Jelling looked at his partner.

"I don't understand," said a puzzled Mallory.

"Don't you read the newspaper?" asked Jelling. "I believe you are the victim of the kissing bandit. At least that's what the paper and other newsies call him. He's pulled this stunt twice before, robs a business, and upon departure gives someone a kiss. The fellow has real style."

Being lumped in with two other kiss recipients didn't make Mallory feel any better.

"Why does he do this?" she asked.

"Sweetheart, if I knew the answer to that I'd be making more money than I am," said Jelling. "Was this man wearing dark clothing and a grayish hooded jacket?"

She nodded, yes.

"And did you see his hands or face? Was his left hand in his jacket pocket?"

"How did you know that?" Mallory asked with surprise. "I didn't get a good look at him even though he was close. I guess I was sorta stunned. But I believe he was a Negro. His right hand was black and his talk sounded Negro."

"And tell me, Miss Mallory. Was he kindly and courteous? I'll bet his manners were impeccable, like he was at some sort of country club soiree."

"You sure know an awful lot about him," said Mallory.

"Just so you'll know, I'm not some clairvoyant," Jelling looked at Mallory, then the others. "All of this – his dress, his mannerisms and most of all his departure kiss – is part of his MO. In police talk, that means method of operation. And his physical description closely matches accounts in all three robberies."

"Officer," said Cathy Peterson, "what you said, about his manners. That's right. Before he left, he bowed to the customers here. It was quite strange."

"You can say that again," said Jelling. "I've seen a lot of unusual cases in this town, some real characters, but this fellow ranks among the top. He may have the elegance of a prince, or trying out for an Academy award, but he is a robber."

The two officers looked at each other and smiled.

"Maybe a prince of a robber," Jelling said, "but still a robber, and he's going to jail. We'll find him."

Chapter 27

Ambrose, who had watched the hooded stranger stroll through the back of the restaurant, hadn't come up front until after the crime had occurred and the robber had left.

He had suspected something and seen nothing. He mingled with customers and fellow workers for five minutes before Brochman asked if he had informed the owner of the robbery.

"God, no! I guess I got caught up in all the goings on out here," Ambrose replied.

Discomfited by his inaction, he bolted toward the back and Dawson's office. For various reasons, including the volatile Miss Keller, employees were instructed never to enter the office without knocking and then waiting for the owner to invite them in.

Ambrose rapped on the door several times, but there was no answer.

"Mr. Dawson!" Ambrose called. "Are you in there? Mr. Dawson! The restaurant has been robbed. You should come right away."

He rapped again, but no one answered.

Circumspect by nature, Ambrose was not about to trigger Dawson's temper, so he returned to the front of the restaurant just as police arrived. He was standing near the counter when he overheard Jelling ask Brochman about the whereabouts of the owner.

"Tony," Brochman yelled. "Did you inform Mr. Dawson of the robbery?"

"I knocked on his office door, but no one responded," Ambrose replied.

"Did you call out his name?" Brockman asked.

"Yes," said Ambrose. "I rapped several times and shouted his name, but there was no answer. You know the policy about just barging into his office."

Brochman assured Jelling that Dawson had been at the restaurant, and that the owner never left without informing someone at the front counter.

Wilson, hearing the exchange, walked over to Jelling, and whispered in his ear.

"I don't like this picture," Wilson said.

"What do you mean?" Jelling asked.

"One of the windows in the rear of the building was pried open," Wilson explained. "My guess is the robber came in through the back end. He may have made a stop in Dawson's office."

"Shit! We'd better check back there right away," said Jelling.

He raised his hands above his head and waved them about.

"Could I have your attention, folks?" he addressed the group. "Officer Wilson and I have to check something with the restaurant owner. I would appreciate it if you could remain here a little longer. If any of you must leave now, please jot your name and telephone number on a piece of paper and give it to Mr. Brochman. We'll be back here in a few minutes."

The two officers asked Ambrose to direct them to Dawson's office. At the same time, Brochman attempted to call Jim Bussaloni, the restaurant manager, who had taken the night off. He decided on his own to place a "closed" sign on the front door, and asked other waiters to attend to his customers.

"Is this the only access going from the back to the front of the restaurant?" Wilson asked Ambrose as they walked to the rear of the building.

The two officers glanced in all directions for any indication that something may be amiss.

"Yes," the chef replied. "There is a central corridor that extends to the back of the building and rooms on either side. The office is the first room on the left once you open the corridor door. The rest is mostly storage.

"I suppose I should tell you," Ambrose said sheepishly. He stopped and looked at Officer Wilson.

Motel Sepia

"Tell us what?" Wilson said.

"Well," and Ambrose struggled to explain it in the best light, "I saw this man walking past the kitchen area shortly before the robbery. He –"

"This man?" Wilson followed up. "What are you saying? You think you saw the robber?"

"I guess so," said Ambrose. "I feel terrible. I should have done something."

"Why do you say that?" Wilson asked. "The man could have been returning from the restroom. Or, he could have just been wandering around, looking for someone or something."

"The man I saw had some sort of covering over his face and wore a hooded jacket," Ambrose went on, his level of embarrassment and red face escalating with each sentence. "But he wasn't in a hurry. He didn't seem threatening," Ambrose launched his meager line of defense.

"He didn't appear to be armed. He didn't say a word, didn't look at anyone. For whatever reason, he didn't seem menacing. I know that sounds weird."

Why, you dumb ass, Wilson muttered to himself, invoking the entire chapter on police department protocol, restraint and public relations to calm his tendency to be openly sarcastic. His tongue fought the urge to unfold in reproach.

"Do you have masked men come through the kitchen often?" Wilson inquired, prudence temporarily forfeited. The words had barely been dispensed from his voice box before he felt regret.

"No, sir. I know I should have done something."

"Well, perhaps you acted in the correct way," said Jelling. "We usually advise the public not to confront robbers or burglars. It's possible you, co-workers or customers could have been hurt in any encounter with the robber. Don't be too hard on yourself."

Ambrose pondered the officer's mitigating words.

"Thanks," he said as he opened the door that led to the back of the building.

The corridor lights were on. Ambrose pointed to the first door on the left even though it was clearly marked "Office."

"Stay here please," Jelling asked Ambrose. "We want to make a quick check in the back."

The two strode to the rear of the building. Wilson opened the far southwest door, switched on his flashlight and entered. The beam immediately found the open window. He pointed and Jelling nodded. Nothing seemed askance, no boxes knocked down, nothing strewn on the floor. After a 10-second survey, they turned and left. They poked their heads in the other rooms. Nothing. They returned to the office.

Both men drew their .38 revolvers. They knew witnesses saw the robber leave. But did he have an accomplice? Would restaurant owner, Dawson, if he was in there, be armed? Was he wounded and willing to shoot at the first sound of any new intrusion? What about all of the other possibilities that could occur? The cops could recite some of them from past episodes. And, of course, there was Murphy's Law, the notion that if something can go wrong, it will – at precisely the worst time.

Jelling removed a handkerchief from his back pocket and carefully cuffed the top and bottom of the doorknob. He cautiously opened the door, just enough to see inside. Slowly, he proceeded further into the office.

Wilson watched from the door where he could see both inside and maintain a view of the corridor.

Jelling spotted the safe behind the desk. He took another step and saw a crumpled form. Moving forward, he shifted his gun from his right hand to the left and leaned over the figure. He pressed his two forefingers on the man's neck. The jugular vein revealed no pulse.

Jelling was not surprised. The victim's blue blazer and tan pants, and the floor around the body, were a spectacle in blood, some of which was already partially dried.

After a few moments, Jelling stood, took a deep breath, and motioned to Wilson. His partner stepped forward, carefully avoided the fatal mass and made a similar inspection.

Wilson looked back at Jelling and gave a slight shake of his head. He agreed. The man was dead.

Both retreated to the corridor, and Jelling pulled the office door shut. They conferred in a whisper.

Jelling looked at Ambrose.

"Let's return to the front of the restaurant. Officer Wilson will stay here."

The puzzled chef obeyed, with questions written on his face. No one spoke. Jelling didn't want to make a dozen explanations. Once they returned to the cash register area, he requested Ambrose and Brochman to assemble everyone, staff and customers, to the front section.

"I need to check something in the squad car. I'll be right back," Jelling informed them. He ran out the entrance and opened the door to the 1954 Ford Crestline cruiser and punched the call button on the hand-held radio receiver.

"Headquarters, this is Car Six."

"Go ahead Six."

"Our 10-20 is the Gourmet by George restaurant. Could you please send an ambulance right away? Notify Lt. Byrne, and you may as well send two detectives and the fingerprint man. We have a robbery, possible 187. Over."

"Understand Car Six. Out."

Police hated to communicate sensitive information over the radio. Too many people had radio scanners, especially newspaper and broadcast newsrooms that tuned into police radio traffic for tips on breaking stories. Jelling chose that route – even though good reporters knew 187 meant a possible homicide – over a telephone call in front of a room full of jittery people.

He went back inside.

"Folks," he motioned for everyone to be quiet. "Could I have your attention? The detectives will be here shortly to investigate this robbery. I would like all customers to please jot down your name, address and telephone number so we can get in contact with you, if necessary, in the coming days. Once you have done that, you may leave."

Jelling wanted the restaurant cleared as much as possible, except for those who directly witnessed the robbery. He mentioned nothing about a body. The last thing the police needed was a theater atmosphere as detectives launched a murder investigation and ambulance personnel hauled out a body.

Within minutes, people began to depart. Only restaurant employees and the Petersons remained.

The officer collected his thoughts, trying to determine the best way to inform the group of Dawson's murder. How much should he tell them? He removed his cap and scratched his head.

"An ambulance crew will be here shortly," Jelling began, looking individually and directly at those who remained.

He was feeling his way, like a person inching down a dark hallway in the middle of the night. Robbery was one thing. Murder changed the picture dramatically. It wasn't Jelling's inaugural at a murder scene, but this was different. The preliminary math didn't add up.

The man kissed the cashier. He bowed to restaurant customers. All this genteelness on the outside cohabitating with a killer instinct on the inside? How does that happen? How can that happen? Why isn't there an internal debate that explodes in some sort of schizophrenic showdown? The victim was stabbed several times, a vicious and brutal attack.

There are so many things that define a good cop. A sense of inquiry. A sense for justice. Fairness. Calmness. Prudence. Sensitivity. Jelling had no notions that he was the perfect policeman, a candidate for cop of the year. He had two bosses, the official city as represented by the police chief and the public at large. His goal was to serve both as best as he could.

"Mr. Dawson has been injured," Jelling continued, bending the truth. "I can't tell you any more than that now. The detective crew will also be here soon. My guess is they will want to interview most of you. I know you must have questions. They'll have to wait for the time being."

Jelling and the others were startled by a pounding at the front door. It swung open and was slammed shut as the person strolled in. Nothing refined here.

Anger preceded the woman as she waltzed through the entrance as if she were the Queen of Sheba. She was shouting, but her words scattered like buckshot before forming a sentence.

Jelling wondered if her tiara was short a few jewels.

She shoved past him and addressed the only person she knew, Ambrose.

"Was it you who hung up on me?" she demanded through a layer of lipstick. Her voice dropped a half octave lower.

"I'm not used to having people do that," she snarled. "It's happened twice tonight, within a few minutes."

Her red hair was on fire. Her blue eyes cut through Ambrose like an ice pick. Her only redeeming feature, at first glance, was a low-cut blouse, but Ambrose was afraid to focus there. Tighter skirts and higher bustlines were the incoming look, and she definitely endorsed both trends. No lampshade dress style for her. She was full and slim in all the right places.

Just as a light went off in Ambrose's head about her identity, she raised her voice again.

"Is everyone here as dumb as you?" she looked at Ambrose. "Didn't you understand my question?"

"Yes, madam. I know who you are," Ambrose stammered. I –"

"I am not a madam, goddamit, no matter what you people here might think!" her eyes bored into him.

Ambrose thought he spotted a glint of tear in at least one of those blue blazers. He began to feel sorry for her, in spite of her oral offensive. He suddenly realized he was a whole lot more secure as the restaurant chef than she was as the restaurant owner's girlfriend. She didn't even know what had happened, that Dawson was injured, perhaps seriously, maybe worse.

"I know you are Michelle Keller," Ambrose said gently, "and I know you are Mr. Dawson's girlfriend."

She seemed to soak in his temperate response. A calming began to set in, arresting her anger and apprehension.

"I want to introduce you to Officer Jelling," Ambrose said to Keller. "He is here to investigate the robbery."

"Robbery?" her eyebrows elevated.

"Don't you recall?" injected Brockman, stepping forward. "I'm the one who hung up the telephone on you because I was in the process of calling the police. I told you there had been a robbery here at the restaurant, and I had to call the police. That's why I hung up, for crying out loud. It was not meant as an offense to you."

Jelling interceded.

"Miss Keller, I'm Officer Jelling. Did you say someone hung up on you twice? Was there a time other than when Mr. Brockman hung up because he had to dial the Police Department?"

"Yes," she replied, as she inhaled the seriousness of the air. Her voice and attitude had shifted somewhat to match the environment.

"Actually three times," she said. "I had been talking with George, that is, Mr. Dawson. He hung up on me, and then some minutes later I called back, and another person hung up. And then, then what's his name, Brockman, hung up on me."

"Miss Keller, think back to your conversation with Mr. Dawson," Jelling asked. "Did you have an argument? Was he angry? Did he hang up abruptly? Why do you think he ended the conversation? Take your time."

There was silence for at least 15 seconds.

"We were talking about our relationship." She paused again, and glanced at the ceiling in search of the right words. "I want it to be more than it is and I feel he, that he –"

"Doesn't want to get married," Jelling interjected.

"Yes. I love him, and he says he loves me. When that happens, if people really mean it, they're supposed to get married."

"Yes, I agree, Miss Keller. But what else did you talk about? What were the exact words, if you can remember?"

"Well, George said, 'O.K., my love,' and then there was another voice in the room, a man's voice."

"Could you hear what this other man said?" Jelling asked.

"Not real good. George was surprised, I could tell."

"Why is that?"

"By what he said."

"What did he say?"

"I don't really want to repeat it. It's not proper language for a lady."

"Well, we excuse properness at times like this," Jelling coached. "You can tell us."

"Alright, then," she said. "I suppose it's O.K. George said 'What the hell is going on here? Who are you and why are you wearing a mask'?"

"That was all?" Jelling prodded.

"No. George then said, 'What the . . .'"

"Go ahead."

"George said, 'What the fuck are you doing?' That was the last he said before the phone went dead."

"There was no other conversation? You didn't say anything?"

"I didn't say a word," she said. "I didn't know what was happening."

"And the stranger didn't talk?" Jelling asked.

"He said, 'Thank you.' And then nothing but a dial tone."

"The stranger said, 'Thank you'?" Jelling repeated.

"Yes. Why would he say that?"

"I don't know," said Jelling.

The ambulance, a 1953 Pontiac Chiefton, arrived with a hospital emergency room night crew before any more questions could be asked.

Jelling requested witnesses to wait while he directed the medical personnel through the restaurant and to the back office. It didn't take long for one on the medical team to signal what Jelling already knew.

Dawson was dead.

"Detectives are on their way," Jelling informed the ambulance crew. "You can't do anything for this poor soul, so wait around until the officers are able to get all they need at the crime scene. It may take a while."

A couple of detectives arrived as Jelling walked back to the restaurant entrance alcove. Wilson remained at what was now officially a murder scene.

Chapter 28

If early morning in summer was Mother Nature at her finest, then dusk had to be a competing reprise.

The setting sun's fading light escorted the day's torrid temperatures out of town. The strongest stars began to muscle their way into the eastern sky. There was a scant rustle among the oaks and willows along Indian Creek, sighs of relief from the hot afternoon. The brush of a breeze made no one wish for a sweater. It was more like a window fan on low, a comforting massage after a blistering August day in Iowa.

"Anyone care for more cherry pie or ice cream, or both?" Lillian Sanders asked the Motel Sepia guests.

"No thanks, Mrs. Sanders," Ann Dolan said. "It was delicious. Such a wonderful treat, but I'm thinking of turning in." She looked at her watch.

"Good gravy! I can't believe it's after 9 o'clock already. By the way, your pie crust was exquisite. Do you make it with lard?"

"Actually, I use Crisco. It's better for you than lard," Lillian replied. "I believe good crusts come in the blend of flour and shortening and the kneading. But I still haven't mastered my mother's crust. She didn't measure anything. Said it was in the feel."

"I buy into that," Matt Kilburn jolted the conversation. "Feel is the essential ingredient, and I feel like another piece of your pie, please."

The Kilburns and Dolans had been busy getting acquainted with the Ericksons. They exchanged all the usual information, home towns and jobs, quickly moving to the complete dossiers on the Dolan and

Erickson offspring – ages, school status, sports proficiencies, awards, plans for the future, hair styles, dress styles, love of shoes, the rock 'n' roll craze and the latest cute actions by the Erickson's youngest and Dolan grandchildren.

Then, according to the Pavlovian order of gender discussion, chairs mystically shifted into a segregated pattern. The three women continued homemaking talk while the three men steered their conversation from family to work, sports and politics.

Roy Sanders wished the two black couples would move over 25 feet and join the natter. It was a mystery of human physics, he pondered, how black and white seek to separate. He knew this wasn't a scientific phenomenon, but rather one entwined in years of cultural history.

The black guest from Mississippi and the white farmers from Iowa had talked earlier, but that brief interracial encounter had dissolved into the familiar and conventional. One small step at a time, indeed.

"Four daughters? Wow!" Harold Erickson looked at Ben Dolan. "What was the record time you had to wait to get into the bathroom?"

"Hey," Matt busted in laughing before Ben could respond. "That's where Ben learned to dance, waiting outside the bathroom."

"Sure, sure," said Ben, always willing to play the good-humored target. "That's an old Bob Hope gag. He has daughters, too. Where did you say you live, Harold, Eau Claire?"

"No. Monica's parents reside there and she works there, but we live in Chippewa Falls," Harold explained. "It's a small place, about 11,000 or so, with 10,900 being German and Norwegian Lutherans." He laughed. "No, that's not right. Make it 10,500.

"Our town is about 10 miles north of Eau Claire," Harold continued, "maybe a little more than 90 from St. Paul. Have you ever heard of Jacob Leinenkugel?"

"Can't say I have," Ben answered.

"Leinenkugel beer? Not a bad way to wash down the dust of a hot summer's day," Harold advised.

"Is there a bad beer?" Matt wanted to know.

"Well, yes," Harold said, weighing if he should persist in playing the role of a German brew master. He decided to proceed.

"Wisconsin people are pretty good judges of beer, and my taste buds could never say much in praise of a beer called Potosi. Neither could my stomach lining. There is a story that the clever folks at Potosi Brewing – it's at Potosi, Wis. – attempted to attract better reviews at far-away places. They went to California with an ad campaign that tried to elevate their beer from the hoi polloi to Nob Hill. You have to admire that."

"Were they successful?" Ben asked.

"I don't think so," said Harold, "not with the hoi polloi or the affluent. Some people like it. One young man from our area was stationed with the Navy in Long Beach. He said a six-pack of 12-oz. Potosi cans cost 85 cents out there, 89 cents in Wisconsin. Price is everything when you are young and in the Navy."

"All we see and hear on the TV ads in Iowa is the dancing Hamms bear," Matt injected. "Some tom-tom drums beating to words about the land of sky blue waters. I guess it sells beer. Just for the record, what's a hoi polloi?"

"That would be us, Matt," Ben responded, and quickly switched the subject to farming. Roy was still mulling how he could blend black and white. After all that was part of the reason, at least in his mind, for starting Motel Sepia. He certainly didn't want to point blank suggest they come together. Lillian would have a fit over that.

There was general agreement that plentiful June rains in the Midwest had boosted subsoil moisture, sending the corn crop on a bountiful path. The potential yield and the price, $1.38, put most farmers in a good mood, enough so as to take vacations. Farmers, by nature, never crowd the optimism line.

"I think we have enough residual moisture to get the corn crop through in spite of this heat," Ben proffered. "Even so, these record temperatures have caused a good deal of burning along the edges of fields. You expect much of third crop, hay Matt?"

"Yeah, we'll be fine. I don't think we will need to buy any hay for the Holsteins."

"We complain about weather in Iowa, but you have to feel sorry for those along the East Coast," Ben said. "First Hurricane Connie, and then five days later, Hurricane Diane. I was watching Douglas Edwards on CBS a week ago, and the flooding in Connecticut was way worse than I imagined. They are even taking up a special collection at church."

"In Wisconsin, we say, 'If you don't like the weather, wait 10 minutes,'" Harold said. "What I want to know from you fellas is whether we should be talking war again over this tiny place called Formosa."

He waited a few seconds to see if his comment would produce any disagreement. Hearing none, he went on.

"Good grief, we just stopped fighting in Korea. The other day Eisenhower and Dulles mentioned use of an atomic bomb if we get into war with China. That's nuts, and I'm Republican."

"I sure can't disagree with you, Harold," Ben said. "I realize Mr. Eisenhower is a highly respected military leader, but we can't solve everything by shooting. I guess the question boils down to our own security and how we defend friends."

"Hell, we ain't got no friends in Formosa," Matt blurted. "It's leftover politics of Chiang Kai-shek. Roosevelt cuddled up with him, too. Seems we have a knack for siding with corrupt and incompetent foreign leaders in places we shouldn't stick our noses."

"That's pretty broad, Matt," Ben tempered. "You don't believe, then, that the Communists want to expand from the Soviet Union and China into all of Southeast Asia? Where do we draw the line? We're in what they call a Cold War, but the talk seems to get pretty hot from time to time.

"They build missiles, we build more," Ben continued. "They spread their system into Eastern Europe, we fortify the West. They push in Korea. We push back. We can kill each other a hundred times over, even as we huddle in our bomb shelters. It's crazy. But gentlemen, it takes two to tango. If the Communists would mind their own business and not try to spread their rot, we'd all be fine."

"You sound a little like our Senator McCarthy," Harold injected.

"No. Don't lump me in with that Commie-under-every-rock paranoid," Ben answered quickly. "At the same time, the philosophy of Communism is a real threat to freedom and democracy. It is anti-religion, anti-private ownership and really anti-independence. I don't get it. Communism boasts itself as the great path to an egalitarian society, but in practice it's those in power controlling those who are not. I pray, our church prays, that the Russians will change."

"Speaking of change, boys, when do you think Iowa will put up a decent challenge to the Badgers in football?" Harold segued with more than a tint of taunt.

"Wow, Harold," Ben replied. "You don't wait long to get into the meaty issues. I have to be honest, I'm not interested in State University of Iowa sports. I follow Iowa State, and for whatever reasons, Iowa and Iowa State haven't played each other since 1934. Cold War, I guess."

"13 to 7, Mr. Harold." said Matt. "That's your answer."

"What do you mean?" Harold asked.

"That was the score last fall when Iowa beat Wisconsin," Matt smiled.

"Yeah, but before that we beat Iowa five or six in a row." Harold countered.

"Who won the Big Ten in basketball last season, huh?" Matt maintained the volley. "Which team won two NCAA tournament games last year? It was the Hawks. Final Four, here we come!"

"Is anybody refereeing this debate," an eavesdropping Roy Sanders inquired. He and Lillian arrived with coffee and tea.

"Are you ladies hashin' over current events?" Roy turned his attention to the wives.

"Oh, not yet," said Monica, glancing at Harold, "and we're deliberately avoiding the mundane. Like sports. But we are getting into movies and books. Here's a question for you, Mr. Sanders. What do you think of 'East of Eden?' Seems a tad too steamy a topic for August. What do you think?"

"Well, we heard it was on the risqué side, but I can't rightly say, not havin' seen it," Roy said. "I guess if I'm itchin' to spend my hard-earned money, I'd be leanin' to see somethin' else."

"Okay, then." Monica continued. "How about 'The Lady and the Tramp?' Has anyone seen it?"

Caroline and Matt nodded in the affirmative. Lillian and Roy said they hadn't viewed it, either. Ann said she hadn't seen it, but her daughters and grandchildren had.

"The kids loved it," Ann said. "They have told me about it so many times I feel I have it memorized. How can you go wrong with a romantic story featuring dogs?" she laughed. "Disney's cash register must be ringing with vigor."

"I want to see "*Marty*" again," Caroline said. "Who can resist the lost and lonely finding love?"

In a gesture of vicarious enchantment and empathy, she tossed back her blond hair and gently placed the back of her hand on her forehead.

"It should win the Oscar for best picture, and Borgnine could be the best actor."

"I'm not so sure," Harold gave a derisive snicker. "Ernst Borgnine has to own one of the ugliest faces in Hollywood. He makes Phil Silvers look like a poster boy for Brylcreem. Now, if you are looking for sexy, I recommend '*The Seven Year Itch*'. Marilyn Monroe struts her stuff as if among a bunch of swabbies just off ship after three months at sea. Wow!"

"Really, Harold!" Monica responded, not just a little piqued. "I didn't realize you were such a big fan of pseudo-adultery."

Her comment hit him like a wave of claims after a wind storm. After a brief consultation with discretion, he decided to keep quiet. Ben bailed him out.

"What do you ladies think of this rock 'n' roll craze?"

"What's not to like?" Matt injected.

"I guess some of it's OK," Ann said. "Young people like '*Rock Around the Clock*.' And, swoon with the McGuire Sisters to '*Sincerely*.' Personally, I lean toward Frank Sinatra and '*Learnin' the Blues*' and big bands like Benny Goodman, Glenn Miller, Les Elgart, Stan Kenton. And, how about the jazz sound of Duke Ellington and Ella Fitzgerald?"

"I agree, Mrs. Dolan, the great arrangements by the big bands, especially Ellington, are good," Monica said. "But at the top of the list, for me, is "*Don't Cry Baby*" by Billy Eckstein and the Count Basie orchestra. That rendition is enough to make a grown woman weep."

"Who likes Duke Ellington?" Roy popped in on the conversation.

"Mr. Sanders," Matt injected with disregard to the question. "You are a lucky man to have a wife who makes cherry pie this good."

"Well, yes and no," Roy replied. "I'm lucky because it seems to be a favorite of our visitors. Personally, I prefer lemon meringue. Cherry wouldn't make my top five list."

"I love the creative work of Ellington," Ann said, returning to Roy's question. "I especially like his '*Mood Indigo*' and '*Caravan*.' No, wait. The best is '*Take the A Train.*' That great blend of saxophones and trumpets, which then back off for Ellington's piano. Gracious, that's a treat to the ear."

"I met Duke Ellington," Roy said evenly.

"Now just a minute Mr. Sanders," Matt fired in a questioning tone. "I never met Glenn Miller and he was born on a farm near Clarinda, Iowa, a mere 30 miles from Ben's place. I thought Duke Ellington grew up in New York, Harlem to be exact. How did he get all the way out to Iowa? And don't tell me he took the A train."

"No, sir," Roy answered. "Duke Ellington was born in Washington, D.C. He wound up in New York City, and that's where he teamed up with other jazz people. But like everybody else, the Depression threw entertainers into the financial dumps. Ellington was forced to hit the road, look for gigs wherever he could find them. He toured, and one of the places he brought his band was Cedar Rapids."

"You met him at a dance here, then?" Matt asked.

"No, Mr. Matt. I met him at my house," Roy answered. "I suppose I was a teenager at the time, but my mama would take in black entertainers and one of them was the Duke. My mama's hospitality and home cooking became famous. Louie Armstrong, Blanche and Cab Calloway, Sonny Price, they all performed in Cedar Rapids and stayed at our house.

"When the great saxophonist Coleman Hawkins came to town, his first call was to mama. He always requested his favorite meal, ham and beans, greens and cornbread. Heck, we were practically on a first-name basis with Count Basie and the Step Brothers. The King Cole Trio stayed at our house. Peg Leg Bates. There were white entertainers who boarded with us also.

"If memory serves me right," Roy said, "the Duke and his band played right before Christmas, I think in 1943, at Danceland. That's a fancy ballroom in downtown Cedar Rapids. I know the war was goin' on. Later on, Satchmo Armstrong played there."

"Well, I guess that's a good history lesson for all of us," Matt said. "I'm assuming black entertainers couldn't stay at hotels at that time?"

"With some exceptions," Roy explained. "Marian Anderson was so respected and admired that when she came to Cedar Rapids to perform she was allowed to stay at the John Adams Hotel. The story is that she had to use the freight elevator to get to her room. Hotel management apparently thought the presence of a Negro on the main elevators would offend white guests, would hurt the hotel's business.

"There is also the story that Nat King Cole – he was originally with the King Cole Trio – was turned down at the John Adams," Roy went on. "This was not so long ago, after he struck out on his own. I can't vouch for it, but the rumor was that an agent for Capital Records picked him up at the airport and brought him into town, not imaginin' that Nat King Cole would be refused accommodations. The flabbergasted agent called the mayor. The mayor was so angry he called the hotel owner. Cole said it was nothin' new, and said he would stay with a friend in Iowa City."

"I'm really sorry to hear that," Ben said. "I would have thought Iowa had advanced beyond that, looked at his talent rather than the color of his skin. Nat King Cole's *'Unforgettable'* is one of my favorites." He looked directly at Roy and Lillian.

"Have you or your family ever been the subject of discrimination?" Ben asked.

"Well, there have been some issues," Roy said, glancing at Lillian, "but I would rather not talk about that. Lillian and I have, for the most part, been treated well here. I like to think on the positive side. I believe people are basically the same, even if they are different color or creed. We are all on this Earth for a short while, and there ain't no other place to go and ain't no time to hate."

"I remember Nat King Cole's rendition of *'The Blue Gardenia'* in the movie of the same title," said Ann. "I think it came out a couple of years ago. His voice is so smooth, so mellow."

Quiet took charge, except for Matt's fork clanging on the plate, rounding up the last bits of cherry pie.

"Prejudice can come to anybody," Roy broke the respite. "My Dad told that right after World War I ended some families of German descent suffered bad treatment. People called 'em Krauts, and they were run out of town in some places. This may be hard to believe, but the house of a German doctor, who lived a block away from us, was blown up."

"You are a gracious man, Mr. Sanders," Ann said, after his remarks settled on their minds. "Catholics and Irish know discrimination, too. I think we are all capable of hurting other people, those we don't really know and those we know. The Ku Klux Klan, which targeted Negroes, also hated Catholics and Jews."

She considered the pain endured by some families in southwest Iowa.

"I remember my grandparents talking about the Klan," she continued. "After World War I, they expanded from the South and had followers in the Red Oak area. They preached that the Pope was anti-American, was going to make "papists" out of everyone. Of course, the Know Nothing Party right after the Civil War was viciously anti-Catholic and influential in Iowa."

"I hear you 'bout the Klan, Mrs. Dolan," Roy said. "When I was a kid, local folks started the first black Boy Scout group here. They even let us camp out with the white kids, a place out near Stone City. That's a village about 15 miles east of here. It's where Grant Wood, the artist, had his school. One night we saw this light shinin' through the tent flaps. Some thought the place was on fire. We ran outside and saw this giant cross burnin', and hooded people runnin' around. Scout leaders gathered and came up with a plan of action.

"The next day, they had horseback ridin' scheduled," Roy explained. "The counselors said everyone was going to ride into town, blacks and whites together, to send a message. So we did. We jumped on the horses and rode into town, just like the Old West. I don't know if any Klan saw us or not. Who knows?

"My older sister saw the Klan in Iowa City," Roy went on. "For awhile – times were tough – she and her husband lived with Eta and Duke Slater. Duke was a great football player for Iowa. All Big Ten in 1920. Won all sorts of awards. I don't recollect what year it was, but the Klan marched in front of their apartment carrying signs, saying 'Down with Niggers, Catholics and Jews.'"

He shook his head in disgust at the memory.

"We can't let smallness be bigger than the rest of us," Ben said. "It's crazy, but it seems some people find joy in hate."

Ann rose from her lawn chair and looked at Ben, a silent signal that it was time to turn in. He stretched his arms overhead, the corresponding response.

Before anyone said anything more, flashing lights and sirens cut through the summer night darkness. All attention focused on two vehicles speeding down the hill east on Mount Vernon Road. Both slowed and swung sharply onto Bertram Road. Front tires spit gravel as the cars maneuvered into the Motel Sepia drive.

The manner of approach was a declaration of trouble. One of the Linn County Sheriff's patrol cars quickly pulled into the area where motel guests were congregated. The other stopped at the entry point. Eyes shifted to the nearest vehicle and the officer inside.

White motel guests stood in baffled curiosity. Silently and spontaneously, the Negro couples rose, but with an inner alarm. They walked toward Roy Sanders and the others.

Sgt. Morris Weber stepped out of his vehicle and walked briskly toward Sanders and the group.

The prattle of four mingling conversations, friendly discourse that directed an almost beguiling babble into the leafy overhang, yielded to mute uneasiness.

"What can I do for you, Morris?" Roy extended his hand. Sanders knew a few of the county patrolmen and several city officers. Weber frequently patrolled the eastern portion of the county.

"Roy, how are you?" Weber said. "Looks as if you have a busy night."

"We do. Seems you have extra business, too. What's the problem?"

"There's been a robbery and murder at the Italian restaurant in town, the one on Mt. Vernon Road not too far west of here."

There were several gasps accompanied by Ann Dolan's "My Heavens!" "Yes, I know the one, Morris." Roy said. "That's terrible. When did all this happen?"

"Not long ago. Maybe around 8:30."

There was at least a 10-second pause in the unfolding drama before Weber picked up the dialogue.

"We received the call from Cedar Rapids police around 8:47 and were asked to check the main entrances to the city," Weber continued. "Witnesses said a black man approached the cashier, ordered her to remove money from the register, and then calmly departed. And before he left, get this, he kissed her on the cheek."

Lillian, Roy and their guests stood in shock.

"He didn't kill her?" Roy asked.

"No. But we think he murdered the restaurant owner," Weber said grimly, shifting his eyes to the ground. "Officers found his body in the back office soon after arriving. Vicious killing, and the office safe was cleaned out."

Weber again looked at the Motel Sepia guests.

"Have you seen anything unusual Roy, a car speeding by, a car turning in?"

Roy read the full implication of the question.

"Nothing unusual, Morris," Roy replied. "Wasn't there a story in the newspaper a few days ago about a robbery where the suspect kissed the cashier?"

"You have a good memory," Weber acknowledged. "Actually, there were two other cases where that happened. The paper labeled him the 'Kissing Bandit.'"

"Do you think it's the same guy?"

"Don't know," Weber shrugged his shoulders. "Could be. Too early to tell."

Sgt. Weber paused, gave a 180-degree scan of the area, and then looked back at Sanders.

"I'm sorry about this Roy, but I'm going to have to ask that your guests not leave in the morning."

He said it loud enough for everyone to hear, and glanced directly at the black guests.

"I would talk to everyone now, but we're patrolling the entire perimeter of the city, the main highways. We want to set up a road block east of here. You'll call if you spot anything unusual?"

"Of course, Morris," Roy nodded agreement. "When will our guests be able to leave?"

"I would say by noon tomorrow," Weber said. "Just want to clear up the whereabouts of everybody over the last couple of hours. We'll be back in the morning."

Morris and the patrol cars left with the same urgency as they had arrived five minutes earlier.

Chapter 29

Suddenly, the warm August night had a peculiar chill that was not born in any weather pattern. A dozen people remained standing in the shadows of the trees surrounding Motel Sepia, the silence deafening.

Even the canopy of leaves hushed, ignoring any slight movement of air. Nearby Indian Creek, hidden in the darkness, seemed to moderate its mild gurgles. It was if everything in this little corner of the world was holding its breath.

A half-moon and yard lights revealed a stunning sameness on people's faces, a blank look that one finds on those searching for answers, knowing none are immediately forthcoming.

Roy Sanders studied them. The faces slowly reconfigured into a quizzical fabric of uncertainty. He struggled to comprehend how a peaceful evening suddenly turned into dank disquiet.

Were they in danger? Was this killer nearby? How did Motel Sepia and its guests get involved in this? Why detain them until noon? What is this world coming to?

Sanders looked directly at the McDowells and Taylors. Surely, they don't think they are under suspicion by deputies, somehow involved. Is that what's passin' on their minds? We're black, we're suspect? Is this different from Mississippi?

"Perhaps they will clear this up overnight," Roy said, breaking into the quiet collision of thoughts. "I know Sgt. Morris of the Sheriff's Department. He stops out here sometimes on patrol. I'm familiar with some city detectives, too."

He hoped to allay any range of fears his guests may be holding, particularly those of Negro travelers.

"Are there any black police officers in your town?" Matt asked. The question shot straight out of the thick apprehension, like a cannon volley from a once silent front.

Roy was surprised at the source.

"Yes, there are, Matt," Roy replied. "In fact, Virgil Howell heads up the fingerprinting in the detective office. He's a good one, too. I hope Virg is involved in this investigation."

Lillian spoke.

"Why don't we all sit down a few minutes to relax and digest things," she proposed. "I'll make some more coffee. Is there anything else I can bring? I still have pie left."

"Oh, it was good, Mrs. Sanders, but I'm afraid everybody would send a curious look my way if I had a third piece of cherry pie," Matt attempted to ease the tension.

"Okay, then. I'll go get the coffee going," Lillian said. She read the dangling unease like a veteran fortune teller. Any intentions of quick sleep had been detoured by the news of a murder.

"Well, this is certainly a fine start for our trips," George McDowell said. "First murder, maybe mayhem down the road?"

"That's not like you, George, to see the glass half empty," Viola replied. "We'll be fine. Get to California and do everything we want."

George looked at his wife and then at everyone else in the group.

"This won't dampen our vacations one bit," Ida Taylor said, leaving her husband surprised at her upbeat attitude. "All of us will be on our way by noon tomorrow. Wait and see."

"You're right, Mrs. Taylor," Ann Dolan chimed. "This crime has nothing to do with us."

"Mr. Sanders. Do you have many killings in your town?" George asked. "In Chicago, murders are a three-inch story on page 20 of *The Tribune*. During the summer, sirens blend in with the shrill of the cicada bug. You hardly notice them."

"To be honest, I don't rightly know how many murders there are in Cedar Rapids," Roy responded. "One is too many. My guess is most result from family fights. But this killin' at the restaurant doesn't sound like a feud among kin. It sounds planned. It has a coldness to it that makes me uneasy, too. I'll admit it."

"Did you know the man who was murdered?" Ben inquired.

"No, I didn't," said Roy.

He thought a minute as to whether he had ever met the owner of Gourmet by George. He and Lillian had never eaten there. It seemed a little too fancy for them. Some businessmen he knew who had been there said the food was good, but expensive. He couldn't even remember the owner's name. Morris hadn't mentioned it.

"We never ate there," Roy continued. "No particular reason, 'cept for Lillian's home cooking and what I hear is a pricey menu. I prefer drive-ins, hamburger joints, especially the A&W on the west side. We occasionally eat at the Lighthouse Inn just east of here. I never met the man who owns Gourmet by George. I don't think he was a member of the Chamber of Commerce. I can't say his name. Maybe Lillian remembers his na –"

He was cut off by a wailing siren from a police squad car with red lights slicing through the roadside darkness, racing past Motel Sepia. It was headed east on Highway 30. The car continued beyond the Lighthouse Inn.

After that Roy couldn't see the flashing lights, only hear the waning howl of the siren. It took less than 30 seconds, but the speeding police car added a layer to the anxiety that engulfed the small group of travelers, different people headed in different directions who were now surrounded and bonded by a common cloud.

Roy had intended to say something about the reported history of the Lighthouse Inn, but after measuring the pervasive worry he decided against it.

The story was that Al Capone himself once ate at the Lighthouse. There was even a claim that John Dillinger sat in a booth just to the left of the entrance, where "his gun went off and left a hole in the wall." No need to mention any of that.

"I would have to say, not knowin' the statistics, that a killin' such as this is a rare thing in Cedar Rapids," Roy suggested, as several of his guests still followed the fading siren fold into the eastern hills. "Rare in Iowa, I think. For the most part, Iowans are a peaceable people, a carin' people, always willin' to help a neighbor in distress."

"I think much of that is inherent in a farming society," Ben advanced. "We may regard farmers as independent cusses, happy in being their own boss, but the deep truth is that they are more dependent on friends and neighbors than most people. Sometimes, out in the middle of nowhere, you just need to go over to the fence line and talk, find out what your neighbor is thinking."

"I would have to agree," said Vernon Taylor. "I think that same sort of rural neighborliness exists in Mississippi. People have trouble puttin' in the cotton crop, others come to their aid. I know in my business it's true. I operate a mortuary, and a couple years ago I had a funeral where I was so sick my wife forced me to stay in bed. Another funeral director took over for me."

"Mr. Taylor, we heard on the –"

"Please call me Vern."

"OK then, Vern, long as you call me Ben."

Taylor smiled and nodded. The two had had that salutation excursion earlier, but convention has a tendency to endure.

It was sort of a miracle, Roy thought, glancing around at the group. He certainly didn't want to appear disconnected in his preoccupation, but it was intriguing. Half the night his mind searched for ways to bring his black and white guests together, to produce some fulfillment of his quest to advance racial interaction. All of a sudden chairs and people shifted and they began to talk.

White men. White women. Black men. Black women. Crazy mathematics, Roy mused, but all of a sudden four became one. It took news of a murder to create a bond, a common thread with which to stitch new relationships. They were suddenly thrust into the same boat, faced with the same predicament.

"We heard on the radio coming out here about the Chicago boy being kidnapped in Mississippi," Ben said. "That anywhere near your town?"

"Yes, sir, it is," Vern said. "About 40 to 50 miles northeast of our town, jus' other side of Greenwood, Mississippi. It happened in a tiny place called Money. It sits right on the Tallahatchie River, a meanderin' stream that on a map looks like it's lost and don't know where to go. It runs all over the Delta like a braid in a girl's hair. In some places, I think it runs into itself."

Ben wasn't sure if he should laugh. The air was too dense with dark news, and he regretted having added another grim topic.

"Till was the boy's name," Vernon proceeded without prompting. "Emmett Till."

Chapter 30

Joe Ellis casually exited the Gourmet by George Restaurant, turned right toward the rear parking lot and began the two block walk south to where he had parked the rental car.

It was shortly before 9 p.m.

He calmly and confidently strode in the shadows of brush and trees bordering the crumbling blacktop. The moon, sliced in half by celestial maneuvering, struggled to penetrate the leafy canopy and overcome the last vestiges of daylight.

Before he arrived at the car, he yanked off his hooded jacket and the net that covered his face. Sweat began to seep from his pores.

Goddamn summer heat, he muttered.

Ellis unlocked the car and tossed the elements of disguise into the back seat. Goddamn town, he thought to himself. Is this the city's edge, he wondered as he gazed south? Again he looked around.

Only sporadically did a house or shed interrupt the elms and oaks in what quickly turned rural. Beyond the first block, beyond the restaurant area to the south, there were no street lights. A cow bellowed in the distance, a mournful call to a wayward offspring.

A mosquito drilled into the nape of his neck. Ellis swatted and swore again. It wasn't Korea or the jungles of Chicago, but he was not entirely free of nerves. His tough calm was interrupted by a different, more familiar sound. He didn't expect to hear a siren so soon.

Why would cops be on their way already? This one-horse place couldn't have more than a half-dozen cop cars patrolling on a weekday night.

214

The siren was still some distance away, but it altered his plan. He wasn't about to turn the car around and meet the cops coming in. He opened the car trunk and retrieved a bar of Lava soap and a small container of water.

First, he scrubbed off the black grease-like concoction that he had used to darken his hands. It was a material similar to a substance used by athletes to reduce eye glare, except he had modified it by adding coal dust. Satisfied that he had discarded his "Negro" hands, he bent downward, washed his face, and poured water over his entire head. He shook his head like a dog exiting a pond and used the jacket as a towel.

Ellis felt refreshed, as if he had not only rid himself of sticky sweat but the more complex residue of a gruesome criminal act. Except in his case, there was no moral aftermath of a grisly crime, a murder. Remorse was neither a part of his lexicon nor conscience.

Human life, if it was in the way, was of no more concern to him than a stray cat crossing a highway. His mind wasn't detoured to some somber and goofy pondering of probity and virtue.

His job as a paid killer employed the precision of a railroad watch and the emotional entanglement of winding it.

Some in his outfit in Korea had mentally struggled with the reality that they had just killed another human being, even though the enemy. It was traumatic for them to watch life drain from another person. Company commanders used death, death of yourself or your buddy, as motivation to kill.

Ellis was never troubled with killing in Korea or in his work for Rhino Ralston. His heedless mind projected no images of killing someone's brother, someone's son, or maybe even a husband and father.

He closed the trunk and entered the car. The sirens were louder. After he started the big Chrysler, he slowly drove south, looking for side streets. The further he advanced, the more the undulating road narrowed. Within a mile it became a country road with little gravel, and shortly after that dissolved in a dead end. This was the goddamn end of town.

Frustrated, he turned around. At the bottom of a hill he swung west on a side road. It turned out to be a dirt lane to nowhere.

Returning to the north-south street, he chose another option for the moment. He pulled into a grassy area and stopped inside a small clearing. He turned off the lights, got out of the car and examined the location. A fence lined with seven-foot sumac, a mammoth cottonwood tree and several hickory and oak trees seemed to create the perfect place to hide a black sedan at night.

It was, he thought, a good place to cool his heels and allow semi-normalcy to return back at the restaurant. Some cops would still be there, but everyone else would be gone.

Ellis sat there for nearly two hours, dozing off before a barking dog returned him to the desolate Iowa street.

Abruptly waking, he sat erect and regained his bearings. Quickly he dismissed any danger. Time had silenced the sirens. The quiet caused him to review the past evening, bolstered his ego at accomplishing the macabre, a job done well and with style.

If the Better Business Bureau gave out awards to criminals for customer satisfaction, reliability in execution of a plan and a squeaky-clean record of not leaving an evidence trail, Ellis could be named Man of the Year. His proud boss could recite his flawless work record and completion of assignments without a fluff of worry.

Self-preservation governed everything.

Ellis looked at his wrist watch. It was 10 minutes before 11. Things would have calmed down back at the crime scene.

He kept front windows down and ears tuned to the north, but only the crickets and other bugs that danced and sang at night could be heard. He couldn't just sit in a field all night, sucking in the developing dew and pollen from ragweed and corn tassels.

Curiously, even though alone and unthreatened, he had a slight sensation of being cornered. It was not a feeling he liked, tumbling inside his brain, seeking to compete with his crowned invincibility. It harkened back to the deep holes of Korea, when his mind would create fences as he sneaked along a mountain ridge en route to a sniper's destination.

Unconsciously, he began humming, *Twinkle, Twinkle Little Star.* His nerves, like cobwebs quivering in the wind, quieted.

Ellis thought. He analyzed. It was always a good way to tear down doubts and encroaching barriers.

He walked around the car, took a deep breath and opened the back door. He removed his sweaty white shirt, stuck it in his suitcase and pulled on a fresh t-shirt. He neatly draped his suit coat on a hanger and hung it on the car's side hook.

Ellis grabbed the hooded jacket and face net and walked 200 feet into the timber. He tossed them beneath a red cedar and with a stick poked them into oblivion. The towel and lava soap followed. If he were stopped, he wanted no evidence in the car. He took his prized knife and heaved it down an embankment beyond a forest of horseweeds.

He was ready.

The Chrysler's eight cylinders purred like a puma stalking a laggard fawn. He kept lights off and edged back onto the dirt and rock road. He coaxed the big sedan with minimal gas. A deer shot out before him and he hit the brakes.

Relax, he told himself.

Again the car crept forward on the roller coaster road. He was back on a surfaced section, now just blocks from the restaurant and the main east-west road.

Soon he would come over a crest of a hill and the restaurant complex would reveal itself. The question was, would he be naked in the dark, attracting peering cop eyes, or could he slither through?

His adrenalin began to build. Like a sniper, he crept along the desolate road, alone and in the middle of the biggest manhunt in the town's recent history. Instead of being the hunter, he was the hunted.

Then he remembered, and he scolded himself for his oversight. There was an alley, south of the restaurant, which ran west. It did not go east. He could turn there and nurse the sedan to the next north-south street and avoid any assemblage of law enforcement at the restaurant.

It was his best option, and he took it. He saw no one and assumed no one saw him. It had been a good bet, and he was proud and relieved.

The road, more like a cinder path, was rough and in some places washed out. The good part was that it was clothed in brush. He intentionally plodded along, fearful of hitting a log or rock that would rip the oil pan or damage something else. Limbs scraped along the car sides.

He came to a clearing and the street lights revealed a sign. It read "Moore's Turkey Farm."

Then, the road twisted north, and he could see a few cars on Mount Vernon Road. He was off the ridge and safe.

Car lights on, he slowly drove east on Mount Vernon Road and past the restaurant on his right. As he proceeded up a slight grade out of town, he glanced back toward the Gourmet restaurant. There were several cars in the front area, including two marked police cruisers. He smiled and gave them a goodbye wave in the dark.

Mount Vernon Road gradually swings north and converts to Highway 30 as it winds east through a grove of trees and then abruptly angles southeasterly down a long hill.

Ellis was grateful he wasn't involved in a chase. The serpentine highway would have made it like the Indy 500. But he was in no hurry. He stretched his hand out the rolled-down window, guiding the cool breeze of freedom into the vehicle and across his face.

As the car entered a straightaway, he noticed flashing red lights in the distance, perhaps a mile away. A roadblock, he thought.

"Sonofabitch!" he muttered to himself. "Fucking Moses! Maybe I underestimated these hick cops."

Fluster rippled through his veins and befuddled his sense of location. Where was that damn turnoff to the motel? Just then the curtain of roadside trees ended and the blinking Motel Sepia sign revealed itself like an oasis in the desert. Now he knew where he was at. Now his compass was pointed in the right direction.

"Naw," Ellis said to himself with a cocky smile. "I estimated fine."

He laughed satisfyingly.

The sedan slowed down. Ellis eased off the brake and steered right into the motel.

Chapter 31

Jennifer Jennings had dozed off in a lounge chair and hadn't heard the car pull up in the Motel Sepia parking area.

When the cabin door opened and closed with a slight squeak, she bolted erect and glanced in that direction. He slipped in like a discrete disease.

The air draft had caused several magazine pages to flip. The lamp across the room produced a golden glow and highlighted his grim countenance.

Even though Rhino Ralston had scripted the entire undertaking, directing their movements like opening night at the Chicago Theater, Jennifer was wary of Joe Ellis' mercurial personality.

She didn't like him, and she didn't trust him.

"Have a nice nap, Rosemary?" he whispered.

Rhino had even assigned them phony names and credentials. Jennifer's role was the fake bride, Rosemary Jones.

"Resting while I do all the work, take all the chances," Ellis snarled mockingly. "Is there something I can do for you darlin', something I can get for you precious?"

When you become as encumbered as Jennings, a pawn in the mechanics of the underworld, the ground where you stand always seems to be moving. She had the perpetual feeling that she was caught up in an earthquake in the making. It was not just the precarious life of staying a step ahead of the law, but the environment of constant fear of severe injury and even death.

In recent months, her mind more and more had drifted to a path out, a way to escape the shackles of the mob and the degrading life she led. Ralston had hinted that she may be able to perform more meaningful work for his businesses, perhaps accounting, once this assignment in Iowa was finished. It may not be total freedom, but the idea conveyed was that she would no longer be part of his mattress squad.

Ralston's plan had been simple. Jennings and Ellis would go to Iowa, pose as a honeymoon couple, and thus provide credibility to their presence and a launching point for Ellis to conduct the real business at hand. Her role was solely that of a new bride, but Ralston made it clear that there was to be no honeymoon activity. They were employees, not lovers.

Deliberately, she had not changed her clothes. She had not bathed. The brown slacks and gold blouse were wrinkled and unattractive. She wore no perfume and no makeup. Her hair was a tangle and strands hung over her face as if they, like her, had lost their way.

There was a time in high school and the first two years at college where she could turn the eye of any male who was awake. She was as pert as Debbie Reynolds and as charming as Audrey Hepburn. She could dangle the physical and trump with the intellect. No grass grew on the path to her door. And then, almost overnight, weeds overtook her future.

"Perhaps I can pour you a nice glass of wine and you could slip into something a little cozier," Ellis continued his mockery. "It doesn't have to be all Rhino business."

She watched as his hulk moved toward the sink. He washed his hands.

The thought that he was rinsing away the life blood of someone he had just killed caused her to shiver. Why should she be shocked? Jennifer knew the purpose of their trip. She knew what role Ellis held in Rhino Ralston's employee diagram.

"Just stay away," she glared at Ellis. "Just stay away or you can answer to Rhino. I will scream my head off. I will throw chairs. I will break every window in this place if you lay one hand on me."

Ellis walked over to her chair.

Even though he had just brutally murdered someone several hours earlier, his adrenaline began to surge. His body quivered with contempt. Their eyes met. The hate exchanged was as blinding as the hot summer sun's glare off a tin roof.

She feared he may explode, but she held her glare.

"Don't torpedo this entire business trip," she said. "It may look bad on your resume."

The audacity of the statement shook him, tossed his whole being into neutral. His curdling veins froze. No one, not even the toughest sergeant in the Marine Corps, had ever caused him to back down like this. A flimsy broad! He could break her in two.

He stopped cold in his tracks and stepped back.

"You know, whore," he said with bitter loathing, "I have to acknowledge, you've got the body of a gazelle and the guts of a lion. There will be other times. I think I'll go to bed. I'm tired, mostly of you."

Chapter 32

Roy Sanders was past tired. He had one eye shut and the other foggily focused on his flat pillow. The only thing that kept his weary body erect, that deflected the call of sleep, was the shocking news of a nearby murder. It persisted on keeping his eyelids open.

Like a zombie, he stumbled over to the office light switch. He had to order his legs forward.

August 29 had started early for him. That was not unusual. During the summer, 6 a.m. would frequently find him along Indian Creek, sipping his first cup of Folgers and aligning the day's agenda in his head. Perhaps, he would analyze a few of the world's problems in between.

Fifteen minutes later, he was back at the office where he poured a second cup of coffee. On this day he had finished reading the Sunday paper.

While the lead story outlined financing problems for two new high schools, the weather was the hot topic. Cedar Rapids on Saturday tied an 1899 record of 97 degrees. It hit 107 in Sac City in northwest Iowa. Sunday was the fifth day of the heat siege, and the gauge on the Motel Sepia office at 6:20 Monday morning had read 75. The paper claimed relief was on the way.

Early on, Lillian directed him to fix a screen on one of the cabins.

"And don't forget to water my flowers."

There was a leaky faucet outside the main house and the mailbox post needed shoring up. He had to check wholesale prices and labor costs in order to give a job quote on carpeting a room at the

Armstrong house. Then he had to follow up on a complaint pitting his rug-cleaning employee against a customer over a missed floor stain at a private home.

Too many balls in the air at one time. Roy shook his head.

He was 42, but by noon he felt like he was 62.

The afternoon and evening had revived his spirits as he welcomed guests and witnessed the intermingling of blacks and whites. But that uplifting experience was deflated by flashing red lights and the arrival of the sheriff's deputy shortly after 9 p.m. A killer was loose in the area.

He and Lillian talked about the murder until she went to bed at 10:30. This kind of news was a rarity in Cedar Rapids.

How could she fall asleep so quickly? The crime news had put Roy on edge and he had a feeling some of the guests were uneasy, too. You don't hear reports of a murder just down the road and fall into bed and a serene slumber, even if you are half asleep.

Roy, moved by some inner need to inspect the outside darkness, to passively review the encompassing shadows that concealed a terrible crime, stepped out to the front yard to think and listen. He walked the 100 feet down to the gravel road with no particular intent in mind, and slowly returned to the house. Here and there the moon left its splotchy mark on the lawn. The wind had gone to sleep, too.

He heard nothing more than the night's usual assembly of noises. The more he murkily pondered events of the day, the more entwined his thoughts became until they collaborated with the rhythmic songs of the crickets and cicadas to produce a sort of hypnosis.

As he re-entered the house, Roy's brain concentrated on one object, sleep. He reached for the office light switch. In a blink before he pushed the off button, his mesmerized mind sensed the sound of a car motor. His hand dropped to his side. The engine became louder before the car's lights flashed against the office windows, removing any doubt it was an illusion.

The quick combination of sensory stimulation imposed a reawakening that gradually shifted Roy to a sense of warning. He rubbed his eyes to reaffirm he had not fallen asleep standing up, and pulled the curtains back on the office window.

The driveway yard light revealed a large black sedan.

It was unusual to have someone looking for a motel room after 11 o'clock at night.

Roy checked his watch: Make that 11:15.

Headlights flicked off, replaced by parking lights. The car door opened.

A big man of maybe more than six feet, with broad shoulders and a muscular neck, rose out of the vehicle slowly and gently closed the door. He walked past the wooden sign that read, "Office, Motel Sepia," and followed the accompanying arrow.

Roy unhooked the office screen door. Like most everyone else, they seldom locked the main door, especially on hot summer nights. Air circulation was a premium.

The man seemed startled when he saw Roy holding the screen door open. That didn't surprise Roy. Except for Negro travelers who may have learned by word-of-mouth or from travel agents about Motel Sepia and the Sanders, no one expects to be greeted by a black person at a lodging place. Except, of course, if the black man is a porter.

"Please, come in," Roy greeted the man. "Are you looking for a room, or do you need directions? How can I help you?"

"Are you the manager?" the big man asked, barely audible.

"My wife and I are the owners of Motel Sepia," Roy replied.

"I see," the man said, his voice a mixture of need and reluctance.

"I guess I'll take a room if you have one," the man said. "I have a meeting in the morning, not far from here."

"You're in luck," Roy responded. "We have one cabin unoccupied. I'm afraid we don't have TV or air conditioning. There is a shower."

"Okay, then. I'll take it. How much?"

Roy provided the information and asked that the man fill out the registration form. He placed the key to Unit 5 on the desk top.

"I see from your t-shirt that you are a St. Louis Cardinals fan," Roy made conversation.

"Not really. It was a gift. I'm not much for baseball."

"Tough day on the road?" Roy asked, as the man filled out the form.

"Yeah, I guess so," was the terse reply.

The man placed a $5 bill on the desk. Roy provided change.

"Do you," Roy glanced down at the registration where it said Mike Brown, "Mr. Brown, do you need a Cedar Rapids map or any other information?"

"No need," Brown said.

"One other thing," Roy said. "I forgot and I apologize. There has been a terrible crime in the city and the sheriff's department has asked that our guests not leave tomorrow until noon. Just in case they want to ask any questions. I'll refund your money if you wish to stay somewhere else. Again, I'm sorry about that."

"That makes things rather difficult," Brown said. "My sales appointment, you see, is at 9 a.m. I was hoping to leave first thing in the morning."

"I understand. You are certainly welcome to try another motel."

Brown was visibly upset. He looked directly at Roy, and for a second Roy had the feeling those eyes bored right to the back of his skull. It made him uneasy. There was something about the man's demeanor, cast in the milieu of murder, that bent the night's normalcy even more.

"No, this will be OK. Probably the same down the road. Perhaps I can call my contact in the morning and reschedule."

There was an uncomfortable pause of about 10 seconds.

"What sort of crime?" Brown asked.

His eyes again penetrated Roy's.

"The deputy said it was a robbery and murder," Roy answered.

"That's terrible alright," he said. "Terrible."

He picked up the key to Unit 5 and left.

Roy watched the car back out of the drive. He looked down at the registration pad. It said: "Mike Brown. St. Louis. 1954 Buick."

Roy's once drowsy eyes stared into puzzlement and speculation.

Chapter 33

At five minutes after midnight on Tuesday, Aug. 30, 1955, the booking log at the Cedar Rapids Police Department listed the following entry:

"Curtis Moore, 22, Cedar Rapids, arrested on three counts of armed robbery and one count of suspicion of murder. Subject being held in Linn County Jail."

Officer Charlie Jelling rang the doorbell at the home of Annie Pearl Moore. His partner, Kenny Wilson, had his department-issued Smith & Wesson .38 revolver drawn, and stood several feet left of the front door. It was 11:30 p.m., Aug. 29.

Both officers had been down this road before. It could be full of nasty surprises, or come off without a wrinkle. You prepare for the surprises, and pray for no wrinkles.

The procedure was mapped out by department policy. Only circumstances at the scene altered the script.

Over the years, four Cedar Rapids police officers were killed in the line of duty, but thankfully none had been killed in the last 34 years. In the most recent death, a 1921 shooting, the officer was killed and two others were injured trying to arrest a man at the library.

For nearly a week Cedar Rapids detectives had focused on Curtis Moore as the suspect in recent robberies at the Czech Inn and Lincoln Truck Stop, holdups where the perpetrator had become known as the "Kissing Bandit."

In each case, witnesses had said that an amiable man about six feet tall, wearing a dark hooded sweatshirt or jacket, his face and neck covered by some sort of elasticized, pullover net, had entered the business, suggested by mannerism that he had a gun, and asked for money from the cash register. The MO in both cases was similar.

As a departing gesture, he had kissed a female attendant. No one was injured. In both instances, the robber, because of exposed hands, was identified as black.

Moore's troubles with the law five years before in an attempted car break-in now festered anew and broke open into big-time trouble. Fingerprints taken then matched those collected in the first two robberies. Fingerprint specialist Virgil Howell made an easy call when he compared the sloped loop pattern of the middle finger with Moore's prints of 1950.

The loop pattern features a significant re-curve and delta line, hallmarks that constitute two-thirds of all fingerprints. The clincher was a slight, round scar – deemed an old puncture mark in Howell's off-hand opinion – that marred a ridge line.

Howell read fingerprints like Einstein deciphered algebra. Area law enforcement agencies came to him for advice. Fellow cops suggested he take up palm reading as a sideline.

"It's a hit alright, boys," Officer Howell had informed detectives working the case on the previous Saturday.

Howell never made a call until he was positive. With confirmation on the two robberies, and now a murder that fit the profile of the Kissing Bandit, Chief Will Kendra ordered Moore's arrest. He didn't want public stirring over two armed robberies to boil into something larger.

Mrs. Moore was shocked when she turned on the porch light and saw two police officers at her front door. She pulled her housecoat tight in a natural move for modesty, not because of any chill. She stepped to the open door and talked through the screen door.

"Good evenin', Mr. Officer," she said in a quiet, steady voice.

She looked them straight in the eye, respectful and not cowering. She had dealings with the police before, the time when Curtis was in trouble, and once when an officer responded to her own complaint. White juveniles had been shouting outside her home late at night, slinging "nigger" this and "nigger" that, a prelude to worse things, she feared.

"Boys will be boys," was the timid response of the officer who was sent on the call. The racist rogues scattered when the patrol car pulled up, but the incident left a sour taste in her mouth, mostly because of the officer's apparent disinterest and prompt dismissal of her concern.

"You are Mrs. Moore?" Jelling inquired.

"I am," she said, pushing the screen door open slightly. "Is there somehow I can help you? It's gettin' on mighty late."

"I know it is, Mrs. Moore," Jelling said, "but we'd like to talk with your son. Is Curtis here?"

"I believe he's upstairs in his bedroom," she said. "What seem to be the problem?"

"If you would please call him down, ma'am, we'll explain the reason for our being here."

"Well, awlright, I suppose. I hope Curtis ain't in some kinda trouble," she said, her voice trailing off as she went back into the house.

Jelling stayed on the front porch and Wilson circled the house to guard the back door. Much to Jelling's surprise and satisfaction, in about a half-minute Curtis Moore and his Mom appeared back at the front door.

It was then that Moore looked at his mother. She immediately read the confession on his face. He looked away.

"Curtis!" Annie demanded. "Look at me. Tell me what this all about, and then explain it to the officer here!"

Her face wrinkled with a mix of worry and budding anger.

Before Curtis could respond, Jelling broke in just as Wilson returned to the front of the home.

"Curtis, would you please step outside," Jelling requested.

"Do as the policeman asks," his mother ordered, and Curtis did. She also stepped outside.

"We're here to arrest you," Jelling looked directly at the young man, "for robberies at the Czech Inn and at the Lincoln Truck Stop in recent weeks, and for tonight's robbery and murder at the Gourmet by George restaurant."

Wilson stepped forward and placed handcuffs on Curtis as his mother looked in shock. Her shaking hands automatically covered her gaping mouth.

Annie had no misconceptions that her son was up for sainthood, that he always toed the line when it came to what was legal and not so. She had been disappointed before. But not this. Murder was a word like cancer. It imparted an immediate, distinctive and ominous sense of horror. She was flabbergasted, and searched his face for an answer to her previous question.

Curtis looked like someone who just touched a live electric wire. His mouth was open, but words struggled to get out. He looked around as if the answer were somewhere in the still night air. Eventually, the wavy lines assaulting his vision leveled off and his mind grasped reality.

"I swear, Mom," he stuttered. "I ain't killed nobody. With Jesus as my witness, I didn't murder nobody."

He looked downward, unable to maintain eye contact with his mother.

Annie shook her black and white hair in rejecting what the officer had said, the words about murder and robbery, and grabbed her son by the arm.

"Curtis, tell me none of this is true," she begged.

"I can't, Mom. I did go to those two places where the officer said, but it was an experiment," Curtis cried. "I meant no harm. I didn't have a gun or nothin'. I wanted to see how people would react if a Negro kissed a white woman. I didn't hurt nobody and I sure didn't kill nobody."

There was suspended silence in the unfolding drama before Curtis spoke again.

Annie looked at him in disbelief. One part of her wanted to take him over her knee and spank him in front of the police, while another part wanted to hug him.

She had had more than her share of life's trials. The diminutive but determined woman suffered a bum husband who was long gone. She loaned a brother a sizeable amount of money at no interest, only he ran off with the whole amount. A close friend was dying of cancer. She had chronic back pain, probably from arthritis, but kept it to herself for fear of losing her job. Her son acted more like a self-pitying teenager than an adult.

And now this.

"Curtis!" she said his name, a mixture of anger and a mother's love. She hugged him. "You say you robbed them places? Officer, he know far better than that, God as my witness. He heard plenty in the Good Book about lyin' and stealin' and cheatin'. He know right from wrong. Son, why? Even your Daddy wouldn't do that. Why? An experiment? Are you crazy?"

"Mom, I's sorry," Curtis said, his forehead wrinkled in remorse. "This fren,' he a student at Coe College, he be studyin' 'bout how Negroes and whites get along, how they interact," Curtis attempted to explain. "He from Chicago. I tell him that Iowa people use the word 'nigger' just like they do in the South, only maybe they whisper it so's to hide their racism. I bet him if I kissed a white woman it would cause as much a stir as down South. It was a experiment."

"Curtis, son, why don't you think these things through? You knew how such an experiment, as you call it, would end."

Annie Pearl Moore shook her head again as if somehow it would produce an answer. A tear slipped from her left eye.

"I'm sorry that Curtis caused problems," she looked sadly at Jelling. "I'm sorry my boy caused you trouble."

"We're sorry, too, Mrs. Moore," Jelling said as his partner took the handcuffed Curtis Moore toward the squad car. "Sometimes young people just don't think. Sometimes they don' think beyond the present."

"I didn't kill nobody, Mom," Curtis said as he was led away.

Chapter 34

Before taking Curtis Moore to the Linn County Jail, Officers Jelling and Wilson directed a barrage of questions at him, including zoning in on his whereabouts several hours earlier. The three were in the booking area on the first floor of the Cedar Rapids Police Department, located on Second Avenue West a few blocks from the river.

The two-story tan brick building was virtually empty of activity. Aside from those in the glass-caged room that also housed dispatch, a single officer in the traffic department was writing out a report outlining the conflicting details of a two-car accident outside the entry to the giant Quaker Oats Co. complex. No other officers, including detectives, had yet returned from the robbery/murder scene.

"You confess to robbing two places, wearing a hooded jacket, dark clothing, kissing a cashier, and then deny the same type of robbery and MO last night?" Wilson said incredulously. "It all fits, Curtis!"

There was momentary break in the questioning before Wilson's capacity for patience was depleted.

"Do you take us for fucking idiots, that two plus two don't equal four?" Wilson cut loose a mixture of interrogation, flying saliva and colorful adjectives.

"That's like trying to explain to your wife that lipstick on your shirt collar, blond hair on your jacket and the clock reading 2 a.m. merely add up to an unusual night at the Rotary meeting."

Moore was in serious trouble. His shaking hands were more evidence of it. He looked down at the drab, worn, gray carpeting.

"What didja say about MO? Who that?" Moore asked meekly, in barely audible tones.

"It's not who. It's what asshole," Wilson shouted. "It means method of operation. In all three instances, witnesses tell us the same thing. Man, about six feet tall, your height, wearing a hooded jacket, smoothly and deliberately asks for cash and upon leaving kisses the female attendant. Sound familiar, Curtis? Does that fit your experiment?"

"I can't deny it, officer," Curtis said. "I did do that at the first two places you mention, but I didn't rob no place last night and didn't kill nobody last night. I swear it."

"Then I suppose you can tell us where you were between the hours of 7 and 9?" Jelling bore in.

Curtis Moore saw the picture developing before his eyes, and it wasn't pretty. He'd already confessed to crimes that looked like first cousins to the one last night. But this wasn't his doing. How could he prove it? He thought, something he should have done, as his mom suggested, long before. His answers wouldn't be convincing. But they were all he had.

"I was jus' messin' round, I guess, first at a pool hall and then at a gas station," Curtis began. "Ended up with some guys, jus' talkin'. Pockets Jones, he called Pockets 'cause he the best pool player east or west of the river, he brought me home, pro'bly roun' 10 o'clock."

Moore's mind was racing in circles, trying to think who else could account for his time in those hours. Other than Pockets, names just didn't surface.

His concentration drifted to a dark spot in the carpeting. Probably some poor bastard who cops had been questioning, and he didn't make it to the bathroom on time.

"You know what, Curtis?" Wilson said. "That all adds up to one significant pile of bullshit. It tells me you have no alibi. We ain't gonna fuck with you any more tonight, but we'll be back tomorrow just like the morning dew. You'll spend the night on a lovely island with wonderful amenities."

"Mr. Officer, if you don't believe me about this all bein' an experiment, just call my fren' up at Coe College," Curtis offered.

"His name is Deron Campbell. He'll tell you. We talked 'bout all this. He a smart fella."

"If he had really been smart," Wilson fired back, "he would have convinced you not to experiment with stupidity. Save him as a character witness at your trial, Curtis. You'll need all the help you can find, only it won't be an experiment."

The Linn County Jail, located on Mays Island in the middle of the Cedar River, was no four-star hotel. Moore would join the many guests of Sheriff Jim Smyth.

Smyth and his wife lived in an apartment at the east end of the lockup. Sheriff for 20 years, he was somewhat of a celebrity. He and his garden next to the jail were the focus for local and national feature stories. His vegetables frequently ended up as part of the inmates' jailhouse menu.

While the jail was only 30 years old, it began to show wear. The heating system didn't always work. There was no air conditioning, and it was not unusual for cells to be damp and putrid. Ventilation was virtually non-existent.

On this muggy August night, Moore would find it downright nasty.

"If you are lucky, Curtis," Wilson continued his badgering, "you'll get a cell near Pal Hinckleman. He likes to talk, even during the night. He likes to talk about terrible things, and with the heat and humidity, you're in for a dissertation on a wide range of ugly subjects. If you're really fortunate, Pal may let you play with his pet cockroach."

The two cops dropped Moore off at the jail, and then headed back to the crime scene. It was well after midnight. There were two other police cars at the restaurant when Jelling and Wilson arrived.

Detective Lt. Louie Byrne was directing the investigation. Byrne had roused Virgil Howell out of an easy chair snooze in front of the TV and brought him to the crime scene. Howell had his fingerprint kit spread out on one of the guest tables up front.

"Hey, Virg," Jelling greeted the fingerprint expert. "When you are done dusting for prints with that big brush, maybe you can give me a shave."

Jelling rubbed his hands over a six o'clock shadow that had grown into an early morning stubble.

"I need to look pretty for when I get home." They both laughed.

"I'm sorry, Charlie," Howell replied. "I jus' don't have enough time to make you look pretty."

That brought an even louder response from those present, and a couple of "Amens."

"Besides, if I brush your face I might find some strange fingerprints on your delicate cheeks," Howell joked. "And if that was the case, I'd be bound to testify about my findings."

"OK, OK, can we trim the persiflage and get down to the nitty-gritty here?" Detective Byrne barked, cooling the tomfoolery.

Byrne was a 25-year veteran on the force. It was not unknown for him to sponsor a few shenanigans of his own, but he also knew when it was time to get down to business.

Byrne was a third-generation cop. There was not much left of his reddish hair, that is to say, white had consumed most of his closely sheared top. He was 5-foot-11, about 185 pounds, and proud that he worked out several times a week at the YMCA. He could handle himself in a fight. But in truth he was a pussycat, the first to come to the aid of someone in need. He spent most Wednesday nights, if he wasn't on duty, serving meals at a downtown walk-in for the poor and homeless.

In Byrnes early years on the force, fellow officers had tagged him with the moniker "Bump." He had a mole above his lips, just below the right side of his nose. It sometimes itched, and he would rub it gently, assuming discrete indifference. But frequently someone would laugh and refer to the "itchy bump." He didn't like it, but it was part of the price of group chemistry.

"Persiflage, detective?" Jelling rejoined. "That sounds like something off the menu here." There were more guffaws.

"I guess that's why they pay you the big money."

Byrne and Jelling walked back through the restaurant to the office where other detectives were busy taking pictures and sizing up the crime scene. Veteran or not, Byrne was visibly shaken by the blood-spattered room. He squinted reflexively, as if to clear away the savageness. The mauling was unlike anything he had ever witnessed; like something you'd expect after a grizzly bear attack.

"I have to think some kind of animal did this," Byrne said to no one in particular. "It's difficult to imagine one human doing this to another human being." No one could add anything. Other than procedural utterances, everyone quietly went about their business in solemn shock. Byrne again looked at the ripped torso and silently said a prayer for the deceased restaurant owner.

Just a few hours ago this man was enjoying life. How can this be? Byrne fought off the impulse to consider that killing was part of man's nature, an inherited trait that was not discarded after the Stone Age. Do we exit our mother's womb with an intrinsic proclivity to harm others? Is the belief of most religions that man is basically good – is that wrong?

"Lieutenant, are you okay?" Jelling inquired.

"What? Oh, yeah. Charlie, would you please make another sweep on the outside of the building," Byrne ordered, "and take one of the young officers with you. Kenny, see if they need any help up front. We have interviewed a dozen or so witnesses, employees and customers, and as you know, they indicate that everything seems to fit with those other two robberies."

"Right," Wilson said. "Except, nobody in those first two cases ended up looking like a Thanksgiving turkey."

Jelling and the rookie cop, Steve Connick, headed out into the cooling night air. It was a welcome relief from the repressive ambiance of the murder scene.

"If this summer weather gets any hotter, I may put in for nights," Jelling told Connick. "Let's give another look at the rear of the building, where the assailant broke in."

They walked around back.

"Shine your light over here at the window," Jelling asked. Both eyeballed the sash.

"See here where he used a small bar to jimmy the window loose?" Jelling pointed.

"I do," Connick said. "Whad'ya suppose he done with the crowbar?"

"Well, he didn't bring it in the building with him," Jelling stated the obvious. "So he must of ditched it somewhere. Let's look around."

They headed for various shrubbery and brush behind the building. It didn't take long for Jelling to spot the black, 20-inch pry bar in a half-dead hedge.

"Well, well, lookie here," Jelling said. Connick went to reach for it.

"Don't touch it with your bare hands," Jelling yelled. "There may be prints on it. We'll tell Howell about it. I think he's still inside."

They continued to search the old alley road and found little of interest other than empty beer bottles, cigarette butts and other trash.

The two were about to turn back toward the building when Jelling shined his flashlight at some small trees further back along the alley.

"What's this? Look here Steve. See these saplings? It looks like a couple of branches have been broken off. I'd say it's fairly recent. The break in the wood looks fresh. What do you think?"

"I'd have to agree," Connick said. "What do you think it means? Is there a connection with the crime?"

"I don't know, but we'll mention it to the detectives. They can check again tomorrow when there's more light. Let's report in to Byrne."

Chapter 35

"Virg, have you had time to run those prints from the restaurant? And did you find any on the pry bar they found outside?"

Detective Byrne shifted into what he called "roundup time," where he pulled in all the information collected so far in a crime investigation and then tried to assemble the jigsaw-like pieces to come up with a partly finished puzzle.

"Not quite, boss," Powell replied, "but I should have a report for you in an hour. Answer to your second question, yeah. There were prints on the pry bar."

"Jelling!" Byrne barked.

"Yes, sir."

"What's your take on Curtis Moore? Did he say much last night when you arrested him? Did he make any attempt to escape? Was he resistant in any way? Feisty?"

"You know the routine, Detective," Jelling responded. "He denied he killed anybody, but then I've never run into anyone accused of murder who confessed on the spot. They are always innocent. He was," Jelling paused. "I would say he was quite adamant that he didn't kill anyone."

"Did he resist, threaten you?" Byrne asked.

"No, he didn't."

"Was there any problem at all in making the arrest?" Byrne persisted.

"There was none," Jelling replied. "We rang the doorbell. His mother answered. We asked to see Moore. She went to get him, and they both showed up at the front door."

"In your professional opinion, did he act like a killer?"

"That's hard to say, sir. He just said he didn't kill anyone."

"What about the first two robberies?" Byrne asked, flipping through interview notes. "According to your report, he confessed to those up front. Is that right?"

"Yes, it is."

"So he confessed to the robberies at Kreiji's and West Side, but not the one at the Gourmet restaurant?"

"That's correct."

"Jelling, do you find that unusual?" Byrne asked, rubbing the mole on his cheek. "He confesses to two crimes, but not the third?"

"No, I don't," said Jelling. "The last one involves murder. There's a big difference between serving 10 to 20 and hanging at the end of a rope."

"You are absolutely right." Byrne looked down at his clipboard and then glanced around the room. "Wilson? Where's Wilson?"

"He's home," Jelling replied, "getting some sleep."

"Get him down here. This is no Cinderella operation. He can sleep later."

Chief Kendra walked into the review room. He was accompanied by Jim Busman of the county attorney's office.

"How we doing here, Bump?" Kendra inquired.

The chief was the only person in the department who wasn't shy in calling Byrne "Bump." Perhaps, Byrne thought, it was the chief's way of saying he was the chief. Byrne didn't like the nickname, and professional protocol demanded he be addressed as lieutenant from equals or less. He detested the alliterative "Bump Byrne," and once called out an assistant chief who had used that combination. That little scene made the hallway rounds and hadn't been heard since.

"We have a man in custody, I know," Kendra said. "How did the interviews at the restaurant go?"

"We're still talking to some people, Chief, and Virg is processing the fingerprint stuff, but we should have most of the dangling details wrapped up this morning," Byrne replied. "Then it's just a case of getting it all in order and see if the pieces fit. We're finding that the description of the suspect given by restaurant patrons is similar to that in the first two robberies, and so is the MO and demeanor of the subject, but you knew that."

"You don't sound convinced," Kendra said.

"Well, there are subtle differences," Byrne noted, his hands spread outward to convey his thoughts.

"The suspect from the robbery and murder last night seems to have had a deeper voice. Most characterize it as bass-toned, more like Ezio Pinza than say Robert Merrill. The voice in the other cases was described as more baritone or even tenor. Last night's suspect, in my mind's eye after listening to the interview tapes, is slightly bigger in the shoulders."

"Holy Moses, Byrne!" Kendra said. "Didn't know you were an expert on classical voice. Do you direct the choir at church? Or do you just specialize in how suspects sing?"

"Funny, Chief. No, I don't direct the choir or sing. If I did, I'm afraid the congregation would leave. But voice can be a good identifier."

"Voice IDs can be tricky," Kendra said. "Head colds. Time of day. Proximity to the last drink, especially something hot like coffee."

"Oh, you're right about that, Chief," Byrne nodded, "but Miss Mallory, the cashier at Gourmet by George, said she smelled no coffee on the man's breath when he kissed her. Instead, she recalled this morning that there was a minty smell to his breath, perhaps like Wrigley's Spearmint chewing gum, to use her words."

"She has quite a keen memory."

"Last night she could barely talk she was so shocked," Byrne informed Kendra. "She also noted today that he kissed her on the left cheek."

"And that's significant?"

"Don't know, but Dorothy Dotson in the Kreiji robbery was kissed on the right cheek."

"And the lady in the truck stop robbery? Where was she kissed, and did she smell minty gum?"

"We aren't sure. We're double checking."

"I never thought I'd live to learn that kissing is a crime," Kendra said in a departing crack.

The laughter of those in the room was shut down by Byrne's order for the team to get back to work.

"Jelling," Byrne requested, looking as if a light bulb just went on above his head. "Go down to the radio room and check through old teletypes and fliers to see if there has been a stabbing, a vicious stabbing murder, anywhere else in the last year. Especially in the Midwest. Get someone to help you sift through the file."

"You mean the National Crime Information Center reports?" Jelling asked.

"Yes, those, and perhaps the FBI circulars."

"What's on your mind, lieutenant?"

"Jelling, you saw that mangled body of the restaurant owner," Byrne said slowly, thinking out loud. "It's difficult to believe that robbery was the only motive in this killing. You don't use a howitzer to rob a hot dog vendor. This murder had meaning, it seems to me, involving more than a few bucks out of the cash register. There was a message in the mauling. The profound depravity here is signature."

Byrne let his appraisal of the murder dangle in reflective calculation.

"I see where you are coming from," Jelling said.

Others in the room nodded assent.

"Also, dig deeper into the restaurant guy's background," Byrne continued. "What did George Dawson do before he sold pasta and Italian wine?"

"Boss, does kissing on the right cheek mean the suspect is right-handed?" Jelling inquired.

"Interesting question," Byrne muttered. "Radio the officer who is re-interviewing people out at the truck stop. Have him ask the lady, I guess she would be the kissee, if she was kissed on the right cheek."

Five seconds passed.

"Oh, and if she smelled minty gum on the kisser's breath."

Byrne scratched his chin as if it were a source of probing powers. Then, seeking additional reflective energy, he again rubbed the mole on his cheek.

Those in the room were waiting for his words of wisdom, pearls of police hypothesis. This case was taking on more peculiar elements than a Halloween vampire movie.

"Do you people remember that Nylon Stocking Caper pulled off by the Little Old Lady from Cottage Grove Lane?" Byrne asked those in the room, but received no response. "Well, this 87-year-old woman, very wealthy, a couple years ago walked into the Me-Too supermarket one Saturday night and while grocery shopping stuffed several Hanes stocking containers inside her blouse.

"Store clerks spotted her and called police," Byrne went on. "She had never been arrested for anything before."

"She didn't exactly commit murder," Jelling jumped in. "What did she get? Twenty years at hard labor?"

"No. No," Byrne answered, slightly miffed that Jelling didn't appreciate the analogy. "The judge gave her a deferred sentence. It's just that weird things happen in this business.

"Kissing," he said, shaking his head. "And gum. Unbelievable! This is one the station wags will be chewing on for a long time."

Chapter 36

Tuesday morning had afforded no early commune with nature's tranquility for Roy Sanders.

A walking zombie the night before, Roy didn't sleep well after his meeting with the Motel Sepia's late-night guest. He sat at the kitchen table, staring at his coffee. There was something about this man that generated questions. Businessman? Wearing a baseball t-shirt? Arriving after 11 p.m.? The brusque demeanor. He had mentioned all this to Lillian last night, but she was half asleep and little of it registered.

Mix all this with the fact a murder and robbery occurred hours before, only a couple miles down the road, and you have reasons for a sense of discomfit and churning stomach.

Roy refilled his coffee cup and wished he had made it stronger. He turned on the 7 a.m. news out of habit and was greeted by a Smulekoff furniture store ad about the comfort of Ethan Allen sofas, but it didn't relax any part of his anxious anatomy.

He stuck his nose out the front door long enough to conclude that August 30 would be cooler, a definite sign that the heat wave had run its course. But his mind was preoccupied by late night scenes of an unexpected and grumpy guest.

"And a great Tuesday morning to all of you," Howdy Roberts pronounced in his signature deep voice. Roberts helped wake up Iowans with his "Musical Clock" show on WMT radio. In addition to playing pop tunes, Roberts regularly introduced the station's farm news director, Chuck Worcester, and morning news announcer Bob Bruner.

In Iowa, the world could be coming to an end, but all that would wait for weather information. Weather was the irrefutable first news. And so it was that Roberts dutifully read the predicted temperatures and prospects for rain. A cooler day is what everyone wanted, and Roberts gleefully delivered a forecast that accommodated. Now, for other news and he handed the mike to Bruner.

Not surprisingly, his lead story was about last night's robbery and murder at the Gourmet by George restaurant, which happened to be one of the station's advertisers.

Police had issued the barest of information about the murder, none of the gory details of how George Dawson died. Dawson was identified as the victim, but there was no information how he was killed. Moreover, the police statement said an arrest had already been made in the case.

Roy was surprised, and vastly relieved.

"Police," the announcer said, "believe that the alleged killer is the same man who robbed two other restaurants in the city earlier this month. As in the first two cases, the assailant wore a hooded jacket, a face covering of some kind and gave a goodbye kiss to the female cashier after taking her money. The woman, according to reports, was not injured.

"Charged around midnight last night with murder and armed robbery is Curtis Lee Moore, 22, of Cedar Rapids," the announcer said. "Moore is being held in the Linn County Jail without bond. We'll have more details on this heinous crime as they become available. In other news, the Iowa Farm Bureau –"

Roy ran upstairs. Lillian was getting dressed.

"Lillian," he said in a half whisper, "I just heard on the early news that police made an arrest in last night's murder at the restaurant. You can't imagine what a big relief that is. I was going half-crazy after that guy came into our place late last night. I actually – Lillian, are you listening? Did you hear what I said last night when I came to bed?"

"Sort of," she answered.

She was still only half out of sleep, similar to her state last night of being half into sleep.

"Somethin' about a business man wantin' a room and wearin' a St. Louis Cardinals t-shirt. What in God's name was that all about, Roy? I do remember tellin' you to quiet up and get to bed."

"Lillian!" He reached out with both arms, put them on her shoulders, and gave a gentle shake. "Look at me."

She did.

"Good," Roy sighed. "What I was tryin' to tell you then and I am tellin' you now is that I thought this fellow who checked in around 11 could be the man who killed the restaurant owner. He jus' seemed strange, like he was wrapped in a foreboding bubble."

There was silence.

"Did you hear what I said?"

"Yeah, I heard you, Roy. Bubble? Just because a guest comes in late, I don't see how you can jump to the conclusion that he is a bad person. Any number of reasons why he's late. Other motels full. Miscalculated mileage. Got a late start. Who knows?"

"Well, I don't think you get the picture, Lillian. This guy made me uncomfortable. But now the radio says they have arrested someone in that murder and robbery, and I take great comfort in that."

"Comfort?" Lillian responded with her voice on the upscale. "A person is dead. Lives are disrupted."

"Yes, Lillian. Comfort for me in knowing that we aren't housin' a killer."

"You've always had a great imagination, Roy, but this time I think you let it run down the road a little too far." Lillian gave him one of her patented looks. "What it does mean is that we can tell our guests they are free to leave this mornin'."

"Well, not until we hear from Deputy Weber," Roy said. "Weber said that guests should stay until noon and that he may want to talk to some of them."

"I don't see what for," Lillian said as she headed downstairs pulling on her housecoat and giving a big yawn. "An arrest has been made. Why should our guests have to hold up their travels? Makes no sense."

"Maybe not," said Roy, as he warmed up his Folgers. "If I don't hear from Weber by mid-mornin', I'll give him a call."

He finished his breakfast and headed outside to attend to the day's chores. Part of the wood fence along the highway needed repair. Two

1x8 inch white boards hung on short 4x4 posts to form the decorative fencing. One of the boards had come loose and sagged to the ground.

Lillian enjoyed breakfast and a smidgen of peace before the kids and hotel duties took over.

Around 8:30 a.m., Ben and Ann Dolan returned from a walk down Bertram Road. Ann was a devout walker. She proselytized the benefits of an early-morning walk, not the least being how it cleaned out the overnight cobwebs. Ben argued that cleaning out the hog pen had the same effect. He said he absorbed enough exercise just in the ordinary course of farming and didn't need to put more mileage on his body.

On this day, to avoid a sermon, he joined his wife in a one-mile trek.

"Fixing fence, I see," Ben greeted Roy. "That seems to be a never-ending job on a farm. Some say good fences make good neighbors. Others say fences put up barriers to friendship. I do know fences keep the neighbor's bull away from our heifers, and that –"

He was cut off in mid-sentence by Ann.

"I'm not sure Mr. Sanders is interested in the fate of your heifers," she said with intent to redirect the conversation. "I must say that walking down your road is a delight, a mixture of cool morning air, shade from so many trees and the sounds of all the birds. Ben identified a bald eagle. We saw a fox and heard a pheasant. It was like going to the zoo."

"And we saw and smelled ragweed," Ben tossed in with demon delight. "Enough to keep allergists in business for years!"

"Now, Ben," she cooed. "Be like Bing Crosby and the Andrew Sisters. Accentuate the positive," she said referring to the song. "Don't be Mr. In Between."

Roy laughed at the couple's back-and-forth bantering, evidence, he thought, of a man and woman confident of who they are and where they're at.

"Speakin' of Mr. In Between," Roy told the couple, "I gotta admit that's where I was last night. Had this car pull up outside the office around 11, just as I was headin' for bed."

He retold how the last-minute guest was gruff and made it sound as if he had horns coming out of his head.

"With all the talk 'bout that robbery and murder a few miles down the road and Deputy Weber askin' to be on the lookout for anythin' unusual, I have to admit I was concerned. I didn't sleep all night."

"You seem somewhat relaxed this morning," Ben offered.

"For good reason," Roy replied. "The news this mornin' quoted police sayin' they have already made an arrest. Seems like they caught up with the same guy who robbed two other places. I can tell you, it was a big relief."

"That's wonderful news," Ann said with a gleeful tone. "I'm sure the entire community is glad to hear that. What an awful thing, Roy, a town coping with a murder. I'll have to say I was uneasy, too, after the sheriff came by last night. Ben, that means we can get on our way. I'll go tell Caroline and Matt."

"Well, I think we need to wait until we hear from the sheriff's office," Roy said reluctantly. "I'm sorry, but Sgt. Weber asked us to hold tight 'til he called. I hate seein' you people bogged down here, but I'll tell you what. If he doesn't call by 10, I'll call him. Does that sound OK?"

"That will be fine," Ben answered. "We'll get everything packed. I must tell you, Roy, unlike yourself, I slept like a log. I don't think I rolled in any direction all night long."

"You had to say that, didn't you?" Ann frowned.

"What?" Ben answered with a tone of proffered innocence.

Chapter 37

By nine a.m., most of the other lodgers had emerged from their cabins.

Without formality or direction, chairs were arranged in some semblance of a circle out front on the Motel Sepia lawn. A few were placed in full shade and others where there was a dapple of morning sun. It was almost as if some undefined spirit was convening a mid-morning social séance, except there was no paranormal agenda.

Ben and Ann had spotted the others, and spontaneously invoked back yard protocol. One by one, motel guests drifted toward the outdoor roundtable like cautious shoppers drawn to a sale. It was this unspoken sign of invitation and acceptance that pulled them together. Black people, white people, farmers, a school administrator, nurse, housewives, a mortician and an insurance salesman.

Aside from their humanity, they held the common role of traveler – delayed traveler.

"Good mornin' ya'll," Vernon Taylor injected his southern drawl into the pleasant Iowa day. "Trust everybody slept well despite the news of last night. I know I sure did. Ida and me was wonderin' how long it'll be before we can be on our way. There's fish in Minnesota waitin' to run onto my hook."

"Yes, I hope we get the green light before long," Harold Erickson tossed in with benign assent. He was sporting a cap with the Wisconsin Mutual logo.

"Need to fill up the Mercury with gas before we get too far down the road," he offered as conversation filler.

"Interesting," said Matt Kilburn, without elaboration.

"What, pray tell, do you find interesting?" Caroline inquired.

She was dressed in a pale pink skirt and white top, with a matching pink ribbon corralling her ponytail.

"Well," Matt gestured, "here's Harold and Monica, Wisconsin people headed south, and Vernon and Ida, southern people headed north."

"Yes, and the point is?" Caroline asked.

"No point, I guess," Matt said sheepishly. "Just interesting. Should be a lot cooler up in Minnesota," he changed gears and picked up on Mr. Taylor's fishing fantasy.

"Have you ever tried night fishing?" Matt asked. "We seem to have better luck, even in Minnesota, going out after 8. Lake has usually calmed down by then and the sunsets are fabulous. Soon after that, you get a songfest from the loons and on a clear night the entire sky opens up. If you are real lucky, you may get to see a big light show – the Northern Lights. It's like cathedral heaven."

He reflected on such celestial wonderment.

"Saves you the time of reading the Bible."

"Don't know 'bout that, Mr. Matt," Vernon laughed, "but it sounds mighty appealin'. But after all that sunset, all that loon singin' and star shinin', do the fish bite? That's the important part."

"Can't argue there," Matt said. "Sometimes they do, and sometimes they don't. Sometimes all you catch is the other guy's line. Seems my best success is a fat leech on a hook decorated with a red and white spinner."

"Don't get Vernon talkin' fishin' or we'll be in a boat all mornin'," Ida implored.

She stepped into the prattle sporting a simple yet attractive red dress. A wide belt, a deeper red, wrapped snuggly around her trim figure. Her coal black hair was rolled up in a big forehead curl.

"One way to shut off Vernon's fishin' talk is to mention the times he came home empty-handed," Ida quipped.

Her comment cast an end to fishing talk like a northeast cold front shuts down hungry walleye.

Lillian eased into the assembled chatter, a tray of kolaches in hand. Her flowered housedress was graced by a fancy white apron. Roy was close behind with two pots of coffee. Their son, Joseph, unconcerned about the rip in his denim overalls, trailed with a basket of cups and acting as if they were lead bricks.

"Good morning everyone," she said. "Don't you be dropping those," Lillian coached Joseph. "And, you forgot the napkins."

She placed the tray of fruit-adorned pastry on a table. Roy nodded to guests and parked the coffee containers on the ground beneath the table. He then retreated for the napkins, knowing Joseph would ignore the hint from his mother.

"Please," Lillian invited the guests while pointing to the pastry, "and be prepared for an exceptional treat. You can't stop in Cedar Rapids without sampling our famous kolaches. There's an assortment of fillings, cherry – just for you Matt – and apricot, blueberry and prune, all fresh from yesterday's baking at St. Ludmila's church kitchen."

"This is so kind of you Lillian, and unexpected," Viola pronounced.

There was a chorus of agreement and thank yous. It wasn't standard fare, but considering the previous night's news and delay, Lillian decided it would make conditions more acceptable.

"Can I have one with the big raisins?" Joseph beseeched.

"Those are prunes, son, and yes, you may have one. The Czechs," Lillian explained, "are famous for their kolaches, and sometimes I think the ladies from St. Ludmila and St. Wenceslaus parishes are competing for the town kolache crown. Help yourselves."

Two minutes later Roy arrived with the napkins. He asked who wanted coffee and heard no refusals.

While pouring, he deemed it a good time to inform everyone on the latest developments in last night's robbery and murder and the subsequent arrest. In a calculated attempt to soften reality, he substituted the terms murder and robbery with "events."

"Some of you already know the mornin' news about events from last night," Roy began. "Some don't. So, I'll repeat what I heard on the radio. Police late last night arrested a local man for the crimes. Said the fella was the same person who robbed two other eatin' places in the last coupl'a weeks. I'll say this much. It brought sunshine to my day."

"You mean we can leave now?" Harold said hopefully.

"Well, like I says to Ben here," Roy answered, "I think it's best if everyone wait until we hear from Deputy Weber. But if he don't call by 10, I'll give the sheriff's office a ring. Sure hate to hold up people from getting' on the road, and delay Vernon's limit of walleyes."

That detail taken care of, Roy continued to fill coffee cups.

He was delighted to hear the conversations among guests evolve. Old comfort zones seemed to gradually give way to new relationships. They may not become close friends, Roy thought, but they had become friendly. The hesitations and uneasiness of the night before seemed to melt in front of his eyes.

More small steps, Roy chuckled internally, satisfied with his cultural maneuvers. "More small steps," he said, only this time he couldn't restrain his joy.

"What did you say, Roy?" Caroline turned her ear in his direction.

"Oh, sorry, Mrs. Kilburn," Roy said. "I was just mumblin' to myself 'bout havin' to take more steps to get all my chores done today. Lillian has another long list of things to do."

Caroline quickly returned to her conversation with Ida. After an exchange of cursory family information and vacation plans, Ida conveyed her worry about events in Mississippi. She explained the growing racial strife and that she was anxious to hear the latest news about the disappearance of Emmett Till.

Caroline said she was unaware of who Till was, and sought the complete story. She was shocked by the information of Till's kidnapping and the burning racial climate in Mississippi. Ida had told all she knew about Till's case.

"I apologize for not being more aware of conditions in your state and not knowing of the Till matter," Caroline said. "I'm sure your son Will is fine and that your parents know how to handle things."

She patted Ida's arm as a comforting gesture and then thought to herself that she'd never made such a show of concern to a colored person before. She'd never sat down and talked, really talked, with a Negro before.

"We can only pray that things will improve," Caroline added, "all over our country." There was a long pause.

"This Emmett Till matter is so sad." Caroline shook her head. "To kidnap a 14-year old boy for, for what? Maybe he whistled at a white woman?"

Roy had been listening to the talk of the Till case.

"Mrs. Taylor, Mrs. Kilburn, you may be interested to know they have arrested two men in the Till boy's disappearance," Roy said.

"They have?" Ida said with surprise. "Excuse me a second."

She tried to get her husband's attention.

"Vernon! Vernon!" she yelled.

Vernon had been listening to Matt's revived epistle on Minnesota fishing. He looked in the direction of his wife. The others did, too.

"Vernon, Mr. Sanders says that they have made arrests in the Emmett Till case," Ida proclaimed. "Isn't that right, Mr. Sanders?"

"Yes. As I was telling Mrs. Taylor and Mrs. Kilburn, the CBS news reported this mornin' that two white men have been charged with kidnappin' the Till boy. Seems they came in the middle of the night, early Sunday mornin', and took him from his uncle's house at gunpoint. One of the men told the sheriff down there that the boy was released, but he hasn't been seen anywhere. They are still lookin' for him."

"That's good news about the arrests, but it will be better news when the young fella shows up," Vernon said to no one in particular.

He was hoping the arrest information would help settle Ida's nerves. He silently acknowledged that with two white men in jail and the boy still missing that tensions were not likely to fade, but intensify. And if young Till were found dead, well, who knows what would happen then.

"Anyone want more coffee?" Roy asked.

A few raised their cups in answer.

"Mr. Sanders, what did the radio say about the weather?" Ben inquired. "It seems like both the temperature and humidity have improved from yesterday."

Weather and its changeability, Roy thought, seem to be the universal grease for discussion, at least among men. Sports may be a close second. Both transcend race, religion, age, political party and any other cultural contrast. He was happy with that, happy for any communication between whites and blacks.

"Oh, yes. The weather. It is better," Roy said, "and from what I heard the heat spell is over. Imagine, coolin' off and no storms with it. There's no rain predicted. At least not for Cedar Rapids."

"Actually, we could use some rain," said Ben. "The corn has tasseled, and rain always helps fill out the ears. But I think we'll have a good crop. Do they grow much corn in Mississippi, Mr. Taylor?"

"Some, but down home it's mostly cotton," Vernon responded. "Our gumbo seems more suited for that. But there is a young fella, a 4-H boy up near Tupelo who's experimentin' with fertilizers. Says he's gonna break world corn records. Claims he will get over 300 bushel per acre. Can you imagine that?"

"Well," said Ben, "if he does that it'll be big news. I better get his name so he can speak at our next Farm Bureau meeting. That kind of production is unheard of."

"Maybe you have better weather down there," Matt glanced over at his brother-in-law. "Sure can't be they have better farmers in Mississippi. It's the weather, ain't that right, Ben?" Ben braced himself for an in-law jab.

"Ya take ole Ben, here," Matt continued. "Nobody watches more weather reports than he does. Even though we're going on vacation, Ben needs to know about the weather. He listens to weather reports in the morning and at noon, and watches TV weather at night. That's what he'll tell you, that he's always up on the weather. The truth, I'm told, is that he falls asleep at the ten o'clock weather and snores at the TV test pattern for an hour."

"Matt, you ever think of trying out for TV comedy?" Ben tossed back. "May do better at that than raising corn."

George laughed. He enjoyed such exchanges, especially between relatives.

"Say, fellas," George's impish side surfaced. "Maybe we or Mr. Sanders should invite that newlywed couple out for morning tea." His graying eyebrows wiggled up and down like dancing caterpillars.

That produced an interspersed mixture of laughs and dubious reaction.

"I can just see the covers flyin' when we knock on the door," George hooted. "Rap, rap. 'Be right there,' a sheepish soprano voice would say. 'Just a minute please while we, ah, while we find the key.'"

"Oh, take your time," George cackled, concluding his vicarious dialogue.

George was his own biggest fan, applauding his ad lib scene. He grabbed his sides and laughed, then slapped his knee for punctuation. Viola was less enthusiastic.

"You want to do a U-turn to California, George?" Viola rejoined. "We can do without the crude attempt at humor."

Among his many talents, George was a quick read.

"Vernon, how big is Belzoni, and what's the main business?" George asked, averting further collisions with Viola.

"Oh, I 'spect 'bout forty-five hundred people," Vernon said. "There's a half- dozen cotton gins in town. I think Clower's is the biggest. Most of the cotton is still hand-picked. Nasty work. Pickin' already started. When they compress that cotton, after removin' the seed, it comes out in 500-pound bales. They have smaller bales, too, ones they ship directly to cloth manufacturers."

"Any of them clothing companies in Belzoni?" George inquired.

"Well, they have a place that makes jockey underwear, but they hire mostly white people. Belzoni a pretty segregated place. Your Viola, she from Tennessee, I understand. You get down there often?"

"Maybe once a year we see Viola's kin," George said. "She got an uncle who can hang in there with the best of the yakkers and jivers. He's about as handy with a jibe as Bud Abbot is with a straight line. Uncle Moses – they call him that because he looks older than Moses – says to me after we've been visiting a couple days, he says, 'Remember, George, Santa Claus has the right idea.'"

"What's that, Uncle Moses?" I ask.

"Visit people for a brief time once a year.'"

George laughed and slapped his knee, and Ben and the other men couldn't help but join in the silliness.

Viola was less entertained. She had long accused George of having a condescending attitude about her family. She hesitated to bring it up in mixed company, but only for few seconds.

"Now, George," she began. He knew that constituted a prelude to a lecture. "Don't you be sayin' mean things about my Uncle Moses. Like I told you before, meanness doesn't just happen overnight. And you shouldn't be gossipin' 'bout my relations."

"Vi, that's not mean. I admire your Uncle Moses. You know I admire all your kinfolk. Uncle Moses and I are as close as 99 is to a hundred."

That sent up renewed laughter. George was on a roll.

"Gossip, you say? I rest my case by quoting Viola herself. I've heard her say to her friends, more than once, 'What's the good of knowing something if you can't repeat it?'"

George McDowell was flirting with a U-turn.

"Uncle Moses liked to brag about his chili," George continued, encouraged by his audience. "Said he was the best chili maker in Tennessee. Claimed he could make chili that would remove the focus from your eyeballs."

"Mr. McDowell, did you say you were a school principal in Chicago?" Monica asked, giving George an avenue away from trouble.

"That's right. This will be my fourth year as principal."

"I'll bet your sense of humor serves you well in school administration," Monica said.

"It sure does, Mrs. Erickson. When you try to please students, teachers, parents and the school board, it takes creative dancing. Like waltzin' on a bed of glass."

"What gets under your skin most?" Harold wanted to know.

"That's an interesting question, Harold," George grinned. "How much time do you have?"

That brought a new round of laughter.

"Come to think of it, I'd have to mention two things," George explained, shifting to a serious side. "The first involves people who jump to conclusions.

"Like the parent who complained to the school board because his son didn't make the honors squad. Said the teacher had it in for his son. We had to prove that the young man failed to show up for class on the day a required paper was due. Then this fellow, like a grasshopper who flings himself with abandon into a pen of chickens, suggests the lad wasn't told of the assignment.

"When informed his son was one of the students who handed out instructions pertainin' to the assignment, this fellow says maybe his son forgot to give himself one of the outlines. Good thing it's against the rules for a principal to bash a parent.

"But worse than that, far worse I believe, is stereotyping – in school, everywhere. It happens all the time, even in novels and movies. Negroes are lazy. In Chicago, Poles are dumb, Italians are crooks and, Mr. Dolan, you probably know this, the Irish are all drunks."

The litany produced abounding silence. It was a point in the interaction where thoughts and impressions meandered among the small gathering like motorists looking for a parking spot, a place to settle into, a place to fit. Ben broke the contemplation.

"I think you could add the notion of some city dwellers that farmers are backward and uneducated." That gave the group more to chew on.

"I'm surprised, Mr. McDowell, that you didn't mention segregation in answer to Harold's question," Ben said. "Mr. Taylor tells me that in Mississippi there are all forms of segregation, in schools and other public places."

"True enough," George concurred. "Not so much in Chicago. But I can see the day when segregation will run out of a legal leg to stand on. I can see the day when Jim Crow and all of his friends will be little more than bad memories. It's in the hearts of people where hatred and stereotyping will survive," he said. "God only knows for how long."

The words filtered through their minds, finding pathways guided by individual experience. They locked on all manner of personal history. It seemed as if they carried extra meaning having been uttered among a mixed assembly beneath the trees of Motel Sepia. It was an unexpected side trip for many of these travelers. It was a time, albeit a brief time, that most would remember all their lives.

Viola broke the meditation.

"George," she probed with an almost hushed inquiry, "when do you suppose you will run out of jokes about my relatives?"

He was speechless. Harold and Vernon failed to control their snickering. Some looked away to disguise their smiles.

Friendly chatter continued to kindle a warm atmosphere among these traveling strangers. Within 20 minutes, they had removed some of the masks of discomfort and uncertainty, and cautiously revealed a part of who they were. Skin color faded as they looked each other in the eye and listened to each other's stories.

Suddenly, the discussion and discovery was interrupted by the bang of a cabin screen door. A muscular man walked slowly toward the group.

Chapter 38

Roy Sanders eyed the approaching guest, the man who arrived late Monday night, and intuitively decided to walk forward to meet him feeling a little as if this was the OK Corral at high noon. Clearly, he was still not comfortable with this fellow.

The man was dressed in a three-piece tan suit. Its look of luxury gave credence to his claim as a businessman bound for a meeting. The white shirt, dark brown tie with narrow green stripes and brown wing-tips expanded his corporate appearance, and would ordinarily ease misgivings.

Roy half wondered if all that finery concealed sidearms.

Daytime also revealed what was hidden by the shadows of night. The man's bulbous, pinkish nose had cheap whiskey inscribed on it. At least, that's how Roy read it. It seemed to clash with his dapper attire.

"Good mornin', Mr. Brown," Roy offered his hand in greeting.

There was neither a corresponding salutation nor extended hand. Brown's eyes, fixed and hard, transmitted a coolness that produced chills on an otherwise warm, summer's day. The veins in his stubby neck seemed as if they wanted to burst free of his confining, buttoned-down collar.

Ears that seemed too small hung on the side of his skull like ornaments. His large head was planted on broad shoulders. Roy glanced at the molded flat top, a stubble field of hair that stood at attention like a miniature bed of nails.

If he head-butted you, Roy thought, it could be fatal. Moreover, he had the feeling that Mr. Brown would take great pleasure in killing you with his hair if not that hidden snub-nose revolver. His suspicions reignited. While he scolded himself for such rambling, paranoid notions, the kind of prejudgment he often condemned, his sixth sense worked overtime.

The color of the man's hair was a sickening yellowish-blond, as if it had been dipped into a vat of Pall Mall dregs. The man's mane was as distracting as his scowl. Follicles were lined up in rows, held erect by some sort of wax and as orderly as a Nazi parade.

To anyone's assessment, this was an immense and powerful man.

"When are we going to be able to leave?" the man asked in a quiet, level tone, but with underlining disdain.

In the far north Midwest sky, scattering puffs of cottony clouds began to interrupt the vast blue dome, a blemish to its pureness. Savvy weather watchers could detect the marks of a developing front. Though a little cooler and less humid, summer held tight to its job of putting finishing touches on the farm products of the plains.

But in the shade-dabbled lawn outside the cabins of Motel Sepia, Roy wondered if a different kind of storm was brewing. He gathered his bearings.

"Well, the deputy sheriff requested last night that guests remain until noon," Roy answered. "He suggested officers may come back to determine if we had heard or seen anything that might help them with the investigation. But –"

"And did you?" Brown's eyes smashed into Roy's.

A lot was being communicated without a lot being said.

"And did I what?" Roy replied with full understanding.

"Did you or any of the others see or hear anything?"

"I don't think so," Roy said cautiously. "Truth is we didn't talk about it much. As I was about to say, and told the others, the radio news this morning said someone had been arrested for last night's robbery and murder. I think that eased everyone's mind, and not a lot more was said about the events."

"What do you think?" the man asked with piercing exactness.

"'Bout what, Mr. Brown?"

Roy was a man who by nature sought to round the rough edges of conversation, smooth out any sharp turns of discourse. Still, he wasn't going to submit to any po' Negro role of a doormat to be stepped on.

"What is it that's on your mind Mr, Brown?"

Brown backed off.

"I'm happy to hear they arrested someone," he said. "But I'd like to be on my way."

Brown's cement truck face suddenly softened. It displayed more of a winning sneer than a joyous smile. The flat lines in his brow relaxed and curved into a semblance of relief. For a few seconds, Roy mused and took comfort. Brown looked like a regular human being on his way to a business meeting.

"I suggested to our other guests," Roy said, "that if I didn't hear from the sheriff's office by 10 o'clock, I would call to see if everyone could leave."

"And you are going to do that now?"

"I can," Roy said, still uneasy. "It's nearly 10."

"Good," Brown said. "I'll be waiting in the cabin." He turned and walked away.

"Hey, Roy!" Matt yelled as Sanders returned to the assembled guests. "We are planning to take Highway 30 east to New York City. Is that what you would recommend?"

"Yeah, I think so."

Roy was still trying to rinse Brown's rigid hair and riveting eyes out of his mind.

"Excuse me, Mr. Kilburn. I have to make a call to the sheriff's office. Check to see if you all can leave."

George McDowell was ready with advice on directions eastward.

"I think you could take the Lincoln Highway to Pittsburgh and then hop on the Pennsylvania Turnpike, if you don't mind paying a toll. Least for a while. When you get to Harrisburg, you might want to take U.S. 22 for the trip into New York. Else, Route 30 will take you into Philly. Best to avoid that, unless you want to see the Liberty Bell."

Ben, thumbs stuck in his beltline, gave a pensive look.

"Oh-oh," Matt groaned, reading Ben's pondering expression with a dire interpretation. "Let's not get ole Ben off the beaten path. Next thing you know he'll want to stop at some museum that claims to have the world's biggest spittoon, or a house made entirely of ear's wax. Once off the farm, he's a nomad type."

"Kinda like Ben Franklin, eh?" George laughed.

"Hadn't thought about swinging through Philadelphia," Ben said. "Give us a dose of liberty and freedom before we're bound up by all that New York shopping and entertainment stuff."

"I hear you," George said. "I enjoyed Philadelphia more than New York when we were out East."

"Guess we don't think much about liberty these days, not like during the war," Ben said. "I mean, World War II."

"Ya'll lost a son in the war, Matt tells me," Vernon looked at Ben. "I'm sorry to hear that."

Ben stared at the ground. He wished he hadn't mentioned the war. He and Ann didn't solicit sympathy and really didn't like talking about Brad's death.

"Yes, we did. He was killed in France, along with thousands of others."

There was another lull in the conversation.

"I imagine the word 'liberty' goes begging for a Negro in Mississippi," Harold looked to Vernon for a response.

Vernon didn't reply, but Ida did.

"When I was in seventh grade in Mississippi," she said, looking into the eyes of those surrounding her, "we said prayers and Pledge of Allegiance every morning before school started. Right there in the Pledge of Allegiance, it says 'liberty and justice for all.' It doesn't say for some. It says for all."

The picture in her mind was that of a small country school in the depths of rural Mississippi. There were no white students. Whites had their own school.

"I knew those words weren't true for me, but I felt they had potential. Someday." She glanced at her husband. "I guess we's still waitin' for someday."

"Have there been many improvements since you were a child?" Ann inquired, her mellow voice imploring a positive answer.

"Oh sure, there are a lot of fine white folk in Mississippi," Ida said. "We have a few white friends. But that's in private. In public, Negro and white don't mix. We drink from public water fountains labeled 'Colored.' Same with restrooms at gas stations. Separate. When I shop for a hat, I'm careful to only look, and not handle. If the hat touches my head, the clerk says I have to buy it.

"I have a friend who volunteered for the United Way couple years ago. She and other Negroes couldn't attend plannin' meetin's with white people," Ida continued. "Had to have a separate meetin'. After a fuss was made by some of the whites, coloreds were allowed in the same room the nex' year, but had to sit in the back row."

"It ain't just Mississippi, Ida," Vernon noted with emphasis. "I don't know the situation today, but a few years back Negro servicemen had separate places in El Paso bars and theaters. I doubt it's changed much. They could serve their country, serve along a white man, but couldn't drink with him. I know a white man from Jackson who became friends with a Mississippi Negro while in basic training in Texas. When they went to a movie, the Negro had to sit in the balcony."

"I'm sorry for your treatment, Mr. and Mrs. Taylor," Ann said.

Ann spoke softly, but always commanded attention, as much or more than a person who raised their voice. She was not one to burst forward and gush an opinion, but soaked up what others said before carefully releasing her own words. Ben and their daughters knew that well.

"Have you had any problems with the Klan, Mr. Taylor?" she asked.

"They around," he said solemnly. "They stay out of the daylight, but they're in the stores, in the fields, in the churches. I've had no problem, but they around."

He knew Mississippi had more lynchings than any state. He knew the recent history not far from Belzoni. He felt the pain and fear of the drama unfolding in the swamps along the Tallahatchie River, but he suppressed it so as not to alarm Ida even more.

"Heard you talk about the Klan and Catholics," Vernon said. "Maybe you know the story of how the Society of the Divine Word, which is a Catholic missionary order, started the first seminary for Negro men in Greenville, not far from us. 1920, I believe it was. Oh, there was opposition from lots of people in the area, including white Catholics."

"No, I didn't know that. Did the seminary survive?" Ann asked. "Did they ordain Negro priests?"

"Yes, but the Society had to overcome claims by the Klan that white women were actin' as scullery maids to the young Negro seminarians. A few years later the pressure became so great the order moved the seminary to Bay St. Louis on the Gulf. It's still runnin' down there. Change is slow, Mrs. Dolan."

"Time can be a big healer," she said, knowing the scars from her son's death had not disappeared. "But it's difficult to wait for justice and truth to penetrate culture. We say everyone is born equal, and has rights to life, liberty and pursuit of happiness. Sadly, what we say and reality are not always the same."

Quiet again took its turn, and then Ann spoke once more.

"There will come a day when justice sees its full light. There will come a day. There is a proverb, I don't know the source. It says that after the game is over the King and the Pawn go into the same box."

Chapter 39

9:55 a.m.

"Sheriff's office. May I help you?"

"Yes ma'am'. I'd like to talk to Deputy Weber please."

"One moment. I'll see if he's here. Who's calling?"

"This is Roy Sanders out at Motel Sepia."

"Please hold."

Roy glanced at Lillian, who was preparing the remainder of guest bills. Most had already paid, but the Taylors and honeymooners had yet to settle up. He cupped his hand over the receiver.

"Should I say anything to Sgt. Weber about this impolite Mr. Brown?" he whispered. "There is something about him that doesn't fit."

Lillian shrugged her shoulders, providing no counsel. It wasn't like Roy to assign negative behavior to anyone, but this Brown fellow worked overtime at portraying a peevish personality. Maybe he had a fight with his wife before he left home. Maybe he was vetoed for a promotion. Maybe he –

"Hello, Roy. What can I do for you?"

"Sgt. Webster. How are you doin'?"

"Good, Roy, and you?"

"Fine. Jus' fine. Sergeant, have you heard any more about the progress of the investigation?" Roy asked. "I heard on the news this mornin' police arrested this young local fella. That must have been a relief to everyone. I know it was for me. So, I was wonderin', can we tell our guests they can be on their way? Some are gettin' sorta anxious."

"I don't see why not, Roy," Webster replied. "One of our detectives who's working with the police just returned. Let me talk to him. Could you hold a second?"

"Sure can, but I have to tell you, Sergeant, this one guest of ours sure acts like a surly criminal," Roy said. "I probably shouldn't say anything, but he showed up after 11 last night, just as I was goin' to bed. Lillian had already retired. He's drivin' a big, fancy black sedan. Creeps up the entrance way like he's got somethin' to hide. I almost called you."

Roy looked at Lillian, but she raised her hands, palms up, as if to say, 'This is your imagination on the loose, not mine.'

"Says he's a businessman, but to my way of thinkin' he ain't got the disposition for a good businessman," Roy continued. "Too unfriendly. Almost hostile. Said he had an appointment for 9 this mornin'."

"Well, he's missed that," the deputy responded. "Roy, he just may be having a bad time of it. We all have them kind of days. Do you want me to stop out and visit with him? Could remove all doubt, maybe improve his attitude."

"No, no. Thanks," Roy responded. "It's just my naggin' suspicion is all." He paused. "More an uneasiness. Lillian, I suspect, thinks it's silly, and maybe it is."

"Well, okay then. Just hold on, and I'll be back on line in a second."

Roy regretted he had brought up the issue of Brown. It wasn't right. Just because the man's disposition resembled an alligator with a bad toothache is no cause to put up a wanted poster. The more Roy pondered the issue, the more he felt he owed the man an apology. What was the Christian admonition about judging others?

"Roy?" Weber said, getting back on the line.

"Yes, Sgt. Weber."

"Go ahead and tell you guests they are free to leave. Our detective seems to think police are comfortable they have their man. This fellow they arrested fits the MO, that is, the pertinent details of two previous robberies. No need to hold up folks on vacation."

"Good, sergeant. They will be glad to hear it. I'm happy this murder business is cleared up. I sense the town has been a little on edge."

"You sense right," Weber said. "And more than just citizens. The sheriff, police chief, mayor and a lot of others have been as squirmy as a cross-eyed centipede. I hope everybody gets settled down now."

"Well," Roy said. "I hope so, too. Thanks again for the information. I'll tell the travelers right away. Stop out any time. Goodbye."

Roy hung up the phone and turned to Lillian.

"Sheriff's office said our guests can leave. I'll run down and tell everyone."

He left without confronting what was behind Lillian's raised eyebrows and wrinkled forehead. Roy decided to inform Brown first. Perhaps that would put him in a better mood and get him on his way to his business appointment. He walked across the road and headed for cabin 5. Matt Kilburn popped out the door of his cabin and intercepted Sanders.

"Heard anything yet from the sheriff's office, Mr. Sanders?" Matt asked, jingling his car keys.

"Yes, Matt. They say you can be on your way. Sorry you had to wait up. Thanks for staying at Motel Sepia. Have a great time in New York. Say goodbye to Lillian before you go."

He was almost to cabin 5 when Brown stepped outside. Suitcase in one hand, Brown motioned with the other as if to brush off lint from the sleeve of his tan suit coat. He glanced down at his shiny shoes, and then raised his head, jaw leading as he approached Sanders.

Roy, not yet dismissing his doubts about Brown, gave him a quick once-over. Brown wearing brown. Seems to be a fit uniform, Roy thought. Dark. Dressed like he's meeting the president of Collins Radio Co. and the entire board of directors. Or, dressed to kill.

Roy scolded himself for such ideas. Before he could talk, he was hit with a question.

"Have you called the sheriff's office yet?" Brown asked briskly.

"Yes, Mr. Brown," Roy replied. "I just came to tell you that everyone is free to go. Sorry to hold you up. Hope you have a good meeting today."

"Sure." Brown curtly replied.

Brown walked to his car, tossed his suitcase and briefcase in the back seat and took off. Rear tires spit out gravel as he headed toward the Lincoln Highway. At that point, he turned east instead of into town.

Roy scratched his head, and all his misgivings about Brown re-bloomed with renewed color.

Maybe it was just one of those times when two people – in this instance, a white man and black man – rubbed each other the wrong way right from the start. It was out of character for Roy to pre-judge, something he generally condemned. But here he was the subject of his own censure.

And now this guy turns east out of town? Like a wrong-way Corrigan, though this was no navigational error Roy was willing to bet. As Dad use to say, Roy mused, it sure smells like bad fish. He walked to the honeymooners' door and rapped. No answer. He rapped again.

"Everyone is free to go. I just talked to the sheriff's office."

"OK. Thanks," a female voice responded meekly.

To no one's surprise, the honeymooners were the last to leave. The woman paid their bill with minimal words. Lillian inquired automatically: Were accommodations satisfactory? "Yes." Any problems at all, Roy asked. "No," she replied with one of those fabricated smiles. Do you need any maps? "No."

The couple drove out of Motel Sepia by 10:20. Roy watched and waved as their car slowly rolled toward the highway. Ah newlyweds. The bliss of young love. She was sitting next to him, cuddled in his right arm. Truth was she didn't look all that honeymooner happy.

Roy looked at Lillian and gave her a double eyebrow lift.

"Interesting group of customers, eh?" he said.

She smiled, picked up the dust pan and broom, clean sheets and headed out the office door.

"Hey, mister," Lillian looked back at Roy. "Get a pail of hot water and cleaner and follow me."

Joe Ellis eased the Chrysler east onto the Lincoln Highway toward Chicago.

He smiled. It was smug homage to himself, and it forced a thaw in his usual steely jaw. He had the same feeling two years ago when Rhino Ralston's main attorney maneuvered an acquittal verdict in Cook County after a two-day trial in which Ellis had been accused of attempted murder.

Funny thing about prosecutions. It makes it tough when the main witness fails to show up.

He hated the assignment to drive to Podunk, Iowa, to do business. It was like taking Miss Ugly to the school prom. That was another chink deep in his ego. No girl ever accepted his request for a date in high school. Even then, it didn't take an A+ student in chemistry to detect his self-centered boorishness.

He held the steering wheel of the big, black sedan with both hands, as if the car might attempt to go off on its own. In an unusual interruption of his programmed mind, perhaps triggered by the inert residue of a lawless lifestyle, Ellis began to wonder about the future.

It didn't, he assured himself, have anything to do with the danger of the job. Morality and ethics were not an issue. His moral make-up was as solid as shadow. There were no ghosts of victims keeping him awake at night. It was more like boredom with the scenery. Maybe he should leave Chicago, move to Florida, and work for the brethren in warmer temperatures.

He hated Rhino Ralston.

Chapter 40

10:12 a.m.

"Lieutenant," Jelling addressed Byrne as he entered the briefing room. "It seems that neither woman in the first two robberies recollects any smell of Spearmint gum on the kisser-crook or anything else unusual in the smell department. Annnd," he held the word out as if it was the biggest crime-busting clue since the Lindbergh kidnapping case, "both confirmed they were kissed on the right cheek."

"Good. Thanks, Jelling," Byrne replied. "Did you find any helpful information concerning any vicious stabbing crimes in the Midwest in the last year or so?"

"As a matter of fact, the guys in records found a couple of cases, one in Indianapolis and another outside Chicago," Jelling responded. "The latter is an interesting case from June out of Naperville, Ill. Seems a man was stabbed a number of times near a church on a Sunday morning. Pretty unusual combination for murder. Sunday morning next to a church?"

"Now you're thinking, Jelling. Give Naperville police a call and see what else you can find out."

"Already in progress, lieutenant. One of the fellas is talking to their detective bureau. He should be up here with a report at any time."

10:18 a.m.

"Perkins, what do you have?" Byrne inquired.

Jim Perkins had worked in records for 11 years. When it came to retrieving documents and reports, he was like an IRS bloodhound. Other cops marveled how he magically pulled out circulars and "wanted" posters from filing cabinets they loathed to disturb.

"Look at this, lieutenant," Perkins offered a crime report while filing a sheaf of additional paperwork under his arm. "On June 19 in Naperville, Ill. – that's outside Chicago – a man's body was found in a church yard. This crime bulletin says he was stabbed many times, and I quote, 'in a vicious, sadistic manner.' The victim was identified as Aldo Arezzo, who, according to his wife, was out for his usual Sunday morning walk. Police there described it as the most depraved killing they'd ever seen."

"And it remains unsolved?"

"Well, no one has been charged," Perkins answered. "We talked with detectives there, and they believe it was organized-crime related, a hit job meant to send a message."

"A message to whom? Who was this Arezzo guy?"

"He was retired, but previously worked as a bookkeeper/accountant for some shady Chicago operation, maybe mob related."

"Holy crapping Moses. Mob related?" Byrne exclaimed. "You could have gone all day without painting that picture." He let that soak into everyone's mind. Mob, as in gangster, was not a word familiar in Cedar Rapids crime lingo. "Any good evidence at that Naperville crime scene, fingerprints?"

"Yes, but that's also the problem," Perkins explained. "They found smudged prints on a park bench, not sufficiently distinct to make a credible ID. They were interested in our murder, especially the debased nature of the killing, and, of course, the similarity to their case."

"OK. Good work, Perkins," Byrne said, slapping him on the shoulder. "I may want to call them back for more information. We need to clear up what they mean by message, and who they think it was meant for. Some peripheral character who was holding out? Or one of their own people?"

10:40 a.m.

Officer Kenny Wilson, gasping for air after his run up the stairs at the CRPD, thumbed through a tablet of notes. He sidled up to Byrne.

"Lieutenant, we just finished re-interviewing some of the people out at the restaurant, including Michelle Keller, the victim's girlfriend. She was pretty devastated last night, so we didn't talk to her long then. Ninety-nine percent blubbering, if you know what I mean."

"Anything really helpful?" Byrne asked.

"She said she had called George Dawson, apparently just before he was murdered," Wilson said, glancing at his notes. "And get this, it seems she talked to the killer right before he hung up the phone."

"What! She thinks she talked to the killer? How does she know that?"

"Well, she doesn't, but – give me a second here – it was someone who was with George Dawson right before he died."

"Kenny," Byrne injected, as he stared at the puffing Wilson, "you really ought to get more exercise, maybe do swim laps at the YMCA." He shifted back to business at hand. "Did this man – it was a man she talked to?"

"Yes, it was a man," Wilson replied.

"What did he say to her on the phone?" Byrne inquired.

"He only said, 'Thank you'."

"No explanation of why he said that?"

"None." Wilson said, his panting subsiding.

"And did she describe his voice? Did he show signs of panic or any inflection at all?"

"She said the man had a deep voice, and he spoke softly."

"And why had she called Dawson?"

"She said she was upset that Dawson was not taking their relationship to the next level. She wanted to get married. He didn't. Now, it doesn't make any difference."

"But Dawson didn't give any hints about the other man? Who he was?"

"No sir," said Wilson. "She said it seemed clear that Mr. Dawson was surprised by this visitor."

"What could she tell us about Dawson? How long has he been in Cedar Rapids and running the restaurant?"

"Well, she wasn't exactly sure, but it seems Mr. Dawson has been here for a couple of years. He took over the restaurant about 15 months ago."

"And before that?"

"Apparently he didn't share a lot of his background with her, but she says he came here from the Chicago area."

"Chicago area?" Byrne said with a tinge of surprise. "Talk to her again and ask if her boyfriend ever mentioned or suggested employment with Chicago's mobsters, but don't say mobsters. Say old line business or mysterious operation. Have we found any records in his office that would give us insight on his past?"

"Not yet, sir. We'll keep digging."

Wilson started to leave but stopped. He nearly forgot an interview point from his notes that he had highlighted with a question mark.

"Oh, one other thing, lieutenant. I don't know if it means much, but one of the restaurant staff, this chap Zwingler, hung around out there until near midnight. He said about 11 or so he was outside smoking a cigarette when he saw a big, black sedan drive slowly past the restaurant on Mount Vernon Road."

"Lot of traffic on that street," Byrne said, "but by 11 at night, maybe not so much. Thanks for all the information."

10:55 a.m.

"I'm afraid I have some bad news, Lt. Byrne."

Virgil Howell stepped into the detective office, his hands juggling documents of some kind that seemed to be floating a step ahead of him.

"What's the bad news, Virg?" Byrne asked, looking back at the fingerprint expert. Byrne usually wasn't ruffled by "bad news." As a veteran investigator he had been down more than one path that turned out to be less than productive. Like any cop he preferred cases where all the arrows pointed in the same direction. But U-turns were not uncommon.

Howell organized a handful of inked papers and concentrated on the top two sheets. He had examined his collection of prints a number of times, came to a conclusion, then examined them again. He wanted to leave no room for doubt.

"Well, them fingerprints we picked up at the restaurant crime scene?" Howell first pointed to the top sheet. "They don't match the ones we lifted at the first two robberies."

He spread his findings on an already cluttered table.

"As you could expect," Howell said, "that restaurant counter was a jumble of hand prints and smudges. But based on where witnesses said the culprit leaned, we picked up a partial that matches more defined markings from the pry bar, the one they found out back of the restaurant.

"And the pry bar gives us a pretty good picture of this fellow," he noted as if holding an 8X10 color photograph.

Howell leaned over the table and positioned the prints from the restaurant counter next to the pry bar impressions. Beneath those sheets he carefully juxtaposed the fingerprints pulled from the Kreiji and truck stop heists. He orchestrated the production like some Leonard Bernstein turned crime buster.

"See here." He showed Byrne and others in the room differences in the swirls. He handed Byrne a magnifying glass to make the images more visible.

"See the differences?" Howell inquired, pointing at the prints with his pencil. Byrne nodded.

"That means the prints – to say it another way – obtained last night don't match those of Curtis Moore," Howell said. He straightened up and looked around the room for reaction.

"Curtis Moore ain't the man who robbed the Gourmet restaurant, lieutenant. And, by extension, I would be bettin' he ain't our killer."

Knowing the intensity of the case, the pressure within the department to make an arrest and assure the town all was well, Howell expected his news would be a shocking turn of events. It was as if the bride changed her mind after the groom slipped the ring on her finger.

"Not bad news, Virgil," Byrne said, looking back at Howell. "Maybe not expected news, but it is what it is."

Howell was surprised. He expected, at best, the head man would be shaking his head in disgust and disappointment, or, at worst, cussing a blue streak and wiping the table clear of every paper and stained coffee cup. Because his information meant starting again from square one.

"It's good news," Byrne professed with a sprinkle of vexation, "in the sense that it firms up the direction the investigation is heading anyway. No use chasing the wrong varmint down the wrong road. There you have it. Curtis Moore is the Kissing Bandit, but not a killer. The chief won't like that because it means we still have a murderer on the loose. And neither will the mayor. But that's the way these things sometimes turn.

Byrne was a good leader, a good cop. He could not openly show disappointment at the results of police investigation that steered the case in a new direction. It was his job to focus on the new evidence, scour a new path, rally the troops and, perhaps hardest of all, convince the police chief and mayor that progress was being made.

"It's the right way, Virgil. It's what we do, at least what we're supposed to do. Investigate, interrogate, sift the evidence and follow what's left."

There was a momentary pause as everybody in the room absorbed the new information and shifted gears.

"Notify everyone in the investigation that we are looking for someone other than Curtis Moore as the killer," Byrne instructed his secretary, Judy Shoff. "Call the sheriff's department and state police. I'll talk to the chief and mayor, and I'll call a news briefing in a half-hour. Virgil, I want you at the press conference, and it will begin at 11:30 sharp. Oh, and Judy, call the newsies."

"Newsies" was the umbrella tag for reporters used by many in law enforcement. Some cops, not Byrne, attached a cynical connotation to the term, as if to infer that the news media were not a professional endeavor with a job to do, but more a pestilence to be dealt with.

"Judy, one other thing. Call Curtis Moore's mother and tell her that her son is not being charged with murder. Tell her the message is from me. And have someone at the jail tell Curtis."

There was a scattering propelled by reality. Minds reviewed and refocused. Byrne touched base with everyone involved in the case, looking for new direction, and information that would guide the investigation along new paths. He had to prepare his comments for the news conference. Before that, he had to explain the situation to the chief and mayor.

"Lt. Byrne?" his secretary popped back into the room. "I just talked to Sgt. Weber at the Sheriff's Department about the new developments in the case? But they already notified area motels that guests were free to leave."

"That was reasonable," Byrne said, "seeing how we had a man charged with the murder until things changed a few minutes ago. Did Weber talk to any travelers?"

"No. He phoned the motels," she said.

An afterthought prompted her to turn back to her boss. She leaned on the door frame, her curly head poked into the investigation room while the rest of her body stuck out in the hallway.

"Actually, Roy Sanders out at Motel Sepia had called Webster around 10," she said, her voice ending on an up-pitch. She was one of those people who had a habit of making a question out of a statement.

"It seems Sanders was upset with one of his guests, said he was gruff and rude," she continued. "Webster knows Sanders well and said it takes a lot to get him riled. I can't see where that adds up to much of anything."

"Anything else Sanders say about this Mr. Crass character?" Byrne asked.

"Sanders told Sgt. Weber this man had a business meeting, but he said he didn't act business-like."

"Well, just because he acts like last night's supper is stuck in his craw isn't grounds for police questioning," Byrne noted. "Did he say what kind of car the man was driving?"

"He did. Said he was driving a black sedan."

Chapter 41

"The noontime news is brought to you by Killian's Department Store, in the heart of downtown Cedar Rapids.

"This just into the WMT newsroom. Cedar Rapids police announced minutes ago that they charged the wrong person last night in the murder of an east side restaurant operator. Curtis Moore, the local young man implicated in two previous robberies in the city, has been cleared of the killing.

"Police Lt. Louis Byrne told reporters that new evidence, including fingerprints taken at the restaurant, shows that Moore is not the person who stabbed George Dawson Monday night at the Gourmet by George restaurant on Mount Vernon Road SE.

"Moore had been taken into custody hours after the homicide and because of similarities in two previous robbery cases – dubbed the Kissing Bandit capers – was charged with Dawson's death.

"In the fast-developing case, Byrne said that even before the fingerprint comparisons there were indications that pointed to a suspect other than Moore. He declined to go into detail. Police Chief Will Kendra said that while the investigation is headed in a new direction, quote, 'The citizens of Cedar Rapids can be assured we will capture the killer.'

"Police have refused to give details of the murder, except to say that Dawson was stabbed to death and that the assumed killer also robbed a cashier of an undisclosed sum of money. As in the two previous robberies, the suspect then kissed the cashier and fled.

"A newspaper reporter asked Byrne for comment on where the case was headed now that young Moore had been cleared of the murder. Byrne responded with a terse 'No comment.' The reporter then specifically asked about a rumor that a black sedan may have been involved in the case. Byrne replied, 'We have nothing more at this time.'

"We will bring you more information on this horrible crime as soon as it becomes available. Now, for the weather –"

Roy Sanders was a news addict. He seldom missed a morning, noon or evening newscast, and read the paper front to back. He sat at the kitchen table, stunned, chewing on a peanut butter sandwich and the radio news he had just heard. For a minute it was as if the world stopped turning, his mind paralyzed and fixed on events of the last 12 hours.

Was the real killer a guest at Motel Sepia? Had he turned him loose two hours before? The late-night scene of the man seeking a room, his muscular build and surly disposition all replayed from his memory like a bad dream. What should he do? Finally, inertia surrendered.

Lillian was still in the laundry room, washing sheets from the cabins. He didn't even tell her about the newscast or discuss what should be done. All of his suspicions raced into reality. His mind flattened discretion like a football runner hell bent for the goal line. Immediately he decided to call the sheriff's department. He waited earnestly for Sgt. Weber, who happened to be in the lunch room.

"Hi, Roy," Weber came on the line. "I bet I know why you are calling."

"You probably do. That fella I was tellin' you 'bout, he left around 10 and the strange thing is he headed east on the Lincoln Highway even though he said he had an appointment here. I had doubts about that guy all along."

"I'm glad you called, Roy," Weber said, and then filled him in on the new developments of the case. Roy had heard most of it on the noon news.

State police had already issued a regional alert on the investigation's U-turn, but the truth was that authorities had little new information to go on.

"I was just ready to call you," said Weber. "Did that fellow you are talking about, did he leave any license information?"

"Actually, he did," Roy replied. "Said he's from St. Louis, but the black Buick carries an Illinois plate number, LNX-4329. Least, that's what he wrote on the registration, and I remember lookin' and seein' the LNX part."

"Did he list a model number or year for the Buick?"

"No model number, but he put 1954 on the motel registration."

"Thanks, Roy," Weber said. "That's a great help. We'll find this guy. I'll call Cedar Rapids police and we'll put out an APB right away."

Weber's information about the black sedan reignited the investigation and everyone's hope for a quick solution to the murder. But Byrne knew there was a long span between suspect and convicted killer. He wouldn't relax until that bridge was crossed.

Roy scolded himself for not being more assertive about his gut feelings, but what else should he have done? He sought out Lillian for validation and solace.

"Oh, there you are, Lillian."

He told her about the news report and the reversal by police from murder solved to killer still on the run.

"I just called the sheriff's office about our guest, Mr. Brown. You didn't talk to him, Lillian, but this fella had suspect written all over him. I shoulda had Weber come out and interview him."

"I wouldn't be too quick to condemn, Roy. Like they say, don't judge a book by its cover."

"Well, maybe so, but I hope they find him soon. I think It will be a big relief to me and a big relief to the community."

Roy's wish was quickly fulfilled.

A police officer in Mount Vernon, Iowa, a small community 15 miles east of Cedar Rapids, spotted the late-model Buick in a parking lot on the campus of Cornell College shortly after 12:30. He radioed the Highway Patrol and Linn County Sheriff's office, and within 10 minutes the black sedan was surrounded like a hive at a bee convention.

Soon after, a sober-looking Brown haltingly walked out of the college administrative offices toward his car and a battery of law enforcement officers. Two state troopers approached him with caution, hands ready to draw their sidearms.

"Are you Mike Brown?" one of them asked.

"Yes, I am," he said, stung by the array of uniforms. "What the hell is this all about?"

"You stayed at the Motel Sepia last night, just outside Cedar Rapids?"

"I did," Brown replied. "So what? Is that a crime?"

"Where were you before you checked into the motel?"

"Strange as it may seem, I was driving."

"Listen mister," one of the troopers shot back. "I don't need any bullshit or smartass attitude. Where were you driving from?"

Brown quickly read the seriousness if the situation and that he had best chuck the tough guy posture.

"Sorry officer," he shifted his tone apologetically. "Like I said, I was driving into town. I came up on 61 and 218 from St. Louis. Got a late start. Wanted to be up here because of an early morning meeting here at the college, a meeting, which by the way, was delayed by more than an hour."

"Who did you meet with?"

"I met with the college purchasing agent," Brown answered. "I sell textbooks. What is this all about, anyway?"

"And the purchasing agent's name?"

"Tom Earlandson."

"Just stay here while we have a visit with Mr. Earlandson," the trooper ordered. "Do you mind if we check your car?"

"Be my guest."

Brown's bad start to a day had suddenly worsened.

A book salesman, underwhelmed by his title and unsatisfied with his job, had just undergone an involuntary attitude adjustment. His gruff guy/nice guy juggling routine was suddenly neutralized. In a matter of seconds, he found his conflicting personality on a tilt-a-whirl excursion.

This unplanned spin, a character building experience you can't find in a library of research material, was relatively short.

Within 20 minutes, Brown was cleared of suspicion of murder and was on his way selling books.

Chapter 42

Sgt. Weber informed Roy of the quick clearance of Mike Brown. Officials at Cornell College in Mount Vernon, Brown's employer in St. Louis and other sources confirmed Brown's statements and the time line he provided to police.

At 1:20 p.m. on Aug. 30, 1955, the gods of crime-solving had called strike two on Cedar Rapids law enforcement. The hunt for George Dawson's killer was back to square one.

One of the most difficult things in life for a human being is to confront his own errors, and Roy Sanders was at that rampart. The brain's section on self-worth and fulfillment depends, in part, on affirmation. Sanders suddenly faced this universal truth and the accompanying pain in admitting a mistake.

He approached Lillian timidly.

"I was wrong," he said softly, looking squarely into her deep brown eyes. Then he relayed what Weber had told him and prepared for a backfire of all his past proclamations about pre-judging, stereotyping and jumping to conclusions.

Instead, she smiled. She was more pleased with his forthrightness than upset by his lack of prudence.

"We all make miss-steps, Mr. Snake Hips. Where does Sgt. Weber think the investigation will turn now," she asked mildly.

Among many reasons, Roy loved her for her acceptance of his foibles.

"I'm not sure, honey, if they know where to turn," he said with a sigh. Weber didn't say much about the investigation." He paused.

"I sure jumped off the deep end, didn't I? But this Brown did a good job of imitatin' a jerk."

"I'm glad you are proficient at installing floors," she looked at him with those penetrating eyes that first overwhelmed him many years ago. "Your detective skills are not all that strong." She smiled. "You had good intentions."

She let that settle into his blank-looking countenance.

"Help me put clean sheets on the beds," she said, a stack of linens in her arms.

1:24 p.m.

"Damn it! Where's Jelling?" Byrne barked. "Where's that information from the Naperville police department? It was supposed to be here more than an hour ago!" He railed at anyone within listening distance, the upshot of a floundering investigation.

"And who was going to call this Michelle Keller back for further questioning?"

He was fuming at himself as well as everyone else. He knew the intensity of the investigation had relaxed, both when evidence pointed to Curtis Moore, and again when Mike Brown was a prime suspect. It was like a basketball team that was ahead by 12 points with less than two minutes to play, taking for granted that victory was in the bag.

Suddenly it was overtime, and Byrne aimed to employ a full-court press to motivate the entire team. He was looking for any spark that could re-energize his group of investigators.

"And get hold of Weber at the Sheriff's Department. I want information on all the people staying at the Motel Sepia last night and every other goddamn motel and hotel in the area."

One of Byrne's assistants had telephoned the detective bureau in Naperville, Ill., in late morning. Lunch time and the sometimes infirmity of human communication combined to produce inertness.

A telegraphed summary of the June stabbing death in that city had finally staggered over the wire at 12:50 p.m. It was misplaced and didn't find its way to Byrne for another 40 minutes.

When Jelling delivered it and explained the delays and detours, Byrne was livid. If it had been mid-winter, the steam rolling out of his ears would have merged with that hissing out of cast iron registers to more than heat the second floor of the PD. He released four-letter words until he ran out, words his wife Marge had scolded him about on other occasions. He finally cooled off.

Byrne looked at the telegraph report for two minutes, and then reread it. The detective was mesmerized by the similarities in the two killings, the horror depicted in both stabbings, the words used by investigators, where prudent police calculation pointed to a signature crime – a killing meant to send a message.

At 1:45 p.m., Weber again reached Motel Sepia. Roy was in the office, glancing at the evening's guest list. He looked up just as the deputy was about to rap on the door.

"Come on in," Roy motioned. "Tell me you have a new suspect in mind for that murder. I sure goofed up on that book salesman."

"Roy," the deputy responded as he walked through the door, "you did the right thing. We just have to keep plugging away at this. Could you give me the rundown on your other guests last night? We're checking all hotels and motels just in case we run into a stroke of luck. I doubt it will lead to anything. The killer didn't likely check into local accommodations." He paused. "The suspicion of Mr. Brown notwithstanding."

Exasperation oozed from his voice.

Roy gave him the rundown on the guests from Wisconsin, Illinois, Mississippi and Iowa, including information from registration forms. Weber then telephoned all of the data – names, car makes, colors and registration – to Cedar Rapids police.

"Thanks Roy," Weber said. "If there is anything else you can tell us about your guests, information you think would be useful, don't hesitate to call. We'll get this sorted out." The officer left and Roy reviewed events of the last 24 hours.

Back at the Cedar Rapids police department, the new information was added to the shifting puzzle. Byrne's head and his investigation were spinning, but it sure couldn't be said he was clueless. As usual it was the sifting process, fitting the right pieces together, that challenged his team.

Cops had a good set of fingerprints from the pry bar found in the bushes outside the restaurant. Those prints, Howell had confirmed, were the same as the less-defined swirls deposited on the restaurant's checkout counter. Interviews of some two dozen people began to produce a picture of the killer. He was a strong man with a deep voice. He chewed gum, witnesses said, or at least they thought he did.

His manner projected a sense of confidence and foreboding. It wasn't swagger. He displayed all the mettle of a brain surgeon treating a bad cold. From the looks of the crime scene, he possessed an extraordinary portion of depravity and was seemingly unburdened by morality.

It was 1:50.

Byrne wanted to personally chat with his counterpart in Naperville, to collectively chew on the assembled facts and ruminate over the MO in both cases. He wanted to telephone them before people on day shifts began to head home. Before he could ask a secretary to place the call, Perkins rushed into the room with some scribbled notes.

"Lieutenant, I've been going though that batch of records brought back from the restaurant last night, and I think our Mr. Dawson came here from Chicago, alright," Perkins said confidently. "He has receipts from Chicago hotels, phone numbers of Chicago restaurants and a Rolodex with quite a few people with Chicago addresses. So far, I haven't found any information that points to family or next of kin."

"Great work, Perkins," Byrne said. "Was his girlfriend, what's her name, Keller, able to shed any more light on Dawson's background?"

"Not that I'm aware of. But there must be someone else familiar with his history. She said he was a golfer, so we'll check that angle."

Within minutes, Byrne's call to Naperville was ready.

"Detective, we have a Capt. McNabb of the Naperville Police Department on line two."

Byrne grabbed the receiver and punched the phone button.

"Capt. McNabb, this is Louie Byrne of the Cedar Rapids, Iowa, police detective bureau."

Small talk, cop palaver and department information preceded the main topic. They weren't long into a crime comparison when McNabb popped the question.

"You think we're talking the same man here?"

"I don't know, Captain," Byrne replied. "But let's assume the killer is the same person. Where do we go with that assumption?"

That produced a lull in the discussion.

"I understand your fingerprints are iffy," Byrne said. "Why don't we mail you a copy of what we have? Maybe your guy can draw a conclusion from that."

"We can try it, but I don't know if it will produce anything that would stand up in court," McNabb said. "And besides, we still don't know who this guy is. Send the fingerprint pics and photographs of the stab wounds. Together, that might help settle the question of a common perpetrator."

Byrne agreed to get the material in the mail immediately.

"Your victim was Aldo Arezzo?" Byrne asked.

"That's right," McNabb confirmed.

"He was retired and played golf?"

"Yes."

"And his wife said he worked as an accountant in Chicago?" Byrne continued.

"Arezzo kept the books for a company or companies that have less than a sterling reputation in the opinion of both Chicago P.D. and the Cook County Sheriff's Department. They are suspected of running front operations for gambling, prostitution and a host of shakedown scams. Mostly they stay one step ahead of the law with a battery of lawyers who could be charged with obstruction of justice.

"You won't find them on the Better Business Bureau approval list," McNabb said as an afterthought.

"Was the wife able to provide you with any names of associates?" Byrne asked.

"He had a few contacts written in his phone book. Some were golf buddies. Some the wife didn't know. None were names we could trace back to his employment. However, we have a man still working on the case. I'll check if he's come up with anything new."

"Good," Byrne said. "Captain, could you please telegram us a copy of those names and telephone numbers? Again, assuming our killer is the same as yours – and that may be a long shot – perhaps there are common names in the records kept by Mr. Arezzo and our victim, George Dawson."

"That's certainly worth checking," McNabb agreed. "Instead of wiring the information, why don't I have my secretary read off the names when we're through talking? It will speed up at least that part of the comparison."

The two concurred, and Byrne said he would relay names from Dawson's files to Naperville.

For some reason, perhaps it was years of investigative experience or maybe hope that he was overdue for a break, a feeling began to bloom in Byrne's gut that they were headed in the right direction.

Chapter 43

Joe Ellis slowly ushered his rented black Chrysler eastward down the Lincoln Highway as if he were in a funeral procession.

He had thoughts of Florida, sunshine, warm beaches and bountiful broads, a life unfettered by the constraints of his bosses in Chicago. He imagined a life full of pleasure. His mind was not encumbered by a single concern of the bloody and mangled body of a Cedar Rapids restaurant owner.

Even though there were no posted highway speed limits, Ellis took pains not to attract attention of Iowa police. The last thing he wanted was to be stopped by a two-bit town cop for coasting through a stop sign or failing to hand signal a turn. Why would they stop him? And if they did, perhaps one of those safety checks, not to worry. The car was only a year old and in perfect condition.

Besides, his new "bride" was sitting beside him, and cops don't mess with honeymooners. The back window told everyone, "Just Married!"

After several miles, Jennifer Jennings – the alias Rosemary Jones at Motel Sepia – deliberately moved out and away from his grasp and sat silently and glumly next to the passenger door. She quickly divorced herself from any marital appearances.

The highway was bordered by 10-foot tasseled corn, a corridor now and then interspersed by green alfalfa and golden oats-stubble. Here and there the pancake landscape was interrupted by red barns, white clapboard houses and the poignant smell of grist and corn that had been processed via the digestive system of pigs.

He drove through the towns of Lisbon, Mechanicsville, Clarence and Lowden without even reading the names. They were foreign to him and he was a foreigner there.

His buoyant mood was not only out of character but to Jennifer, almost unnerving. She didn't feel comfortable around him at any time, and now a peculiar sense of unease squirmed through her body. She rolled down the car window, half closed her eyes and took a deep breath.

The serene landscape provided no comfort. Her shoulder-length blond hair waved at the passing countryside.

"Dreaming of becoming a farmer's wife, Miss Rosemary?" he laughed at her. "I can just see you feeding chickens and milking cows."

She ignored him.

Jennifer hated every mile of this trip. She detested her role as Rosemary, and she had come to loath her life as much as she abhorred Ellis. Here she was, 26 years old and a commodity. She was a company moll. Rhino Ralston owned and managed her. Drugs and booze had escorted her to indenture and kept her prisoner.

She had grown up a proud free-thinker, part of a counter-culture crowd in an elite section of Park Ridge. Now she found herself trapped and alone. Why? Had she intended to merely reject her parents' lifestyle only to end up fully alienated from them? Did she want to punish them because, she thought, they favored her brother? Show them she didn't need their help or coddling?

For whatever reasons, she made choices that led her down unintended paths. Bad decisions often breed more bad decisions. Her mind drifted in a quick rerun of these recent years. She watched in a daze as the symmetrical corn rows filed by and wondered how she could re-order her life.

Nobody walks out on the Rhino. She knew that from company stories and personal experience, the latest still unfolding at an Iowa restaurant where a mangled body gave testimony to mob canon. You paid Rhino and his pals in one way or another. Her body and soul were part of this whole ugly scene. She slept with whomever and wherever "business" demanded.

"Park your ass over there by the door when we are in pig-shit territory if you must, but when we stop, I want you next to me," Ellis barked.

His mood could change faster than a trouper in a one-man play.

"When there's people around, I want you acting as the devoted wife," he directed his surly announcement with a spray of saliva.

His white T-shirt was void of any emblem or words. He belonged to nothing and was devoted to nothing, except his own ego. The shirt's cotton sleeves stretched to accommodate his bulging biceps. He admired that, as he did his entire being. To say that he was vain would be a gasping understatement.

Ellis drove with his right hand. His left arm rested on the door frame that housed the rolled-down driver's side window. He mulled switching on the car radio, just to fill the vacuum of silence. "Miss Rosemary" wasn't going to talk, and, truthfully, he preferred she keep her mouth shut. He turned the knob. Two attempts at tuning yielded farm markets, rural staples that may as well have been in Chinese. Ellis swore as he snapped the radio off.

"Pass me a stick of Spearmint, Rosie babe," he ordered, holding out his hand and snapping his fingers.

She hunted through the glove box for his precious gum.

You are a like an addicted cud-chewing cow, she thought, but with a personality more like the rear end of a horse.

"We'll stop down the road for a sandwich," he informed her. "You are probably hungry from all that honeymoon work." She said nothing. "Damn, Rosie, you're not only strange, but slow."

After another 10 minutes, he found an A&W drive-in on the edge of DeWitt, Iowa, another in the endless string of towns along the Lincoln Highway. He pulled under the canopy and looked at the menu board. Ellis spit his gum chaw at the feet of a teenage girl on skates, part of the chain's car-hop brigade, and ordered for both of them.

Basking in over-confidence can be dangerous, and it was something usually shunned by Ellis. As a Marine sniper, he never took anything for granted. As a paid killer, and working for the mob, that was even more paramount. Every move, no matter how small, was subject to deliberation and anticipation of what may come next.

Ellis was in no hurry and envisioned nothing that could detour his smooth return to Chicago. If need be, if he decided, there were a number of towns where they could stay the night, from Clinton, Iowa, to Naperville, Illinois, though he would rather avoid the latter. Aurora, Ill., would be a better choice. Or Dixon.

The car-hop, dressed in a snazzy red outfit with a dainty white apron, skated up to the black sedan, a tray full of food balanced in one hand. She attached the tray to the car, then circled back to retrieve the drinks.

Ellis ogled the slim, paleness of her legs exposed between the short dress and white knee-length stockings, tight knits that were topped by red and blue rings. He restrained his emotions to thoughts, lest any verbal expression might draw more attention than he wanted.

Jennifer's mind was more focused on changing her life than hot dogs. But, she acknowledged, you have to eat. The whiskey and even worse that had numbed her system and hardened her personality in recent months did not obliterate her love of root beer. For a few seconds the cool mug and drink brought back memories of more tranquil times.

Ellis devoured his order and considered seconds. Who was he to deny himself? He summoned the car-hop, again surveyed her anatomy and put in his supplemental request.

"You have catsup seeping from the left side of your lips," he told Jennifer. He grunted a hybrid sneer-laugh delivered with an air of superiority. "I like it. It sorta looks as if I smacked you around. I could'a done that last night."

"You lay a hand on me and Rhino gets the full report," Jennifer snapped.

That was her major trump card with Ellis, and he knew it. Ralston ruled, and he was forced to live with that.

The money was good, but Ellis was tired of being a marionette jerked around by Eddie Ralston, a Charlie McCarthy manipulated by Edgar Bergen. Ellis, too, fantasized about ditching the Chicago mob and moving somewhere else.

He knew Ralston's reach matched that of the FBI. If Rhino wanted to find a person badly enough, he would, and that usually meant an ugly conclusion. At least, that's what Ralston wanted you to believe. Ellis' off-hand, albeit callow, notion was to merely evaporate from the Chicago scene, giving Ralston no reason to hunt him down, no dangling debts.

Sure, he could be arrested somewhere and attempts made to have him testify against the mob. But to what end? Implicate himself? Cut a deal? No, no. Too many had driven down that dead alley. And Chicago cops could haul him in any time, if they wanted to. So, he thought, calculated, that if he departed quietly without obligations of any kind, commission or omission, he could safely start a new life. Or could he?

For all those reasons, he kept his hands off Jennifer's private parts. This woman with catsup on her mouth might be a slave, but he rejected that role for himself. In his mind, he was an essential part of the mob enforcement lineup, someone active in the business. His cocky, egotistical nature obscured his own passive role.

Neither could he envision succumbing in perpetuity to a scumbag like Ralston.

"Like your hot dog, Rosie?" Ellis sneered, still munching on a hamburger and cheese curds. "I really do appreciate you, Rosie. You're quiet, unlike most chicks. You sit there, content, eating, sipping, all in the presence of great studness. Maybe I'll ask Rhino for an extra favor when we get back."

Chapter 44

There was a time when Jennifer Jennings proudly anchored the "A" affirmative sophomore debate team at Northwestern University. She could assemble an assertive argument and conduct visceral interrogation like a seasoned state's attorney. She pummeled opponent positions and needed no coaching on the art of persuasion.

While she wasn't skillful in athletics and displayed little interest in stylish clothing, Jennifer had no shortage of opinion and academic savvy. If there was something to protest, something she cared about, she lined up with chin out front and attitude in assertive gear. She quit the school newspaper upon being informed that news stories were supposed to be unbiased. She was attractive and smart. And independent.

"Resolved: *That the Congress of the United States should enact a compulsory fair employment practices law.*"

That was the national debate question then and Jennifer grabbed onto it with vigor. Under the rules, students must prepare to argue both sides of a question, but she convinced the debate team advisor that she couldn't put "my soul" into defending the status quo. Damned if she was going to exert time and effort on behalf of something she didn't believe in.

You would have thought by her tenacious presentation that she was working in a sweat shop sewing clothes for 25 cents an hour. She not only argued with passion, but relished slicing up opponent's reports. It was unfortunate her doggedness excluded scrutiny of her personal life. Had she stayed in school, she often thought privately, she may have helped Northwestern finish first in the nation in the 1955 debate tournament instead of third.

All that, and her 3.75 grade point average, had left town with a guy named Lee Gibson.

Gib, as friends called him, invited her to an "adventure beyond Meister Brau Blue Fiesta." At the time it had sounded as inviting as a drinking and polemics excursion with some modern Thomas Paine. Looking back, she couldn't imagine the degree of her naivety and what it had cost.

Her potential as a student and successful adult in the world withered like a budding rose swarmed by aphids and parched for water.

Old Gib, all of 25 years of age and a dropout denizen himself, introduced her to off-beat thinkers and tutored her taste to Four Roses and one Jim Beam. They partied. It was almost as if they had dropped off into Lake Michigan, and indeed, she often felt as if she were drowning in freewheeling over-indulgence.

Her parents were crazed with worry. Eventually, her father hired a private investigator who contacted college friends, which led to revelations about Gib and Jim Beam. Jennifer was found to be lost. She had opted for a new lifestyle, and told her parents so.

Gibson, when she first met him, was a scrawny 5-foot-8 with thick, straggly brown hair that looked as if it hadn't seen a comb in months. He was a likable sort, had a keen wit and was one of those people who attract by rumpled ineptness.

He was malleable, Jennifer believed, an unthreatening type she could shape into the character she wanted him to be – sort of like a toy yet to be defined. Both envisioned a life void of the rules they grew up with.

Those initial designs, certainly not rooted in any concept of commitment for each other, faded into a casual ramble. Over the months, Gib and Jennifer matriculated to pep pills, frequently mixed with alcohol, and then to barbiturates and opiates, the favorite of Beatniks. Her once sparkling eyes became leaden and mournful, vivid signals of dismay and dysfunction.

The two young people, sadly but not surprisingly, became easy targets for an unsavory world. They entered different dark alleys, forced there by the rude reality of economics and survival.

"Damn Rosemary, I'm proud of you," Ellis slipped into his mocking alter ego. He could rally smugness and derision without effort and relished referring to her by the fake honeymoon name.

"You didn't have the shakes much the last two days. Are you weaning yourself from Buddy Beam? When I first met you, Rosie, you smoked like a chimney and drank like a camel. You stunk from Pall Malls and shook like a hootchie-coochie dancer."

She suppressed her tongue. In truth, she had changed, a little. Rhino demanded it. It was nothing she could take pride in, and she didn't. It was just the way things were. She couldn't be a sexual instrument, valued female merchandise, if she smelled and looked like hungover nicotine. She still drank an occasional Falstaff and risked a drag or two on menthol Kools.

For all of that, she hated Ellis, and she hated herself.

They finished the last of their root beers at the A&W, a rather peasant meal for big-city high rollers. Ellis checked the gas gauge and decided a fill-up could come later.

"I have to be honest, Rosie baby," he crowed. "Even if you came on to me like a Rock Island locomotive, I would have to switch you to a side track. You don't jiggle enough in the right places to suit me, if you get my meaning. You may think you're steam engine hot, but if I had to put you in a full train lineup you'd be the caboose. You are just not my type. What do you say to that, Rosie baby?"

"I'm grateful," she said softly, staring out the rolled down car window.

Jennifer was well aware of Ellis' short fuse. She would prefer to say more, but feared she had said too much.

She watched the young car-hops and wondered if they were among the unspoiled creatures of nature, or if misfortune's long reach had somehow wiggled its finger into rural America, too. It was a depressing thought.

Ellis looked at her with savage scorn as he backed out of A&W and pulled onto the road.

"You consider yourself better than most of us, coming from money, and patted on your talcumed ass by a nursemaid in a rich suburb," he spewed his spite. "But Rosie, that was then. Now you are simply a college dropout whore, a commercial whore. Whatever knowledge was pounded into your reluctant head is worthless.

Your talents reside between your legs, and once Rhino sees sagging mammaries you'll be working out of Rush Street."

Aware of the swelling heat in her body, Jennifer leaned into the window's passing air stream. However, the slight wind could not dislodge visions of an imaginary pistol in an imaginary drama. If I had a loaded gun, she thought, I would plug him right here. I'd put a round between his snaky eyes, another in his foul mouth and empty the chambers in his crotch.

She was fuming inside and fought to keep it concealed on the outside. She hunted for diversion, anything to suppress her seething hate for Ellis and to keep from provoking him further.

"Do you mind if I turn on the radio?" she asked, forcing formality through the grit of her teeth, "maybe find a nice song by Fats Domino?"

"You like them nigger singers, hey, Rosie? Well, go 'head. That would seem to fit. From what I've seen, you take on all comers. Course, you don't have much choice in the matter, do you."

Her illusory theater continued.

After shooting him, she would then go to the trunk, retrieve the tire wrench, and smack him squarely in the testicles – for fun, not practical effect. She chuckled at a vision of Joe Ellis writhing in pain, not knowing if he should sooth his bleeding forehead with his hands or console his throbbing privates.

"What the hell are you laughing at, whore?"

She fiddled with the radio knobs. Stations faded in and out with crackling and whistling static. Oscillating strains of Georgia Gibbs and "Dance with Me Henry" mingled with "Sincerely" by the McGuire Sisters. The red line of the radio dial then landed on a strong signal out of Cedar Rapids.

"Police have refused to give details of the murder," the radio blared the news, and she quickly turned down the volume, "except to say that Dawson was stabbed to death and that the assumed killer also robbed a cashier of an undisclosed sum of money. As in the two previous robberies, the suspect then kissed the cashier and fled."

Jennifer glanced at Ellis and knew immediately he was the subject of the radio story. She felt sorry for the cashier, not for being robbed, but for having been kissed by this ape.

"Turn that news a little louder," Ellis ordered. She did.

"A newspaper reporter," the radio account continued, "asked Byrne for comment on where the case was headed now that young Moore had been cleared of the murder. Byrne responded with a terse 'No comment.' The reporter then specifically asked about a rumor that a black sedan may have been involved at the crime scene. Byrne replied: 'We have nothing more at this time.'

"We will bring you updated information on this horrible crime as soon as it becomes available. Now for the weather. It looks as if there could be pop-up showers in Eastern Iowa this afternoon, but no storms are anticipated."

Ellis had bent his ear toward the radio with obvious interest. The news report sent a sour streak through his A&W lunch. His confident composure sagged like a heavyweight champ who just took a left punch in the gut. The words "black sedan" put a dent in his arrogance.

"Turn that goddamn thing off," he commanded as the forecasted temperatures filtered through the radio grid.

Jennifer did as she was told.

"What time is it?" he muttered.

He looked at his own watch. It was seven minutes past noon.

"'Black sedan', bullshit! That's what it is, Miss Whore," Ellis mumbled in an attempt to reassure his nicked composure. "News people like to take a rumor and run with it like a courier takes off with unstamped hootch. They throw that 'black sedan' thing out there to create interest, sell newspapers. It's all bullshit."

He had driven only a few blocks when, without forewarning, he whipped the Chrysler into a Mobil station at the east edge of DeWitt.

Ellis had two things on his mind. In spite of the "black sedan bullshit" he was preaching a minute earlier, he decided to get a full tank of gas just in case of an emergency, such as the need to take some side road where there may not be a filling station. And he wanted to wipe off the "Just Married!" sign from the back window.

"Guess what, Rosie, we're getting a divorce," he smirked. "I don't want you to get all sniffley on me, but our married days are over."

Jennifer would have liked to yell "Hallelujah!" but she refrained. Instead, she pictured his privates quivering like a bell that just struck midnight. She was still holding the tire wrench after taking a Babe Ruth swing.

Strike three, she giggled internally.

"Get your ass out here and scrub the rear window clean," he directed.

The station attendant offered to check the oil and clean the windshield and rear glass, but Ellis declined.

"She can clean the back window. That's what a good wife is supposed to do, the cleaning. Don't you agree?"

The attendant said nothing, but headed for the gas pump.

"Would you like regular or ethyl?" he asked Ellis.

"Now what do you think, farm boy? A big car with eight cylinders? Don't you think perhaps it would take high test?" Ellis responded in haughty derision. "Wash that window Rosie."

And she did, as if she were scrubbing him out of her life.

Chapter 45

When Lt. Byrne hung up the phone after talking with McNabb in Naperville, another ember of information suddenly glowed in his mind. That reporter at the news conference had mentioned "black sedan." And someone on the investigation team had mentioned a black car driving slowly past the restaurant last night after the crime. Another long shot?

"Judy, those people checking the motel and hotel guests, have them ask about other black cars, especially large black cars," he ordered his secretary. "And who was it that saw the black sedan?"

The answer came out of a cloud of Lucky Strike smoke.

"I know about that," Officer Kenny Wilson said as he re-entered what had become investigation central. "Zwingler, the restaurant guy, mentioned a black car. Want me to see if he remembers anything more about it?"

"Pronto," said Byrne, "and take that nicotine fume factory with you."

It seemed as if a fourth of law enforcement in Cedar Rapids was running down leads in the Dawson murder. Byrne's bloodhound senses were engaged. This, he thought, was the sort of energy necessary to find killers. He knew that every hour that passed made the trail more difficult to follow.

He unconsciously shifted into Eliot Ness gear.

"Lieutenant, Weber at the Sheriff's Department just called in," Perkins from records informed Byrne. "He didn't have much new information, but get this. When I asked him about a big black sedan, other than the Buick driven by the book salesman, he checked his notes and said that another of the guests last night at Motel Sepia, a woman who said she was on her honeymoon, listed a black Chrysler on the registration form. Roy Sanders, the motel owner, confirmed it."

"Good, Perkins." There was a pause as wheels turned. "Let me ask you, when you went on your honeymoon, Perkins, did you drive a big car?"

"No sir. Didn't have a car," Perkins laughed. "Borrowed my brother's 1949 Ford. Let me tell you, Lieutenant, that was one nifty rod, it –"

"Never mind that, Perkins," Byrne interrupted. "Don't you find it a little unusual that honeymooners would be driving a fancy, late-model vehicle?"

"Hard to say, sir. Not if you had an old man with lots of dough."

"Point taken. Get Sanders on the line. I want to talk to him."

2:05 p.m.

Wilson returned after talking with Zwingler. There was nothing Zwingler could add to the car's description, Wilson said. "He couldn't identify the make, only that it was bigger than a Ford or Chevy sedan.

"It wasn't so much the type of car that caused Zwingler to take note," Wilson explained to fellow officers, "but rather that it was driving abnormally slow."

This section of Mount Vernon Road, particularly late at night, can sometimes mimic the Hawkeye Downs Speedway. Fast cars are the rule. Slow ones stand out. It's the get-out-of-town zone.

"Zwingler said this guy poked along like a driver hunting for a parking spot downtown," Wilson said.

"OK, people, listen up," Byrne ordered. "Think like the killer. Before the commission of the crime, he didn't park his car on Mount Vernon Avenue. There's no parking allowed on the street there. That means he either parked in the restaurant lot, not a likely thing, or somewhere nearby, perhaps south down 42nd.

"After the murder and robbery, as he left, the chances are that he did not exit on the street along the restaurant's front door," Byrne continued. "Too chancy. If he had parked down the street, what were his choices for egress? He couldn't go south on 42nd. That's a dead end. What were his other options?"

"Well," Wilson said, searching his memory and rubbing his chin as if reasoning powers resided there, "that cinder track of an alley runs east-west just south of the restaurant. It's rutty. The city doesn't maintain it, and I don't think people use it. But didn't Officer Connick say some saplings had been knocked down along there? It was close to where they found the pry bar."

The phone rang. Byrne answered.

"Yes? Thanks, Mr. Sanders for calling back. This is Lt. Byrne down at the Cedar Rapids Police Department. Sorry to bother you, but I have a couple of more questions. You had a female guest yesterday at Motel Sepia who drove a black car, is that right?"

"Yes," Roy replied. "As I mentioned to Sgt. Weber, it was a black Chrysler. Pulled in shortly before 5 o'clock, I think."

"And this woman in the black Chrysler, she said she was on her honeymoon?" Byrne's voice conveyed his skepticism.

"Yes sir, Lieutenant. That's what she said. And I noticed when they pulled out this mornin', in the back window of the car, there was 'Just Married!' letterin'."

"Was she accompanied by a man when she registered, and if so, did you notice if they left their accommodations at any time Monday night?" Byrne questioned.

"There was a man in the car when she registered, but he never came into the office," Roy said. "In fact, I saw very little of him and only at a distance. She listed her name as Rosemary Jones," anticipating Byrne's next question.

"Rosemary Jones? Interesting," Byrnes mused. "Did you notice a wedding ring, by chance?"

"Sorry, Lieutenant. I really didn't look for one."

"No reason to, Mr. Sanders. And the car's plates? Illinois?"

"That's right."

"And you didn't see the honeymooners leave at any time?"

"I sure didn't Lieutenant. If they left, I didn't notice."

"No other black cars in your lot last night?"

"Jus' this one, and, of course, that black Buick."

"Did you talk to this man, the groom?"

"No. As I said, I only saw him from a distance."

"Please, Mr. Sanders, describe him for me, as best you can," Byrne requested. "Tall? Short? Skinny?"

"Oh, no, sir. He wasn't skinny. Hard to say how tall as he was sitting in the car when they pulled in, but later I spotted him outside their cabin for a few seconds. Hard to say. Maybe he was around six feet. Strong, like."

"Anything else unusual about the honeymooners, their arrival, activity or the car?" Byrne asked, jotting down notes.

"Well, Lieutenant, they came in late afternoon and we didn't see much of them. I'm sure that had somethin' to do with the activity, if you get my meanin'."

"I'm reading you, Mr. Sanders," Byrne laughed. "This black car. Was it clean? It didn't look like it traveled on any rural roads, dusty?"

"No sir, it was a handsome vehicle, shiny like new. Four-door. Might have been a New Yorker. Had a busload of chrome, white walls. I believe I remember it had a radio antenna. Can't think of anything else. Come to think, there was one oddity, least for otherwise fancy car."

"What was that Mr. Sanders?"

"I noticed a scratch on the passenger door when they pulled out of Motel Sepia," Roy said.

That caused Byrne's antenna to perk up.

"Was there a dent in the door?"

"I don't believe so, sir. Just a nasty scratch of the paint, like it rubbed somethin'."

"Right." Byrne pictured how it may have happened. "And when did they leave?"

"Most of the guests were gone shortly after 10 this morning," Roy replied. "The honeymooners departed later, maybe around 10:30 or a tad later. But then, there's that activity factor, Lieutenant."

"Yes, I see what you mean, Mr. Sanders. And when they left, this Illinois car, it headed east on the Lincoln Highway? Is that correct?"

"Yes sir, real slow-like."

"Did she list a plate number for this black car?"

"Yes sir. Just 'bout to give that to you," Roy said, rustling through his registration book. "It's 954-697, then underneath those numbers was Illinois with 19 on the left and 55 on the right. Saw it when they left, too."

"Thank you, Mr. Sanders," Byrne said. "If you think of anything else, please call." He gave Roy the direct number to the detective bureau. "If you don't mind, Mr. Sanders, we'd like to check the cabin where the honeymooners stayed. Is it OK if I send some people out to do that?"

"Of course, Lieutenant. I'll tell Lillian some of your people will come by."

Byrne sensed progress.

"Wilson, get back out to the restaurant site and check that alley for tire marks," Byrne directed. "I want to know the width of any tracks and tread. Get another person to go with you. Then stop at the Motel Sepia. I want the cabin area where these honeymooners stayed checked. Scour the cabin and examine the ground where their car was parked. Let's see if the tire tracks at the two places have anything in common."

Wilson moved toward the door before a shouting Byrne stopped him.

"And radio the information. From both places. I want a report in 30 minutes. Preferably sooner."

2:25 p.m.

Perkins no longer knocked before entering the room usurped by Byrne's investigation. Nobody did. The two-way movement in and out of the place, which was not much larger than the holding cell down the hallway, could have used a traffic cop for control. What had been independent bodies coming and going had merged into a team scrum. Byrne had them thinking and acting as one.

"Whoa, slow down there, Mr. Perkins," Byrne advised, balancing a fresh cup of coffee in his right hand. "The hubbub in this place is beginning to resemble a Jane Russell press conference. Whaddya have?"

"I compared the two lists of names, the ones we found in Mr. Dawson's books at the restaurant, and the ones given over the phone by Naperville police of names in Mr. Arezzo's files," Perkins explained. "If Dawson and Arezzo knew one another, sad to report, they didn't call one another. Or, at least, we found no direct connection from these lists."

"In other words, you struck out?" Byrne said.

"Well, maybe not entirely," Perkins responded. "There was the name of Eddie Ralston on one of Arezzo's old financial forms. And we found R. Ralston listed in an old telephone register kept by Dawson. The number is no longer in service, but it was a Chicago listing."

Byrne took a sip of his now cold coffee.

"I think we can begin to assume that these two victims were once connected, a kinship shrouded in a shadowy past and, unfortunately for them, bound eternally by similar brutal deaths," Byrne pronounced. "Let's get McNabb back on the phone to see what he knows about this Ralston fellow."

In a few minutes, the Naperville officer was again on the telephone and providing the shady background of one Rhino Ralston.

McNabb was about five paragraphs into Ralston's rap sheet when Byrne was interrupted by his secretary. She was swinging her arms like an umpire declaring someone safe in a bang-bang play at home plate.

"Excuse me, Capt. McNabb. Could you hold on for just a second?" Byrne requested. "I'm getting an emergency wave from one of my people."

"Sure, Lieutenant," McNabb said. "No problem."

"What is it, Judy?" Byrne asked, covering the phone mouthpiece with his hand.

"Wilson is on the other line with information about some tire tracks," Judy said, pointing at the phone's blinking light.

"Yes, I'll get the line," Byrne said, putting McNabb on hold. "Go ahead Wilson."

"Lt. Byrne," Wilson reported. "The car tire tracks in that dirt alley behind the restaurant are about six inches wide. I checked with the Chrysler dealer, and he confirmed that size for a New Yorker. We are now at Motel Sepia. The tread marks and tire width are similar out here, where that black Chrysler was parked."

"Fine work, Wilson. Did you find anything inside the cabin that would help us?"

"No sir, but we are still checking."

"Good. Call back if you find anything significant." Byrne clicked off Wilson and reconnected with McNabb. "Capt. McNabb, are you still there?"

"I am."

"I believe we are on the right trail."

Bump Byrne caressed the mole above his lip as if he were a fortune teller rubbing lines of a palm. He updated McNabb on the new information.

Chapter 46

"Are you Lt. Byrne? I need to visit with Lt. Byrne," an excited and overly anxious Deron Campbell addressed an officer in the front lobby of the Cedar Rapids Police Department.

"What's the problem, young man? Lt. Byrne is extremely busy right now. My name is Jim Perkins. I work in records. Is there something you want to look up? File a complaint? What can we do for you?"

"No, I'm not here to file any complaint," Campbell said. "I just want to talk to Lt. Byrne. I understand he is the officer in charge of the murder investigation."

"You have information about a murder?" Perkins asked.

"Only that Curtis Moore is no murderer," Campbell said frantically. "I'm Deron Campbell, a student at Coe." He offered his hand in greeting and Perkins accepted.

"How do you know Curtis?"

"He and I are sorta friends," Campbell said. "We meet now and then to talk. Curtis has had some tough times, finding a job and all. He likes to jaw about things, mainly life things. I tell him about growing up in Chicago and he tells me about Cedar Rapids.

"Couple weeks ago, I told him about this summer class I have. Sociology class. We exchange ideas about religion and racial things. How people get along. Is it any different here in Iowa than it is in Chicago, things like that. What sort of friends we have. Do we experience discrimination, or hear people say things that put others down."

Perkins nodded to indicate he got the drift of what Campbell was trying to explain.

"OK, OK. What does that have to do with murder?"

"Well, sir, one day Curtis heard me say something about conditions in the South, where a black man cannot even look more than two seconds at a white woman or his intentions are questioned. Or worse, the assumption is made that he plans to do something to this white woman, like touch her.

"It wound up with Curtis claiming it was no different in Cedar Rapids, that if he kissed a white woman, he would be tossed in jail. Said he was thinking of an experiment, that's what he called it, an experiment, where he would kiss a white woman just to see what would happen."

"Curtis Moore is not charged with kissing a white woman," Perkins injected. "Mr. Campbell, is it?"

"That's right."

"He's charged with armed robbery," Perkins said. "Two instances of armed robbery. He's become known as the Kissing Bandit. But before he kissed these two women, he took money from two businesses. He's been cleared of last night's murder and robbery at the restaurant on the east end, if that's what you're talking about."

"Yes," Campbell sighed, tossing his arms in the air as a gesture of relief. "That's good to hear. Someone told me Curtis was charged with murder, but I knew he couldn't kill anyone. That's not his nature, to hurt people."

"Did you know he could rob someone?" Perkins asked.

"I don't know what happened," Campbell replied, "but I find it hard to believe Curtis really wanted to steal money. It was part of this stupid experiment he kept talking about. I tried to talk him out of it, but he seemed determined to go ahead with it."

"Unfortunately, Mr. Campbell, the law doesn't excuse stupidity," Perkins said with a shrug of his shoulders. "If he did it, whatever the motive, he did it. If you want to make a statement on your friend's behalf, I'll get one of the clerks to help you. But, he isn't charged with murder."

"That's a comfort. I know Curtis wouldn't harm anyone," Campbell repeated. "Yes, I would like to write something out about his dumb experiment."

With that, Perkins referred him to a student helping in records and returned to the main task, solving a murder. It was after 3 o'clock. He took two steps at a time up the stairs and skipped toward action central, where he was greeted by a ringing phone.

He picked up and heard the voice of Kenny Wilson.

"This is Perkins, Kenny. What's up?"

"I talked again with Miss Keller," Wilson related. "She gave me the name of Dawson's regular golfing partner here in town, over at Ellis Park. I just talked to him."

"Yeah? Did he have any worthwhile information?"

"Well, he had a couple of names, fellas Dawson told him were good friends in Chicago and one in Naperville. One of these guys, a Ken Soloman from Naperville, actually came to Cedar Rapids to play golf, twice. Jelling and I couldn't reach the Chicago guy, but we did talk to Soloman. We asked him what he knew about Dawson and if he was aware of this Arezzo character."

"And?"

"Soloman said he knew Arezzo and Dawson. Said the three played golf in that area a number of times, once in a tournament."

"I'm surprised the Naperville police didn't know about that," Perkins commented.

"They interviewed Soloman and were aware of his friendship with Arezzo, but not of Dawson's connection. They had no reason to bring up that name."

"What else did Soloman tell you?"

"He said Arezzo, on more than one occasion, mentioned his past association with the dark side of Chicago, including this Rhino Ralston mobster. That's why police there picked up the tie to the mob, but never produced enough evidence to file charges. They want a solid case against the Ralston crowd before they go to a grand jury."

"Where does that leave us?" Perkins asked.

"Good question," Wilson replied. "It leaves us with an Arezzo-Dawson link. That's important. I think we can take it that if Arezzo was associated with the mob and possibly died at its hands, it's not far-fetched to assume that Dawson may have worked in the same quarters and died from the same disease. Their deaths are similar. I'm guessing their lives were similar."

"I'll pass this along to Byrne," Perkins said, realizing the importance of the connection. "But like Naperville, the lieutenant will want more than assuming and guessing before getting too excited." "Agreed," said Wilson. "We'll keep digging. At least this gives us one more piece in the puzzle."

Before McNabb and Byrne concluded their conversation, they reviewed all that they knew. While the picture on the horizon was still fuzzy, both sensed a sort of coagulation of information that was beginning to come into focus, possibly on the Lincoln Highway toward Chicago.

Should they put out an APB on the black Chrysler, the honeymoon car? Stop the passengers and search the vehicle?

There was no doubt that Byrne's opinion and hesitation were colored by the false alarm involving another black car, and the swarming of the book salesman in Mount Vernon. He didn't want a repeat of that. It left the department looking a little like the Keystone Cops.

McNabb was about to conclude their telephone powwow when Perkins high-signed Byrne again. His waving arms projected urgency.

"Just one more second, Captain," Byrne requested. "I have this fellow Perkins acting like an orangutan at feeding time."

"I'll hold," said McNabb.

"What is it Perkins?" Byrne inquired.

"Lieutenant, Jelling and Wilson have found a tie between Arezzo and Dawson. The two were golfing buddies in Illinois. And, another golfer they talked to mentioned that the subject of Rhino Ralston came up more than once during their visits. I believe we can conclude that Dawson, Arezzo and Ralston worked together at one time, certainly ran in the same circles."

"Good, Perkins."

Byrne conveyed the additional information to McNabb. Again they analyzed the evidence at hand, albeit mostly circumstantial. But Byrne's nose was twitching.

"Excuse me! Excuse me, Lieutenant," Judy cried excitedly as she ran toward him.

"One more second, Captain," Byrne sighed.

"Lieutenant, Jelling just radioed from the Motel Sepia. They were rummaging through the honeymooners' cabin and found a Spearmint gum wrapper."

Chapter 47

It was a few minutes past 1 p.m. when the "newly unmarried" couple exited DeWitt, Iowa.

The silent treatment was in full mode. But their private thoughts were bulging with urges to escape, she from him and a life gone sour, he from cops and Rhino Ralston's pervasive thumb.

Jennifer pulled up the collar on her white blouse, an almost mechanical motion designed to insulate her from Ellis' piercing eyes. The navy peddle-pushers covered all but the lower part of her legs.

If only they were back in Chicago, she thought. What a pitiful notion, that she should seek refuge from an autocratic lowlife like Ralston. She was between two evils and it created bile that was tough to swallow. She had to deal with the present, and that meant Ellis' mercurial moods. She didn't trust him.

Ellis drove 50 mph east on Highway 30, pondering what speed was best not to attract attention. His left arm rested on the door's turned-down window, fingers tapping on the steering wheel. He alternately glanced ahead and then in the rear- view mirror, watching for anything unusual, or for anyone who may be watching for a black sedan.

The news report and those two words, "black sedan," had become etched in his mulish mind. They produced tiny warning signals that zipped around in this brain like tense magnetic flecks between two poles.

However, he would never acknowledge to anyone that he was nervous. He had been in much tighter spots than this and always found a way out. He was invincible, certainly not threatened by any hayseed cop.

The tasseled corn, some of its yellowing leaves reflecting strains from the heat, placidly ignored the passing travelers and their personal concerns. To a mind set in neutral, staring ahead in preoccupation, it would be like moving through a mesmerizing tunnel. Only it seemed as if the endless rows of corn were the travelers, filing by, leaving everything else stuck in vacant time.

As the corn sentries slid by, on both sides of the road, they sedated all but seasoned nomads. The two-lane highway appeared to stretch into infinity. The intermittent white middle line zipped by in hypnotizing cadence. Up close, the concrete road produced waves of reflected heat and then, in the distance, evolved into what looked to be a ribbon of water. The black sedan's tires slapped at the highway's joints, adding a rhythmic component to a near psychedelic setting.

Approaching cars grew from envisioned ants to a metallic whoosh as they passed into obscurity.

The two people, entangled in the rigors of bad decisions, traveled through one of the most bountiful regions on Earth, but were bound in the poverty of mutual anxiety. The marrow of their existence was soured by servitude. It was a tragedy in which a crime was consummated, and the usual joyous condition of love and honeymoon reduced to contrivance.

Jennifer locked on the serene countryside and again reflected on her life.

How had she become so hardened in college? Why had she gone beyond seeking elbow room, a normal exercise of maturation, and, in so many ways muscled her family out of her life? Was it necessary to jump off the bridge to find new water to swim in? Her older brother seemed to accept the obsessive protection without leaping into the shallow end. He had completed law school at the State University of Iowa, and now was an adviser in the Illinois State House.

Ellis glanced to the left where a farmer baling hay interrupted corn's domination of the landscape. He was oblivious to this blip in prairie scenery. A spewing geyser would have caught no more of his attention.

Maybe, he thought, he should talk to Rhino, tell him that he was sick of the Midwest, its winters and familiarity. He couldn't just say he was tired of Rhino and his Chicago associates. He wanted out. It was time for something else, new undertakings.

He nearly laughed out loud. Right, like this was a request to the home office to be transferred to Miami.

Good ole Rhino, compassionate Rhino. "Sure Joe," Ellis imagined Ralston saying, "check out Tampa, the Gulf Coast, Miami. See what you like."

DeKalb Hybrids. Funks G. Pioneer. There were more seed corn signs in Iowa than liquor advertisements in Chicago.

Would Rhino react violently if Ellis just disappeared? Or would he write it off as an insignificant matter with no direct threat to his businesses? Trying to figure Rhino was like trying to understand Einstein's theories.

A self-pitying gloom enveloped Jennifer. She wished she could have been like her brother, more accepting, less bull-headed, more understanding and less self-centered. But doesn't everyone reject what their parents want? Mother always had a soft spot for "sonny." Her brother could do no wrong. Why did they expect her to be like him?

Ellis slowed down. The hazy blue sky had given birth to a few puffy clouds, some in the distant north marked with dark eyelashes. He sensed a wind change, too, and the air transported the slightest scent of rain. The corn tassels became animated, joyously waving in expectation of a soothing wash by Mother Nature.

"I'm going to pull off on this gravel road," Ellis announced. "I've got to think. I want to make some contingency plans."

A pang of fear trickled through Jennifer's body like a mild electric charge. Surely, he wouldn't attack her in broad daylight. If he stayed away during the night, the rule of Rhino keeping things in order, he certainly wouldn't try something now.

She kept telling herself this as the skin on her arms and legs crinkled into goosebumps. She kept quiet. She squeezed closer to the door.

He drove less than a half mile on the rural gravel road before stopping. He looked at her.

"You have a high regard for your desirability," he said point-blank, sensing her uneasiness. "If I wanted any part of your cold body, I would have had my way long before now. You are laughable, squirming in your seat like a worm strung on a fish hook."

He looked back at the highway and saw only the shimmers of the hot sun on the hot fields.

"Rosie, baby, you are one icy strumpet, quivering like a lost polar bear cub in the desert, looking for its mommy." His insults were on parade and he wallowed in devious fulfillment at hurling the phony honeymoon moniker.

Jennifer's insides pulsated with revulsion. Again her imagination placed a target on his forehead. If she had possessed a gun, she would have emptied the chamber's contents in his skull.

Ellis pulled out some maps. He could either stay on Route 30, or, go north and take Highway 64 into Chicago. The latter would be slightly longer but bring them directly into the city via North Avenue. The question, he thought to himself, was which route had fewer cops and police departments that monitored APBs out of Iowa? He knew for sure he wanted to avoid the Quad Cities.

There was another thing to ponder. Should he stop in Clinton and call Rhino, tell him of the radio report about George Dawson's murder and the "black sedan," or was that asking for more trouble? What would Rhino do? What could he do? Rhino wouldn't want to be pulled into any situation. Shit. Would he get the rest of his money for the Iowa job?

The more Ellis thought about that prospect, not receiving the balance for committing murder, the more he despised Ralston. It was a paranoia spasm he had to control. He dismissed the idea of calling Rhino. Who knows what insane action that would trigger? One thing began to congeal in his mind. He had to leave Rhino and the Chicago mob. It was suffocating him.

"Rosie, I think we'll stop at a gas station and find directions to a gun shop or hunting store, a place that sells knives. I need to find a nice machete-like slasher like the one I ditched near the restaurant. Just in case we run into some hand-to-hand combat. We must adapt, improvise and overcome, Rosie, in order to win the battle. There is nothing like a sharp knife to instill confidence. Time to reload, baby!"

Jennifer was stunned.

This guy was totally nuts, she thought. She must be totally nuts to have allowed herself to be part of this, to place herself in this situation.

"I think we should check out this little town," Ellis said, pointing to a dot on the map called Low Moor. "We'll ask about a hunting store there. Does that fit with your plans, Rosie, the Cold Queen of Park Ridge? If you aren't dreaming of becoming a farmer's bride, maybe you're anticipating whoring up with one of Rhino's business partners."

His derailed demeanor delighted in spewing taunts, basked in inflicting discomfort and fear.

"Ah yes, the cold rich bitch, making herself available for all of Rhino's slime balls. Quite an occupation. You'll have to insert something in the Northwestern Alumni quarterly. Perhaps they will want to interview you about your work. That would make your family proud."

He was smiling, sneering.

"Your father could brag about you at the country club."

Jennifer took her right hand and dug her fingernails into her cheek. She pinched and twisted as though his eyes were the target.

She didn't just want to produce pain. She wanted to maim. She wanted to scar. Her hand shook in fury. Lost in bewilderment and consumed by an intense loathing, she began to convulse like a victim of fever. Her soul gasped for respect.

After a minute or so, the released tears soothed some of her anxiety, like a spring rain softens remnants of a harsh winter. Her hand and body began to relax.

She noticed blood on her fingers. He had managed to cause her to harm herself. What kind of insanity is that? she shuddered.

"What are you doing over there?" Ellis demanded. "Is that blood on your hand? What's going on?" he shouted.

His paranoia again bloomed and produced a picture of cops hunting for a black sedan and now asking about blood on the car seat.

"You damn whore. I should've insisted you stay in Chicago. I didn't need you or a honeymoon ruse to do this job."

He yanked his handkerchief from his back pocket.

"Take this and wrap your finger," he directed. "Don't get any blood on your clothes or the car seat. You bitch!"

His acrid reaction even left a bitter taste in his mouth, a signal of worry. He sought to suppress it.

"How did you cut your hand?" he asked with a slight nod toward civility.

"I didn't cut my hand," she said softly between persistent sobs. "I cut my cheek. I pinched it and scratched it, pretending it was you. Pretending it was your eyes. You are an evil bastard."

Ellis' momentary lapse in restive behavior was quickly overtaken by his vile nature. His right arm coiled like a snake. He smacked her hard on her left cheek. Jennifer screamed as her head twisted violently and bounced off the molding of the car door. Lucky for her, the window was rolled down.

"The next time my hand won't be open," he stared bitterly into her eyes. "The last thing I need right now is lip from a scrawny bitch like you."

Jennifer cowered all the more, shifting the handkerchief from the self-inflicted wound on the cheek to the growing bump on her forehead.

Chapter 48

Jennifer dabbed the scratch on her face with the handkerchief. Her right cheek was still bleeding and the self-inflicted wound released a burning tingle. The left side of her face had red welts that looked like imprints from a bear paw.

Her head pounded in pain. Maybe her profound hatred for Ellis, in a curious ricochet of impulse, would leave a scar where her fingernails gouged her cheek. It certainly would leave a wound on her emotional well-being.

Her eyes were closed, focused on the darkness in her life. Like a bad movie, the scene flickered from Ellis to the depths of her own existence.

Was she staring at shame, depression? Was that what her life had come to, a hopeless abyss? Was there any light at the end of the tunnel? Was there even a tunnel? Could she crawl on her knees to Rhino to seek release?

She had to find a way out. She had to reclaim her future. For God's sake, she had to reclaim herself.

Suddenly, there was a break in the darkness, a fracture in the bleakness. She saw a tiny light, like that flashed by a home movie projector. People were talking in the backyard, her backyard. Children were playing, running. She was skipping, curls flying from side-to-side, running toward the swing under the huge elm tree. Up she jumped, grabbing ropes in each hand. She was laughing and then screaming as her father pushed her higher and higher.

"Faster, Daddy, faster," she heard herself beg, as if it were yesterday. The clouds in the sky raced toward her, and then retreated, all in rhythm. Tiny ripples of tickle spun through her stomach.

Oh, it had been wonderful. The joy, the happiness. Uncles and aunts and cousins, everyone wrapped in the comfort of family, forgetting petty squabbles like the time smartass cousin Rollie pushed her in the mud. He was careful not to get dirt on his fancy brown and white shoes. He had laughed as she looked at the dirt on her pretty red dress.

Actually, she had to admit, she had rather enjoyed it.

"Not too high, not too high," her mother cautioned like a swing coach. She transported another pitcher of lemonade to the thirsty revelers.

Was that Uncle Jack over there, playing catch with Mark? Mark, the oldest cousin, who wanted to grow up and become president of Mars Candy Co.?

"Higher, Daddy, higher," her excited child's voice rang from memory.

Uncle Jack yelled. He had looked at the little radio that was perched on a folding chair. It was plugged into a long extension cord that snaked its way beneath the screen door and into the house where it sought the electrical energy to give voice.

"Bert Wilson just called the final out," Uncle Jack had rejoiced. "Believe it or not, ladies and gentlemen, the Cubs won! The Cubs won!"

Her Daddy had cheered. She really didn't care.

"One in a row! Break up the Cubs," her Daddy had yelled. She didn't understand.

"Higher, Daddy! Higher!"

Ellis pulled into a Sinclair station.

Jennifer looked up from the backyard scene of her memory to see instead an empty human being seemingly void of happiness. Ellis appeared not as a man of character, or someone with moral sensibility, but a sack of bones and muscle, barren of spirit and compassion.

She felt a twinge of sorrow for him. It departed quickly. She gazed up at the little green dinosaur on the station sign.

An attendant asked if they wanted a fill-up. Ellis said no, but asked for area maps.

"By the way," he attempted to sound and act like a tourist. "Is there a hunting and fishing store in these parts, perhaps some place that sells fillet knives? May check out the backwaters of the Mississippi for some black crappie and largemouth bass."

Ellis had never been fishing in his life, but once heard a man who had been in his Marine Corps outfit talk about fishing in the myriad of sloughs off the main channel of the Mississippi River.

"There's a real fine store in Clinton that sells knives of all sorts, and fishing gear, too," the attendant said. "And, they have a guy there who can direct you to some of the hot fishing spots along the Mississippi. Friendly fellow. I can give you his name if you –"

"Never mind," Ellis interrupted. "I have my own techniques. What's the name of the store?"

"Well, OK. The store is Bob's Grocery on Fourth Street in Clinton. Can't miss it as you drive into town a mile or so."

"I ain't interested in groceries."

"They have a lot more than groceries," the attendant tried to be helpful. "Big kitchenware department, you asked about cutlery. You won't find a bigger selection of knives in Iowa. Why, they've got more knives than a hog slaughtering plant."

He laughed. Ellis didn't.

"And just about everything else," the man quickly added, sensing the sticky atmosphere produced by Ellis' churlish nature. "Quite the place. The missus there would have a real good time looking around at Bob's."

"Well, she ain't my missus, and she ain't looking around," Ellis blared. "See ya, Bub. Oh, one other thing. Do you know if they sell guns?"

"I don't think they deal in guns, but I can tell you one thing, sir. They will know where you can purchase hunting equipment. Say, you're quite the outdoorsman, fishing and hunting. But this ain't really the season for –"

"No matter," Ellis hopped back into the Chrysler, maps in hand. He made a U-turn back to the main highway.

He continued to drive extra slow, like a snail laboring through January molasses. Once back on Route 30, he accelerated to 50 mph. A small aircraft had just lifted from a nearby runway, its wings wobbling like a fledgling bird. Ellis watched it for several seconds, and quickly dismissed its importance.

Traffic began to pick up as they approached Clinton, a town stuck on Iowa's eastern nose. It's where the Hawkeye state pushed the river in a bulge toward Illinois.

"I want to be a writer, Daddy," Jennifer's recall activated again. "I love stories. I'm going to write a story how my Daddy pushed me so high that my toes touched the clouds. And how my tummy tickled when I came down."

Jennifer had been on every school newspaper since seventh grade. She wrote essays and poems and anything that required the combination of nouns and verbs. She had intended to major in journalism at Northwestern.

She shook her head in dismay. Jennifer, you must find your way back, she said to herself. You must find your way back.

Ellis drove past a cemetery and then slowed down as he reached an intersection. An arrow pointed right to the town of Camanche, but he wanted to continue straight ahead.

"What's that goddamn awful smell?" Ellis proclaimed eloquently as they entered the south outskirts of Clinton.

He drove down a four-lane blacktop street, past gas stations, drive-ins and a huge industrial complex that was belching steam and other things. Inside a huge train repair shop sparks from welding operations popped like firecrackers. After a mile or so, the road swung right, and he resumed swearing as he entered a confusing intersection. Unsure of where to turn, he opted to pull into a DX station.

The big Chrysler rolled over the snaking air tube, sounding the "ding-ding" that harkened a station attendant.

"How can I help you?" asked a middle-age man whose cap displayed the familiar DX diamond logo.

"Can you direct me to Bob's Grocery?" Ellis asked. "I think it's on Fourth Street."

Chapter 49

"**M**e thinks Kilroy was here," Byrnes mumbled into the phone after relaying the chewing gum information.

"What's that about Kilroy?" McNabb asked, scratching his head in befuddlement at the other end of the line.

"Sorry, Captain, I was just ruminating out loud. You remember Kilroy, as in 'Kilroy was Here'? That goofy caricature that was popular during the war? It was graffiti, a sort of a GI calling card."

"Oh sure, I remember," McNabb said. "I was with the Infantry in North Africa. We saw one of those bald-headed, big-nose Kilroy scrawlings somewhere in Morocco. What's he doing in Cedar Rapids?" he laughed.

"Well, he's not. I was just assigning the mysterious name of Kilroy to our allusive killer," Byrnes explained. "I believe we are on the right track with this so-called honeymooner and black Chrysler. What do you think? We know the man who was stabbed here and your victim in Naperville were acquaintances. The crime MO is similar, brutal with aforethought."

There was a lot of police processing zipping over the phone line in between the spoken words.

Byrne sensed a heightening of what he called "investigative itch." To hear him explain, it consists of sore feet, telephone ear, creeping underwear, coffee breath, and the disintegration of underarm deodorant, all crowned with an intense passion to solve a case.

Byrne and McNabb had been talking for nearly 10 minutes as new information dribbled in and was mingled with the old. Things were beginning to add up, come to a junction. The puzzle, once again, was being filled in, piece by piece.

"We believe the killer and this Rosemary Jones were accomplices, probably fake honeymooners," Byrne continued. "And the killer also used as cover the highly publicized Kissing Bandit capers here in Cedar Rapids, making like he was the same person who robbed two other businesses. We know George Dawson's killer was a big, strong man and probably chewed Spearmint gum.

"We believe a car that was in an alley behind the restaurant murder scene was also at the Motel Sepia. Tire tracks match. This car, a black Chrysler, hauling alleged honeymooners. And, we found that gum wrapper at the motel.

Byrne shuffled through his notes to see if he left anything out, and to give his counterpart time to digest the accumulating evidence.

"Captain, when you receive the copies of fingerprints from the crime scene here, I'll bet you a six-pack of Falstaff that they will resemble the partials you found on that park bench in June," Byrne said. "The same killer, mob connected, as apparently were both of the victims at one time. I think we have our man, and he's on the way back to Chicago with his make-believe bride.

"I say we move in. What do you think?"

"Don't like Falstaff beer, Lt. Byrne, but I believe you are right on the money on these murders," McNabb replied. "What's your best guess on their location?"

"Well, they left here about 10:45 this morning," Byrne said. "They were headed east, and assuming they would continue in that direction they would have arrived in Clinton around 12:30. Let's say they stopped for a sandwich. They probably didn't leave Clinton until around 1 or 1:15. Pull out a map, Captain, and help me coordinate."

The two cops mumbled details of their activities into their phones as they spread highway road maps on their desks. Twenty seconds later, the muttering and shuffling gravitated to coherence.

"Okay, let's say they left Clinton around 1 p.m.," McNabb calculated, "and now it's almost 2:50. Assuming they continued east on Route 30, they would be – good grief – they would be half way across Illinois by now. Maybe near Shabbona or Waterman. Is that how you see it?"

"That's a fair estimate," Byrne said. "Looks like our killer is coming home to you."

"Another possibility," McNabb added, "is that the black Chrysler jumped north somewhere and is on a different highway or state route."

"And," Byrne injected, "they could have been sneaky and left Highway 30 somewhere in Iowa. But I think we have to assume they followed familiarity, and that would be Route 30, likely the way they came into Iowa."

"Let's get out an APB to both the Illinois and Iowa state patrol," McNabb suggested, "and we'll notify police in Illinois towns. In fact, we'll send a couple of cars west, one on Route 30 and another on State 64."

"Sounds good," Byrne agreed. "We will alert Clinton police and send a couple of our own cars in your direction. We'll try to keep communication tight. Let's plan to have phone contact at least every 15 minutes to update any information from the field and coordinate any changes in the hunt."

"Good plan," said McNabb. "We will keep one line dedicated to the search."

McNabb paused, deliberately, for five seconds to underscore his next words.

"Lt. Byrne, make sure that everyone knows this man is extremely dangerous. If this is who we think, he kills indiscriminately. It's his business. He doesn't ask questions. Doesn't care who you are or what you are.

"As we understand it," McNabb continued, "and we've reviewed all of our notes from June, this guy is a paid hit man. His name is Joe Ellis. He served in Korea as a sniper, and he is focused on two things. Killing his prey, and that's how he looks at it, and surviving. He has no respect for human life except his own, and he covers his tracks well."

"Do you think we will be able to take them alive?" Byrne asked.

"I don't know," McNabb replied, his voice colored with disquiet. "I just pray we don't lose any of our people."

That marked the seriousness of the hunt.

"I'll make sure all the people on our end realize that," Byrne said.

"One other thing, Lieutenant," McNabb said. "When this is over? I'll have a Pabst Blue Ribbon."

Chapter 50

"**D**amn one-way streets!"

Ellis mustered his patience in the name of keeping a low profile. No need to flag the cops by driving the wrong way on a one-way street. Now that he was in a larger city he didn't know if the danger of being spotted was less or greater. He was as unsettled as a stomach besieged by flu.

He finally managed to spot Bob's Grocery after a maze of street connections produced a mini tour of the town's south side. He pulled slowly along the high curb, two doors down from the store.

The two-story building with a fancy roofline cornice looked like it was out of the late 1800s. The brick front was neatly complemented by colorful awnings draped over high windows that revealed enough merchandise to make ole Richard W. Sears' mouth water. Grocery store was a misnomer of substantial proportions, although it had a wide variety of foodstuffs, too.

Just inside the front door large glass bottles with side-skewed lids lined up on shelves like plump recruits on a parade ground. They were full of various candies. The next isle featured barrels of licorice. Nearby were pinwheel lollipops big enough to use as spare tires. Chocolate bar chunks were stacked in sinful rows, singing beckoning refrains to bug-eyed children.

There were jawbreakers of all colors and sizes, some of adequate diameter to look natural on a golf tee. They came wrapped individually or displayed with flamboyance in square glass containers.

Parents couldn't be blamed if they blindfolded their progeny. It was a mouth-watering array of sweets, a stomach ache waiting to happen, sugary bedlam! It was a confectionary carnival.

Within view of this candy exposition were walls of tools in every shape and for every job. Close by were bins of bolts and their partners, nuts and washers. Nails came in every penny size, and there were enough spikes to start your own railroad. Brooms and mops consorted with pots and pans.

It was fair to say that Bob's Grocery was a destination store. Clinton, Iowa, a long, narrow town cuddled between bluffs and the Mississippi River, has a history centered on lumber production. But in the mid-1950s Bob's Grocery could legitimately occupy a place of fame in the town.

The store had enough knives to outfit a battalion of pirates.

Ellis came in to look for knives, but knew immediately he wanted to purchase several ten-packs of Wrigley's Spearmint Chewing Gum.

At first he had ordered Jennifer to remain in the car. Her eyes must have betrayed her; a glint that implied she may run. That and nature's calling.

"I have to use the restroom," she said mechanically, not looking at him. He changed his mind and told her to come along. She grabbed her small black clutch purse and exited the car.

Ellis half pushed her up the steps and into the store. The stone steps were grooved with years of foot traffic. The place, no architectural wonder, nevertheless produced the kind of awe sensed at the fireworks finale at the state fair. It was an astonishing exhibit of merchandising where volume was everything and order was forgotten.

Bob's Grocery was a like a museum that had expanded several times into adjoining businesses that were less successful. Stamped tin ceiling squares were interrupted by walls to mark where former businesses were married to Bob's. Large black fans dropped from the high ceilings and labored to counter summer's heat. Two floor fans added their meager efforts.

"Good afternoon," a portly middle-aged woman greeted Ellis and Jennifer. "Has it begun to rain out there yet? We could sure use some rain. My garden is beginning to look – oh my, young lady! What happened to your face? Did you take a fall? Oh my!"

"Yes, that's what happened," Ellis replied before Jennifer had any chance to speak. "We were at a park and she slipped and hit her head on a picnic bench."

"Goodness. Can I get some salve and a bandage?" the clerk asked. "She should keep that cut protected."

"It will be fine," Jennifer offered meekly. "Really, it doesn't hurt."

"We would like to look at some fillet knives," Ellis quickly interjected. "Might do some fishing in the Mississippi and one has to be optimistic." He faked a laugh. "I'm a knife collector and was told you have a sizeable selection."

The clerk gestured in the direction of housewares.

"I think you'll find what you need over there," she said, still concerned about Jennifer's wound. "Are you sure young lady that you don't want a Band-Aid for that cheek?"

"I'll be fine," Jennifer said, casting her eyes downward. "But I would like to use your restroom."

"By all means. Do you see those corrugated bushel baskets over on the far wall?" She pointed to the rear of the store. "When you get to the bushel baskets, turn right into the next room, walk past the boys' T-shirts and pants, and if you look left, you'll see the "toilet" sign. We just have one place for men and women."

"We'll find it," Ellis said, sending her a look of disgust that would curdle eggs. They walked in the direction she indicated.

"Why don't you just pee in one of those bushel baskets?" Ellis sneered. She ignored him and proceeded to the restroom. "I'll be keeping an eye on the door," he said with all the savoir-faire of a skunk.

Relief achieved, their shopping commenced.

Ellis looked up, down and sideways, away from the kitchen cutlery to the utility and hunting knives. He spotted several that he liked. Jennifer watched and squirmed as he picked up a knife and felt its business side. Never had she seen a person so consumed, so emotionally engaged by an object of utility, an object that could kill.

He caressed the blade as if it were the cheek of a lover. His eyes bulged, his lips curled into a circle of wonder. Small beads of sweat seeped from his forehead. For a second, she thought he was going to kiss the shiny metal in some sort of erotic impulse. It was sickening.

This was the moment Jennifer made up her mind.

She slowly walked over to a section featuring butcher knives. Almost immediately, she envisioned thrusting one deep into the belly of Joe Ellis. She was twisting it, ripping his insides. Now his eyes were bulging for a different reason, lips quivering, sweat building. She shocked herself. What had she become? How could she be like him?

"What the hell are you doing?" Ellis confronted her. "You look like you're going to be sick."

"I am sick," she said softly, "sick of myself."

"Well, that makes two of us," he snarled.

Ellis returned to his task of shopping on behalf of death, a proxy for sadism. He strolled the store looking for small arms, but couldn't find any guns. It was about the only thing Bob's Grocery didn't have.

After a half-hour, they left the store with four knives and a sack of chewing gum. He tossed the packages on the floor in the back seat, got in and inserted the key in the ignition.

It was nearly 2 o'clock.

Ellis studied the Iowa and Illinois road maps. With the newscast's "black sedan" report still bouncing around in his mind, he tried to think like a cop. If police were focusing on him, and it was an assumption he was forced to accept, they would look first along Route 30. That was a given.

He had to avoid Highway 30, pick an alternate route back to Chicago, he said silently. Maybe follow Route 67 in Iowa, and then angle over to Illinois 64 or 38?

He was edgy, and drove aimlessly north in the city. He went by the YMCA and ignored a sign giving direction to the courthouse. They passed a park and homes nestled among trees, and then drove by Mercy Hospital. He recognized nothing. His mind was everywhere, but nowhere.

Traffic lights relit his sense of place. The overhead sign said Main Avenue and simultaneously he saw an arrow for Route 67. Out of the corner of his eye, he spotted a commercial sign for "B.J.'s Gun Shop." He swung the Chrysler right and found a parking place.

Again, Jennifer was ordered to tag along. The store was small and looked more like a place where stolen guns were pawned or ditched on the cheap. Guns were not his preferred choice for execution, but now Ellis found himself in a different circumstance. The place featured peeling paint and cracked windows. Inside, cigar smoke competed with body odor, both emanating from the old timer behind the counter. His sweat-stained cap advertised "Bill's Bait & Stuff."

Ellis spotted an old single-shot .22 Remington, worthless for his purposes. What was available in handguns? Not much. But then he was drawn to a corner case section with small weapons, and his eyes lit up like a six-shooter in the hands of Tom Mix. The .38 Special improved his disposition like a shot of Jack Daniel's calms the nerves.

Within ten minutes, Ellis had purchased the .38 and a Colt .50, ammunition for both and a fancy, brown-handled switchblade with a wavy edge and a tip that spelled pain. He wasn't concerned about Mr. Geezer reporting the transaction. It was unlikely the clerk was on a first-name basis with the sheriff.

Once again on the road, Ellis drove around the block and followed the U.S. 67 North marker. About a mile up the road, a sign pointed to Eagle Point Park.

Still formulating his future, Ellis slowed and turned into the Mississippi overlook with the unstated purpose of gathering his thoughts, which continued to focus on the words "black sedan." He pulled into a parking lane. There was no one else around.

Ellis had fashioned himself as untouchable, able to defeat and destroy anything and anybody who tried to block his path, except, maybe, for Rhino and his ilk. He deigned himself to be beyond society's moral and legal restrictions. Now he sensed a tightening in his chest.

He rolled down the car window and began tapping on the steering wheel. His self-bestowed invincibility on trial, he shouted a stream of swear words that sought to dent the placid countryside, interspersed a host of body parts and functions and naturally asked a deity to condemn all of it.

Jennifer glanced at him, surprised to see what she diagnosed as a mini-meltdown. She hesitated to call into question the unbreakable image he accorded himself. Still, the hateful acid in her stomach churned. The venom sought release. She continued to stare at him. Curiously, he avoided looking at her.

"Bad case of anxiety?" she said boldly. "It must have been those cheese curds you had at the drive-in." She intended to editorialize further about the sickly look on his face, but before another word exited her mouth, his open right hand landed across her lower jaw. Again her head slammed into the door frame.

"You goddamn mouthy whore," he said, glaring at her like a wild ape. "I swear if you utter one more thing about how I look, I will retrieve one of my new knives, carve you into pieces and toss your chopped up ass over this bluff."

Jennifer didn't dare review his raging face again. She began to doubt if her life could be protected by Rhino's long arm. She understood, clearer than ever, that she was accompanied by a beast.

Pain reverberated in her head. Thoughts rattled inside her brain, and she started to sob and tremble. Quickly, she mustered all the strength she had to sooth her battered soul.

Rather than stoke her hatred for Ellis, she began again to silently condemn her life decisions and the cauldron she'd created. Strangely, her shaking stopped. Her confidence and collective being rallied, bolstered by an expanding vow of new direction.

They sat there several minutes before Ellis slowly got out of the car, maps folded under his right arm.

He walked toward a concrete picnic bench that had been decorated by local birds. Jennifer quickly grabbed her purse and frantically hunted for paper and pen. Ellis placed his right leg on the picnic bench seat and stretched it, pushing down on it. He repeated the exercise with his left leg.

In panic, she pulled out the yellow Motel Sepia receipt.

Ellis shook his head like a wet dog so as to free it of cobwebs. Arms held skyward, he stretched his back. Jennifer watched him, then scribbled nervously.

"HELP. BLACK SEDAN", she wrote on the back of the receipt.

He surveyed the expanse of the Mississippi River Valley, looked at the maps again and mumbled a few words. He nodded agreement with himself and took note of a change in the sky.

Clouds had replaced the blue Midwest dome and began to roll like Ellis' upset stomach. The wind picked up and thunder echoed in the distance. Far below in the main channel of the Mississippi River, he watched a string of empty grain barges being pushed northward out of the locks. A black-capped chickadee sprung from a bull thistle flower in pursuit of a doomed insect.

He returned to the car and tossed the crumpled maps on the front seat, in the middle that served as a demilitarized zone. The eight cylinders jumped to life and gravel spit from the Chrysler's rear tires. Silence governed the ceasefire as the pair headed north.

Jennifer sat on the note she had written like a goose on a golden egg.

Chapter 51

3:05 p.m.

"Carroll County Sheriff's office," a man in a raspy voice answered.

"Is that you, Jack? This is Tom Tegland at the Clinton P.D."

"Yeah, Tom, it's me," Jack laughed. "I'm still able to answer the phone."

"I know that, Jack. You are a man of many talents," Tegland joked. "I was momentarily taken aback. You're usually out rounding up bad guys."

Jack Yeager, like many small town law enforcement officers, worked in obscurity, tending to neighborhood spats and cats that decline to come down from trees. A really bad day was when the local café ran out of cinnamon rolls.

"Well, if you didn't know," Yeager said, "when it's time for Trudy to take her coffee break, she goes. The world could be coming to an end and sweet strains from the harp drifting down from heaven, but by golly, Trudy is going to get that coffee break in before it's all over. Everybody else on duty is out on the road. What can I do for you this fine day?"

"I hope it stays fine, Jack. Just wanted to check if you received that All Points Bulletin out of Cedar Rapids, Iowa, and Naperville, Ill., regarding a late- model black Chrysler sedan. Occupants are suspects in murders in both cities."

"We sure did, and we've coordinated the advisory with counties to the east along Route 64," Yeager replied. "Understand these could be some bad folks. Mobster types out of Chicago? We don't get much of that out here in the boonies."

"Know what you mean, and I hope we don't get any of it today. Stay in touch. And Jack, give my regards to Trudy."

"Roger wilco, Tom. Keep us posted."

Tegland was a 15-year veteran of the Clinton Police Department. Before becoming a cop, he worked in security at the DuPont plant. These kinds of days made him question if he should have left the quiet and boredom of DuPont, even with the rotten egg chemical smells out there. Or, better yet, he should have pursued a career in home construction. He loved to tinker in woodworking.

Chances were that the subjects of the APB were already in Illinois.

Tegland hoped that was the case. He had no more desire to confront a Chicago hood than the next law enforcement officer. Contrary to what some might think, most cops don't become cops because they like to get in people's faces and shoot guns. It's a job, sometimes dangerous, sometimes rewarding, sometimes as boring as walking the grounds and buildings of a factory.

He looked out the west window of the police station. Leaves on the old elm tree across the street began to dance at the direction of a northwest cold front. Further on the northwest horizon, thunderheads began to coalesce as the mixture of summer air collided. Rain had been forecast on morning news.

He walked down the hall to the radio room.

"What's the latest on that case out of Cedar Rapids?" Tegland queried the dispatch officer.

"Nothing new," he was told. "Although there was a repeat message warning that the suspect, who is traveling with a woman, is one mean character. He's a hired killer, a veteran of Korea, and takes no prisoners as a matter of mission."

Tegland didn't like the image of some small town police officer coming face to face with a professional hit man. Or worse yet, innocent bystanders crossing the path of a wholesale psychopath. He was making no assumptions that the danger had left Clinton. He couldn't just wait. He decided to make some calls.

In addition to phoning other area sheriff's departments, Tegland touched base with town marshals along Route 30 in the Clinton area, on both sides of the river. He advised them to check with gas stations along the highway and anywhere else the black Chrysler might stop.

He suggested they talk to town idlers, those people who watch traffic go by, individuals who make it their business to know everything that's going on. Town cops know who they are, and they can be useful resources.

Tegland asked local police from Dubuque to Muscatine to immediately contact bridge attendants along the Mississippi River, in person if necessary, and inform them of the hunt.

What else could he do?

Chapter 52

"Have you heard anything more about the search for the restaurant killer?" Lillian Sanders asked her husband, Roy. "Any additional information on the news?"

"I have heard nothin' more, either on the radio or from the sheriff's department," Roy replied. "All the attention is still on that black Chrysler heading east. But where is it? Where are they?"

Those questions were on a lot of minds. For Roy the questions shrouded circumstances that either ended in peaceful arrests or tragic loss of life. For Lillian it was more a reflection on what could have happened at Motel Sepia, and it sent a post traumatic shiver through her body.

The questions were on the minds of thousands of people in a broad area of the Midwest as news spread about a dangerous killer on the run. It gripped farm country in a live drama, akin to radio's "The Shadow," except this one wouldn't end with the turn of a knob.

Lillian was finishing the last load of laundry – sheets, pillow cases and towels that would be re-circulated at Motel Sepia cabins in the days to come. For the first time she grasped the danger posed by someone who only last night had been a guest at Motel Sepia. For the first time she considered the perils of running a public business on a busy highway.

She knew hard work. She had experienced long days. She, like Roy, had felt the unspoken questioning aimed at black business operators. Lillian had sensed the uncertainty that goes with any business undertaking. But this was new. She had never considered criminal danger.

Roy was looking at the registration records from the day before. He stared at the signature: Rosemary Jones. Glenview, Illinois. Lic. #: 954-697. The line for a home telephone was left blank.

"How could we have suspected these two were big-time bad apples?" Roy asked, knowing there was no answer to his soul-searching. He had been the victim of deception, and that added to his impulsive response to the book salesman, was a semester's worth of education in humility.

Lillian brushed back her dark hair with her left hand, an attempt to get run-away strands out of her eyes. She was tired. The events of the last 24 hours had dumped an extra layer of weariness on her. Running a house, a family and bunch of cabins was one thing. Getting mixed up in a murder case was beyond the pale.

"I could use a glass of iced tea," she said, hoping Roy would take the hint.

He had to chuckle inwardly. She was like that, never requesting a glass of iced tea or anything else directly, but couching her desires in a statement that usually required only tacit translation. Frequently before they would go to bed she would ask him innocently, "Are you hungry for a dish of ice cream?" Well.

"Would you like some tea, Roy?" and she made a move toward the icebox.

"No, I'll get it," he said.

"I pray this ends with no more killin'," she sighed, collapsing her body on a kitchen chair. "Just a squeeze of lemon, if you don't mind," she looked at Roy. "I hope no harm comes to that young lady, that Miss Rosemary or whatever her name is. It's a shame people don't devote the same amount of energy toward an honest livin'. As for Mr. Dawson, I'm guessin' if you play with fire sooner or later, you will get singed."

In spite of her exhaustion, Lillian's mind was bent on working overtime. She again shuddered at the thought of a killer sleeping on their property, a killer just next door.

"You know, Roy, this is far from over for us." She took a sip of her tea and looked into the glass as if it contained some sort of hidden message, some residual tea leaf insight. "If they arrest these people, we'll be testifyin' in court here and probably have to go traipsin' off to Chicago to testify, too."

Roy knew that mingled somewhere within her fatigue and frustration Lillian was wondering why they were in the motel business. Three guests had reservations for the coming night. Their business had been steady. Unlike big operations where employees work on shifts, Lillian and Roy worked seven days a week. They did close the cabins from November through April.

"I can't answer that, Lillian," Roy said plainly.

"Can't answer what?"

"What you said. Why some people spend so much time and energy trying to make money by hurtin' others."

"Damn!"

It wasn't a declaration of disappointment, but rather the cohabitation of sureness and cryptic incompleteness. Louie Byrne was expressing the collective sentiment of his cop team. It was partly acknowledgement that they were headed in the right direction. It also carried the specter of unknown dangers that were bound to unfold, dangers housed in a black sedan.

It encapsulated all of the time, the ground work and all of the sweat that comprised the investigation of George Dawson's murder. It was one of the most high-profile cases in recent Cedar Rapids and Iowa police history. And now, he hoped, matters were moving to an end. What that might entail had everyone worried.

He paced around the second floor of the Police Station like an expectant father.

In most cases, there is an investigative gestation period when collected evidence is mingled and assessed. Certain aspects of a case grow into positions of dominance and others diminish in significance. Tests confirm some information and eliminate other elements. And, as in most endeavors, there are false labor pains, where expectancy falters.

Eventually, a conclusion, a summation of the entire team's efforts, is reached. That resolution was at hand in the murders of George Dawson and Aldo Arezzo.

Byrne, McNabb and everyone involved in the investigation were convinced that this time they were on the track of the right killer.

Simultaneously, Byrne had this gnawing fear, a sensation in one's gut as when food is reversed, that something unforeseen and difficult, if impossible to prevent, was lurking somewhere.

"Call Clinton P.D. and see what they know," Byrne ordered.

"We just talked to them," answered Perkins, the records hound who was the department's Harry Houdini for pulling lost documents seemingly out of the air. "Clinton has been in close contact with other area law enforcement. There just isn't anything new in the hunt, Lieutenant."

Byrne, for the 20th time, looked at Iowa and Illinois maps spread on the investigation room table. They produced no answers.

"Damn," he repeated. "Where is that black Chrysler?"

Chapter 53

Eighteen minutes after it left Clinton, Iowa, the big Chrysler halted at a "T" intersection stop sign in the absolute center of Middle's nowhere. Straight ahead was a massive bluff bedecked in scraggly brush, sumac and horseweeds.

Ellis, confused by the remoteness and handicapped by his natural impatience, grumbled and then glanced at his maps again. There was not another vehicle in sight. He turned right on Route 64, feeling his way along in what for him was uncharted territory. It may as well have been the Everglades.

Iowa's landscape, which had quickly transformed from flat cornfields to timber and hills, now suddenly evolved into backwater and lake country.

Raindrops began to collect on the car's windshield like little blisters.

Route 64 led eastward into the small town of Sabula, Iowa. It was a blip of a place, an island created by the Corps of Engineers when it constructed a downstream dam at Clinton. It had become a marine outpost for Mississippi River fishermen and owners of small pleasure craft. It wasn't big enough for a killer on the run to hide.

After two blocks, the highway elbowed north, surrounded by tiny shops more geared to a river culture than farming. Within three more blocks, Ellis, his mind preoccupied with "black sedan" radio reports and cars with flashing red lights, suddenly awoke to geography that looked like the bayous of Louisiana.

The road north of Sabula floated on a berm surrounded by canals and swamp vegetation. It would have been no surprise to him if an alligator slithered onto the highway.

For a few minutes, Ellis' mind was redirected and soothed by the canopy of foliage that all but concealed the gathering storm. After two miles, tranquility ended as the misplaced jungle surrendered to the wide open Mississippi River Valley and the looming iron bridge into Illinois. A bald eagle dove like a P-51 fighter plane, aiming for a surfing catfish.

"STOP" a sign over the toll booth window said. Ellis pulled over. From the casual demeanor of the toll agent, there were no signs that anything was amiss, nothing to suggest that his nerves had been put on alert by an APB alert.

"That'll be 25 cents," the man in the booth said with a friendly smile. "Twenty cents for the car and driver and a nickel for the passenger."

He was dressed in a khaki uniform and wore an olive drab cap with a black bill. He stepped out of the booth and walked toward the car.

"Howdy, Miss," he said, placing his thumb and index finger on the tip of his cap as a sign of respect for a woman.

Ellis handed the change to Jennifer and she relayed it to the bridge attendant.

"Thank you and have a good day," the attendant said, waving and turning back to the booth.

Jennifer shifted in her seat as Ellis pulled away. Was this the right place, the right time? What would be a better opportunity, a better chance? She was like a person in a canoe, 50 yards from plunging over the waterfalls, who suddenly spots a nearby rock. Should she swim for it?

Slowly, set on staving off panic, she reached beneath her buttocks and crumpled the motel receipt in her right hand. Her left hand covered her mouth as she faked a sneeze and, in the same motion, dropped the "HELP" note out the car window onto the ground.

Did Ellis notice? Would the attendant see the crumpled paper? Would the surging northwest wind carry her emergency message and hopes into oblivion? She let out a big breath.

Ellis focused on the approaching narrow bridge, its steel cantilever trusses stretching up and down to form two points high above the mighty Mississippi River.

The Chrysler's wide tires slapped the open steel grid of the bridge floor, sending off a hum resembling a swarm of bees.

Jennifer looked out the car window and for a second, as she peered downward through the holes in the bridge decking, was startled by the river's whitecaps churning far below. For some reason, she saw it as a metaphor for her disjointed life and uncertain future.

Just downstream, a lone fishing boat plowed through the wind-molded waves, laboring to find shelter as the storm expanded and the rain spigot began to open wider. Sheer bluffs on the Illinois side grew taller as they crossed the river, ominous barriers that forced the highway to find a new direction.

Once across to the Illinois side, Ellis, for no specific reason, turned right toward Savanna. After about a half mile, he pulled onto a side street next to a Zephyr gas station where a waving mechanical arm invited potential customers.

He parked and again consulted his maps. As best as possible, he wanted to avoid major highways. Satisfied, he turned back north on Route 84.

The wide river sprawled to the left. Some distance to the north, looking like twin black logs, a double string of coal barges moved upstream. The tracks of the Chicago, Burlington and Quincy hugged the river's bank. The scene was breathtaking, but the occupants of the black Chrysler were of no mind to appreciate the beauty.

Ellis focused on taking the safest route back home, one least likely to be watched by cops with APB chatter on their radios. His mind's eye envisioned a crisscrossing of Illinois that would carry them safely back to Chicago. A short distance past the towering Palisades State Park, he swung right at a rusty sign marking Mill Hollow Road.

A boom of thunder reverberated through the hillside trees. The rain intensified and the narrow, dirt road became slick. Ellis' plan of sneaking his way home on remote back routes literally took on water. At one point, the Chrysler's tires spun and struggled to push the vehicle to the top of a ridge. They came to a junction with Scenic Ridge Road. A faded sign peppered with shotgun pellets pointed left to Derinda Center. Ellis turned right.

He was relieved that this road seemed to have more gravel, was more stable, even if it had a corrugated surface. The car picked up speed to 15 miles per hour when another junction forced another decision. He chose left and swung onto Zion Road. The windshield wipers worked furiously to ward off the heavy rain.

His mind became fuzzy, as if he had just slammed a double Jack chased by a Fox De Luxe stout. The swelling storm clouded his perspective. Uncertainty stepped in. Another stop to recheck maps was in order. Satisfied, his mind eased and the plan solidified in his mind. He confidently wended the Chrysler through cornfield corridors, past farmsteads and smelly hog lots.

His zigzag plan unfolded.

Chapter 54

"**H**ey, Miss!" the toll booth attendant yelled, but the car was already on its way, approaching the bridge.

A gust of northwest wind rippled the flag adjacent to the booth. The lanyard snapped against the pole. A small piece of paper was scooped up and bounced across the road toward the toll booth like a miniature tumbleweed. He thought she had dropped it in the process of paying the toll. Maybe it was there before, but he hadn't noticed.

He bounded after the elusive message, grabbed it as another car was approaching and stuffed the little paper in his pocket like so much trash. It was ten minutes before he thought about it again.

Casually, he took the note from his pocket.

"HELP. BLACK SEDAN," it read in scrawled cursive.

Within seconds his memory was jogged. It had been only a half an hour earlier that a Savanna, Ill., police officer had stopped by to tell him of the APB and the black Chrysler. The attendant immediately notified Savanna police.

It provoked a tide of communication among law enforcement agencies. From Naperville, Ill., to eastern Iowa, attention was switched to the Savanna area, now ground zero in the search. Illinois deputies blanketed the main highways from Freeport to Rock Island. Information was fed to local radio stations asking the public to watch for the black sedan.

The hunt was at maximum intensity. It blossomed to become one of the biggest assemblage of authorities in Illinois since Jefferson

Davis and Abraham Lincoln were involved in the Army's chase of Sauk Chief Black Hawk some 120 years before.

McNabb and Byrne, back in radio contact, reviewed the fast-breaking developments.

"I can't believe he is still in western Illinois," McNabb told his Iowa collaborator.

"What's your best guess?" Byrne asked. "Did he go north, east or south from Savanna?"

Byrne rubbed the mole on his cheek as if he could summon an answer to his own question.

"I doubt he went south," McNabb replied. "The only thing we know for sure is he hasn't made a U-turn and crossed back to Iowa. All of the bridge people are on high alert. Illinois State Police are coordinating the search. We are in communication with all sheriff's departments and local police. This guy is not going to escape. I pray we have no casualties."

The thunderstorm which had brewed in northeast Iowa now vented on western Illinois. The clash of electrified clouds sent a shudder through the skies. The prelude of lightning provided a back glow to thunderheads ready to open their spigots. Then, without the benefit of any more drum rolls, the blackened dome exploded.

Townspeople scurried for cover. Shoppers headed home, leaving most streets barren of life. Farmers who were baling hay cussed mildly as they hastily hauled partially-filled wagons into barn lofts. It would be a couple of days before alfalfa and timothy windrows would be dry enough to resume work.

Everyone was watching the storm. No one was looking for a black sedan.

At one point the rain fell in sheets. The moaning wind whipped the rainstorm in a diagonal marching order. Pellets of ice peppered vegetation and all in its path in a most impertinent affront.

Wipers on the black sedan labored unsuccessfully to clear the monsoon-like deluge. Conditions were so intense that Ellis, driving in strange territory with eyes squinting, at first slowed and then pulled into a grassy access lane next to a cornfield.

For the moment, at least, his plans and cast-iron will were humbled and detoured by nature. No more than 100 feet from the roadway, the grassy strip became more of a path that curved and evolved into an untilled waterway designed for erosion control. He could park there, hidden from traffic, the tall corn acting like armed sentries.

He left the motor running and the windshield wipers whipping.

Lightning blitzed the dusky farm fields, and thunder took its cue and bellowed against the countryside. For a few minutes, it took on a metallic sound, as if someone was beating against large sheets of metal with gigantic logs. Day had turned into night. The swollen thunderheads were stenciled against an angry sky as part of a celestial light show.

Corn stock tassels pelted by rain dripped like thousands of lawn sprinklers. Some corn leaves were ripped from their moorings and hurled aloft. The wind continued to howl, as if insulted by some meteorological relative. Angry clouds exchanged lightning punches.

Would it ever quit, Ellis wondered. It seemed as if they had been transplanted into a tropical gale. For a second, the outlandish scene caused him to ponder if Nature was casting its opinion about his soulless life. His imperious core quickly dismissed such notions.

With the windows rolled up, air inside the car became stale and steamy.

A few of the new Chryslers had air conditioning. Ellis' rental did not, and it was further reason to cuss Rhino Ralston. Rhino was a cheap bastard, except when it came to his personal desires, and those didn't include comfort of employees.

And now Ellis was parked in the middle of a cornfield, with torrential rains, a bitchy broad, and cops perhaps sniffing at his trail. He was not happy.

"How do you like being stuck in this romantic get-away?" he finally severed what had been a long silence. She said nothing. He poked her with his finger.

"Get it? Get-away?" She remained silent and looked away.

"Hey, I give you permission to talk now, you prissy whore," he snarled. "What a joke you are. Trying to be highfalutin and Rhino's mattress pad at the same time. Does the truth hurt, Miss Rosemary? Go ahead. Speak up. How about some of that fancy Northwestern rhetoric you like to brag about? Give it your best shot."

She tried to mentally block out his insults, peering through the foggy window streaked with rain. Maybe there was truth in what he said, but it still roiled her innards. Where did a lowlife like Joe Ellis get credence to criticize her? And why did he loathe her? She hadn't volunteered for this gig. Maybe it was his way of expressing self-hatred, or evidence of a leak in his armor.

She clamped her jaws shut.

"Come, come. I know you want to converse," Ellis mocked. "Perhaps provide some insight on your work. How would you outline your job description? Tell what it's like to have Rhino as your pimp. You should give out Green Stamps. Customers would have books of them. Maybe, Rosy, you can provide an anatomical review. Your legs must be strangers; they have been apart so many times."

Only the boom of a nearby lightning strike stifled the angry words about to exit her mouth.

She squirmed, fury building in her body like the atmospheric fireworks that surrounded them. Her mind was a kaleidoscope of competing images wrapped in rage.

She was running toward the swing, yelling *"push me Daddy, push me,"* arguing with her mother, gulping a Jim Beam, shivering to the touch of a stranger's hand, the entire drama directed by a laughing and taunting Ellis.

"You're sweating," he snickered. Beads of perspiration trickled down and around the mark on Jennifer's cheek. "I have the feeling you want to tell me something."

She began to tremble.

"Are you getting the hots for me?" he uttered with salacious breathing. "Look at me." His eyes slithered from her smooth lips to heaving breasts that appeared to him as being larger than when this odyssey began.

The rumbling clouds raced eastward, and the rain began to taper.

Life for a skilled professional killer and befuddled mob moll, already an unlikely melodrama, had progressed to sinister surrealism. Their world had shrunk to a black Chrysler sedan parked in an Illinois cornfield being bombarded by an August thunderstorm.

Hormones were stirring out of control inside his body, angst building in hers. She could smell the danger.

His right hand reached out. She pushed hard against the door. He tossed the unfolded maps in the back seat.

"I've got to take a piss," he announced.

In addition to his powerfully honed body and expertise with knives, Ellis was proud and confident of his ability to look ahead, to anticipate. Planning had served him well in Korea, and he took pleasure in crafting a scheme for handling Rhino's execution orders. Only once had he come close to the grips of a prosecutor, and the mob's money and inability of a dead witness to testify suppressed that.

There was that time after he crawled on his belly for five hours to get the shot he wanted to kill the overseer of a North Korean POW camp near Pukchin only to find himself being hunted from three sides. He had to find a different route back to safety. Knowing the terrain through research and planning had saved his life.

The rain had almost stopped. He walked to the back of the car and unzipped his pants. In addition to relieving his bladder his rising testosterone levels sought liberation.

Ellis looked skyward and saw scantily clad women in Miami, voluptuous vixens in Key West. They were the future, but Miss Rosemary was the present. His loins began to do his thinking, and he forfeited his vaunted discipline.

The car's engine suddenly roared and the Chrysler leaped backward. He spun to the right to evade the massive machine, but the bumper slammed into his right knee and spun him to ground. Jennifer shifted the car to low, pulled forward, spun the steering wheel and then rammed the gear shift into reverse, aiming a second time at the flailing Ellis.

"You are dead!" he shouted, writhing in pain and holding his twisted leg. "I will kill –" and his words were cut off by the black sedan's second thrust. The car was now her knife. This time, both of his legs were struck and the car was about to pin his body when it became mired in the cornfield mud.

Ellis, legs mangled, his right arm crushed, and pants ripped and unzipped, lay frozen in a field of muck.

Jennifer turned off the ignition key and began to sob.

She exited the car and slowly walked to where the mud-spattered Ellis was lying. Her heart pounded like a boxer on the verge of a TKO. She stared at his supine form. One of his legs displayed a bone that had pushed through the skin just below the knee. Blood oozed from the wound and also spurted from a tear in his arm.

He was motionless, stripped of vanity, exposed. The tension in her body eased, and slowly her visceral hatred for Ellis evolved into a serene sense of satisfaction. A small smile pushed her lips apart. Relief filtered slowly through her bloodstream as if her old buddy Jim Beam had entered the door. There was not a speck of remorse in her body.

"You worthless piece of humanity," she said quietly.

She kicked at his twisted leg. He clenched his teeth to hide the pain. She spoke louder, supposing he could hear.

"I have witnessed a lot of hell in the recent few years of my life, much of it my own fault, but you give evil a good name," she said. "A hungry maggot would puke at your remains. You are scum. On a scale of one to ten you are minus ninety-nine, a piece of shit."

She gazed at him with cold defiance. Her eyes traveled to his unzipped trousers, and she chuckled. Then she pointed.

"I'd say you have been de-wackered."

Jennifer turned in triumphant satisfaction and scanned the horizon for the nearest farm house.

Chapter 55

The massive left arm of Joe Ellis lashed toward her legs like a giant scythe sweeping against vulnerable grain.

Crawling in the mud, his body flaring in pain, he roared revenge. His bloody paw smacked her left ankle, and she crumpled to the ground. Jennifer, shocked and terrified, screamed and fought to escape. He squeezed her leg like a vise, his powerful fingers stopping blood flow in its tracks. She desperately tried to squirm away, digging her hands into the soil to seek leverage.

She found none.

Enraged, Ellis clamped his hand around the calf of her right leg and attempted to drag in his prey. His face bulged with searing hostility, and turned scarlet to reflect his boiling blood being pumped at maximum pressure.

Jennifer's thrashing left foot bounced off his slippery head. She was sliding toward him. In blind panic, she reached out and snagged the sedan's bumper with her left hand. But it was a temporary stop and no match for his strength. Her grip dissolved.

Instinctively, she grabbed a handful of mud and slung it at his head.

Ellis grimaced. His bared teeth seemed to convert him into a wild beast. She picked up more mud. Like a late-inning reliever, she mustered all her strength and aimed at his eyes. It was not a direct hit, but she sensed a loosening of his grip. His partially clogged eyelids begged for a cleansing swipe, but he doggedly maintained his grip.

A volley of mud balls followed. One centered on his scowl, offering prime Midwest soil for an unscheduled lunch. He sputtered. His caked face sought relief.

In a frenzy of yanks, she freed her leg. As he peeled off dirt from his face, Jennifer staggered to her feet and scrambled away in trembling terror. Half-crazed, she ripped loose a corn stalk and began beating him with its roots. Her fear of again being snared in his clutch was offset by a psychotic urge to inflict pain. Her muddled mind was bent in one direction, directed by reckless hatred.

Ellis again found himself in a battle with Mother Earth. Half blinded by muck, he flailed wildly, batting away clumps of sodden dirt, hoping to find flesh. Instead, he latched onto the corn stalk and yanked it toward him, desperately hoping to pull her within his muddy clutches.

Jennifer, her better senses recovering, released the rope-like stalk and stumbled backward. She regained her footing and hobbled to the car. She pulled the keys from the ignition, and staggered around to the trunk and opened it. In seconds, she removed the lug wrench. Void of restraint, she began beating his feet, then his legs with the tire iron. Now her intense hate found fulfillment.

Ellis met pain on a new level. His shrieks needed no translation. Carefully staying beyond his reach, she sent the tool spinning like a discus toward Ellis' head. He saw enough of the projectile to evade its full blow. One end, however, gouged a chunk from his right ear.

Unflagging fury pushed her to the car's rear door where she removed one of Ellis' knives and returned to the battlefield. She swung the 10-inch blade and sliced his fending arm. Another gash found a major artery in his neck. Blood spurted from his wounds as if he were a sprinkling can.

He mustered his drained body to action, but the response was pitiful and ineffective. Loss of blood and shock had reduced this robust specimen of manliness to a withered mass. His threats had dimmed to pleas that went unheard. No one could hear him as he hummed *Twinkle, Twinkle Little Star,* and shuddered from his wounds and humiliated ego.

Jennifer Jennings had come to know evil up close. She had been immersed in the absence of good long enough to absorb its complete dimensions.

Her whole being heaved with adrenaline. The knife went up and down in vicious thrusts and twists for nearly a minute, replicating most of the lethal wounds that Ellis had so proficiently delivered to his victims. His body shook in response to her bloody foray.

Thunder from the retreating storm echoed through the corn rows. The once shouting winds relaxed to more of an eerie whisper. Rolling black clouds softened to a less hostile slate and created relief with openings of light. The dying drizzle tried to wash the macabre stage, but it could not meet the test.

While the storm had abated, the tempest in Jennifer's life was far from over.

The flashing lights from a Carroll County sheriff's car splashed red over the late afternoon. The deputy pulled into the farm yard and parked under a dripping oak tree. A windmill, exhausted by the thunderstorm's outburst, slowed down to a rhythmic click.

Jennifer was still sitting in a rusting Ford pickup truck, her hair frazzled, her face speckled with mud, her arms and clothes spattered with a blend of her own blood and that of Joe Ellis. She appeared to be in another world, one coated by pictures from hell.

"I was coming back from town," the farmer told the officer. "She was walking down the middle of the road. It had started raining again, and I stopped to see if she wanted a ride. I asked if she'd been in an accident, but she didn't reply. She hasn't said a word since we arrived at my place about 15 minutes ago. Do you have any idea what this is about?"

The deputy briefly explained the hunt for the black sedan and its occupants, and asked for directions to the field near where Jennifer had been walking. He radioed for backup and requested an ambulance.

Within 15 minutes the quiet Illinois countryside was overrun by local and state law enforcement officials and emergency personnel.

A state patrolman took Jennifer to a hospital in Freeport. Ellis' ripped corpse was removed by ambulance to a morgue in Sterling.

A summary of the startling drama was radioed back to Sheriff Jack Yeager. He relayed it to state police commanders and the word fanned out.

The ordeal was over.

"State police told us that two officers are guarding this Jennifer Jennings at the hospital," Naperville's Capt. McNabb informed Lt. Byrne in Cedar Rapids. "She has agreed to tell her story. The entire story."

"It's a big relief," sighed Byrne. "I was really concerned that some citizen or law enforcement officer would be killed in trying to stop him. How do you explain such evil? It appears he was a human being directed by the devil himself. Captain, we can be thankful how it turned out. He is dead, and that also means a lot less paper work for us."

McNabb paused and took a deep breath.

"It's been a helluva day."

Chapter 56

It was only 9 p.m., but Lillian Sanders was already asleep. Roy was half-listening to a sports update on WMT radio when a news bulletin severed regular programming. The black sedan search was over, the newscaster said. One of the biggest manhunts in recent Midwest history ended quietly in a rain-soaked Illinois cornfield.

The suspect, Joe Ellis, was dead. His make-believe bride was in a hospital.

Officers at the scene described the quiet and eerie conclusion to an otherwise frenzied day that portended a volatile outcome for police. There were expressions of relief from Cedar Rapids Police Lt. Louis Byrne and his Naperville, Ill., counterpart, Capt. Jerry McNabb.

Roy's living room rocker came to a squeaking halt.

He and Lillian were bone-tired from the regular tasks of Motel Sepia, she especially. Most of the motel's chores shifted to her after Roy was called to help with a flooring project. They were juggling a demanding list of duties and hadn't heard a newscast in hours.

Perhaps, he reflected, launching Motel Sepia had been a mistake. It was enough to run Fourteen Acres and two flooring businesses. Had he pushed his personal yearning to bring black people and white people together too far, at her expense? Was his one-step-at-a-time formula for racial interaction out of step?

For a second he thought he had drifted off in sleep. Maybe his ears heard wrong. Did his drowsy mind interpret right?

Roy stood, walked over to the cream-colored Philco, and turned up the volume. It was news that would make both of them sleep sounder once they had digested the complete story, one in which they unexpectedly had held a part.

He went to the bedroom.

"Lillian, Lillian," he whispered, and tapped her on the shoulder.

By the time he had repeated the full report, she was sitting upright in bed. Neither said a word for nearly a minute.

"Sometimes, it's amazin' how life can change so fast," Roy said. He gently stroked her hair and then kissed her forehead. "Sometimes it seems like life just wants to stay the same. Either way, Lillian, we keep movin' along – to somewhere. God's ole Earth just keeps spinnin' like nothin's happened."

It was one of those special moments in a couple's life when they breathe in each other's presence and, like Evelyn's father said, know the mystery of two becoming one.

"We are conceived in the womb and thrust into eternity," Roy went on. "We live in the blink of an eye. We must make the most of it."

He saw a tear, then two, slowly slip down the softness of Lillian's cheek. Her brown eyes glistened, and looked up into his.

"What's wrong, Lillian?" he asked.

"Absolutely nothing," she said. "Absolutely nothing."

Afterword

In 1877, Standing Bear and his people, the Ponca, were forcibly removed from their land in northern Nebraska and sent to Indian Territory in Oklahoma. Upon arrival, they discovered that the U.S. government had made no provisions for food or shelter for the tribe. As a result, many, including Standing Bear's son, did not survive the harsh winter.

In defiance of the relocation order, Standing Bear decided to return to his homeland in Nebraska. Many accompanied him. They traveled on foot, begging along the way for food and shelter. Near Omaha, they stopped to visit relatives. Soon thereafter, the Ponca were arrested and held by General George Crook.

With the help of local Indian rights activists and, some say, General Crook himself, Standing Bear sued in U.S. District Court for his right to return home. Judge Elmer Dundy announced that Chief Standing Bear would be allowed to make a speech in his own behalf.

Raising his right hand, Standing Bear proceeded to speak.

> *"That hand* (he said, describing his own raised hand) *is not the color of yours, but if I prick it, the blood will flow, and I shall feel pain. The blood is of the same color as yours. God made me, and I am a man."*

As the trial drew to a close, on May 12, 1879, Judge Dundy ruled that "an Indian is a person" within the meaning of habeas corpus. He stated that the federal government had failed to show a basis under law for the Ponca's arrest and captivity. He found in favor of Standing

Bear, for the first time giving the rights of a U. S. citizen to a Native American.

It was a landmark case, recognizing that an Indian is a "person" under the law and entitled to its rights and protection. "The right of expatriation is a natural, inherent and inalienable right and extends to the Indian as well as to the more fortunate white race," the judge concluded.

Twenty-two years before that, in March 1857, the United States Supreme Court, led by Chief Justice Roger B. Taney, declared that all blacks – slaves, as well as free – were not and could never become citizens of the United States. The court also declared the 1820 Missouri Compromise unconstitutional, thus allowing slavery in all of the country's territories.

The case before the court was that of *Dred Scott v. Sanford*. Dred Scott, a slave who had lived in the free state of Illinois and the free territory of Wisconsin before moving back to the slave state of Missouri, had appealed to the Supreme Court in hopes of being granted his freedom.

Taney, a staunch supporter of slavery and intent on protecting southerners from northern aggression, wrote in the Court's majority opinion that because Scott was black, he was not a citizen and therefore had no right to sue. The framers of the Constitution, Taney wrote, believed that blacks "had no rights which the white man was bound to respect; and that the Negro might justly and lawfully be reduced to slavery for his benefit. He was bought and sold and treated as an ordinary article of merchandise and traffic, whenever profit could be made by it."

Referring to the language in the Declaration of Independence that includes the phrase "all men are created equal," Taney reasoned that "it is too clear for dispute, that the enslaved African race were not intended to be included, and formed no part of the people who framed and adopted this declaration . . ."

Lincoln's Emancipation Proclamation led to passage of the Thirteenth Amendment in 1865 and the abolition of slavery. Three years later, the Fourteenth Amendment reversed the Dred Scott decision and granted citizenship to black people.

Standing Bear gave witness to a truth that was neither new nor old: No matter race, creed or culture, our blood and human nature are the same. No matter if we are rich or poor, young or old, born or unborn, it is our human nature that grants us value and common bonds.

The unresolved lies in men's hearts.

About the Author

Dale Kueter wrote for Iowa newspapers for forty-one years, thirty-five at The Gazette in Cedar Rapids. He attended Loras College in Dubuque, Iowa, and graduated with a degree in journalism from the University of Iowa in 1958. "Motel Sepia" is his first novel.

Kueter grew up on a farm near Bellevue, Iowa. After college, he married Helen Hayes. They are parents of five daughters and have fourteen grandchildren. He and his wife live in Cedar Rapids, Iowa.

CPSIA information can be obtained
at www.ICGtesting.com
Printed in the USA
LVHW042355251218
601725LV00001B/118/P